Mad about You

Mad about You

SINÉAD MORIARTY

PENGUIN BOOKS

PENGUIN BOOKS

Published by the Penguin Group
Penguin Books Ltd, 80 Strand, London WC2R ORL, England
Penguin Group (USA) Inc., 375 Hudson Street, New York, New York 10014, USA
Penguin Group (Canada), 90 Eglinton Avenue East, Suite 700, Toronto, Ontario, Canada M4P 2Y3
(a division of Pearson Penguin Canada Inc.)
Penguin Ireland, 25 St Stephen's Green, Dublin 2, Ireland
(a division of Penguin Books Ltd)
Penguin Group (Australia), 707 Collins Street, Melbourne, Victoria 3008, Australia
(a division of Pearson Australia Group Pty Ltd)
Penguin Books India Pvt Ltd, 11 Community Centre,
Panchsheel Park, New Delhi – 110 017, India
Penguin Group (NZ), 67 Apollo Drive, Rosedale, Auckland 0632, New Zealand
(a division of Pearson New Zealand Ltd)
Penguin Books (South Africa) (Pty) Ltd, Block D, Rosebank Office Park,
181 Jan Smuts Avenue, Parktown North, Gauteng 2193, South Africa

Penguin Books Ltd, Registered Offices: 80 Strand, London WC2R ORL, England

www.penguin.com

First published by Penguin Ireland 2013
Published in Penguin Books 2014
004

Copyright © Sinéad Moriarty, 2013
All rights reserved

The moral right of the author has been asserted

Typeset by Palimpsest Book Production Ltd, Falkirk, Stirlingshire
Printed in Great Britain by Clays Ltd, St Ives plc

ISBN: 978-0-241-96338-8

www.greenpenguin.co.uk

MIX
Paper from
responsible sources
FSC
www.fsc.org   FSC® C018179

Penguin Books is committed to a sustainable
future for our business, our readers and our planet.
This book is made from Forest Stewardship
Council™ certified paper.

To my girlfriends, for your loyalty, love and laughter

Trust: firm belief in the reliability, truth, or ability of someone or something.

Oxford Dictionaries (British and World English)

I pulled a heavy box marked *Miscellaneous* towards me and peered inside. It was full of photo albums. There must have been ten of them, all overflowing with photos of our life together. I opened the first. There was a photo of me and James on holiday in Greece. It was almost painful to look at – we were so happy. James was beaming at the camera, tanned and fit. Beside him, I was white as milk and covered with heat-rash. Why he hadn't dumped me then and there was a mystery.

I couldn't believe how young we were in the photos, young and carefree. Well, if I was honest, I looked a bit hot and bothered. I really didn't need to get heat-rash on my first foreign holiday with my boyfriend. Who wants to have sex with a girl who hides in the shade wearing a burka? The other hotel guests kept asking if I was allergic to the sun. And the sad truth was: yes. No redhead should sunbathe in 38-degree heat; it's not how God made us. He made us to sit under umbrellas in big floppy hats, sipping cold wine. So that was what I did for the second week of our holiday and things were a lot more fun. While James surfed, water-skied and paraglided in the burning sun, I waved encouragingly from my permanent position under a large parasol, surrounded by books and a bottle of rosé. Life was good.

I turned the pages of the album. There was a photo of us on our last night in Greece – the night James proposed. I was absolutely radiant and bronzed (the miracle of fake tan). We were so happy and in love. I rested the album on my lap and gazed around the empty, soulless room. Where were those two people? When had life got so complicated and daunting?

I flicked forward to our wedding day. Wow! Look at my waist! So slim. I was at least two sizes bigger now. I'd have to lose that extra stone this year. I wanted to get back to that slim girl. I wanted to go back to that day. I wanted to be relaxed and joyful again.

Sighing, I flipped forward to the photos of Yuri. I stopped then, overcome with emotion. There was one of us at the airport, coming through the arrivals door, holding our precious Russian angel. My sister, Babs, must have taken it. You could see Mum rushing towards me, holding a bunch of enormous 'Congratulations' balloons. Yuri was fast asleep on my shoulder; James and I were exhausted, but elated. I looked closer: Mum was crying and so am I. Remembering that day still brought tears to my eyes. I peered at Yuri's sleeping face, the baby boy from Russia who saved my sanity and gave me the gift of motherhood.

I shuddered, remembering how I had shouted at him yesterday when he vomited all over me instead of into the bag I was holding for him. The boat trip over had been a nightmare. Yuri had thrown up the whole way from Dublin to Wales. And then his little sister, Lara, had proceeded to vomit the whole way from Wales to London in the car. I thought we'd never get here. But we did.

The room was still dusty, in spite of my best efforts. All of the windows were open to air the house, but it still smelt stale and stuffy. I'd have to scrub it from top to bottom. The walls were painted magnolia and the floors had that cheap, rope-like carpet that rented houses tended to go for because it was low cost and hard-wearing. There weren't many aesthetic touches in this place. The carpet felt rough and scratchy under my toes. I'd buy some big rugs to cover it. I looked around and sighed again. It would take a lot of work to make this house into some kind of home. It was so drab and bleak.

Panic rose in my throat. 'Stop it, Emma,' I scolded myself. 'It's not a big deal. People move all the time. James is happy about his new job. Be supportive. Don't show him how you really feel.' But he wasn't here now. He'd taken the children to the park to leave me in peace to unpack – or to get away from me, my snapping and shouting and general grumpiness. I found it hard to hide my feelings, but I was trying.

It isn't easy to give up everything you love. I'd said goodbye to our house in Dublin, which I'd spent years making into the perfect home. I'd left behind my friends, my family – although, truth be told, my younger sister lived in London and my brother was in New York, but still, I'd left my parents. And I'd given up a job I loved. It was all for James, for his new job, for his career, for his well-being and happiness. I wanted him to be happy, of course I did, especially as he'd been so miserable since the last job fiasco, but I didn't really know anyone in London and it felt like starting all over again. The problem was, I'd loved my old life. Yuri and Lara were so happy at their playschool and everything had been perfect. Well, OK, not perfect. The last six months had been far from perfect. They'd been really stressful, actually, but now I was afraid. What if London didn't work out? What if James didn't succeed? What would happen to us then?

I looked at another photo to try to calm my nerves. It was one of James and me at Lucy and Donal Brady's wedding, about four years ago. We're all standing arm in arm, heads thrown back in laughter. My best friend marrying James's best friend – how perfect was that? We'd all had so much fun together. Their wedding was also the day I found out I was pregnant with Lara, our little miracle. Such wonderful, happy times. I felt a lump forming in my throat.

When I told Lucy we were uprooting and moving to London, she said it would be the making of us, that we'd have all this quality time together as a family and that it would get us back on track. I wasn't so sure about that. We'd been here exactly nineteen hours and I felt desperately lonely and homesick.

I pinched myself in exasperation. 'Get a grip, you dramatic cow. You're a forty-year-old mother of two. Make the most of this new adventure. Work at it, focus on making it a success. Turn this strange house into a home. Make your marriage work. Be nice to James. Be positive. Feel the fear and do it anyway. Forget your troubles – come on, get happy . . . blah blah blah.' The positive rant wasn't working.

My phone rang. I could see from the caller ID that it was my mother. I hesitated, then answered it.

'And they call this summer!'

'Hi, Mum.' I crossed my legs and propped my chin in my hand – if it started with a complaint, it could go on for some time.

'It hasn't stopped raining since you left. Honestly, the weather in this country is a farce. We'll be getting a toonami next, mark my words. I've never seen such rain. It's all that global warning.'

'It's "tsunami" and "global warming", Mum.'

'That's what I said. And, let me tell you, putting your newspapers in a green bin isn't going to stop the ozone layer burning us all to death.'

'I thought you said the tsunami was going to kill us?'

'It'll be one or the other. Your father has me demented, dividing everything into separate bins. He now has a compost heap in the garden. Did you ever? This is a man who has only ever given nature a cursory glance while pounding around the golf course. Now he's insisting that banana skins and tea bags and God knows what else go into this big pot he has on the windowsill. It stinks out the kitchen, not to mention looking awful. Honestly, Emma, he's getting very peculiar in his old age.'

I knew from experience that there was no point in interrupting my mother's flow. I put the phone on loudspeaker and got up to continue unpacking.

'How are my little pets? I think Yuri's grown over the summer. He's still very small, mind you, but that's the awful food they fed him in that orphanage. Hopefully, in a few years' time, he'll be as big as the other boys in his class.'

'Mum!' I warned her. 'I've told you before, don't be negative about the orphanage.'

'Why not? You told me it was a terrible place, and didn't you save him from it?'

I gritted my teeth. 'We didn't save him, he saved us. We're the ones who should be grateful.'

'Well, there's no need to bite my head off. I know how lucky we are to have him. Sure, amn't I besotted with him? He's my favourite grandchild. And before you give out, I love Lara and Sheila, too.'

'Mum! It's Shala,' I corrected her, for the millionth time. 'You know perfectly well how to pronounce it and it's annoying for Sean and Shadee that you insist on saying "Sheila". The child has a lovely Iranian name and you need to accept that.'

Mum sniffed. 'I don't know why my children couldn't call their babies nice simple names. None of this Yuri and Shala nonsense.'

'Yuri was named before we adopted him, and it's a beautiful name, and may I remind you that your daughter-in-law is Iranian and Shala is also a beautiful name?'

'I just don't see why Sean couldn't have married a nice

Irish girl. Why did he have to find an Iranian girl who doesn't want the children baptized or raised as Catholics? It breaks my heart.'

'Mum, Shadee is amazing and Sean is blissfully happy. The fact that she isn't Catholic doesn't matter. She's a great wife and mother, and a lovely person. And, besides, we all know you baptized Shala under the kitchen sink the minute they had their backs turned.'

Mum changed the subject, as she always does when she's found guilty. 'Anyway, that's enough about that. How are you, pet? All unpacked?'

I sighed. 'No, I still have about twenty boxes to go.'

'Well, chop-chop, Emma. James needs a nice home to come back to after work.'

'Thank you, Mum. I'm going as fast as I can.' I childishly made faces at the phone – this was the kind of behaviour my mother often reduced me to.

'It's important that a man wants to come home to his wife, Emma. Put a smile on your face and make the most of it. London is an exciting place to be.'

'But . . . what if we never come back to Dublin?' I said, finally admitting my biggest fear.

'If you don't, you don't,' Mum said, reassuring as always. 'Life isn't straightforward, Emma. You should know that by now.'

'I *am* aware of it. I have an adopted son and I've just moved country for my husband's job. Straightforwardness isn't something I expect or demand.'

'Marriage is all about compromise,' announced the woman who had never compromised in her life. 'You just have to get on with it. London is your home now. Make the most of it. Life is a long and bumpy road.'

I tried to keep the annoyance out of my voice. I loved

Mum to bits, but she wasn't exactly a soft shoulder when you needed one. 'All right, Mum, thanks for checking in with me. I appreciate it. James will be back from the park soon, so I'd better go and sort out dinner.'

'Well, mind yourself and call me if you're feeling lonely or want to talk.' The phone clicked and she was gone.

Life had certainly been bumpy lately. I hoped it would be smoother now that we had made the move. But what if it wasn't? I tidied the photo albums away into a cupboard. I had to leave the past behind. Those carefree days were over long ago. I had to focus on our future, whatever that might be. Smile, Emma, I ordered myself. Everything will be fine.

2

The doorbell rang. I looked through the peep-hole. Phew, it wasn't the journalist, only Babs. I opened the door to see my younger sister dressed like some kind of over-the-top rock-star at ten in the morning. She was wearing dark sunglasses, skin-tight jeans, six-inch heels and a tank top, with Dolce & Gabbana emblazoned across the chest.

'Subtle top, Babs. And, in case you hadn't noticed, it's cloudy so you don't need the shades.'

'Out of the way.' She pushed past me, wheeling a suitcase behind her. 'What time is the photographer coming? You need a lot of work.'

'Thanks! The journalist from the Irish *Sunday Independent* will be here to talk to James at half ten, and they're going to do the photo at about eleven.'

'Thank God for that. I'll need a full hour. Now, for the love of God, make me a cup of coffee, will you? I'm really hung-over.'

'Morning, Babs.' James came in and kissed her cheek. 'You're looking very . . . last night,' he said, with a grin.

Babs grinned back at him. 'You're right, James, these are last night's clothes.'

I spun around. 'Where did you stay?' I asked, hoping Babs wasn't sleeping around. She had to grow up. At twenty-seven, she needed to calm down, stop shagging random men and meet a nice guy.

'Chill, Emma, I crashed in a friend's house,' she drawled, sticking her head into the fridge, then drinking orange juice straight from the carton. 'A very cute, randy friend,' she added, giggling.

Before I could tell her off, James stood in front of me. 'How do I look?' he asked, fiddling with his tie.

He looked very handsome. He was wearing his one and only suit – dark navy with a blue shirt and red tie. I noticed he was thinner. The suit was a little too big for him now. His brown eyes searched my face for approval. Where had my confident, self-assured husband gone?

I went over to kiss him. 'You're gorgeous. Even cuter than when I first met you.'

He smiled, relaxing.

'You look like an accountant,' Babs said. 'You should lose the tie. You're a rugby coach, not a banker.'

'Ignore her,' I told him. 'You look very distinguished.'

'Thank you, darling.' He squeezed my hands; his palm was sweaty. 'Right. I'll leave you two to it. I want to go over my notes.'

As James walked out, the children came running in. 'Auntie Babs!' they squealed, when they saw her, and charged over.

Yuri and Lara adored Babs, partly because she was good-looking – it amazed me that children were so attracted to beauty – but they also loved her because she talked to them as if they were adults. She never censored herself in front of them. She said exactly what was on her mind and the kids loved that. She also bought them completely unsuitable presents. For Christmas last year she had given Yuri a huge toy machine-gun and Lara a big case filled with makeup, glitter, stick-on nails, plastic earrings and bracelets – a true treasure trove of girly junk.

Of course, I was the one who got shot by the little balls from Yuri's gun, and it was me who had to clean up the glitter that Lara stuck to all the furniture and cushions in the

9

house. But they all got on well, which I liked, and the children brought out a nicer side to Babs. She genuinely cared about them. In fact, they were probably the only things she gave a damn about, apart from herself and her career.

Babs held up her hands to stop them. 'Hey, kids, what have I told you? Never call me "Auntie". I'm far too young for that. Just because your mother is ancient doesn't mean I am. Remember, I'm thirteen years younger than her.'

Lara put up her arms. Babs checked her little hands were clean, then lifted her up for a kiss. 'My God, you get more beautiful every time I see you. Not as beautiful as me but, still, you're going in the right direction. Thank God you didn't get your mother's red hair.'

Putting Lara down, she turned to Yuri. 'So, Shorty, what's up? Have you grown?'

Yuri nodded proudly. 'Three centimetres since I saw you.'

'Well, you won't be playing basketball anytime soon, but I suppose it's something. Now, I've got a treat for you.'

'What is it?' Their eyes were wide with anticipation.

Babs pulled a box of Smarties out of her bag. Great, I thought, just what we need: sweets to make them hyper when there's a journalist on the way and we'd like him to see a nice, normal family.

They shrieked with delight. Babs handed the box to them. 'Run for your life, before the witch here gets her hands on them and lets you have just one each.'

As they ripped open the box, I turned to my sister. 'Thanks so much. They'll be bouncing off the walls now.'

'I know, and their teeth will fall out and I won't be the one bringing them to the dentist and paying for fillings, blah blah blah. Come on, Emma, live a little. It's a box of Smarties, not crack cocaine.'

I decided to change the subject. 'Did you ask your work

people about Putney? Do any of them know this area? Any advice or tips for me?' We'd been in Putney three days now, but I still had no real feel for the place.

Babs reapplied her lip-gloss while the children gorged themselves on Smarties. 'It's where all the boring people with kids live so you'll fit right in.'

'Gee, thanks. I'm so glad to hear that,' I said, giving her a fake smile.

'Seriously,' she said, looking around, 'this place is depressing. All the houses on the road look exactly the same. I don't know why you didn't listen to me and get a cool loft in Soho.'

I shook my head. 'Because lofts are for people like you – young, selfish and single – not for someone like me who has two small kids. I need a garden so the children can run around in circles and tire themselves out instead of trashing the house.'

'Fine, whatever.' Babs polished off her coffee and ordered me upstairs for my make-over.

The suitcase, it turned out, contained a whole bunch of outfits Babs had borrowed from the wardrobe department at the TV show she presents, *How To Look Good With Your Clothes On*. An hour later, having managed to squeeze myself into one of the fifteen dresses she'd brought, I was ready.

'Give us a twirl,' Babs said, and I obeyed. 'If I say so myself, I did a damn good job. Green is definitely your colour. It tones down the red hair – and, with the super-suction Spanx, the dress actually looks like it fits you properly.'

I heard the bell ring, and James opening the front door. He was greeting a man – it must be the journalist.

I studied myself critically in the mirror. My makeup was good, at least I was able to do that myself, and the dress was very flattering. Babs had insisted that I wear six-inch heels, to make my legs look thinner, and I had to admit that, although the shoes were torturously uncomfortable, they made a big difference. I smiled at myself. I was pleased with the overall result. I really wanted to look good for this photo. I knew it was important to James. He was determined to make sure his new job went smoothly and a good first impression was vital. He was still haunted by what had happened with the Irish team, and I knew he was determined not to put a foot wrong this time.

We went back downstairs. I still hadn't dressed the children, who were running around like lunatics in the garden in their pyjamas, high on sugar. I was waiting until the very last second to put on their freshly pressed clothes. James's interview was in progress. Babs and I watched them through the glass door that separated the kitchen from the living room.

The journalist was dressed very casually in a crumpled shirt and chinos. He was younger than James. His Dictaphone lay on the coffee-table between them, but he was taking notes as well. James was sitting bolt upright on the couch, his hands clasped together in his lap. He seemed very tense.

'Are you worried you'll end up like your predecessor, out on your ear after nine months?' the journalist asked him.

Nine months! James hadn't told me that. He'd said the previous rugby manager hadn't worked out, but he hadn't mentioned the very brief timeline. Would we have to move again in nine months? Would anyone hire him if this job didn't work out, just like the last one? My stomach twisted.

James smiled stiffly. 'I'm planning to bring all the experience and success I had coaching Leinster to London Irish. I'm confident I can turn this team around and have a long and fruitful career with them.'

'But your last position, as assistant coach for the Irish team, ended after only six months. What makes you think this will be different?'

'Ouch,' Babs muttered. 'Look at James's face.'

Damn! Why the hell had the journalist brought that up? It was so unfair. It hadn't been James's fault.

James crossed his arms and frowned deeply. 'The Irish position didn't work out because of a clash of personalities between the head coach, Frank Gallagher, and the Irish Rugby Federation. Unfortunately, I was a casualty of that disagreement. The only reason I was let go was because the new coach they hired, Jackson Hadley, wanted to bring his own assistant coach with him.'

'Good answer,' I whispered.

'Yes, but his body language is really defensive,' Babs whispered back.

James was sitting with his arms folded tightly across his chest. The Irish job fiasco had really knocked his confidence. I hated Frank Gallagher with a passion. If he had just been a bit less pig-headed and got on with managing the team, none of this would have happened and we'd be back home in Dublin, living our lovely life, and James would be his old self-assured and contented self.

'He's going to have to be tougher,' Babs said. 'He should tell that journalist to stick his stupid questions up his arse.'

'Keep your voice down!' I warned her. The last thing James needed was the journalist to hear insults being slung at him from the next room.

'Seriously, Emma, James needs to grow bigger balls. He can't go around being defensive and poor-me about his old job. It didn't work out. He should put some kind of a spin on it and make it sound like he walked out on them, or he was keen to move back to his hometown London, or something.'

She had a point. He'd need to be smoother and more polished for future interviews.

The journalist tapped his notepad with his pen. 'Is it not

also true that you were let go because the captain of the Irish team, Barry O'Brian, didn't respect you?'

James dropped his arms to his side and sat forward. 'No, that's not true at all. I've no idea where you got that information, but it's false.'

'Really? I heard it from Barry O'Brian when I called him about you. He said, although you were highly valued at Leinster, the Munster players on the Irish team didn't rate you. He felt a lot of your success was based on luck and the fact that Donal Brady was a brilliant captain and player. Brady also happens to be a good friend of yours, am I right?'

James's face went an alarming shade of red. Gripping his knees with his hands, he snapped, 'Barry O'Brian never said any of this to me. When I coached him, we got along just fine. As for Barry and the Munster players thinking I wasn't a good coach, frankly, that's bullshit. In fact, Munster tried to poach me when I was training Leinster. They offered me more money to move down to Limerick and train Munster, but I refused because I was loyal to Leinster and to the team. As for the comment about Donal Brady, yes, he is a close friend of mine and I think he's a tremendous leader and player, but he's not a coach. *I* coached that team to victory and I will not have anyone saying or implying otherwise.'

'Way to go, James.' Babs was impressed and I breathed a sigh of relief.

'Are you surprised by O'Brian's comments, then?' the journalist asked.

James sat back. 'Yes, I am. I thought he was more professional than that, but I'm certainly not going to get into a slagging match about it. O'Brian is a fine player and a good captain for Ireland. I wish him and his teammates well.'

The journalist smiled. 'That's very magnanimous of you.'

James grinned, his face finally losing its tension. 'My wife's

Irish and my children are half Irish. I had a wonderful time living and coaching in Dublin. But I'm in London now and I want to look forward, not back. I intend to be the most successful coach London Irish has ever had.'

'Fighting words.' The journalist jotted down the quote.

James nodded. 'I *am* a fighter and I have the utmost confidence in my abilities.' Standing up to stretch his legs, he asked if the interview was over. It was obvious he'd rather have been eating the guy's toenail clippings than answering his questions.

'More or less, but I wonder if I could ask your wife a few questions? I'd like to get a sense of how she feels about the move,' the journalist said.

What? I froze. That wasn't part of the plan. I didn't want to answer any questions. I was prepared to smile at the camera, but I certainly hadn't agreed to an interview.

'Emma!' Babs nudged me roughly. 'Get your arse in there.'

'But – I don't know what to say!'

'Just smile and say very little. Keep your answers short and don't ramble.'

'I never ramble.'

Babs rolled her eyes. 'Hello! You spend your whole life rambling and ranting and going off on tangents, just like Mum.'

'I do not. I am not like Mum in any way. I never rant and, besides, you're a fine one to talk about –'

Babs held up a hand in front of my face. 'Zip it, Emma. Now, get in there and help your husband out. He needs it.'

James looked at the door, smiled when he saw us hovering there and walked over to usher me in.

'You were amazing. I'm so proud of you,' I whispered in his ear. He squeezed my hand.

Introducing me to the journalist, he said, 'Emma, this is

Joe Kendal. He'd like to ask you a few questions. Is that all right?'

I proffered my hand and plastered a smile on my face, but something caught my eye: it was Babs, waving at me from the doorway. 'Psycho smile,' she mouthed. 'Tone it down.' I tried to relax my facial muscles into a less alarming grimace.

Joe Kendal smiled at me and I couldn't help feeling like a mouse in a snakepit. 'So, Emma, how do you feel about the move to London? You've got two small kids so it can't have been easy.'

I felt James's body tensing again beside me. I knew what the hack was probing for, and there was no way I was going to give it to him. It was time for me to take control.

'I'm delighted to be in London, Joe. I married an Englishman, so we're a half-English family anyway. It's such a wonderful city, so vibrant and with so much to do and see. We're very much looking forward to settling into our new life here. And I think Irish London are very lucky to have James as their coach.'

I heard a groan from the doorway. 'London Irish, you dope,' Babs hissed. James threw back his head and laughed. I was blushing wildly, but he didn't seem bothered by my mistake. Wrapping an arm around me, he said, 'Emma has been very supportive of my career. I'm very lucky to have a wife who puts up with all the upheaval that this job entails.'

'You won't print that Irish London mistake, will you?' I asked Joe. 'I mean, I don't want people to think I'm stupid or slow or mentally challenged or something. Not that there's anything wrong with being mentally challenged, of course. I mean, loads of people are and they're great and they lead really full lives. I'm not being racist or bigoted, or whatever the word is. I know people who are mentally challenged –

sure what difference does it make? We're all God's creatures, right? I mean, I have friends who –'

James was looking at me aghast, as was Joe Kendal, but I couldn't stop the torrent of nervous words that was pouring out of me.

'Put a sock in it, Emma.' Babs strutted into the room. 'Hello, Joe, I'm Barbara Burke. You probably recognize me from my show, *How To Look Good With Your Clothes On.*'

Joe stared at her blankly.

Babs carried on: 'You'll have to excuse my sister. She's not used to the media. But I can tell you one thing, James is a bloody brilliant coach. He transformed that Leinster team. London Irish are lucky to have him on board. Make sure you print that.'

Joe took out his notebook. 'What did you say your name was?'

Babs frowned. 'Barbara Burke, host of the very successful *How To Look Good With Your Clothes On.*'

'Never heard of it. What channel is it on?' Joe asked, as James and I tried not to laugh.

'Lifestyle,' Babs snapped. 'It airs at two o'clock on Mondays, Wednesdays and Fridays. It's a very popular show.'

Joe nodded and scribbled. 'OK. Well, thanks very much, James and Emma – and Barbara. I'll just pop out and ask Eddie to come in for the photos now.'

James and I shook his hand, exchanged a relieved glance, and I ran out to wrestle the children into their clothes.

While the photographer was setting up, I watched Lara and Yuri sitting beside James on the couch. Yuri looked adorable in his little blue shirt. With his fair hair and chocolate brown eyes, he would have melted anyone's heart. And as for my little princess, she hadn't inherited my red hair, as Babs had pointed out, so she wouldn't have to go through school being called 'Carrothead' or 'Fanta'. She had beautiful blonde hair. It was very fine, so I kept it shoulder-length. But Lara's best assets were her navy blue eyes and her killer smile. When she smiled, two big dimples appeared, one on each cheek. It was adorable.

I marvelled at my two beautiful children and silently thanked God for giving me the gift of motherhood. Although my infertility, Yuri's adoption and then Lara's premature birth had been really difficult times, there was never a day went by when I didn't feel grateful that it had ended like this. These two children were my miracles, and I appreciated them all the more for having struggled so hard to have them.

As I watched my beautiful little ones snuggling into their dad's arms, I willed myself to be positive. We were a family, a unit, a team, and together we would make it work. I shook my hair over my shoulder and shot the most convincing smile I could manage at the camera lens.

3

Once I saw my own linen on the beds and our clothes hanging in the wardrobes, the house felt less alien. The children's rooms looked out onto the back garden and ours faced the main road. As I was putting away Lara's clothes, I glanced out of the window. To the right I saw two very blond children in a paddling pool. To the left a woman in shorts and a T-shirt was digging a complicated vegetable patch, with rows and rows of plants and a small glasshouse in a corner.

The sun was shining and I began to feel more positive. Putney seemed a nice area. I was glad we had chosen to live there. James's new boss had recommended it as a pleasant suburban village not too far from the London Irish training ground, where James would be working. There was a gorgeous French coffee shop and patisserie five minutes from the house, a good selection of restaurants and one really cool boutique on the high street.

Even though the area looked promising, I was still worried about filling my days while James and the kids were at work and school. James was already deeply involved in his job while Yuri and Lara would start nursery school soon. What would I do then? I didn't know anyone and, besides, I was used to working. Back in Dublin, I'd loved my job as a makeup artist on the TV chat show *Afternoon with Amanda*. Amanda had been a great boss and I'd really miss her. I knew the competition in London for makeup artists would be fierce. I wasn't sure how to break into the industry. I'd have to talk to Babs. She worked in TV, so she could put me in touch with whoever did her makeup. I could ask them how to go about getting work. For now, I'd just have to stay focused on getting the children settled and finding my bearings.

I went downstairs to make some coffee and try to sweet-talk James into agreeing to do a big shop – we needed everything to fill the fridge and cupboards. He was standing at the kitchen counter, trying to persuade Yuri and Lara that dry toast was nice.

'But I want butter on mine,' Yuri said.

'I know, but we don't have any. Mummy will do a big shop later.'

We'll see about that, I thought, with a smile.

'But I don't like bread with no butter. It's yucky.'

'Yuckity-yuck,' Lara added.

James was relieved to see me. 'Oh, look! Here's Mummy now – she can sort this out. Daddy has to go to work.'

'Work? I thought you were going to be around for a week, to help me settle in.'

'We finished unpacking the last boxes yesterday,' James reminded me. 'We're settled.'

'But I don't know where the nearest big supermarket is.'

James shrugged. 'Nor do I, darling. I've never lived in Putney before. Why don't you ask one of the neighbours?'

I tried not to get too annoyed in front of the children. If they hadn't been there to act as a buffer, I'd have whacked him over the head with the nearest weapon I could find. 'I don't know them. I don't want to go banging on doors yet. Come on, James, please. You can go in tomorrow.'

James ran a hand through his dark hair, pushing it back from his eyes. He looked tired. He had tossed and turned all night. 'Sorry, darling, but I have to show my face today. I want them to know how keen I am. I really need to make a good impression. You'll be fine,' he said, giving me a quick hug before picking up his kit bag. 'Besides, Imogen said she was going to pop in to check on you today.'

I stopped dead. 'What did you say?' Had he really just casually announced that my nightmare of a sister-in-law was coming over?

James was walking towards the door, making a quick escape. I grabbed his shoulder. 'Excuse me. Imogen?'

He sighed. 'She knows the area – she lived here as a student – so she can help you out.'

I glared at him. 'You know I can't stand her.'

'What does "can't stand" mean?' Lara asked. 'Does it mean you has wobbly legs?'

'Nothing,' James and I answered in unison.

'It means you hate something,' Yuri informed his little sister.

Lara's eyes widened. 'Mummy, do you don't like Imogen?'

'No! Of course I do,' I said, desperately trying to do damage control. Lara had a habit of repeating everything she heard at home. 'I meant I can't stand her to come here when we have no food in the house and it's still messy.' I pulled James aside. 'Why didn't you make up an excuse?' I hissed.

James put up his hands defensively. 'I'm sorry, Emma. Look, I was talking to Henry last night and she came on the phone and offered to call in. I couldn't very well say no.'

'Yes, you could. "No" is the easiest word in the world to say.'

'It would have been rude.'

'Imogen has skin like an elephant's. She's incapable of being insulted.'

James grinned. 'That's a bit harsh. She means well.'

'No, she most certainly does not. She goes out of her way to be nasty.'

'She's just a little direct at times.'

'She's a cow,' I muttered.

'She's my brother's wife,' James protested, a bit alarmed. I'd say he was worried about the reception Imogen would get from me.

'Why are you talking all quiet?' Lara asked.

'We're just discussing Daddy's work,' I said brightly. Then to James, 'You can't leave me now.'

James peered at his watch. 'Sorry, darling. I said I'd meet the management team at nine thirty. I have to go.'

'James, this is not a good start to our new life. You may come back to an empty house,' I grumbled, my earlier positivity evaporating.

'You never know, you may have fun.' James winked at me, then legged it out of the door.

I was in the middle of a whirlwind effort to tidy the kitchen when I heard Imogen's loud, horsy voice bellowing outside.

'Come along, children, we have to visit poor Aunt Emma. She's never been to London before so she needs our help. She's not used to big cities. She won't be able to manage at all.'

Yuri looked up from the jigsaw he was doing. 'Is that Imogen?'

I nodded.

'Do you think Thomas is there, too?' He looked terrified.

I peeped out of the window. 'Yes.'

'*Muuuuuuum!*'

'I know he can be a bit of a pain, Yuri. Why don't you just

try to stay away from him? Hopefully they won't stay too long.'

The bell rang. Damn! No time to run up and change. I reluctantly went to open the door, with Lara at my side. My three-year-old daughter was dressed from head to toe in a frog outfit she'd found in one of the boxes when my back was turned.

Imogen was standing at the door in her usual uniform of white shirt, navy blazer, cream chinos and sensible slip-on shoes. She was all about smart, practical clothes. I'd never seen her in heels. She'd once told me that she thought my clothes were very 'jazzy' and that my 'sky-high shoes' were 'utterly ridiculous'. Apparently I'd develop bunions from wearing them. Imogen's idea of glamour was putting a scarf – probably dotted with horseshoes – over her navy blazer.

Her brown hair was cut in a short bob, which she held back from her face with an Alice band. She always wore one, even though I was pretty sure they'd gone out of fashion in the eighties. Mind you, I was in no position to criticize anyone: I'd answered the door in an old pair of tracksuit bottoms and the T-shirt I'd slept in.

Imogen's children were dressed like clones of their mother: cream chinos and white shirts. I looked at Yuri, who was wearing a T-shirt that said *I Hate Homework* and red pyjama bottoms with bright green aliens all over them. I cursed James under my breath for landing this on me. 'Hi, guys,' I said, plastering a smile on my face while Imogen took in my unkempt, trailer-trash look.

'Just up?' she asked, brushing past me, followed by Thomas and the twins.

'Uhm, kind of, yes. We stayed up late unpacking.'

'Hello, Aunt Emma,' the twins said. Thomas ignored me. Nothing new there.

I smiled at the twins, who were sweet girls. Luckily for them, they had inherited Henry's sunny disposition and so far had avoided their mother's sharp tongue and large posterior – we're talking Kim Kardashian plus J-Lo *and* Beyoncé. I felt positively petite beside her. Every cloud . . .

I bent down to the twins. 'Girls, please just call me Emma. "Aunt Emma" sounds so formal and makes me feel ancient.'

'They address all of their aunts and uncles like that. I don't see why they should make an exception for you.' Imogen was looking around the hall, wrinkling her nose.

'Come on in. I'll put the kettle on,' I said, praying it would be a flying visit. The older children went into the lounge, but Lara followed me into the kitchen. 'It'll just be black coffee, I'm afraid, Imogen, I haven't had a chance to find a supermarket.'

Imogen lowered her oversized posterior into a seat and arched an eyebrow at the general clutter. I moved towards the kettle and clicked it on.

'Ribbit,' Lara said, hopping like a frog.

Imogen looked at her. 'Oh, hello. Are you off to a fancy-dress party?'

Lara shook her head. 'Ribbit.'

'Is she still not talking?' Imogen asked.

I took a deep breath and willed myself to remain calm and serene, two very alien emotions in my life. I'd have loved to be both calm *and* serene all the time. 'I like you. You're feisty,' James said, when he first met me. 'Feisty and spirited.' I wasn't sure how thrilled he was by my feistiness now, but in the beginning he'd thought it was great.

I was very touchy about anyone commenting on Lara's speech because she had been late to talk. She hadn't said a word until she was almost three, which everyone kept commenting on, of course. But once she started, she came out with complete sentences and hadn't stopped since. We'd had five months of non-stop chatter and she had an opinion on everything.

'Lara, say hello to Imogen,' I said, desperate for my daughter to show Imogen how wonderful her vocabulary was.

Lara blinked. 'Ribbit.'

'Oh dear. It's getting serious now, Emma. Have you considered that she may have –' Imogen leant in and whispered loudly '– learning difficulties? I know a marvellous woman who deals with children who –'

I cut straight across her: 'Lara does not have learning difficulties. She's pretending to be a frog. She's very creative.'

Imogen sat up. 'How can you be sure if she doesn't speak?'

'She speaks perfectly well.' I turned to Lara and eyeballed her. Keeping my voice neutral, I urged her, 'Come on, sweetheart, talk to Imogen. Show her how clever you are.'

Lara stared at me, unblinking, then turned and hopped away shouting, 'Ribbit.' Right then and there, I wanted to kill my own child.

Imogen looked at me as if I was living in denial and her point had been irrefutably proven. 'I'll text you the woman's number later. It's useful to have.'

'Lara is not – Oh, never mind.' I slammed two mugs of coffee onto the table, slopping them.

'It's a pity you didn't consult me before renting this place.' Imogen took out a large handkerchief and wiped her coffee cup. 'The other side of Putney is so much smarter. This road is a bit, well, mixed.'

Imogen had been in the house ten minutes and I already wanted to slap her. I fantasized briefly about wrapping a whole roll of masking tape around her mouth. 'What are you going to do about the awful décor?' she continued.

'As we're renting, there isn't much I can do. But I'm going

to cover the walls with paintings and photos and get some colourful rugs to put over the carpet. We'll fix it up so it looks more homely.'

'Have you put the children down for schools?'

'They're going to attend a Montessori ten minutes' walk from here. I had a quick visit to it the last time I was over and it seemed nice.'

'But isn't Yuri five?'

'No, he's four and three-quarters, so he can go to big school next year. I'm happy for him to be a bit old for his class – he had a difficult start in life.'

'I see. I presume you explained to the teacher about Lara being different?'

I gripped the table to stop my arm shooting out and punching Imogen. 'Lara isn't different. She's perfectly normal.'

As if on cue, Lara hopped in, grabbed a biscuit and said, 'Ribbit.'

Thomas came in behind her, scowling. 'I'm bored, Mummy, let's go.'

'Not yet, darling, I'm trying to help poor Emma find her feet. She has no idea what to do in London.' Imogen put her hand on Thomas's shoulder. 'Thomas goes to St David's College. They start aged six. And from nine years old they offer weekly boarding, which Thomas does. It's one of the best schools in the country. It has an excellent equestrian centre. You should put Yuri down for it. Of course, it's impossible to get into, the waiting list is never-ending, but . . .' Imogen paused for effect '. . . I'm one of the governors, so I could get him a place next year.'

As if I would consider sending my angel boy to some horsy boarding school with his wretched older cousin. Did she think I was completely certifiable?

'He wouldn't last a day.' Thomas snorted. 'A midget like him couldn't handle St David's.'

'Do not call him a midget,' I snapped.

'All right, dwarf.'

'Yuri is not a dwarf!' I was now sitting on my hands because I didn't trust myself. I was definitely going to punch someone.

'There's no need to be so defensive, Emma,' Imogen said. 'The child *is* extremely small.'

I turned on her. 'My son is not a midget or a dwarf. He had a shitty start in life at the orphanage, but he is growing all the time, and although he may never be ten feet tall, the doctors have assured me that he will end up being of average height.'

Thomas took a biscuit and stuffed it into his mouth. 'Your house smells.'

'It just needs to be aired.'

'It stinks.'

So do you, you little brat, I thought darkly.

Yuri came in. 'Mummy, can I have a biccie?'

I swept him onto my lap, inhaling the scent of his hair. 'Of course you can, pet.'

Imogen leant over. 'Yuri, wouldn't you like to go to the same school Thomas goes to one day? It's a boarding school. You sleep there from Monday to Friday. Doesn't that sound like fun?'

Yuri shook his head vigorously. 'Please don't send me away, Mummy.'

I put my arms around him protectively. 'I'd never send you away. You're my lucky charm.'

'Mollycoddling boys is bad for them, Emma, mark my words. You don't want him to turn into a mummy's boy. He'll be bullied at school.'

I hugged Yuri closer. If I could, I'd never let him out of my sight. I felt a tap on my shoulder. It was the twins, followed by the hopping frog, who was beginning to look a bit sweaty in her polyester frog suit.

'Uhm, Aunt Emma, we're trying to play with Lara, but she doesn't seem to be able to speak. Is "ribbit" the only word she knows?'

I shrugged. 'What can I say? She's a Method actor.'

After insulting my house and my children, Imogen left to take her own children horse-riding. Naturally.

I shut the door and breathed a sigh of relief. James's sister-in-law would have to be discouraged from calling again. She brought out a very violent streak in me. Why couldn't Henry have married a sweet English rose? How on earth had Imogen managed to get James's brother, a lovely guy, to marry her? It remained a complete mystery to me. James reckoned she must be incredible in bed. I doubted it, unless she was very bendy from all the horse-riding. Maybe they did role plays: Imogen was the jockey and Henry was the stallion and they used props, like riding boots and hats and whips . . . The thought made me giggle and feel nauseous in equal measure.

'Mummy.' The frog finally spoke. 'I'm hungry.'

'Lara, why didn't you speak when your cousins were here?'

Lara pulled her frog mask off. 'Because frogs don't talk.'

'I know, pet, but now Imogen thinks you can't speak.'

'Actually, Mummy, I don't like her, she's very shouty.'

'Me too,' Yuri agreed, nodding emphatically. 'And I don't want to go to Thomas's school. Promise you won't make me go there, pinkie promise.'

I hugged them both. 'I will never, ever, ever send you to the same school as Thomas, and we're not going to see Imogen or your cousins often because we're going to avoid her like the plague.'

'What does "avoid like a pague" mean?' Yuri asked.

'It means that we're going to be too busy to answer the phone or call over to her.' I was rewarded with two grateful smiles. 'Now, come on, let's get dressed and go exploring.'

Several days later, when I had cleaned the house from top to bottom, hung the paintings and bought a big rug for the living room, I decided it was time to make an effort with the neighbours. I really needed to make some friends before the children started at nursery school so I wouldn't go mad with loneliness.

I called into the house on our left, but there was no answer, so we went to the house on our right, number seven. I rang the doorbell. A supermodel opened the door. She was tall, slim, tanned, with cascading dark hair and green eyes. She was wearing teeny-tiny denim shorts and a bikini top.

'Yez, can I 'elp you?' she asked, in the sexiest French accent this side of Brigitte Bardot.

'Hi, I'm Emma. I've just moved in next door. Do you live here?'

'Yez. I am the au pair of theez family.'

'Oh, right, OK.' Thank God for that. I didn't fancy befriending a mother whose thighs were the same width as my middle finger. 'Is the mum around?'

'No, she eez shopping. She like to shop very much. I think she will be back at about five o'clock, but I am not definite about theez.'

'No problem. Will you just tell her I popped over to say hi?'

'OK.' The supermodel closed the door.

'Mummy, she looked like a princess!' Even Lara was impressed.

'I know. But she's not the mummy, she's the minder.' I didn't want Lara thinking that any mother looked like that.

'I want a minder like her,' Lara said.

'Come on, let's go home and have some ice-cream.' I wanted to distract Lara from the stunning au pair. I wanted to distract myself from her, too – she had reminded me of someone I'd rather forget.

I'd always felt really secure in my marriage. James was solid, steady and devoted to me. He was very English – reserved and measured – and had always loved my Irish lack of restraint and impulsiveness. I felt safe with James. But then one day, about five months ago, I'd called on him at work at the Ireland training ground. I wanted to show him a painting I'd bought. When I arrived I saw him talking to a young woman. She was wearing tight leggings and an Ireland sweatshirt – not very flattering, but you could tell she had a killer body underneath. Even from a distance, I could tell he was trying to impress her. I could see how animated he was. He was telling some story and she was laughing hard. I knew it couldn't have been that funny, because James is no comedian. She had her hand on his arm and she was leaning into him and he was leaning towards her, too. You could tell from a mile away that they liked each other. There was an intimacy about them that stopped me in my tracks.

Lucy did point out that it wasn't as if I'd found him having hot sex with someone in the storage cupboard, but I still felt sick. I could see he was flirting with her. You know when your husband fancies someone . . . because he acts the way he did when he used to fancy you.

When I came up behind them, James jumped and then went a bit red in the face. He hadn't been expecting me and was suddenly flustered. He introduced me to this Mandy person. She was at least ten years younger than me and a whole lot more pert. Her boobs still stood up and her face was almost devoid of lines.

I put out my hand and shook hers very firmly – if I'm being honest, I crushed it a bit. Well, a woman has to stand her ground. I wanted Mandy to be under no illusions as to who she was up against. 'And what do you do, Mandy?' I asked.

'I'm a physio,' she said, shaking her bouncy ponytail.

'Really? And how long have you been working with James?'

'About two months,' she said. 'He's been so great to me, showing me the ropes and making sure I feel included in the squad. And he's so funny – you must laugh all the time at home. You're so lucky.'

Two months! Two months this flirtation had been going on and James had never mentioned any new physio coming into the squad. And who the hell was Mandy to tell me how lucky I was? And James wasn't that funny. He could be amusing sometimes but not hysterically so, like she was making out. I was furious and, actually, I felt threatened and suddenly very insecure.

'Well, I'd better go. I'll see you later at training, James. Nice to meet you, Emily.'

'It's Emma,' I said.

'Oops, sorry.' Mandy bounced off, leaving me seething with a shifty-looking James.

I turned to my hilarious husband. 'So how come you never mentioned Mandy before?'

He shrugged. 'What's to say? She's one of the new physios, that's all.'

I glared at him. 'I think there's a lot to say, actually. She seems to find you very amusing. Apparently you went out of your way to make sure she felt at home. You seem to have taken a very keen interest in her.'

James dug his hands into his tracksuit pockets. 'I always try to make new people feel comfortable.'

'Oh, she seems very comfortable to me. You're doing a great job there. She looks very at home.'

'She's a good physio and fun to be around. All the guys love her.'

I bet they do, I thought grimly. 'Is that right? Well, bully for her.' I tried to keep my voice neutral. I didn't want James to see how rattled I was. I wanted to be calm . . . but, unfortunately, that is not in my nature.

'Do you fancy her?' I blurted out.

'No.' He was avoiding my eyes.

'Oh, my God, you do. I can see it in your face.' I was shocked. I'd never been remotely worried that James would meet someone in work, because 99 per cent of the people he worked with were men. Besides, I just hadn't imagined he fancied other women any more. I'm not saying he didn't think some women were good-looking or sexy . . . but actively fancy them? No. I'd never seen him like this with any of our female friends or his colleagues' wives or anyone else we socialized with. James was always polite and charming, but never flirty.

'For goodness' sake, Emma, don't start making a drama out of nothing. She's a new colleague I get on well with.'

'Very well, by the look of things,' I muttered.

'She's easy to work with. There's no crime in that,' he snapped.

I opened my mouth to protest, but decided to shut it again. He was annoyed and defensive. I didn't want to push him right into Mandy's arms. I needed to step away and think about what to do. I changed the subject and tried my best to be breezy, but it was difficult through gritted teeth.

For the next month I'd watched James like a hawk and

popped in, at different times of the day, to visit him at work. I checked his phone and his laptop when he wasn't in the room, but didn't find anything. As Lucy said, it was probably just a little flirtation, and there was no harm in it. But I didn't feel so blasé. A flirt can lead to a lot more if it isn't nipped in the bud. A flirt means you're bored at home. Happily married men don't flirt.

James got more sex in the weeks that followed my meeting with Mandy than he knew what to do with. I cranked it up big-time – new lingerie, scented body lotion, candles and even some dirty talk. James seemed very pleased and participated enthusiastically. It ended up being fun for both of us. But I had been shaken by what I'd seen. I realized that I needed to make more of an effort at keeping our marriage interesting and fresh. And although most nights I just wanted to put on my fleecy pyjamas and eat chocolate biscuits in bed while watching bad reality TV, I had to remember that there were two of us in our relationship.

Then, of course, James had been fired and Mandy was no longer an issue as our life was turned upside-down.

As I walked the children back to our house, I resolved that this was the night to christen our new home. I'd bought a black lacy body in Dublin, before we left, and I was going to root it out, open a bottle of wine and give James a little reminder of why he'd fallen in love with me.

I was lost in thought, planning my evening, when I heard, 'Hey, Sis. Hey, Shrimp. Hey, Gorgeous.'

It was Babs, climbing out of a taxi, looking amazing, with perfect hair and makeup. She was wearing a ballet-length, halterneck red dress.

'I know, I look ridiculous. This dress is so conservative, but they've had complaints about me showing too much flesh on the show. Apparently some frigid cow in Devon thought it was disgraceful to have so much cleavage and thigh on view on an afternoon show. I bet her husband loved it and she just got the hump with him ogling me.'

I never ceased to wonder where Babs got her confidence. It was colossal. I wished I had half of it.

'You should consider wearing clothes that don't show off so much flesh more often. You look much nicer and less available,' I noted, behaving every inch the older sister. But, then, it was true.

'I love your dress. Do a twirl, Babs, do a twirl,' Lara demanded.

Babs obliged with a couple of spins. 'I've come straight from the studio to give you the good news. I'm the best sister in the world and you can grovel at my feet.'

I put my key in the door and ushered the kids through the kitchen and into the back garden. 'Go on – I'm waiting with bated breath.'

Babs threw her enormous bag onto a chair. 'I've got you a job.'

'What?'

'The makeup artist on our show just handed in her notice. Before they had a chance to start looking for someone else, I said they had to hire you.'

'You're kidding! Really?'

'Yes. I'm not all bad, you know. Anyway, they asked about your history and blah blah blah. I bigged you up, of course. I said you'd worked for the best show on Irish TV and done all the celebrity weddings in Ireland. So they said they'd give you a three-week trial, and if that works out, they'll hire you on a six-month contract.'

'But when do they want me to start? What sort of hours? What about the kids?' I was thrilled and nervous all at once. It was too soon – I had so much to sort out and I didn't know

London at all. I'd have to get a nanny. How would I juggle everything?

Babs opened the fridge and poured herself a glass of wine. 'You start Monday week so you've got plenty of time to sort out your stuff.'

I sat down at the table. 'And the hours – what do you think they'll be?'

'Usually from about nine thirty or ten in the morning till about five, sometimes later, depending on how the show is going. Some of the women need a lot of encouragement to get undressed and look in the mirror. Sometimes it takes hours, which is such a pain in the arse. On those days we always run late.'

'Will I have to travel?'

'Not really. It's mostly shot in London – we don't have a big budget.' Babs rummaged in the cupboards. 'Do you have anything decent to eat?'

Wow! A job, and so soon. It had been much easier than I'd expected. It would do me good to work, though. I wouldn't have time to dwell on the move or my loneliness. Plus I'd be earning my own money and hopefully I'd meet nice people. It was great. Except for one small detail: my sister was the star of the show.

As if she could read my mind, Babs, who had found a box of animal-shaped crackers in one of the cupboards, said, 'Obviously I'm the most important person on the programme so you can't try to boss me around or behave like my sister. You have to be super-nice to me and treat me with respect.'

'Can't I just ignore you?'

Babs waved a lion cracker at me. 'I'm serious. This is my show.'

'Isn't that what all presenters think until they're replaced?'

'I'm not going to be replaced. The public love me.'

I resisted the urge to laugh. 'Whose makeup will I be doing?'

'Mine, although obviously you won't have much work to do on me, and then you'll have to do the women we're making over. Some are shocking-looking, so you'll have your work cut out for you.'

'You have such a lovely way with words.' I held out my hand. Babs passed me a giraffe cracker.

'So, are you in?'

'Absolutely. Now I just need to find a childminder.'

Yuri and Lara came running in from the garden.

'Guess what?' I said.

'We're going home!' Yuri ran around the kitchen, cheering. 'Yeah. I can go to Connor's house for a play.'

My heart sank. The poor little guy missed his friends in Dublin so much. 'No, sweetheart, we're not going home, but Mummy's got a new job.'

Yuri looked crestfallen.

'Is the beautiful girl going to mind us?' Lara asked, still dazzled by the au pair next door.

'No, Mummy's going to find a different minder.' One who looks like an old troll, I thought. An old troll with rotten teeth and severe acne so Daddy won't be tempted by her.

'Can I have a cracker?' Yuri asked Babs.

She shook the box. 'Sorry, Short-fry, I ate them.'

'But I want one.' Yuri looked as if he was about to cry. 'It's mean to eat them all. It's not fair.'

Babs laid her hand on his head. 'Listen, Squirt, I've just got your mum a job. And if your mum has a job, that means she makes money. If she has money, that means she can buy loads more of these crackers for you, and more toys and sweets and all that stuff, so don't give me a hard time. OK?'

Yuri nodded. 'OK.'

I couldn't believe it. If I had eaten Yuri's crackers, he would have had a complete meltdown, but the kids never freaked out with Babs. Maybe if the TV presenting dried up she should consider childcare. I smiled to myself. Somehow I doubted any woman of sane mind would have Babs in her home.

'Right, *amigos*, I have to go. I've got a show to tape.'

After the children had had their snack, I decided to enjoy the lovely sunshine and sit outside on the patio. I wanted ten minutes of peace to read my magazine, so I told Lara and Yuri to do races up and down the garden. I was reading a very good article on why women are never happy with their bodies when Yuri pushed Lara. She fell down, scraped her knee and proceeded to scream like a banshee.

'For God's sake, Yuri, I've told you a million times not to push your sister.'

'Blood!' shrieked Lara.

I examined her knee. 'No, pet, there's no blood. Now, stop screaming.'

'She pushed me first. I hate her!' Yuri shouted.

'Don't say that,' I snapped. I couldn't stand it when they were mean to one another. They only had each other in the world, and when James and I died, I didn't want them fighting and falling out. Because I had one adopted and one biological child, I was even more determined to make them close. Siblings had to look out for each other. I was close to my brother Sean, but he lived in New York now and was hopeless at keeping in touch. When we met up it was always great, but I only spoke to him about once every six weeks. As for Babs . . . When we were younger, the thirteen-year age gap had seemed huge, but we had got closer over the years, although she still drove me crazy and we did argue a lot.

'Apologize to your sister,' I ordered Yuri.

'No way.' Yuri crossed his arms.

'Yuri, I'm going to count to three and you'd better apologize or you'll be in big trouble. One . . . two . . .'

'Uhm, hello?'

I turned to my right. A woman was leaning over the fence, waving at me. Damn. I really hadn't wanted my neighbours to hear me shouting at my children.

'Hello!' my neighbour said again.

I jumped up and went over. 'Sorry. Hi, I'm Emma.'

Close up, the neighbour was pretty in a very natural way. Her hair was cut short and she was very tanned with bright blue eyes.

'I'm Carol. Carol Richards. Number nine.'

I shook her hand. 'Nice to meet you. We've just moved over from Dublin.'

Carol leant on her spade. 'I thought I heard an accent. How are you finding it so far?'

'It's fine, thanks. I've just been unpacking and getting organized, so I haven't really had a proper chance to look around or meet people.'

'Who's this, then?' Carol pointed to Lara, who was peeping from behind my leg.

'Oh, sorry, this is Lara, she's three, and that's Yuri, he's four.'

'And three-quarters,' Yuri said, coming over to inspect the new person.

'Three-quarters is very important. Nice to meet you, Yuri and Lara. What beautiful names you have.'

'I'm adopted from Russia. My mummy says I'm her heart baby,' Yuri piped up.

'Wow, lucky you,' Carol said, smiling at him.

Yuri continued with his life story: 'Mummy said when she saw me in the orf'nage, she knew I was her little boy. Her

39

heart told her. Some babies come out of their mummies' tummies, like Lara, and some come in their mummies' hearts, like me.'

I stroked the back of Yuri's head. I loved him telling people he was my heart baby. It made me want to weep with love and pride.

'Well, it looks as if you've been filled in on our family history,' I said, laughing.

'It's very heartwarming.' Carol had a lovely smile – very genuine. I liked her immediately. I could tell already that she didn't have any agenda or angles: she was exactly who you saw.

'Do you have babies?' Lara asked our neighbour.

'Lara!' I said, embarrassed. 'I've told you it's rude to ask people that.'

'It's OK,' Carol reassured me. 'Actually, Lara, I have two boys.'

'Are they big or small?' Lara asked.

'Terry is nine and Freddy is seven, but he's tall so everyone thinks he's nine, too. They've gone to the park with their granny.'

'Yuri isn't big at all. Mummy keeps trying to get him bigger. It's cos of the yucky food in the orf'nage.'

What was going on? The kids were never normally so forthcoming with information. Before I could interrupt, Carol turned to Yuri and said, 'I think you're a perfect size.'

Yuri beamed at her and climbed up on a rock to look over her fence. 'Wow! Your garden's a big mess,' he said.

Carol laughed. 'Well, it's actually an organized mess. You see, I grow all my own food.'

'Do you grow cornflakes?' Yuri asked.

'No, but I grow rhubarb and strawberries and courgettes and aubergines and carrots and tomatoes and cucumbers and beans and lots of other things, too.'

'Yuck. Yuck. Yuck. The only thing I like is strawberries,' Yuri announced.

'Yuri! Don't be rude. It's incredible that Carol grows all those vegetables and fruits in her garden.'

'What's a corgette and what's a oberine?' Lara asked.

I could feel my face going red. I was mortified that my daughter didn't know those vegetables. I'd probably have Jamie Oliver knocking on my door tomorrow, berating me for being a bad mother. I'd been very conscientious about vegetables with Yuri because he really needed them to strengthen him when we'd brought him home from the orphanage. But Lara spat out every vegetable I put into her mouth, and dinner time had become a war zone. Yuri would eat vegetables if they were hidden in a sauce, but Lara could spot, smell and sense a vegetable at ten paces. She refused to eat anything except the plainest of food and, if I'm being honest, I'd kind of given up. I knew I needed to try to introduce vegetables again, but I hated fighting with Lara every night and it nearly always ended in tears – either Lara's or mine. Sometimes even Yuri joined in.

'Why don't you come over and I'll show you the garden?' Carol suggested.

'Thanks. We'd love to!' I was delighted to be getting some quality time with someone new. Carol definitely seemed like my type of person, so hopefully we could be pals.

We got to her garden via the side entrance to her house. While our side of the wall between the two houses was black, Carol's was white and it had vegetables painted on it in bright colours. Yuri and Lara were very impressed.

As for her garden, I was stunned. What Carol had achieved with a fairly small space was incredible. I couldn't believe the variety of fruit and veg she had managed to plant and grow. I had killed every plant I'd ever owned, including a cactus, and they were supposed to live for ever. We ate the sweetest strawberries I'd ever tasted – even Lara liked them. I was thrilled that she didn't spit them out. Then Carol served us apple juice, made from her own apples. It tasted fantastic. We all drained our glasses. The fresh fruit tasted so much better than supermarket stuff that I made solemn vows to myself to be a better mother from that day forward and feed my children fresh things. I'd have to find a farmers' market or something.

Carol even had a hen coop tucked behind the glasshouse. She kept four hens, which laid all her eggs. The children went from being curious to enchanted in ten seconds flat – they loved this garden of colours and scents and hidden surprises. Back over the fence, ours contained a paddling pool and overgrown grass.

'Carol, this is amazing! Have you been working on the garden long?' I asked.

She sipped her apple juice, savouring it. 'Ever since we moved in, ten years ago.'

'Well, you've done a fantastic job.'

'Keith, my husband, says I'm a bit extreme. I've gone very green, you see. I get so furious when I see neighbours' bins full of things they could recycle. The worst on this road is Poppy. She puts all her plastic packaging into her black bin. It makes my blood boil.'

Yikes! I sometimes did that too. I tried to be good, but if I was in a hurry or unpacking zillions of boxes, like I had been lately, I sometimes just shoved everything around me into the black bin. I'd have to be careful in future. I didn't fancy Carol going through my bins and calling me to task.

'*Cooeeee!*' a voice called from behind us.

I turned to see a tall, rake-thin blonde woman tottering down the side entrance. She was wearing skin-tight white jeans, a jewelled, fitted kaftan and the most enormous sun-glasses I'd ever seen – they covered three-quarters of her face.

'I saw you from my window so I thought I'd pop around. The side gate was open, Carol. I presume you're our new neighbour?' she asked me.

'Yes, I'm Emma.'

'This is Poppy – she lives at number seven,' Carol said.

'Oh, right, hi, nice to meet you.'

'We wented to your house and sawed your beautiful minder. She's like a princess,' Lara told Poppy.

Poppy smiled at her. 'Aren't you a cutie? And I love your accent. It's adorable. Yes, Sophie is gorgeous. I like looking at pretty things. I couldn't have anything ugly in my house – it would depress me.' Turning to Carol, she said, 'I honestly don't know how you can sit in this garden – it's like being in the middle of a muddy field.'

Carol laughed good-humouredly. 'This garden means that we don't eat awful processed food full of additives.'

'I prefer Valium and white wine to food. It helps me deal with my life.'

Well, well. One of my neighbours was growing enough veg to feed half of London and the other was a lush. London certainly wasn't boring. Curiosity got the better of me. 'Are you having a tough time?' I asked.

Poppy laid a hand on my arm. 'Darling, when I met Nigel he was head of corporate law at Hendricks, Goodge and Farrow. He was handsome, wealthy and married, but unhap-pily so, fortunately for me. Anyway, we had a very passionate affair and he divorced his wife to make an honest woman of me. His first wife took him to the cleaner's. We were left with very little, so we moved here.' Poppy rolled her eyes. Clearly, Putney was a long way down the list from where she aspired to live. 'And then once he had married me there was, as they say, a job vacancy for a mistress. The bastard left me for his secretary – don't talk to me about clichés. So in our divorce I got half of half, which, let me tell you, was not a lot.'

This was fascinating. I felt positively boring next to this tale of woe. 'How long had you been married?'

'Seven years. And the bastard had the audacity to have an affair and leave me, and our two sons, for a woman who is fatter than I am and uglier. So you see, darling, I need my pills.'

I tried not to laugh. Poppy seemed more upset that her rival was unattractive than that her marriage was over.

'What age are your children?' I asked.

'Six and four. I got my tubes tied after I had Charlie.'

'Yuri's four. Maybe the boys could come over and play some time?'

Poppy nibbled a strawberry. 'Anytime. You can keep them, if you like,' she said, with a wicked grin.

'Actually, speaking of kids,' I said, suddenly inspired, 'I'm looking for a childminder. I'm starting a job soon. Do you know of any good local nanny agencies?'

'What line of work are you in?' Poppy asked.

'I'm a makeup artist.'

Poppy whooped. 'There is a God! You must give me all your best tips. I need them. Honestly, since I turned thirty-seven everything has started drooping and I can only afford Botox once a year. And let's be honest, darling, it's tough out there and I do not want to spend the next forty years alone. I need to look my best to get a new man and I'm only interested in millionaires. I've been on several dates and none of them had big enough bank balances . . . yet.' She winked at me.

I laughed. Poppy was fun. 'I'd be happy to give you some tips.'

Poppy lifted her sunglasses onto the top of her head. 'Now, childcare. I got my girl through Outstanding-aupairs.com. I can forward you the details when I get home. There's an agency on Putney High Street called Nanny Solutions that's supposed to be good, too. But actually, now that I think of it, my cleaning lady mentioned that her daughter's looking for work. She's nineteen or twenty and she's Irish too. I'll text Maggie when I get home and let you know. Maggie's fantastic, so kind and trustworthy. I'm sure her daughter will be a decent girl.'

'That would be brilliant.' I was delighted with how things seemed to be falling into place – first the job, now the childminder. 'Thanks so much.'

Carol was crouching to examine one of her vegetables. 'I'm not going to be much help to you. I've never left the children with anyone but my mother,' she said.

'Never?' I was shocked. 'But what if you need to go out and your mother isn't available?'

Carol shrugged. 'I just stay in, or take the boys with me.'

Poppy butted in: 'And, by the way, her mother lives miles away and only babysits about three times a year.'

I was gobsmacked. 'So you've never left the children with anyone else?' Was she serious? It just sounded so . . . inflexible.

'No, and I never would.'

'I'd leave my kids with anyone who'd take them,' Poppy announced.

'Why?' I asked Carol.

'I wouldn't let a stranger look after my most treasured possessions,' Carol said. 'I just wouldn't be able to relax.'

'I've had lots of different babysitters looking after Yuri and Lara, and I've never had a problem,' I pointed out.

'You're wasting your breath,' Poppy assured me. 'You'll never change Carol's mind.'

45

I was taken aback by Carol's attitude. How could she never leave her boys with anyone but her mother? Her oldest was nine. There must have been lots of nights when she'd wanted to go out but had had to stay in. I didn't see anything wrong with using babysitters. I'd always hired nice local girls.

When I'd gone back to work after my adoption leave, Mum had looked after Yuri, but when Lara had come along I'd hired a lovely Polish girl called Natasha, who had minded the two children for the four hours I was at work each day. Natasha had been amazing: she'd baked with them and taken them to the park and was very sweet. If I hadn't had her, I wouldn't have been able to work. Working mums had to hire people to look after their small children or put them in crèches. I didn't have the guts to say it out loud, but I thought Carol was being unrealistic.

Carol could probably guess what I was thinking from the look on my face, and it was her turn to sound defensive. 'I'm not judging anyone else. I just personally wouldn't feel comfortable leaving my children with someone I barely knew. Would you let a stranger wear your clothes or sleep in your bed? No.'

'It's called having a life, Carol. It's called getting out of the bloody house. It's called retaining your sanity,' Poppy said. 'Nowadays children rule their parents' lives. It's all about them. We're just slaves to their needs and wants. I'm sorry, but I think it's utterly ridiculous. A woman is not a monster for wanting to have a few hours to herself.'

'Or for going back to work,' I added, 'which a lot of the time isn't even a choice any more. Lots of my friends have had to go back to work to help pay the bills.'

Carol sat back on her heels and looked at us. 'It's a choice everyone has to make. I'm not saying my way is the only way, but it's the only one that I feel happy with. I contribute to our household bills by growing all the food we eat and selling the extra at the markets on Saturdays.'

Poppy made a dismissive gesture with her hand and dropped her sunglasses back over her eyes. 'Carol, darling, you need to go out some Saturday night, eat an enormous steak, drink cocktails made with tons of additives and live a little.'

Carol grinned. 'I live very well, thanks, Poppy. We're all different.'

'And that's what makes life interesting,' I added, not wanting to alienate either of my new neighbours.

'Give me a Martini over a parsnip any day,' Poppy drawled.

I could see Yuri and Lara in the corner, digging a hole that didn't look like it belonged. I jumped up. 'Thanks so much for the lovely juice and the strawberries. I'd better get the children home and start setting up interviews for nannies.'

'Give me your number and I'll call you as soon as Maggie lets me know about her daughter.'

I reeled it off and Poppy typed it into her phone.

Later that evening, when the children were asleep, James and I sat on the couch chatting. I filled him in on my new job offer and the search for a nanny.

James was clearly relieved. 'That's wonderful, darling. I was worried that you'd seemed a bit lost since we moved here. Now you'll be busy and ready to give London a go.'

I bristled. 'Well, it hasn't been easy.'

James raised his hand. 'I know, and you've been great. I just think a job will get you out and about and you'll have fun.'

'Well, I don't know how much fun I'm going to have working with Babs, but it'll be a distraction and maybe I'll meet nice people. It'll be good to earn some extra money too. Now I just need to find someone to look after the children.'

'I like the sound of the Irish girl. It's always good to have a personal recommendation,' James said.

'I agree. I'm nervous about going back to work so soon. The kids won't have me around to settle them properly into school.'

James put his arm around me and I snuggled against his chest. 'Don't worry, darling. They'll be fine. Kids are very adaptable. They'll have new friends in no time. We just need to find a nice girl to look after them, and you'll be home to put them to bed and read them stories. They'll still see plenty of you.'

'I know. Lara will be fine, but Yuri . . .'

James sipped his wine. 'Henry and I went to boarding school when we were seven and it did us no harm. Yuri will be fine. You mustn't fuss about him so much. He needs to learn to stand on his own two feet and fight his own battles.'

'I don't fuss.'

James looked at me, arching an eyebrow. 'Emma, you worry about him all the time. Constantly. There's no need. He's a great little fellow who is perfectly well able to make new friends and get on at school.'

Grudgingly I admitted to myself that he had a point. I did worry too much about Yuri, but he was different from Lara. He was shyer and quieter, and I could see he was out of sorts with the new house, and now there was a new school to get used to as well.

James put his glass down and stretched. 'God, I'm stiff.'

'How come?' I asked.

'I probably overdid it a bit today, trying to show them all that I'm as fit as they are. I think I'll just watch the training session tomorrow.' He rubbed his shoulder. 'I really need to get this right. I have to make an impression with the first few games.'

'Any gorgeous physios?' I asked lightly.

James shot me a look, then shook his head.

'So, no bouncy Mandy-types for you to ogle?' I kept the tone light, but I wanted him to know that I hadn't forgotten and that it was not OK for him to flirt with people at work.

James took my face in his hands and looked into my eyes, then he kissed me. 'No, Emma, and you know that you're the only woman I want to ogle.'

'I'm very glad to hear it.' I smiled, relaxing. 'Speaking of ogling, check this out.' I flashed the strap of my lacy underwear. James's eyes lit up. 'I think it's about time we christened this house.'

James grabbed my hand and pulled me up. 'I thought you'd never ask!'

5

'Emma? It's me, Lucy. Guess what?'

'Uhm, you've won the lottery and are going to give me lots of money so I can live in Dublin again?'

Lucy laughed. 'No! Donal and I are coming to London, but if I did win the lotto, I'd sweep you away to a tropical island full of gorgeous Ryan Gosling lookalikes.'

'Now that's the way to spend your winnings.' I giggled. 'Oh, Lucy, I can't tell you how happy I am you're coming over! We really miss you guys.'

'I'm dying to see you, too. I've a meeting on Friday afternoon, but I should be finished by six. Will we call over then? We can go out for dinner or stay in, whatever suits. Although it might be easier to stay in with all the kids.'

'I'll throw something in the oven. We can plonk the kids in front of a movie until they fall asleep, then really tuck into the wine.'

'Brilliant. Can't wait.'

'Me neither.' I hung up, beaming.

On Friday, I dragged Yuri and Lara to the supermarket and stocked up on food, flowers, wine and beer. Then we went home and they helped me clean the house – bribed with the promise of sweets when we'd finished. By the time James came home at six o'clock, the place looked pretty good – like a home.

Shortly after James arrived, Lucy and Donal turned up, with Serge in tow. He was a very cute little boy. At two he was still small and a very quiet child. I constantly had to tell Lara and Yuri to be gentle with him as he often found them a bit boisterous and ended up in tears.

Lucy was wearing a gorgeous pale pink dress and jacket, with perfect hair and manicure. She always looked groomed, even when she was in a tracksuit. She just didn't do slobby or messy. Donal was, as usual, wearing a rugby T-shirt and jeans, and Serge, who was in his daddy's arms, was dressed from head to toe in mini-Leinster rugby gear.

After we'd greeted each other, Lara and Yuri took Serge off to show him their new toys and we gave Lucy and Donal a quick tour of the house. They made all the right noises. Lucy was positive about everything.

'Come on!' I laughed when she admired the olive green bathroom. 'You can't say this is nice – it's so kitsch.'

She smiled. 'Yes, but you've put nice touches – scented candles and lovely towels – so it looks as good as it can.'

I hugged her. 'Only a true friend would say that.'

'It looks grand to me,' Donal said.

Lucy snorted. 'Donal wouldn't notice the difference between Italian marble and plastic tiles.'

'Who cares?' He shrugged. 'These things don't matter. A bathroom is a bathroom – am I right?' he asked James.

'Having spent years in boarding school showering in icy bathrooms with cold tiles, I'm really not that fussy.'

'The only thing a house needs is kids to fill it.' Donal stared at Lucy, who froze.

'Don't start,' she hissed at him.

'Well, the bedrooms are over here,' I said, trying to cut the tension.

James cleared his throat. 'Much as I'm sure Donal is enjoying the tour, we might cut it short and go down to catch the rugby match.'

'Good man, James, lead on.' Donal turned on his heels and followed James downstairs.

Lucy and I finished the tour and she made some really good suggestions as to how I could make the place look better. She had a great eye for detail and was the most stylish person I knew. Her house was incredible. Donal had left her to do everything so she had gutted the place and redesigned the interior completely. It had even featured in an interiors magazine.

We went back downstairs and filled up the paddling pool to keep the children happy while James and Donal watched the match. Lucy and I sat down in the sun to catch up over a bottle of chilled white wine.

'Well? How are you? How are things?' Lucy asked, putting on her sunglasses.

'Not bad, actually. I've just got a job – on Babs's show.'

'Really? That was quick.'

'She only told me a few days ago. I've been dying to fill you in. I have to say, Babs has been brilliant for once. She basically forced her producer to take me on.'

'Well, she's always been persuasive.' Lucy's voice had an edge to it.

Lucy was the only person in the world who intimidated Babs. She was four inches taller than my sister and, because of her success in the tough, male-dominated world of business, she was very forthright and didn't take attitude from anyone. There was serious history there, too. At my brother's wedding five years ago, Lucy found out that Babs had slept with Donal while Lucy and Donal had separated briefly. Lucy had gone crazy and threatened Babs. Ever since, I had tried to keep them apart.

Now, as usual, I sidestepped the comment. 'I'm really pleased because it'll get me out of the house and keep me busy.'

'That's good. Staying at home full-time would do your head in. I honestly don't know how anyone can stand the boredom.' Lucy knocked back her wine.

I watched my children, squealing with delight as they sprayed each other with water. I did find full-time motherhood dull at times, but I'd miss them so much when I went back to work.

'How are things going for James? Has he started at London Irish yet?' Lucy asked.

I poured her some more wine. 'He's really nervous about making a good impression. My God, Lucy, I hope this job works out. Did you know the previous coach only lasted nine months?'

She waved her hand. 'Forget about the previous guy. James is brilliant at what he does. He was a great coach at Leinster. He'll be fine. He just needs to get to know the place and find his feet, and I bet London Irish will start winning all their games.'

'I hope so. If they don't, God knows where we'll end up.'

'Speaking of jobs, I've got some news.'

'Another massive promotion?' I smiled. Lucy had a high-flying job as a management consultant and seemed to be promoted every year and given huge bonuses. She was the only person I knew who seemed to be recession-proof. Another friend, Tony, had had his salary slashed. He and Jess were renting out two of their bedrooms to four Korean students to make ends meet.

Lucy shook her head. 'Much more dramatic than that. I'm actually leaving Wright Hodder.'

I was shocked. Wright Hodder was Lucy's life. 'Wow, are you taking time out to spend with Serge?'

Lucy frowned. 'Hello, Emma, it's me, Lucy! Can you honestly imagine me staying at home, not working?'

She had a point. Lucy was never going to be an apron-wearing stay-at-home mother. Not even in a designer apron in her magnificent kitchen.

'OK – so what's the plan?'

'I'm going out on my own with two guys I did some consultancy for. Oh, Emma, I'm so excited. I've wanted to do my own thing for a while now, and when this came along, I jumped at it.'

'That's brilliant. What is it?'

'It's an aircraft leasing company and it's based out of City airport in London, which means . . .' she paused for effect '. . . I'll be over in London every week. Most weeks I'll probably be based here Monday to Thursday. I'll be travelling a lot in Europe, but we'll still get to see each other.'

'Oh, my God! Cheers to that!' We clinked glasses. I was thrilled – my best friend was going to be close by. London was becoming more attractive by the minute.

Lucy smiled a smile that was pure happiness. 'I'm really excited about it. I was chuffed when the guys asked me to join the management buyout team. If it works out, and I think it will, I stand to make a lot of money. The people involved are incredibly dynamic. I'm really impressed with their ambition and drive.'

Lucy sounded so excited. I was genuinely happy for her. She had been very up and down since Serge was born (another name my mother constantly gave out about, but Donal had insisted on naming him after the famous French rugby player), and this was the first time I'd heard her sound so upbeat in ages. On the downside, though, I knew Donal wasn't going to like his wife travelling so much.

'How are you going to work it all out? Will Donal and Serge move here too? Oh, my God, you could rent a house in Putney. We could be neighbours! What does Donal think?'

Silence. She looked away.

'Lucy?'

'I haven't told him the extent of my travelling yet.'

Christ, was she crazy? How could she tell me and hold out on her own husband? 'Because you know he'll go mad?'

'Yes.' She threw back more wine and looked uncomfortable. I wanted to say something helpful and sympathetic, but I couldn't think of a positive spin to put on being away from Donal and Serge four days out of seven.

'It'll be tricky trying to juggle everything,' I said gently, not wanting to rile her. Lucy had a pretty sharp temper when she was annoyed.

She shrugged. 'I'll fly out first thing Monday mornings and fly back on Thursday or Friday evenings – it's only three or four nights a week. Men do it all the time. It's really not a big deal.'

The thought of being away from Yuri and Lara four nights a week made me feel ill. I could never do it. But Lucy was different. She was quite masculine in the way she was able to separate work from parenthood. She loved her work and Serge, and she didn't see why one had to negate the other. When it came to balancing work and spending time with him, her stock response was: 'If I was a man, we wouldn't be having this conversation.'

She was right, but it was different for most women because they didn't want to be away from their child all day. Lucy rarely put Serge to bed during the week because she always worked late. To be honest, I think she was struggling with motherhood. It hadn't come naturally to her. She often complained about how boring it was. But Serge was only two and, like Lara, he had been slow to speak. I knew that when he began to talk properly, and became more of a little companion, Lucy would really fall in love with him. In the meantime, her new job meant that Donal would be left holding the baby. 'It's still kind of tough on Donal, being on his own all week. You'd have to see that from his point of view.'

'He's got the nanny to help out,' Lucy snapped. 'Emma, I know it's not ideal, but this is a once-in-a-lifetime opportunity to make some real money. I could retire in a few years if it goes well. I can spend lots of time with Serge then. I'm not giving this up. No way.'

I reached out and patted her arm. 'Hey, I'm on your side and I'm happy for you. I'm just pointing out that you taking the job makes Donal's life more . . . complicated. So when you're breaking the news to him, you should probably acknowledge that.'

Lucy turned to me, her mouth set in a determined line. 'Donal has a great life, Emma. I pay the mortgage and I organize all the childcare, leaving him free to write his sports column and do his rugby commentating at the weekends. During the week he plays golf and does some volunteer work, teaching inner-city kids to play rugby. Not a lot of men have that kind of luxury. My career is the reason he has the freedom to pick and choose the jobs he wants.'

Again, she had a point, but it wasn't the whole picture. Donal was lucky in some ways. James certainly didn't have the freedom his friend enjoyed. Makeup artists didn't earn much money. I barely made enough to cover childcare, transport and groceries. It was hard for men to have that pressure on their shoulders. Even with all the talk of equality and increasing numbers of women going back to work, the majority of households still relied on the father to bring home the bacon. Most mothers worked part-time because of the horrendous cost of childcare. The onus was generally still very much on the male to be the family provider, but Donal was spared that. Still, though, while Lucy was out working, Donal was putting their son to bed every night on his own. Looking at her defensive stance, I worried about their relationship. It had always been fiery, but what I'd seen of them so far today – the almost palpable tension – made me wonder if there were deep divides between them now.

I tried to put Donal's side across. 'I know he has those freedoms, Lucy, but he's still going to be looking after Serge a lot, so I'm just saying, tread carefully when you're announcing the new travel details to him.'

Lucy sighed. 'I will. I keep putting it off because I'm dreading it. I know he'll go mad. To be honest, Emma, all we seem to do is fight at the moment anyway. Maybe the break will do us good.' She looked so forlorn that my heart ached for her.

'Oh, Lucy, I'm sorry. Look, all marriages run into problems now and again. No one is immune.'

'How are you and James?'

I frowned. 'I don't know. We've been so busy with the move that we haven't really talked in months. I'm trying to be positive and so is he, but he's sick with nerves and I am too. If this job doesn't work out, I'm worried he won't get another, and if he does, it'll be training some crappy team in the arse end of Wales for little or no money. I'm scared.'

Lucy sighed. 'Life is so much more complicated now, isn't it? Donal is still at me to have another kid. He keeps telling me to come off the pill. He doesn't seem to understand how difficult I find having one child. He keeps going on and on about not wanting Serge to grow up on his own.'

'I see his point. It would be nice for Serge to have a sibling, but a baby is a joint decision.'

Lucy threw her hands into the air. 'Exactly! That's what I keep saying, but he just won't listen. He thinks I'm being selfish, but, Emma,' Lucy's voice shook, 'I know that another baby will push me, and our marriage, over the edge. I mean, you remember how unhappy I was when I was pregnant? It was horrendous. I hated it.'

I remembered all right – it had been the longest nine months I'd ever experienced. Lucy had been irritable and overwhelmed from the moment she'd done the pregnancy test. The problem was, she was so used to managing things impeccably that she'd presumed she could manage a child in the same way she did a business deal. In reality, she hated the lack of control over her body that came with pregnancy, and when Serge was born, he had been a huge baby and she had ended up with internal and external stitches. She'd had to sit on a doughnut cushion for four weeks afterwards because the pain was so severe. I'd never seen her so miserable.

I nodded sympathetically. I knew there was nothing I could say that would convince her another pregnancy, another childbirth, another baby was right for her. Deep down I knew she was right: another child would send her over the edge.

'Donal's really good at being a parent – he's much better than me. He's so natural with Serge. From the beginning he knew what to do with him. I was so awkward and clueless. I hated being so out of my depth.'

'All new mums feel that way,' I told her.

'Not to the extent I did. Honestly, Emma, the day I went back to work after five weeks at home with Serge was one of the best in my life. I felt in control again. I felt so useless and incapable as a mother, but in work, I was the person everyone came to for advice. I knew who I was in the office. At home I was just an idiot.'

'But, Lucy, the more time you spend with your baby, the better you get to know them and the better you are at being a mother. It's like any other job – you need to put in the hours to learn how to do it right.'

Lucy sighed again. 'I don't enjoy it. I know it's a terrible thing to admit, but I don't. I love Serge, but I don't feel that I have to be with him all the time, and when I'm in work, to be honest, I rarely think about him. I find the weekends torturous. Wheeling a buggy around a park and sitting in cold, damp sandpits is my idea of hell. I see these other women digging away, making castles with their children, and I admire them. But I don't want sand in my shoes and all over my clothes. I'm a terrible person. I'm a freak.'

'No, you're not,' I assured her. 'I hate sandpits too.'

She gave me a weak smile. 'Yes, but you're totally into your kids, Emma. I actually went to see a therapist about my lack of mothering instincts.'

'Really? What did they say?'

'She told me to stop worrying, that it would come in time. She said some mothers bonded with their children later than others.'

'Well, there you go. You'll probably enjoy parenthood more when Serge is older and a bit more engaged with everything.'

Lucy put down her glass. 'The guilt is killing me. I feel like a bad person. And I keep thinking about my own mother, who showed no interest in me until I was about eight. I'm worried her coldness has rubbed off on me. I never thought I was like her until I had Serge.'

I was astonished to hear that. She had always consciously distanced herself from her mother and made sure she shared as few attributes as possible with her. Lucy's mother was a cold, hard woman and a ferocious snob, who had been shocked when her daughter had married Donal. She'd thought a rugby player from a small town in the west of Ireland was beneath clever, beautiful, successful Lucy. Her own husband had been a smooth-talking, charming, sophisticated businessman, who had abandoned his family for a younger woman when Lucy was only two. Lucy's mother had never got over his betrayal and had spent her life using her large divorce settlement to try to buy her way into the social set she aspired to belong to. She had never, in the almost thirty years I'd known her, looked happy. I'd always pitied her, to be honest.

I took Lucy's hand. 'You're nothing like your mother. You're kind and loyal and generous, and you don't care how big people's bank accounts are or what car they drive. You're a good person, Lucy, and you'll be a great mum. Stop beating yourself up.'

Lucy squeezed my hand and took another sip of wine.

'*Muuuuuuu*mmy!' Lara screeched.

'What?' I looked over to the paddling pool.

'Serge won't give me back my Barbie. He's not a good sharer.'

'Sharing is caring.' Yuri wagged his finger at Serge.

Lucy called, 'Serge, give Lara back her doll. Good boy.'

Serge clung to Barbie and shook his head.

'What's all this about Barbie?' Donal came out onto the patio, followed by James.

'Give me back my Barbie.' Lara pulled at Barbie's legs, but Serge had a vice-like grip on the doll's hair.

Donal went over to the children. 'Sorry, Lara, pet. Poor old Serge isn't used to sharing. That's what happens when you're an only child.'

Lucy glared at him.

'It's fine.' I walked over to Lara. 'Serge is our guest and we share when friends come to play. Now stop all that shouting and play with one of your other ten dolls.'

'No! I want to play with Disco Barbie cos her sparkly dress is the bestest.'

'Spa'ky 'ess,' Serge repeated, pointing to the dress.

'What do you want to be playing with this for anyway?' Donal said, looking at Barbie in her micro-mini silver dress. 'Come here and play with some trucks. Barbies are what little sisters play with, not big boys like you. If you have a little sister, she'd have Barbies. Would you like a sister?'

I had been willing to back up Donal's point of view with Lucy, but this was ridiculous. Using Serge to push his point across and make Lucy squirm was pathetic. It wasn't fair on Serge or Lucy. I could see the tension in her body. She had drawn up her knees to her chest and her mouth was a tight line of resentment. If this was Donal's idea of persuasion, he had already lost the argument.

Serge refused point-blank to let go of the doll, so I decided to distract them all with treats. I knew the offer of chocolate would make Lara forget about Barbie, sparkly dress or not.

As the children gobbled chocolate buttons, I kept up a steady flow of chit-chat, trying to keep things on an even keel. I glanced at my watch – two hours to bedtime: then we could put all the kids down and catch up properly. We just had to steer clear of contentious subjects – of which there were so many – and focus on having a laugh together, like old times.

The children were in bed, Serge tucked up on a mattress in Yuri's room. James fired up the barbecue to cook some burgers and chicken breasts, with Donal on table-setting duty. I opened another bottle of wine and Lucy and I had made some salads. We sat outside under the stars. It was one of those balmy nights when you could pretend you lived somewhere exotic. We'd found our groove again, talking and laughing together easily. James was the most relaxed I'd seen him in months. Donal was good for him – he understood James's job, knew the pressure he was under and, best of all, how to make him laugh.

It was when we had finished our meal and were kicking back over coffee that James asked Lucy how her interview had gone.

'Really well, thanks,' she said.

'What was it for? Some big new job? Emma was hazy on the details.'

'Yeah, it was for a very big job actually,' Lucy replied. I could see Donal tensing. 'I'm joining a start-up company. We're going to be leasing aircraft. I'll actually be over here quite a bit as our head office will be in London.'

So that was how she was going to break it to Donal. I resisted the urge to drop my head onto the table and groan. I couldn't believe she was dumping this on him in front of us.

'Sounds fantastic – congratulations!' James said, holding up his glass to her.

Donal put his coffee cup down with a thud. 'I thought you were still thinking about it,' he said, glaring at Lucy.

'No. I told you I was going to take it. I just needed to iron out the final details, which I did today. We signed this afternoon. I start next week.'

'It does sound like a great opportunity,' I noted.

Lucy leant back in her chair. 'It's an amazing opportunity and it could set us up for life. The earning potential is huge. The only slight downside is that I'll be based in London from Monday to Thursday . . . sometimes until Friday.'

Donal stared at her, stunned. 'What? You'll be away all week! That's a "slight downside"?'

Lucy looked nervous, but determined. 'I'll only be gone three or four nights.'

There was a long silence, and when Donal spoke again, his voice had a hard edge to it. 'So, you're telling me you've just taken a job that means you'll be essentially living in a different country, away from your husband and child, five days a week, and somehow you didn't think it was necessary to ask my opinion before accepting it?'

James looked at me, wide-eyed. I wanted the floor to swallow us both. We should not have been in the middle of this. This conversation was private. It was between Lucy and Donal. Why the hell had Lucy landed this bombshell on Donal in front of us? It wasn't fair. We didn't know where to look. I tried desperately to think of some way of breaking the tension, but there was nothing I could say. I looked down at my hands and held my breath.

'You knew it would involve travel. I told you that.' Lucy was like a steam roller. Nothing was going to stop her now.

'Travel, yes, not bloody emigration,' Donal hissed. I could see that his fists were clenched hard, as if he was controlling the urge to lash out.

'It's not for ever. In a couple of years' time I hope to have earned enough money for us never to have to worry again.'

'I'm not worried now,' Donal snapped.

'I want Serge to go to the best schools and have the best of everything.'

'For what? He doesn't need any of that. He needs his mother to be present, not living in a different country.'

Lucy slapped her chair in frustration. 'I'm not commuting to New Zealand. I'll be spending three or four nights away each week. That's all. Lots of people do it.'

'And what? I'll just obediently pick up the pieces as usual, is that it?' Donal growled.

Lucy's eyes flashed. 'No, Donal, you won't. I've asked Teresa to stay until seven o'clock the nights I'm away. I told her to feed and bathe Serge, so all you have to do is put him to bed. It's all organized. And I've asked Janice to babysit every Wednesday night so you can go out with your friends for a pint or a movie.'

'I see. So Teresa and Janice knew about the job before I did. Is there anyone you didn't tell?'

'Come on, Donal, you knew I was going to take it.'

'Of course I did. But you never mentioned that you were moving to London in the process.'

'Don't make a big deal about it.'

Donal shoved his chair back and stood up abruptly. I felt James tense beside me, as if he feared he might have to intervene physically. I didn't blame him: the air was so charged with emotion, it felt like this could turn really nasty.

Donal's face was hard with anger. 'I'm sorry, am I not being reasonable? Not being fair? Am I supposed to be delighted that you're abandoning your family? Well, Lucy, I hope you'll be very happy, because this job is all about you. Neither I nor Serge want or care about money. What we want is for you to be living with us, not in London making tons of cash that we don't need. I hope you're happy with your decision because I can tell you right now that I'm not and I don't see that changing.'

Lucy jumped up and poked him in the chest. 'Give it a rest, Donal. Stop playing the bloody martyr. Lots of men would love to be in your position, with a wife who earns a big salary so they can do what they want.'

Donal grabbed her hand and pushed it away from him, but Lucy was tipsy so she lost her balance and fell over. James

64

caught her and helped her back into her chair. 'Come on, guys! You both need to calm down.' He was angry now. 'You can sort this out.'

'Really, James?' Donal turned to him. 'Would you be thrilled if Emma here decided to take a job that took her away all week?'

'Well, I . . .' James hesitated.

'Be gentle,' I whispered to Lucy. 'He's really upset. Go easy.'

Lucy reached out towards her husband. 'Come on, Donal, I'll be back every weekend to cover for you when you're commentating on TV and we'll still have a family day on Sunday. Please don't make it into a big deal. If you were offered an amazing job commentating on Sky Sports Monday to Friday in London, I'd be happy for you. I'd encourage you to take it. I'd work around it without making you feel like crap. Why can't you be supportive of me?'

Donal bent down, putting his face close to hers. 'The difference between us is that I'd never take the job. I'd never leave my family because it's the most important thing in my life, not my career.'

A deafening silence ensued. I couldn't think of anything soothing or comforting to say. They were both right and they were both wrong. Lucy did pay the mortgage and look after Serge on Saturday while Donal worked. But I felt sorry for Donal because, no matter which way you cut it, it was going to be tough on him being left all week with a little boy who would be missing his mother.

'Come on, guys, don't argue,' James said quietly. 'How about a little after-dinner drink?' He went to the kitchen, came back with a bottle of Baileys and poured everyone a large glass. 'I know this is hard, you two, but we've only got tonight with you and we want to enjoy it. Do you think you can leave the discussion for another time?'

I silently applauded my husband. His message was subtle but clear: don't drag us into this fight. Donal and Lucy exchanged a look that said the discussion was far from over, but then they sat down and took a deep breath.

'Serge is looking great,' I said, moving onto what I thought was safer ground. 'And he's really beginning to talk.'

'Yeah, he has a few words now, all right.' Donal almost smiled.

'They're mostly sounds, but it's sweet hearing him try,' Lucy said, draining her drink.

'Well, Lara only started talking when she was almost three.'

'It's great when they begin to chat,' James said. 'They're so much more fun and they play so much better together.'

I held my breath. James had just given Donal an opening, and I knew he'd take it.

Donal clinked his ice around in his glass. 'Poor old Serge has no one to play with, and it'll be difficult to sort out a sibling for him with my wife living in another country.'

Lucy flushed. 'You know I don't want another child.'

'Well, I do. That poor little lad needs a sibling. Every kid needs a brother or sister. Don't they, James?'

James coughed. 'Well . . . it's nice to have a sibling. I certainly liked having Henry around when I was growing up.'

I kicked James under the table. What was he trying to do – add fuel to the already raging fire? I tried to help: 'But it's also nice to be an only child because you get your parents' undivided attention. Only children often turn out to be very successful – look at Lucy.'

Lucy smiled gratefully. 'Thanks, Emma. At least someone doesn't think being an only child is the worst thing in the world.'

But Donal was having none of it. 'Every child wants a brother or sister to play with. I love kids. I want a whole pile of them. I want a house full of noisy kids running around, having fun. It's what life's about.'

Lucy slammed her hand on the table. 'I don't want that, Donal. I really struggled after Serge was born and I still don't find it easy. Another child would not make things better. It would make things much worse.'

I caught James's eye and motioned towards the kitchen. Without another word, we got up and went inside, but we could still hear our friends arguing on the patio. It was awful.

Donal groaned with exasperation. 'Life is about kids and family, not a fat bank balance and a big house.'

Lucy threw her hands into the air, her voice rising. 'Donal, all we've done since Serge was born is fight. How can you possibly think another child is a good idea? I'm not good at being a mum. I try, I really do, but it doesn't come naturally to me and I spend all my time feeling guilty about it. Another child would kill me.'

Donal shook his head. 'No, it wouldn't. You know the score now, what to expect. A second child would be much easier. There's no shock the second time – we know what to do with a baby. And it could be a little girl, a lovely little girl who looks just like you.'

Lucy was not budging. 'I do not want another baby. I will never want another baby.'

Donal's voice was like ice. 'Well, I do, so we appear to have a problem.'

'This is bullshit. I'm going to bed.' Lucy stormed into the house and marched up the stairs to the bedroom.

James and I watched her go, then Donal strode into the kitchen.

'Should I go after her?' I asked Donal.

He shook his head. 'She's drunk. Let her sleep it off. Christ, what a night!'

'I'll just check on her for a second.' I tiptoed upstairs, and when I looked into the bedroom, Lucy was fast asleep, fully clothed on top of the bed. I took off her shoes and gently placed the cover over her. I'd never seen her like this, so angry and bitter. I was really worried about their marriage. That had been no normal argument: it had been vicious and hurtful.

When I came back down I could hear James and Donal chatting outside. As I tidied up the kitchen I listened to their conversation.

'She's obsessed with her bloody career,' Donal said.

'It means a lot to her, but then it always has. Lucy's always been a career girl,' James said.

'She's going to be living in a different country from her son.'

James sighed. 'I know, mate. It's not easy.' I knew James didn't want to get into a slagging match – he never did. He was always the measured one, the one who looked at both sides of a story or argument.

Donal's voice dropped lower and he sounded weary. 'What happened to us? We used to have so much fun together, but since she had Serge she's been so cold and distant. She's always running out to work. It's as if she prefers to be in the office than at home.'

'Look, we all have our troubles. Emma and I were at each other's throats before we moved here. But things are good now. You'll get through this. It's just a bad patch.'

I wasn't exactly thrilled to hear James telling Donal about how badly we'd been getting on. These things were private. I didn't want him discussing our arguments with anyone, not even his best friend.

'It's a very bad patch.' Donal stood up. 'It's been going on for a long time, and the frightening thing is, I don't see it getting any better, especially now that she'll be away all the time, getting even more detached. Sure she'll be like a stranger in the house.'

'Hang in there and you'll probably find she's home more once she gets settled into the new job.'

Donal slapped James on the back. 'Good old James, always the optimist. I hope you're right. You're lucky with Emma – she's a great bird and a great mother.'

If I hadn't been eavesdropping, I would have hugged Donal. I waited for James to agree wholeheartedly and praise me too, but all he said was 'I know she is. Now, come on, let's get to bed. The kids will be up in four hours.'

'I'll crash on the couch, thanks,' Donal said.

'Oh, right. I'll grab you a blanket.' James came in and asked me where the blankets were.

'I'll get it. Can you just bring in the rest of the dishes from the patio?' I asked.

While James cleared up, I fetched Donal a blanket and pillow.

'Thanks. Sorry about this and about all the fighting. We weren't very good dinner guests.' Donal looked sheepish, which at six foot five was difficult.

I reached up and put my hand on his shoulder. 'It's fine, but please go easy on her, Donal. She's trying. I know she's obsessed with work and that it's hard on you and Serge. Hopefully, when she gets this company up and running, she can rework her schedule to be more family friendly.'

Donal held the pillow to his chest. 'Will you talk to her, Emma? Please? She won't listen to me.'

'I'll try, I promise.'

'Thanks.' Donal lay down with his long legs hanging over the edge of the couch. The poor man was unlikely to get a wink of sleep.

I went back into the kitchen to help tidy up the final dinner things, but James had finished it all.

'Bed?'

'Yes, please.' As we walked upstairs, arm in arm, I clung to James. 'Don't ever let us get like that,' I whispered. 'I never want to feel such anger and hate towards you.'

He smiled at me and rubbed my cheek. 'We won't, darling. We're not like them. For one, we both want the same things.'

He was right. 'Do you think they'll break up?' I wanted him to say, 'No way.' I wanted him to reassure me and tell me that our best friends would be fine.

'It's possible,' he said.

'What?' I was horrified. Did he really think that? Surely it was just a phase, granted a very bad one but they'd work it out. They had been so happy before and could be again. I believed that.

He shrugged. 'Emma, people break up all the time. Lucy and Donal are at each other's throats. I actually thought he was going to hit her at one point. He's so angry with her and I understand why. It's all about Lucy and her job.'

'Yes, but she is paying the mortgage – and we've all just moved country for your job. The person earning the main salary does kind of dictate what happens.'

James glared at me. 'Lucy doesn't have to take this job. She could have stayed in the job she had. She chose to leave, Emma, but I was forced to. I do not appreciate you comparing the two situations when they're completely different.'

'Sorry, you're right. It's not the same. I just feel sorry for both of them. I hate seeing them so unhappy.'

James put his arm around me. 'Me too.'

'Communication and compromise,' I said, spouting from a book I'd once read about marriage.

'And regular sex.' James grinned.

'Except at two in the morning when your wife is exhausted.' I smirked.

'Fair enough. I'm wiped out, too. Let's get some sleep. Hopefully things will be calmer in the morning.'

But they weren't. Lucy and Donal left without having uttered a word to each other.

6

After the disastrous dinner with Lucy and Donal I realized I had very little time left to find a nanny and get everything sorted. I began to panic. I called Poppy for advice. She was really helpful and gave me the names of a few more websites. Plus she told me she had spoken to Maggie, her cleaning lady, and that Maggie's daughter, Claire, was available for work and, even better, had previous experience in childcare.

By Monday afternoon I had lined up three interviews for Wednesday. The first two were coming through the agency in Putney, a Spanish girl called Elena, who was in her early twenties, and Betty, a local woman, who was fifty-three. I had arranged directly with Claire to meet her too. I was secretly hoping the Spanish girl would work out and that all four of us would be speaking Spanish within the year. Wasn't that how Gwyneth Paltrow had done it? If it was good enough for Gwyneth . . .

James had muttered something about me handling it all, but I wasn't having that. I insisted he interview the prospective nannies with me, arguing that it was important to have two perspectives on the candidates. Hiring a nanny is never straightforward. You want a paediatric nurse who cooks like a Cordon Bleu chef and has *Blue Peter*-type arts and crafts skills. But you don't want her to be so wonderful that your children end up preferring her to you. You want someone who is smart enough to handle any crisis that may come along while you're at work, but you don't want someone telling you how to raise your children. You want someone who is firm with the children, but not bossy or stern. You want someone who will give the children hugs, but not too many. You want someone who will keep the house tidy, but not spend time vacuuming when she could be teaching them the fine art of origami.

The problem is, you want someone who loves and cherishes your children as much as you, but who will not take your place. That's why grandparents make the best childminders, because they love the children as much as you do, but they don't want to be parents again. At the end of their minding, they're happy to hand them over.

I made a list of questions that I wanted to ask, things I felt would reveal the candidates' true personalities and help me make the right choice.

On Wednesday morning, James sat in his tracksuit, jiggling his legs and looking at his watch. Elena arrived very punctually at nine thirty. I flung open the door, ready to love her.

Elena was drop-dead gorgeous and wearing a very short, tight sundress with no bra. I took one look at her and knew there was no way this stunner was getting the job. I opened my mouth to tell her to go straight home, but then I thought it would be rude, so I reluctantly invited her in.

James was texting when we walked into the room. When he looked up and saw Elena, he dropped his phone. He actually dropped his phone – I couldn't believe it. It landed with a thud on the floor. My decision never to hire Elena or anyone who looked like her was confirmed when I saw his face. What was it about older men and young girls? The men turn into complete idiots around them. I'd seen it at work in Dublin all the time. *Afternoon with Amanda* had models on every day to show off the clothes in the fashion segment, and every man over forty would drool as they walked by. It was harmless, but at the same time a bit pathetic.

Women didn't do that. Mind you, I had found myself lusting after Taylor Lautner in the *Twilight* movies. I was appalled when I found out he was only twenty when he'd made the first. I felt like a dirty old woman but he *was* very hot . . .

James jumped up. 'Very nice to meet you, Elena. Please have a seat.' He led her to a chair. 'Can I get you a drink?'

'No, *gracias*, I am fine.'

'Are you sure? It's no trouble at all,' James persisted.

'No, thank you.'

'Not even a glass of water?'

'James!' I snapped. 'She's not thirsty.' I turned my attention to the pretend interview, and asked Elena about her childcare experience.

'Well, I love chil-deren. I am having the brothers and sisters at home in Espain and I am playing with them all the day.'

'That sounds fantastic,' James enthused.

I glared at him, but he was too busy staring at Elena's chest to notice. I tapped the information sheet the agency had given me. 'It says here that you are currently with a family in London. But you've only been with them two months and you want to leave. Why is that?'

Elena looked down. 'The mummy is not very nice to me. She say mean thing to me.'

'That's terrible,' James said, his voice dripping with sympathy and indignation at her plight.

'What kind of things does she say?' I asked.

Elena pouted. 'That I am taking too long in the shower and that I am too slow ironing the clothes and that I am bad at the cooking.'

Was this girl really that stupid? First, she turns up for an interview in a skin-tight mini dress with no bra on and then she proceeds to complain about her current employer.

'She sounds like a very difficult woman,' James said, as if he'd like to go and give her a piece of his mind. 'I can assure you, there will be none of those unpleasant comments if you work here.'

'Are you a good cook?' I enquired, before James jumped in and offered her the job on the spot. I could see her now, prancing about in her teeny-tiny skirts, spatula in one hand and Spanish olive oil in the other. Over my dead body . . .

Elena shrugged. 'I am OK. I can make the toast and the scrambly eggs.'

I suddenly had the urge to laugh. This girl should be on a TV show. She was ridiculous. 'What about ironing? Are you slow?'

'Emma!' James interrupted. 'I'm sure Elena is a perfectly good ironer. Besides, there's not a lot of ironing to do here.' James turned to Elena and smiled. 'I wear a lot of sports gear, you see, because I coach a rugby team.'

Elena's eyes widened. 'I am loving the sports. I like to jogging very much.'

'I can see that you're very fit.'

'James!'

'What?'

'Inappropriate!'

'Maybe you could 'elp me be more fit.' Elena beamed at him.

I'd had enough of this girl. She could go and flirt with someone else's husband. I stood up. 'My husband will not be helping you with your fitness regime. Now, it's clear that you are not remotely suitable for this job.' I frog-marched Elena to the front door. 'Thanks for coming, but let's not take up any more of your time. I would suggest you wear jeans and a jumper to your next interview. Mothers do not appreciate nipples. 'Bye now.'

By the time James had got to the door, it was closed. 'That was very rude,' he said.

'No, James, staring at a young girl's cleavage and dribbling is rude.'

'I was not.'

'Oh yes you were, and if you think for one nano-second that I'd have her going for late-night jogs with you and doing lunges in the front room, you've another think coming.'

James flexed his muscles. 'I was looking forward to showing her some of my moves.'

I raised an eyebrow. 'What moves? The diving-on-the-couch move? The flicking-the-remote-control move? Or your *pièce de résistance*, the opening-a-can-of-lager move?'

James grinned. 'Very witty, darling. I'll have you know that I've been training with the team every day. I'm feeling much fitter.'

He looked it. For a man of forty-three, James was very attractive. Sometimes I wondered what he saw in me. When I was dressed up I looked good, but day-to-day I felt plain. Even though my hair was now a nice auburn colour, I was still an insecure red-headed teenager inside. People, mostly my mother, were always telling me how handsome and charming James was and it made me feel paranoid. I felt as if they thought I wasn't worthy of him, as if he'd somehow married beneath him, punched below his weight.

I made a resolution. It was time for me to lose the extra weight I'd been carrying and shake up my wardrobe. London was a good place to start. Babs could help me pick out some age-appropriate but edgy clothes. It would be easier to diet once I started work. No more home-made flapjacks for the kids – the majority of which I ended up eating. As soon as I started work it would be a skinny latte on the run and a low-fat yogurt for lunch.

As Elena left, the next candidate, Betty, arrived for her interview. The minute I saw her, I felt I had found the perfect nanny. Betty was primly dressed in a long-sleeved blouse, sensible navy slacks and Scholl sandals. She was the kind of woman who wore a strong bra and big pants. There was no fear of James running away with her. She was more vicar's wife than *femme fatale*.

'So, Betty, you said when we spoke on the phone that you have experience in childminding,' I said, after we'd done the introductions.

Betty nodded, placing her handbag on her lap. It was like one of those handbags the Queen carries – a black square with a big clip on the top. 'I do indeed, Mrs Hamilton. I've raised my own four children and I've been a nanny to two other families since. One had three children and the last family had two, like you.'

I loved being addressed as Mrs Hamilton: it was very *Downton Abbey*. I could get used to this. I pictured Betty bringing me breakfast in bed on a big wooden tray with legs. She'd place a linen napkin across my lap and pour my cup of Earl Grey. Then she'd open the curtains and set my clothes out for the day. It would be lovely . . .

'Excellent, and what kind of things would you do with the children to keep them occupied?' I asked.

'I believe that children need a strict routine. The problem with this country is lack of discipline in the youth. Mark my words, if children today had stricter parents, none of this looting and rioting would ever take place.'

James banged his knee with his hand. 'I couldn't agree more, Betty.'

Hold on a minute. I was not happy with the direction

the conversation was taking. I didn't approve of slapping or smacking or the wooden spoon, or any of that kind of discipline. I was no saint, I regularly shouted at the children and I wasn't proud of it, but I did not approve of physical violence and I certainly wasn't about to hire someone who did.

'Oh, Mr Hamilton,' Betty gushed, 'it's so nice to meet a young man who isn't afraid to spank his children. The way some children speak to their parents, these days, it'd make your hair stand on end. I even heard a child in the park yesterday telling his mother to shut up. He couldn't have been more than six. I tell you, if my children had ever spoken to me with such a lack of respect, I'd have given them a good wallop on the bottom and they'd never have done it again. But all this woman said was "Don't be rude." That child will grow up to be a sociopath. A good smack would have sorted him out.'

I was liking Betty less and less by the second. I did not want to come back from work to find Yuri's bottom black and blue. 'Hold on!' I interrupted. 'Let me be very clear here, Betty. There is no spanking in this house. Ever.'

'Except between consenting adults.' James winked and, despite my best efforts to remain in serious interview mode, I began to laugh.

Betty didn't crack a smile.

The third interview was with Claire. She was small with thick brown hair tied back in a ponytail and nice blue eyes. She wore no makeup and was dressed in tracksuit bottoms and a baggy T-shirt, which made her look younger than nineteen. I was very glad to see that she was wearing a bra and, unlike the previous candidates, that she didn't look as if she wanted to either sleep with James or beat up our kids.

'So, Claire, where are you from in Ireland?' I asked.

'I'm originally from Carrick-on-Shannon in Leitrim, but I moved to London with my mum a year ago.'

'Why did you decide to come here?' James asked.

Claire blushed and looked down at her hands. 'Well . . . the thing is . . . you see . . . I . . .' She hesitated, flustered.

'It's all right, take your time,' I said, wondering what on earth she was going to say. She seemed very upset about her reasons for leaving Ireland. I hoped it wasn't anything sinister.

She took a breath. 'I was bullied in school. It got really bad last year so my mum decided it was best to take me out of school before my finals and start a new life over here.' She blushed.

'That's terrible. You poor thing.' I felt really sorry for her – I could see how upset she was. She seemed so young and fragile.

Claire nodded. 'It was awful. The other girls made fun of me because I didn't have expensive clothes or a cool phone.'

'Girls can be cruel.' James was clearly feeling sorry for her too.

'Yes. There was also a teacher who was really mean to me.' What kind of school had she been in? 'A teacher? But that's shocking. Did you report them?' I asked.

She shrugged. 'Yes, but no one believed me. The headmistress took his word over mine. He said I was imagining it, so my mum said it was best if we left.'

'Well, good for your mum. That teacher should be struck off for being mean to you. I had a teacher in school who was awful to me, too. It was my chemistry teacher. I didn't understand chemistry, it was like Japanese to me, and the teacher kept telling me I was either deaf or stupid.'

Claire smiled. She had a lovely smile – it lit up her young face. It was also a good sign: she had a sense of humour.

She'd need one if she was going to be looking after children all afternoon.

James asked Claire about previous employment. 'Is it true you have some childminding experience? Can you tell us a bit about that?'

Claire nodded. 'I worked in a local playschool when I first moved over. It was a maternity-leave cover, but then the lady came back, so I was let go. I worked in Tesco after that, but I really didn't like it. I loved working with the kids – they were brilliant. I have a reference from the lady who runs the playschool.' She handed James a copy. She seemed much more at ease now. She'd found it hard to tell us about the bullying, but I could see that she was actually quite a capable girl.

James and I read the reference together: Claire was helpful, kind, patient and, although she was quiet, she was very good at interacting with the children, especially the younger ones.

'Great reference.' I handed it back. 'The job will also involve doing some light housework and cooking simple meals for the children. How does that sound?'

Claire smiled. 'No problem. I cook for my mum all the time. Not fancy food, just spaghetti bolognese and roast chicken, that kind of thing.'

'Perfect.' I smiled at her. I liked this girl. She was very sweet and gentle. But she seemed very young. Would she be able to manage Yuri and Lara when they had a tantrum?

'How would you deal with a child in meltdown?' I asked.

'Lots of the children had meltdowns in the playschool. I think the best way to deal with them is to distract the child. I find it works every time.'

Great answer! She was a pro. The more she spoke, the more I liked her and the more competent she seemed.

'What would you do if one of the children was really bold?'

Claire became animated. 'I watch *Supernanny* all the time and I think she's brilliant. I'd use the naughty step and crouch down to explain to them why they were on it, then always reward good behaviour.'

Was she kidding me? This girl was perfect. I watched *Supernanny* to make myself feel better about my parenting. The kids on the show were so badly behaved that I always reckoned I must be doing something right as mine weren't nearly that bad. And we had a naughty chair that I used when the children were bold. Claire was exactly what I was looking for. I beamed at her.

James stood up. 'I'm sorry, but I really have to go. Nice to meet you, Claire.' He held out his hand. She shook it shyly.

I walked to the front door with James. 'What do you think?' I whispered.

He shrugged. 'She seems nice, a bit shy, though. I'd worry she'd be too quiet for the children. We want them to have fun. I'd like someone a bit livelier.'

'I think she's perfect. I don't want some loud, over-confident person in the house. I like the fact that she's quiet and gentle and her reference is brilliant and she watches *Supernanny*!'

'Please tell me you're not going to hire someone because they watch a TV programme that you like.'

'Of course not,' I lied.

James stepped outside. 'I've got to go. Don't offer her the job immediately. Let's talk about it later. Say you'll call her tomorrow.'

I went back inside to talk to Claire. I had made up my mind to offer her the job. After all, I was the one who was going to be dealing with her most. James would be at work. I trusted myself more than anyone else when it came to the kids. She'd be kind and caring, and that was exactly what I wanted for them.

'You're hired,' I said, holding out my hand to shake hers.

Claire jumped up from her seat. 'Really?' She grasped my hand eagerly.

'Absolutely. I want someone nice taking care of my children, and the fact that you're Irish is a bonus. It'll help them feel more at home.'

'Wow! I'm so thrilled! Thank you.' Claire blushed again.

'Can you stay for a bit? I'd like you to meet Yuri and Lara. They're just over with my neighbour. Come and say hello.'

I brought Claire around to Carol's house, where Yuri and Lara were having a ball with Carol's two boys, digging up vegetables and playing with watering cans. I introduced Claire to Carol and then to the children.

She muttered a greeting to Carol, then crouched down and shook Yuri and Lara's hands. 'What are you guys doing?' she asked.

They explained, and she asked if she could help. Within a minute, Claire was happily playing with the children, crawling about in the mud, regardless of her clothes. I could see she had a way with children. She seemed more comfortable in their company. She wasn't shy or quiet with them. She was lovely, gentle but fun too. I watched her help Lara fill the watering can.

'She seems very nice,' Carol said.

'I've just hired her. I think she's absolutely perfect. Now I can go to work and not have to worry.'

'And you'll always have me next door in case of emergencies. Be sure to tell her she can call on me anytime,' Carol said.

'Thanks. Really, thanks for being such a nice neighbour. I'm so glad you're next door.'

Carol smiled. 'You're welcome.'

I heard Lara ask Claire if she was their new minder.

'Yes,' Claire said.

Lara looked her up and down. 'Well, you're not beautiful like a princess, but you're a very good helper.'

Claire had the royal seal of approval.

7

The following Monday, I woke up with a pit in my stomach. It was my first day at work and, worse, it was the children's first day at school. Yuri kept asking me who he was going to play with. He was so anxious about his new class and, although I kept trying to reassure him, I could see he was scared at the prospect of a new place and new children. My heart was breaking for him. I had to will myself not to give in and keep them both at home.

After Claire's tale of being bullied, I was even more worried about the new school. I'd have to keep a close eye on Yuri and Lara to make sure it didn't happen to them. The good thing was that they had taken to Claire. In the short time she'd been in their lives, they had become really fond of her. She had come in for a few hours each day, since Wednesday, so they could get used to her and, so far, she had been great with them – taking them to the park, doing Lego and jigsaws with them, painting and baking. I was so relieved to have found her. I knew the children would be happy in her care, which made me feel a little less guilty about going to work so soon.

From today onwards, Claire would be picking them up from school at twelve thirty and bringing them home. I was hoping to be back by five thirty. James was working late a lot, so his times were unpredictable. He was obsessed with winning his first game in three weeks' time, and I could see the pressure he was under so I tried not to nag him about being in work all the time, but it did bother me. I was lonely. I had changed my outfit five times by eight a.m. It was ridiculous, but I wanted to look nice and not as if I was trying too hard, for both the school gate and for work. In the end I opted for a lilac sundress with a cream cardigan and silver ballet pumps. I rarely wore heels to work because makeup artists spend most of their time standing, so comfortable footwear was essential. I had applied my makeup very carefully so I looked fresh and glowy. I appraised my image in the mirror and decided it would do. I could relate to how Yuri was feeling – I was nervous of all the newness, too.

I decided to send Lucy a photo of my outfit and ask her opinion. We had barely spoken since the dinner – she'd been swamped with work and I was sure she was avoiding me because she knew I'd bring it up. She texted back: *Perfect, mad busy, b in touch soon*. I replied, *We must meet up, let me know when u r free*. She didn't reply.

I went downstairs and found Claire chatting to the kids while giving them their breakfast. She had agreed to come in early two days a week to do laundry and light housework. James was trying to make conversation with her.

'Do you live around here?' he asked.

Claire nodded. 'Shepherd's Bush.'

'Excellent. It's just you and your mother, is it?'

'Yes.' Claire went back to encouraging Lara to eat. 'Come on, one more for the elephants . . . one more for the zebras . . .'

James whistled when he saw me. 'Wow.'

'I like your dress, Mummy,' Lara said, between spoonfuls.

'You look great,' Claire added.

'Thanks, guys. I need all the confidence I can get today.'

'Right, well, I'm off. Good luck today, everyone, on your first days. I know you'll all be fine.' James kissed the children and me, then headed off to work.

It was incredible. He just strolled out of the door without

a backward glance. While I was feeling physically sick about the children's first day, guilty about working, fretting about Claire being the right person to look after them and worrying about all the things that could go wrong, James was off to work, thinking only of his day. Men just didn't do guilt. Lucy had been right when she'd said that if she was a man no one would question her focus on work and her lack of guilt. Oh, to be a man . . . or a Lucy.

I put down my toast. I couldn't face eating anything: my stomach was doing too many somersaults.

After breakfast, Claire helped me get Yuri and Lara into their jackets. I asked her to take a picture on my phone of the three of us. As I hugged my two children close, I could feel my eyes welling with tears. This was a first day for all of us – new school, new job, new life.

As we left, I reminded Claire to collect them at twelve thirty sharp. 'I'll call you when I get a break. I'll be dying to know how their first day went. I feel terrible I won't be there.' I tried to hide how emotional I was feeling about it. I felt sick that I couldn't collect them on their first day, but I could hardly ask to leave work early on my own first day.

'Don't worry, Emma, they'll be fine,' Claire reassured me. 'I'll fill you in on every little detail when you get home.'

Yuri and Lara hugged Claire tightly, then we left her to tidy up.

As we walked the ten minutes to Mrs Roberts's Montessori school, Yuri kept asking me if Connor might be there.

'Yuri, I've told you, darling. Connor lives in Dublin and we live in London now. But there will be lots of new children to play with. It'll be great fun, I promise.'

Lara skipped along beside me. 'I can't wait to go to school, Mummy. I'm a big girl now, isn't I?'

'Yes, sweetie, you are, a very big girl.'

As we approached the gates, we were greeted by the unmistakable sounds of post-holiday catching up. Mothers and children swarmed everywhere, with most of the kids shrieking wildly. Some little ones were crying and clinging to their mothers' legs, but most were already back in school mode, racing around, bags sliding down their shoulders and shirts coming untucked. The women were squealing hellos, kissing each other and talking animatedly about their summer holidays. They all seemed to know each other. There was lots of laughter and camaraderie. I felt as if we were behind a glass wall, watching it all as spectators, very much on the outside.

I was glad I'd dressed up. Most of the mothers were very stylish and well groomed. They had perfected the smart-casual school-mum uniform. I was surrounded by glossy hair, skinny jeans, wedges or ballet flats and smart T-shirts with light summer jackets over them. Fabulous silk scarves and perfectly manicured nails were *de rigueur*. I'd have to make an effort every morning if I wanted to fit in here. This school gate was a lot more stylish, and more intimidating, than the one on our estate back in Dublin.

Yuri clung to my leg, while Lara commented on the other girls' dresses. 'I like the sparkly one. I like the pink one. I like the twirly one, but I don't like the brown one. Brown is stinky, like poo.'

I crouched down. 'Lara, remember what Mummy said about giving your opinion? If you don't have anything nice to say, don't say it.'

'But poo is brown, Mummy,' Lara reasoned.

'Yes, but it's not a nice thing to say about a dress. Only say nice things, OK?' I didn't want her going in and alienating everyone on her first day. The school yard was a tough place.

You needed to make a good first impression, even if you were only three and a quarter.

Lara whispered, 'Poo is brown, brown is poo.'

I watched the mothers chat to each other, feeling like a complete outsider. Back in Dublin, I'd been one of those women, thrilled to see the other mums after a long summer. Arm in arm we'd stroll off for coffee and catch-ups before I headed into work at ten thirty. But here I was standing alone with no one to talk to and I had to be in work by nine thirty. I tried catching a few of the women's eyes, but they just smiled vaguely and moved towards their friends. I was clearly not about to be adopted. I'd have to work hard at fitting in.

A bell rang and the teachers came to take the children inside. Yuri was going to be with Mrs Roberts and Lara with Miss Timmons. Lara stood in line behind another girl in her class and began chatting to her about her Peppa Pig runners. She would have no problem settling in. But Yuri refused to let go of my leg. I had to walk him over to the teacher and peel him off me.

Mrs Roberts took him firmly by the hand. 'Come on now, Yuri, let's introduce you to the other children.'

'Mummy,' Yuri cried. 'Don't go. Please.'

I plastered a fake smile on my face and tried to look enthusiastic. 'You're going to have a great morning, darling. Mummy has to go to work. But I'll see you later.'

'I want to go back to my other school,' he sobbed. 'I don't know anyone's name. I don't have any friends here.'

Neither do I, I thought grimly. 'You'll make friends.' I stroked his cheek.

'Don't leave me,' he cried.

'You'll be fine,' I said, tears filling my eyes.

'Come along, this way.' Mrs Roberts half dragged him into the classroom.

I waved, forcing a cheery smile to my face, fighting back tears. I turned to see if any other mothers were feeling emotional too, but they were all standing in little clusters. I was on my own.

As the school door closed, I turned and walked to the tube, sobbing all the way.

At nine thirty I was sitting in the reception area, waiting for Babs. She swept in, wearing enormous sunglasses and an animal-print jumpsuit.

'Morning, Tiger,' I said, grinning at her.

'Leopard, actually.' Babs raised her sunglasses and looked me up and down. 'Not bad, except for the dorky shoes. Flat shoes make your ankles look fat.'

'Thanks for that. I've just left Yuri crying inconsolably and I'm feeling really fragile, so can you tone down the negative comments?'

'Oh, don't get all sensitive. I'm just being honest. Would you prefer me to lie?'

'On my first day at a new job? Yes, absolutely. Feel free to lie for the rest of the day.'

I followed my sister through Reception and into the studio. Babs introduced me to everyone. I met the producer, Gary Mason, who was classically tall, dark and handsome. His wedding ring didn't stop him openly flirting with Babs. It made my stomach turn. It was half past nine in the morning and he was a married man. Babs was all giggly around him. I was shocked – seriously? This married guy? Would she ever learn? I'd have to talk to her about it later. Married men were off-limits.

Babs then introduced me to the two researchers, Hannah and Tania, who were very friendly and bubbly, and to the director, Karen, who was very no-nonsense in a way I liked. Finally, I met two cameramen and a soundman.

The studio was made up of a big open space where they shot most of the show. The room was divided in two: one side was set up as a living room, with couches and chairs; the other had a 360-degree mirror and rails of clothes. To the left of the studio there was a small kitchen, a medium-sized lounge and a small makeup room.

'Right,' Karen said, clapping her hands. 'Let's have a meeting to run through the show.'

Everyone sat down in the 'living room', and Karen went through the running order. Gary sat beside Babs and very subtly touched the back of her neck with his hand as he stretched out his arm. I watched my sister's cheeks flush. Damn, this was bad.

'We have two women coming in today. They're best friends. One is a farmer's wife and the other is a divorcee, whose husband left her for another man, so, understandably, her self-esteem is very low. It's going to be a good show – audiences love a sad story and it doesn't get sadder than being dumped for a bloke.'

'Love it!' Babs whooped. 'A gay husband is brilliant.'

'Just be careful, Babs. No homophobic comments,' Gary warned her.

Babs batted her eyelashes at him. 'But I'm allowed to mention that her husband prefers back entry, right?'

Gary threw back his head and laughed loudly. Far too loudly, as far as I was concerned. It wasn't that funny.

'Was she always like this?' Karen asked me.

I opened my mouth to answer, but Babs cut across me: 'When she's at work, Emma is not my sister, she's the new makeup artist. I don't want anyone asking her questions about me. Let's keep it professional, please.'

How professional is sleeping with your boss? I wondered.

The meeting went on and I tried to follow their quick-fire

chat. Eventually, the schedule was nailed down and it was time for makeup.

'Right, Emma, let's get you to work. We need Babs ready to shoot the opening scene at twelve thirty,' Gary said, sounding every inch the producer.

I jumped up. 'No problem.' I followed her into the makeup room and set to work.

Babs sat back in the chair. 'What do you think of Gary?'

'He's married.'

'He's very sexy.'

I stopped blending foundation into my sister's cheeks. 'Don't even think about it. Remember the last time?'

Babs had slept with her married boss in her last job as a TV presenter and had ended up being threatened by his wife and her thug of a brother.

Babs rolled her eyes. 'That was different. Gary's not like him. He's a great guy.'

'Let me be very clear.' I forced Babs to look at me. 'Stay away from married men. OK? Believe me, it's hard enough for us married women to maintain a good relationship with our husbands, what with kids and work and mid-life crises, without young single girls hitting on them. Gary has a wife and I'm sure she's a very nice person, like me, so leave him alone.'

Babs laughed. 'You're not that nice.'

'Compared to you, I'm Mother Teresa.' Babs closed her eyes as I applied eye-shadow. 'Find yourself a nice single guy and have a normal relationship.'

'You sound like Mum!' Babs said sarcastically.

'Mum has a point. I mean, you're not far off thirty now. Don't you want to settle down?'

Babs looked incredulous. 'And end up like you and James with your boring life, sitting in watching TV? Are you mad?'

'It's not boring, it's secure and comfortable.' I bristled. Sometimes it *was* a bit boring, but I liked my life. It wasn't nice to hear it dismissed out of hand in one sentence.

Babs shrugged. 'All right, so you like it that way. But I don't want the same things as you. I want to be the top-earning female presenter in the UK and then I'm going to America to earn tons of cash over there and buy a massive house on the beach in Malibu.'

I wondered for the millionth time where Babs had come from. Honestly, someone must have switched babies at the hospital. She had completely different DNA from everyone else in our family or, indeed, anyone I had ever met. Mind you, a big house on the beach in Malibu did sound nice.

'Chop-chop, Emma. I need to start filming in ten minutes.' Babs clapped her hands.

I finished doing her makeup and she examined herself in the mirror. 'Much as I hate to admit it, you're very good at your job. I look amazing.'

'Gee, thanks.' I added some lip-gloss. 'I'm serious, Babs. Stay away from Gary. Married men are trouble. A man who cheats on his wife is a scumbag.' I left the other bit unsaid – that a woman who knowingly carries on with a married man is a bitch.

'You don't even know him so stop going on about it.'

I sighed. Would my sister ever grow up? I followed her out to the set.

While they set up for filming the opening segment, I snuck into the Ladies to call Claire.

'They're fine, Emma. They had a good morning,' she said.

'OK. Put them on to me for a minute,' I asked, desperate to hear in their voices that they were not traumatized by their first day.

'Hi, Mummy,' Lara said, sounding so young and sweet.

'School was good. I did colouring and I have a new friend called Bella who has sparkly Peppa Pig shoes.'

'I'm so happy to hear that. You're such a good girl. Will you give the phone to Yuri now? . . . Hi, Yuri, how was school?' I asked.

I could hear him breathing heavily down the phone. 'Well, it was OK, but I don't have any friends. I wish Connor was in this school. I wish we could go back home, Mummy. I don't like London.' Yuri's voice broke and I tried not to cry for him.

'I know it's hard, sweetheart, but you'll make new friends soon, I promise. I'll tell you what, will Mummy bring you home a treat to cheer you up? How about a packet of chocolate buttons?'

'White ones?'

'Yes.'

'A big packet?'

'The biggest one they have.'

'OK.'

'Good boy.'

'Mummy?'

'Yes, Yuri.'

'Are you coming home soon?'

'In a little bit. I have to work for a while longer, but then I'll come straight home. Put me on to Claire.'

'Emma?'

'Hi, is Yuri really all right? He sounds upset. Was he crying when you picked him up? What did the teacher say?'

'Honestly, Emma, he's fine. Both of their teachers said they had a good first day. Yuri wasn't crying. He was a bit quiet, that's all.'

'Well, give them a big hug for me.'

'I will, and I promised to make brownies with them, if that's all right?'

'That's great. Thanks.'

'No problem. Please don't worry about anything.'

I hung up feeling better. They were in excellent hands. Thank God I'd found a nice nanny. I'd known it was going to be hard not picking them up from school, but I hadn't banked on it being this hard. I was worried about them settling in and it was taking a lot of willpower not to dash out of the studio and hop into a taxi. I struggled to compose myself and get my emotions under control. It will all work out OK, I repeated, like a mantra.

'Emma, can we have you back on set, please?' Karen called.

I stuffed my phone into my pocket and pushed back my shoulders. I had to stay focused. Back to work . . .

8

I powdered Babs's forehead, removing the shine, then stood back to watch her work. She sat on the couch and spoke to camera.

'On today's show we're going to meet Mary and Glenda from Devon. Mary is fifty-six, married to a farmer, and spends most of her days in wellies and woolly jumpers. She's badly in need of a fashion make-over. Glenda is Mary's best friend. She's fifty-two and recently her husband left her for – you won't believe this – another man! Glenda's husband didn't run off with the local barmaid, he ran off with the local butcher. As you can imagine, Glenda's confidence is at rock bottom, so I'm going to help her find herself again and, hopefully, next time, she'll meet a man who prefers women.'

Karen brought in Mary and Glenda. They looked nervous and excited. Babs went over to greet them. Mary was small and round, with short black hair and a friendly smile. Glenda was tall and broad, with shoulder-length brown hair.

Karen asked them to sit on the couch and told them that Babs was going to talk to them on camera.

'But we've no makeup on,' Glenda said, sounding worried.

'That's the point. We want you to look as bad as possible so the make-over is more spectacular,' Babs explained. 'Just act natural and answer my questions. Don't worry, I'm brilliant at this. Just follow my lead.'

The camera rolled, and Babs began to give her initial assessment. 'Well, Mary, how long is it since you went to a hairdresser?'

Mary put her hand up to her hair. 'About a year. I've been cutting it myself.'

'I gathered that, and are you cutting it with sheep shears? It's an absolute disgrace. No self-respecting woman would go out like that. We've a lot of work to do on you. Now, is this what you normally wear? Jumpers and saggy, shapeless jeans?'

'Well, you see, I spend most of my days helping my husband on the farm, so I go for practical, warm clothes.'

Babs raised an eyebrow. 'Listen, Mary, if you don't want to find your husband shagging sheep, you need to smarten up. Those baggy jeans are going straight to the bin, along with that awful green knitted jumper.'

Mary looked a bit taken aback. 'Is she always this rude?' she asked Karen.

'She's usually worse. Don't worry, the viewers love it,' Karen assured her. Turning to Babs she said, 'You can't say "shagging sheep" on daytime TV.'

Babs rolled her eyes. 'Listen, Mary, if you don't want your husband to dump you, like Glenda's did, you need to smarten up.' She looked at Karen. 'Was that tame enough for you?'

Karen nodded. 'Perfect. Carry on.'

Babs turned her attention to Glenda. 'Now, Glenda, I know your husband turned out to be a bender, but I have to say, you really aren't going to keep any man, straight or gay, looking like that. There's no excuse in this day and age for a woman to have a moustache. You look like you have a furry animal on your face.'

Glenda's hand flew to her upper lip. 'I – I usually wax it, but I've been very upset lately.'

Babs wagged a finger at her. 'Glenda, we all have problems, and it's still not OK to let yourself go. No woman should go around town with a crumb-catcher like that on her face. We're going to get rid of it. Now, what do you do? Do you work? Are you at home? Do you have kids?'

Glenda, with her hand still covering her upper lip, answered, 'I'm a postmistress and I don't have any children.'

'Well, no surprise there! I doubt there was much going on in your bedroom. Did you never suspect your husband was gay?'

Glenda shook her head. 'We got married late in life, I was forty-two and I just thought he wasn't interested in sex.'

Babs leant in. 'Glenda, *all* heterosexual men are into sex. Anytime, anywhere, anyhow, even when they're ninety.'

She had a point there. James was never not in the mood, even when he was exhausted. The only time he wouldn't have sex was when England was playing rugby. Then he had eyes only for the TV.

Glenda sighed and looked downcast. Babs took her hand. 'But the good news is, I'm going to make you look so hot that you'll be having sex for years to come. Now, we have a lot of work to do. Your arse and boobs are dragging all over the floor. We need to get you into some iron underwear, then find you some decent clothes and a proper hairstyle. Don't worry, Glenda, when I've finished with you, even Mary's husband will be begging you for sex.'

Mary's head nearly spun off. 'What?'

Ignoring her, Babs looked at the camera. 'Now we're going to get these ladies to strip down to their undies so we can get a good look at where their flabby parts are and figure out how to hide them. It won't be easy, but I'm kind of awesome at this so watch this space.'

The two ladies were asked to take their clothes off behind a curtain and then to stand in the 360-degree mirror, with all their bits on view. I would have run from the building screaming if anyone suggested I had to strip down and look at all my flabby bits in that torture chamber. Babs came over to stand by me while the cameramen were shooting.

'Jesus, they're a pair of ugly heifers. I know I'm good, but I need something to work with. Mary's nearly as short as Yuri and Glenda has shoulders like Arnold Schwarzenegger's. How the hell am I supposed to make them look good?'

I watched the two women take turns to be filmed in their underwear and wondered what on earth would possess any woman to expose herself on a show like this. Unhappiness and desperation made people do crazy things. I was determined to make them up so they looked lovely. I studied their faces and worked out what makeup would suit their colouring. 'Have a heart, Babs. Poor Glenda needs kindness, not criticism.'

Babs ate a piece of chocolate. 'I'm presenting a make-over show. It's not *Dr* bloody *Phil*. I'm sorry her husband turned out to be a sausage jockey, but my only job is to make her look better – and it's a big ask. Still, by the time I've finished with her, she'll feel a million times better and she won't look like Whatshisface.'

'Tom Selleck?' We giggled.

'Yes. I'm going to wax her to within an inch of her life. There's no excuse for a woman to have hairy anything. It's disgusting.'

Speaking of waxing, I couldn't remember the last time I'd had my bikini line done. I'd have to sort it out. I wasn't very hairy, but it definitely needed pruning. Babs had a point.

'No man wants to have sex with a gorilla. Hollywood wax all the way.'

'Is the Hollywood the one where you get it all waxed off?' I asked.

Babs spun around. 'Are you telling me you have hair down there?'

'Yes, of course. It's natural.'

'It's gross.'

'No, it isn't.'

'No woman should have hair anywhere down there.'

'I think it's weird to have none. It looks freaky.'

'Well, I haven't had any complaints.'

'Don't give Mary and Glenda Hollywoods – they'll have heart-attacks.' I was genuinely worried about the two women being plucked alive.

'We don't do bikini waxes. The budget only allows for upper lip and legs.'

Karen joined us. 'Right, Babs, we need some commentary about their shapes – go easy on them, stick to pears and apples, all right?'

Babs put her hands on her hips. 'You hired me because I'm honest. Neither of them looks like a pear or an apple. They look like big fat sausage rolls.'

I touched up Babs's makeup and watched my sister stride over to the women.

Gary walked over to me. His jeans were too tight and he was wearing a T-shirt with a picture of Bob Marley smoking weed on it. It looked ridiculous. He was clearly having a mid-life crisis, which I was pretty sure included shagging my sister. I tried not to be repulsed by him. After all, he was my boss too.

'Was she like this as a kid?' he drawled, pointing to Babs.

Was he serious? Did he really want to shoot the breeze with me about my sister? Did he not realize I could see through him? He was pathetic. Maybe the tightness of his jeans was making his brain function slower. I tried to be polite. 'Oh, yes. In fact, she's mellowed a bit since then.'

He chuckled. 'I've only been working on the show three

months, but I've been in TV for fifteen years and I've never met anyone like her. She's a total fireball.'

If he hadn't been my boss and it hadn't been my first day, I would have told him to stay away from my sister and go home to his wife. But I didn't want to get fired yet, and I needed to find out from Babs what exactly was going on between them. I prayed it was just a harmless flirtation, but I could tell from the way they looked at each other that there was a whole lot of sex going on. I'd have to try and talk sense into Babs.

'Are you married, Gary?' I asked, hoping a conversation about his wife would distract him, or at least shame him into taking his eyes off Babs for a second.

Gary nodded, still staring at her. 'Yes, and I have twins, a boy and a girl, so we were done in one go,' he said, with a laugh.

'I have two kids too. I think it's plenty,' I agreed. 'I'm in awe of people who have more.'

'Nutters, if you ask me. Two are a right handful.'

'Does your wife work?' I was determined to say 'wife' as often as possible.

Gary snorted. 'You must be joking. All Val does is spend my hard-earned money.'

'It's not easy being at home all day,' I noted, defending his wife.

'Does any woman really need ten pairs of black boots?'

'Sometimes women shop because they're lonely.'

Gary looked at me. 'Lonely? Her sister lives across the road and her mother's around the corner.'

'Well, being at home with small kids is never easy.'

'Believe me, she tells me how hard it is every day.' He sighed.

Damn. Clearly everything was not good at home, which

meant that Gary probably was having an affair with Babs. I had to get Babs to stop this. Media people were well-known gossips: one affair with a married producer could be described as a mistake, but two, Babs would be labelled a tramp. I needed to save my sister from herself.

Over at the mirror Babs was standing in front of the two women who were now in bathrobes. 'Mary, you're an apple shape. Short and stumpy, with a huge middle-age spread. You need to do more digging and less eating. Glenda, you're built like a rugby player. You're so wide and chunky you have a man's body, which is probably why your husband married you. Now I'm going to show you both some styles that will hide all your flaws and camouflage your flabby bits. Then we'll do hair and makeup, and by the time we've finished with you, you'll be unrecognizable. Let's be honest here, you're not supermodels, but I can improve you one hundred per cent.'

The afternoon flew by. First, wigs were chosen – the budget didn't stretch to taking the participants to get their hair coloured and cut. Next, Babs squeezed the women into super-strength slimming underwear.

When Mary complained that she couldn't breathe and thought she might pass out, Babs glared at her. 'I have a reputation to maintain, and that corset is the only way you're going to fit into the clothes I've chosen for you. You can't go around town with your belly hanging out. So just suck it up.'

Babs dressed Mary in straight-leg dark denim jeans, with very high boots and a vertical striped shirt that she belted at the waist.

'I can't walk in these boots,' Mary grumbled.

Babs bent down and yanked up the zips. 'Stop moaning. You look better than you've ever looked in your life. You have to suffer to be fashionable.'

While Babs dressed Glenda, I worked on Mary's makeup. I warmed up her skin tone with some light liquid foundation and a soft blusher. I highlighted her blue eyes with grey shadow, then made them pop with a very subtle line of liquid eyeliner on the upper lid. Finally, I layered on black mascara and finished off with some neutral lip-gloss. Although I had no experience with wigs, I had to help her put hers on. It was a short black style, not dissimilar to her own hair, but the cut was much choppier and funkier and a side fringe swept across her face. Mary wasn't allowed to see herself in any mirrors, and she was brought to the other side of the studio so Glenda wouldn't see her. Then she had to sit on her own, no doubt wondering what on earth Babs had done to her.

Babs dressed Glenda in beautifully tailored cream trousers, navy and cream shoes with kitten heels and a navy halter neck top with a deep V that made her shoulders look less wide. She added a long necklace, which drew the eye down.

Glenda then came to me for makeup. She had brown eyes, so I decided to give her a smoky look. The poor woman needed to be vamped up. She needed to feel sexy and feminine and attractive again. Losing your husband to a man is about as crushing a blow as you can sustain.

Glenda was very quiet in the chair. 'Are you all right?' I asked. 'It sounds as if you've had a very difficult time.'

She smiled at me. 'I'm fine, thank you. This was Mary's idea. She thought it would be a good distraction for me.'

'Is it?'

'It's certainly different. I've never met anyone like that Barbara before. Have you known her long?'

I decided to be vague. 'A while.'

'She's so confident – I envy her that – so sure of herself.

She'll go far in life. I wish I'd been more like that when I was younger.'

No, you don't, I thought. Babs had no friends because she had alienated everyone at school and in all of her various jobs since then. In truth, she hadn't made one true friend in life, no one she could rely on. She had lots of acquaintances and people to party with, but no one she could call in the middle of the night and cry to. Then again, Babs almost never cried because she never felt deeply enough about anything to get really upset. The only time in the last ten years that I could remember my sister crying was when Lara was born. Babs had come in to see her. Lara was in the incubator and they weren't sure if she was going to make it. None of us could believe it when Babs shed a tear. We were all in complete shock. My mother had referred to it ever since as 'the time Barbara cried', which always made me smile.

I blended Glenda's makeup. 'How are you managing? Are you feeling very low?'

'I was initially, but I've got really good, loyal friends. They've all been round with dinners and bottles of wine and kind words. They even dragged me to a Zumba class last week and I enjoyed myself for the first time in ages.'

'That's wonderful to hear. Friends are so important, aren't they?'

'Oh, yes, love. Men come and go, but it's your friends you can rely on.'

I knew I shouldn't ask, but I was dying to know. 'Did you have no inclination that your husband was . . . well . . . interested in men?' I'd read about women who came home from work one day to find their husband shagging Kevin the milkman, but I'd never met anyone to whom it had actually happened.

Glenda closed her eyes so I could apply shadow. 'I suppose if I look back now, I can see there were some signs. He did love *Strictly Come Dancing* and he stormed out of the cinema when we went to see *Brokeback Mountain*. I thought it was because he couldn't stand to see two men together, but I know now it was because it was too close to the bone.'

'I'm sorry. It must have been awful for you.'

'It really was. But I must confess, now that I'm over the shock, I quite like having the house to myself. He was very moody, you see. I suppose it was all those hormones and suppressed urges. It's much calmer now he's gone. Mind you, it didn't do my confidence much good.'

I put Glenda's wig on, a blonde bob. She looked completely different. The colour was too bright for her, but a similar cut with more subtle highlights would have been perfect. I hugged her. 'You look fantastic! Wait until those locals get a look at you! They'll be talking about how hot you are.'

Babs came to get Glenda. 'Wow, you look great. Good job, Emma.'

Glenda and Mary were brought face to face with each other, their eyes closed. Then, as the camera rolled, they opened their eyes, screamed and whooped and got all teary.

Karen stood beside me, surveying the scene. '*Yesssss!* We love it when they cry,' she exclaimed. 'But I'll need you to fix their makeup for the next shot.'

I rushed over and removed the mascara streaks. 'You're both stunners,' I told them.

Next they were placed side by side in front of covered mirrors. The cameras captured their reaction as Babs pulled the covers back and they saw their make-over. Both women were shocked silent, they kept touching their faces and turning around to look at their raised, perky bums.

'I told you I was a miracle-worker,' Babs said. 'Don't you

look fabulous? Did you ever in your wildest dreams think you could turn into swans? Who would have thought I could make you two look so good? No man – gay or straight – would leave you now!'

Turning to face the camera, Babs added, 'Once again I've outdone myself. If you look awful and want to have your life changed, contact us via our website. I'm Barbara Burke, stylist *extraordinaire* and presenter of *How To Look Good With Your Clothes On*. See you next time.'

9

I couldn't believe how tired I felt after just one day's work. I suppose I was no longer used to standing on my feet all day. I packed up my stuff quickly – I couldn't wait to get home to Yuri and Lara.

As I was about to leave, Karen came up to me. 'Well done, Emma. You were great today. I have to be honest, we were worried you were going to be another Babs, and there's only room for one ego that size on this programme.'

'There's only room for one ego that size in the world,' I said, laughing.

Babs strutted over. 'Let's go. I'm starving. I'm coming back to your house for dinner. I've nothing to eat in mine.'

We walked out and I headed for the tube station.

'Where are you going?' Babs asked.

'The tube.'

'I don't do public transport. The only perk of this badly paid job is that I get taxis on account.'

It sounded good to me – I'd be home quicker. As Babs hailed a cab, a young, dishevelled woman, with a mane of chestnut hair, came timidly towards us.

'Excuse me, are you Barbara Burke?'

Babs looked her up and down. 'Who's asking?'

'I just *love* your show,' the woman gushed. 'You're so funny and honest. It's brilliant. And you're so glamorous and stylish – you always look so cool.'

I watched in amusement as Babs flicked her hair and bestowed a dazzling smile on her. 'Thank you.'

'Would you mind giving me some advice? My boyfriend just dumped me out of the blue and I really want him back. I love him. I know we're meant to be together. I was thinking I'd get my hair cut and buy some new clothes to try and make him fancy me again.'

Babs stared at her, the dazzling smile gone. 'Are you insane? Your hair is your best asset – don't even think about cutting it. Your clothes, on the other hand, are awful. Go out and buy yourself a short, tight black dress, fishnet stockings and black high heels. Men are simple, stupid creatures and a short skirt and high heels always gets them going. If that doesn't work, shag his best friend. That'll get his attention.'

Babs climbed into a taxi and beckoned me to follow her. I turned to the poor woman, whose mouth was hanging open, and said gently, 'Perhaps you could try talking to him and find out why he broke up with you. You might be able to work it out.'

Babs reached out of the taxi, grabbed my arm and yanked me into it. She slammed the door shut.

I rubbed my arm. 'There's no need to be so rough.'

'Emma, you cannot encourage these people. If you get into a conversation with them, you could be stuck for ages and then they might start stalking you. I have to be careful – a lot of nutters out there prey on celebrities.'

'Did you just refer to yourself as a celebrity?'

'Yes, I did. I *am* a celebrity.'

'Please tell me what pills you take. I want to live in your shiny world. It seems such fun.'

Babs turned her back on me and looked out of the window. 'You're just jealous of my success.'

I laughed. 'Oh, Babs, it's not your success I'm jealous of, it's your confidence. It must be fantastic to think so highly of yourself.'

She turned back to me with the hint of a smile. 'Looks like I was born this way, as Lady Gaga might say. And I'm obviously adopted or the result of an affair Mum has never admitted to.'

I grinned. 'And where did that conclusion come from?'

'I don't have red hair, like you and Sean. I'm blonde and gorgeous. I'm incredibly talented and confident, while you two are all needy and insecure. There are no common genes at all.'

I secretly hoped Yuri and Lara would end up with some of Babs's confidence. Not all of it – God, they'd be unbearable – but a little would be great. I had been very shy as a teenager and it was only in my late twenties that I'd begun to feel in any way good about myself. I'd finally stopped trying to wear clothes that were too short and tight and dressed to suit my shape. Then, as if by some miracle, my hair turned from a carrot colour to a really nice auburn.

But, if I'm honest, meeting James was what really boosted my confidence. He was handsome and smart and funny and, for some reason, he adored me. James made me feel ten feet tall. Being married to him gave me such a sense of security and love. He had been so supportive when we'd struggled to get pregnant and all through the adoption. We had seen couples torn apart by infertility, but it had brought us closer.

I looked at Babs's life and felt sorry for her. I'd have hated to be out clubbing and dating a different guy every week. I liked to feel safe and protected. Marriage and children had given me that. James and I had created our own little unit and I loved it. Babs thought my life was boring and mundane, but I was very happy. Well . . . if I was a stone lighter and we won the lotto, my life would be absolutely perfect.

I glanced out of the window as the taxi passed groups of tourists wandering about in the September sunshine. So far,

London had been OK – nice neighbours, new job, great nanny, happy husband . . . So far, so good.

'Babs,' I interrupted my sister's frantic typing.

'Hold on, I'm tweeting.'

'What? That you're in a taxi with your sister? Wow, how fascinating!'

'People are very interested in what I have to say, actually. I have six thousand followers.'

'That just means there are six thousand crazy-lonely people out there.'

She ignored me and kept on typing. I watched the way her hair fell over her eyes, how she pursed her lips as she was thinking. Babs could push my buttons like no one else, but I loved her. I hated to see her wasting herself on men who had baggage and no real intention of making her happy. Why couldn't she see that was all it was?

'Babs, I want to talk to you about Gary.'

'What about him?' She continued to type, her thumb shooting around the on-screen keyboard.

'Just remember that he's married and has two kids, and you do not want to make the same stupid mistake.'

She hit send and looked up at me. 'You don't know anything about it, so just butt out.'

'I'm your sister and I have no intention of butting out. I'm telling you to stay away from him.'

Babs cursed and threw her phone into her bag. 'Seriously, Emma, get off my back. I'm in no mood for a lecture.'

Before we could get into an argument, the taxi pulled up outside the house. I jumped out and rushed through the gate, up the path and through the front door. I was dying to see the children. They were at the kitchen table, helping Claire decorate a cake.

'Mummy!' They jumped down and rushed over to hug me.

I wrapped my arms around them and inhaled their familiar scent. 'I missed you, guys. How are you? Is everything OK?'

'Yes, Mummy. Look, we're making a brownie cake,' Yuri said, beaming up at me.

'Oi, Danny DeVito, don't I get a hug?'

Yuri threw his arms around Babs's legs. 'And what about you, Lara? Come on.' Lara joined in. 'That's better. You should be nice to me – I'm the superstar in this family. Suck up to me because I'm the one who's going to give you inappropriate presents and cash when you're older.'

I went over to Claire. The chocolate brownie cake had 'MUMMY' written in Smarties across the top. 'Did you really make this?' I asked.

Claire blushed. 'It's a welcome-home-after-your-first-day present.'

I was really touched by the gesture. 'Thanks! That's such a lovely treat. How was today?'

Claire began to tidy up the cooking utensils. 'It went really well. I made fresh vegetable soup for their lunch.'

'Oh, no! I should have told you – they hate vegetable soup!'

Claire dried a bowl with a tea-towel. 'Actually, they ate it all. Had seconds, too.'

I frowned. 'Really? Even Yuri?'

'Yes, Mummy, I did. Claire's soup was yummy,' Yuri announced. 'Much nicer than your yucky one.'

I was stunned. 'I'm amazed, Claire. What's your secret?'

'It's nothing. I'm sure your soup is the same. I just put some cream and garlic into it, so maybe that was why they ate it.'

I put my hand on her arm. 'It's OK, I'm not annoyed. I'm thrilled. Please continue to make it and get them to eat it. This is great news.'

Babs came forward and proffered a hand. 'Seeing as my sister isn't going to introduce me, I'm Babs, Emma's much younger sister.'

Claire gave it a weak shake. 'Hello, I'm Claire.'

Babs plonked herself onto a chair. 'I have to be honest, I think you must be mad to want to mind someone else's kids all day. It has to be the worst job out there.'

I managed to stop myself shouting at Babs to shut up. Claire was the reason I could go to work. Claire was dependable. Yuri and Lara liked her, and she had just got them to eat vegetable bloody soup. Babs needed to be muzzled.

Claire busied herself wiping down the kitchen counter. 'I love kids. I think they're great.'

Babs wrinkled her nose. 'Why?'

'Because they're so sweet and innocent.'

'Exactly. Well said, Claire.' I was determined to take charge of the conversation. 'Now, I think I'll have a piece of this gorgeous cake.'

'Easy there, Emma, you really don't want to put on any more weight. If I was you, I'd eat some carrots or celery instead.'

'Thanks, Babs, but I'm going to have some of the delicious cake Claire and the kids made specially for me.'

Babs tut-tutted. 'Suit yourself, but don't come crying to me when your arse won't fit into your jeans.'

'I think Emma looks fine,' Claire said quietly.

Babs put a huge slice of cake on her plate. 'Of course you do. She's paying your wages.'

'What's wages?' Yuri asked.

'It's nothing, sweetheart. Babs is being silly as usual.' I glared at my sister.

Babs took a bite of her cake. 'Mmmm. How long have you been in London?' she asked Claire.

'About a year.'

'Why did you leave Ireland?'

Claire's face went bright red and I jumped in to save her. 'None of your business.'

Babs patted her mouth with a napkin. 'Jesus, did she rob a bank?'

I kicked her under the table. 'Drop it.'

Claire put up her hand. 'It's OK, Emma.' Turning to Babs she said, 'I left because I was being bullied.'

'At school?'

'Yes.'

Babs shrugged. 'That happens to loads of people. You have to move on. Girls can be bitches.'

'What's "bitches" mean?' Yuri asked.

'Babs!' I hissed.

'Sorry.' Babs leant down. 'It's a mean girl, but it's a bad word so don't use it or your mum will kill me.' She handed him a Smartie from her slice of cake.

'OK.' Yuri grinned.

'Kids, go and wash your hands and then come back for cake,' I said. They ran out.

'Was the bullying really that bad? Did you not just complain to the headmistress or a teacher?' Babs asked.

'Actually a teacher was mean to me too,' Claire said, blushing fiercely.

'Really?' Babs licked her fork. 'How?'

'He was just . . .' Claire looked at the floor.

'Did he come on to you?' Babs asked.

Claire dug her hands into her pockets. 'He was always giving me . . . special attention.'

'Oh, my God, did he molest you?' I asked.

'Not exactly, but he was always putting his arm around me, winking and hugging me and squeezing my shoulders, and telling me I was amazing and special. He used to bring me in chocolate and sweets. I think . . . I think maybe . . . he was in love with me,' she stuttered.

'OK.' Babs looked puzzled. 'How is that mean? I'd have loved a teacher who gave me food.'

'It's creepy,' I said. 'Not to mention extremely inappropriate. I'd freak if a teacher did that to Lara. There are boundaries, and he was clearly not observing them.'

'When I asked him why he was giving me so much attention,' Claire went on, 'he went mad and said I was a liar and a stupid little girl who was imagining it. Then he went to the headmistress, told her I was mad in the head, and after that he ignored me and acted like I was invisible.'

'That sounds really strange,' Babs remarked, frowning.

'It sounds awful,' I said, giving Claire a sympathetic look. I felt very sorry for her. Her face was all red and she looked upset at the memory. 'You poor thing, you've had a tough time. I can promise you that no one in this house will bully you. You're safe with us.'

She smiled. 'Thanks, Emma. I like it here. You're a lovely family.'

'Well, the kids are mad about you and anyone who can get my children to eat vegetables is a legend in my book. Now, why don't you head home and put your feet up? You've earned it, that's for sure.'

'I enjoyed today – the kids are great. They're really happy and enthusiastic.'

'Well, thank you for looking after them so well, and for the very thoughtful cake.'

'You're welcome. See you tomorrow. 'Bye, Babs.'

'See you,' Babs said, stuffing another piece of cake into her mouth.

I walked Claire to the door. Yuri and Lara came charging

out to say goodbye. Claire turned around and they ran into her arms to hug her. For the hundredth time I thanked the nanny gods that we had found someone who fitted in so well with us.

When we returned to the kitchen, Babs was still eating cake. I prayed that one day my sister's metabolism would slow down and she'd put on weight, like normal people did.

'That story was a bit odd,' Babs said, as soon as I walked in.

'No talking with your mouth full,' Lara scolded her.

'Honey, when you get to my age you can talk with your mouth full, watch TV all night, eat chocolate for breakfast and drink until you fall over.'

'I want to be your age!' Lara jumped up and down.

Babs smiled at her, then turned back to me. 'Why is she so shy and awkward, and why does she wear clothes that are ten sizes too big for her? You should get her on the show. We could do a lot with her.'

'Lara, sweetie, will you go into the TV room, like a good girl? I just need to talk to Babs for five minutes, OK?'

'OK.' She reluctantly left the room to find Yuri.

I waved my fork at Babs threateningly. 'Claire will not be coming on the show. She will be too busy looking after my children. She's shy because she was bullied, which is why she left Ireland and moved here.'

'She wasn't really bullied,' Babs said. 'A teacher hugging you and giving you sweets isn't bullying. It's a bit odd, yeah, but he probably just felt sorry for her. There's no way he fancied her – the state of her! Bullying is when you get your head flushed down the toilet every day. I'm sick of everyone banging on about being bullied. I bet you half of them make it up.'

I was incredulous. 'What?'

'Seriously, every celebrity interview I read is full of "Poor me, I was bullied in school," or else they're bi-polar. Don't you think it's a bit strange that almost everyone in TV and movies was either bullied or is bi-polar? Half of them are lying just to get column inches. It's pathetic. I did an interview last month and the reporter kept asking about my childhood – did anything terrible happen, was I abused, bullied, molested, flashed at? Pathetic. Then she asked me about my mental health – am I putting on a front, do I suffer from anxiety or depression or eating disorders or mood swings? Eventually I told her that I eat like a horse and the only flashing I'd experienced was me flashing my boobs at a car full of priests when I was sixteen. She kept saying, "But we're looking for misery stories."'

'Really? She actually said that?'

'Yes! The magazines only want stories about people who had their arm ripped off by a lion or found out their father is a transsexual.'

'I don't want to read that kind of stuff,' I noted.

'That's what I said. Who the hell wants to read about miserable ugly people with missing limbs? I hate misery, I hate moaning and I hate bullshit stories about bullying. People called me Horse or Hook Nose all the way through school. It just made me more determined to get my nose job, which, let's face it, turned me from an eight point five out of ten to a perfect ten. I'd call that incentivizing someone, not bullying.'

I laughed. 'You happen to have been born with elephant skin, while most people are a little more sensitive.'

Babs popped the last bit of cake into her mouth. 'Bullshit. Most people are just looking for a reason to blame others for their misery, their lack of success and their shitty relationships. I am so sick of the women coming on our show crying about their husbands leaving them or not paying them any attention. If you want a man to pay you attention, lose weight, buy sexy underwear and ride him senseless. He won't be looking over the hedge after that.'

I made a mental note to get out my good undies and have regular sex with James. I didn't want him looking over any hedges. I felt bad to be treating it like another item on my To Do list, but maybe that was what life with kids was like for everyone: Tuesday, grocery shop; Wednesday, sex; Thursday, bins . . .

Lara came into the kitchen, crying. 'Mummy, Yuri won't let me play with his Lego. He says I'm not allowed cos I'm a girl.'

Babs stood up. 'Let me deal with this.' She marched Lara back into the lounge. 'Hey, Stumpy, let your sister play with that Lego. Get it into your thick head that girls rock, OK? We are smarter, funnier, hotter and can wipe the floor with men.'

'She's really bad at Lego,' Yuri protested.

'Listen, Half-pint, when you're fifteen, spotty, short and desperate for action, you'll be glad you were nice to Lara because you can snog all her friends. They'll be two years younger and gagging to get some experience. Mark my words, it's worth investing in Lara now. Be nice to her.'

'What's "snog"?' Yuri asked.

'When a boy and girl kiss with tongues,' Babs said, sticking her tongue out.

'Charming!' James walked in with his backpack over his shoulder.

'*Grooooss.*' Yuri scrunched up his face.

'Yeah, right! Come back to me in ten years' time,' Babs told him.

'I like boys,' Lara said.

James kissed her head. 'Well, let's hope you haven't inherited your aunt Barbara's penchant for men.'

Babs punched him on the arm. 'I can't help it if men find me irresistible.'

James laughed. 'Irresistible or certifiable?'

Babs put her hands on her hips. 'Is that what you wear to work?'

'Yes. What's wrong with it?'

'It's a saggy tracksuit! Have you no self-respect? You should try dressing like José Mourinho. Now he is hot!'

'I often train with the team – I'm very hands-on. I don't spend my day sitting behind a big desk strategizing.'

Babs grinned, taking great pleasure from winding James up. 'Well, maybe you should. Tracksuits are not a good look on any guy, but especially not on old men.'

'He's not old,' I defended my husband.

'Thank you, darling.'

'He's middle-aged,' Babs said.

'No, he isn't. Middle-aged is, like, fifty.'

'Duh! People don't live to a hundred, Emma. You are both middle-aged.'

I looked at James. 'Oh, my God, are we?'

He shrugged. 'I suppose we are.'

I put my arm around him. 'Well, I like you and your middle-aged, tracksuit-wearing body.'

'Thank you.' James kissed me.

'Yucky kissing!' Yuri shouted.

Babs rolled her eyes. 'I agree. Pass me the puke-bucket.'

'Well, I hope you're not feeling too nauseous to eat, because dinner is ready,' I said, smiling at James.

We moved into the kitchen, leaving the children playing in the lounge.

'Smells good,' James said, going over to the sink to wash his hands.

'Marks & Spencer's finest,' I admitted.

We sat down and helped ourselves. Even though she'd had three slices of cake, Babs heaped her plate.

'So, how was work?' James asked me.

'Good. It went really well.'

'She wasn't bad,' Babs drawled. 'She made two awful-looking trolls halfway respectable.'

'I assume you're referring to two women?' James uncorked the wine.

I grinned. 'Two very sweet ladies from Devon.'

James filled our glasses. 'Poor things, coming all the way up from Devon to be abused by Babs.'

Babs rapped his knuckles with her fork. 'Meeting me was the best thing that's ever happened to them, I'll have you know. I transformed them. The single one might actually meet someone now.'

'Speaking of men, Babs, anyone on the scene?' James asked. 'Any poor unsuspecting London boy being used and abused?'

I bristled while Babs scooped a large piece of the chicken and leek pie onto her fork. 'There might be.' She raised an eyebrow. I stood up to get a glass of water to stop myself shouting at her.

As Babs shovelled another forkful of pie into her mouth, she said, 'By the way, I met Mary Poppins.'

James looked puzzled.

'You know, mousy Claire.'

'Oh, right. Yes, she is rather quiet, isn't she? I thought we should interview a few more candidates, but you know Emma. She decided she wanted Claire and that was that.' Seeing my face darken, James quickly added, 'But I think she was right. Claire is good with the children.'

Babs shook her head. 'She told us this really weird story about her teacher fancying her and then denying it. It sounded

118

like she was making a big deal about nothing. She seems very young for nineteen, doesn't she?'

I nearly choked on my water. 'Do you have any idea how immature you were at nineteen, Babs? Claire is like a mature woman compared to you.'

'I was born mature,' Babs said, as James and I laughed. She put down her fork. 'Just because she made you a cake doesn't mean she's not a bit odd.'

'She's just quiet and lacks confidence,' I said firmly, tired now of talking about Claire. 'Being bullied is terrible. I, for one, am going to be especially nice to her to build up her self-esteem. She deserves to be happy.'

Babs finished her plate of food, wrapped a large slice of my cake in a napkin and stood up. 'Much as I'd love to stay and discuss childcare with you, I have to hit the road.'

'Thanks for eating all of my cake,' I said.

'Better me than you, Fatso!' On that note, Babs picked up her bag and sashayed out of the room.

I followed her out to the hallway. 'Babs, I'm serious about Gary. You have to stop seeing him. You're going to get a reputation and it could affect your career.'

'Back off,' Babs snapped.

'I'm worried about you.'

Babs turned her back to me. 'Drop it.'

'Where are you going? Are you going to meet him now? Don't, Babs. You must know that he'll never leave his wife. They never do.'

She spun around, looking furious. 'Gary's different, OK? For once in your stupid life just shut the hell up and leave me alone.' She stormed down the path and hailed a cab.

I stared after her, mouth open. I knew I was being a bit preachy, but I'd never seen Babs so angry and upset. Did she actually love the guy? I couldn't bear the thought of it because

I knew in my heart he had no intention of leaving his wife for her. She was his bit of fun, sex with no strings attached.

I went back into the kitchen. 'What was that all about?' James asked. 'I heard Babs shouting at you.'

'I was warning her to stay away from Gary, the producer on the show. She's sleeping with him.'

James groaned. 'I take it from your tone that he's married.'

'Oh, yes, with two children.'

'She sounded really angry with you.'

I sat down in a chair. 'She is. I've never seen her so furious. She's bolshie almost all the time, but she rarely shouts and roars. She was shaking with rage. I think she's fallen really hard for him – she could even be in love with him, which is a first for Babs.'

'Well, darling, she's an adult. You can't stop her making bad choices. You have to stop trying to change her. Babs is who she is. She's always going to blaze her own trail. You've been giving her advice for years and she never listens. The only person Babs ever listens to is herself. Perhaps it's time to back off a bit.'

A message flashed up on my phone. I read it, then fell back against the chair, stunned. James rushed to my side. 'Emma? Emma, are you all right? What is it?'

With trembling hands I held my phone up for him to see. The message was from Babs: *Sry 4 shouting. Must b hormones. Am pregnant.*

I was in bed, not even managing to concentrate on *Grazia*, when my phone beeped. I grabbed it, hoping it was Babs replying to me. I had rung her ten times and sent ten messages, but she was ignoring me. It wasn't my sister, it was Lucy, asking if I was still awake and if I was up for a chat.

I was glad of the distraction. It would be nice to catch up with her and I was dying to see how things were between her and Donal. I was really worried about them. I was also worried about Lucy's relationship with Serge. Being away from him so much would surely affect him. They had stressed in our adoption course that you must spend time with a child to bond with them.

The other thing about children is that you need to fall in love with them. The more time you spend with them, the more you love them – even though they can drive you crazy. But if you're away from them all the time, you become detached. It's human nature. I knew Lucy loved Serge, but I was worried she'd regret all this time spent in the office. Kids grow up so quickly and you never get back what you miss.

I dialled her number. When she answered, she sounded tired. 'Hi. Thanks for calling back. I'm not disturbing you, am I?'

'Not at all. I've been dying to talk to you. How did your first day go?' I asked.

'Good, thanks. The office is really nice, and Paul and Alan are great. We've got really ambitious plans. I'm excited.'

'Great. And, uhm, how are things at home?'

She sighed. 'Oh, God, Emma, this morning was bad, but tonight was worse.'

'Really? That doesn't sound good.'

'It was a disaster. I didn't sleep a wink last night. I was nervous and excited about today. I had to get up at four a.m. anyway to catch my flight, so I knew I'd get no sleep, to be honest. Before I left I went into Donal's room.'

'What do you mean "Donal's room"?'

'He's been sleeping in the spare room since I took the job,' she admitted, sounding a bit embarrassed.

'Oh, Lucy.' This was not a good sign.

'He hates me at the moment, but I still didn't want to leave without saying goodbye. He was awake, so I just told him I loved him and that I didn't want to fight any more.'

'Good on you. What did he say to that?'

Lucy sighed. 'He said he'd never like this set-up, but that he did want to stop fighting because the atmosphere in the house was bad for Serge.'

'Well, he has a point. Our kids hate it when we argue. It does upset them.'

'I know, I know.' Lucy sounded frustrated now. 'Anyway, I suggested the two of us going out for a nice dinner this weekend, but Donal is working Friday and Saturday until late, so . . .'

I snuggled down under my duvet. 'At least you tried. And you should keep trying. He'll come around eventually.'

'I sat on the plane over here, going over the conversation in my head. The reality is that Donal's going to be really busy for the next eight months, with almost every weekend taken up with rugby commentating and writing his column. But we'll just have to try to make some time to spend together or we'll be like ships passing in the night.'

'How about making Sunday your date night?' I suggested.

'I thought about that, but I want to go to bed in good time on Sunday because I'm up so early to catch the first flight to London.'

'I forgot about that. Will Donal be working a lot of Saturday nights?'

'Well, he'll be travelling to the UK and France for some of the away matches, but most of the time he'll be in the studio commentating and then writing his column afterwards, so he's never normally home before about ten.'

'God, it's going to be hard to find time between both of your busy lives.'

Lucy sighed. 'It'll take a lot of effort to make this work. I know that by the end of the week I'll be exhausted, and I'm going to be looking after Serge all weekend. Honestly, Emma, I feel tired just thinking about it. But I know lots of women with high-flying careers also manage a home life, so I'll have to figure it out.'

'Well, if I can help at all, let me know. Now, tell me about work.' I decided to get her to focus on her job: she liked talking about that.

Lucy's voice immediately took on a different tone. She sounded happy and enthusiastic. 'Well, we hit the ground running. We had back-to-back meetings and conference calls all day. But the best part of it is that I'm completely in charge. It's brilliant, Emma. This is my company, my creation, and I'm really excited about it. I think we make a fantastic team. Alan and Paul are bright, ambitious and energetic. So, yeah, a good first day. I actually think Image Leasing is going to be a big success, if I don't jinx it by saying that!'

'Oh, Lucy, that's great to hear.' I was glad she was positive and upbeat about something in her life. While I might not see eye to eye with her on working away all week, I did want her to be happy, and her career had always been hugely important to her. It was a very big part of her identity. I suppose I had never considered that it would be a bigger part than being a mother. I still couldn't get my head around that.

'Did you have a drink to celebrate?'

'We did. I was sipping a glass of brandy, looking out of our boardroom window at the view of St Paul's Cathedral, soaking in the wonder of this new venture and the possibility that I could really make some serious money, if it goes well, when I remembered.'

'Remembered what?'

'That I'd promised to Skype Serge before he went to bed.'

My hand flew to my mouth. 'Oh, no, Lucy.' How could she forget?

'I ran into my office and called home, but there was no answer, so I left messages. Then I got a text from Donal saying, "As you know Serge goes to bed seven thirty. He was very disappointed not to hear from you." He actually put "very" in capitals, just to be sure I'd feel every ounce of it.'

'Oh, God, Lucy.'

'I felt really awful, but then Alan and Paul came in. When they saw my face, they knew something was up, so I explained. And they just laughed.'

'What do you mean?' I asked, puzzled.

'Alan laughed and said Donal sounded like his wife. He said she's permanently in a grump about something. And Paul told me that Donal is bloody lucky to have a wife who earns so much. He said he'd love it if his wife worked, rather than just shopping on Bond Street and spending his money.'

It was all very well for Paul and Alan to laugh, but they weren't thinking about Serge. What about his disappointment? It wasn't just about Donal being annoyed, and he had every right to be. This was also about a little boy excited to talk to his mum, who had forgotten to call, and a dad having to pick up the pieces of that let-down. I tried to play down the fact that I thought her colleagues sounded like selfish tossers. I didn't want to make her feel worse, so I didn't mention Serge's disappointment either.

'Men don't have the guilt gene. When James goes away, he doesn't feel the need to call home every day. I do. I couldn't not talk to the kids.'

'I don't really have that gene,' Lucy admitted. 'Paul was saying that his kids grew up with him working long hours and that if your kids have never known any different, why would they be damaged by it or hurt? He says he only ever sees them on the weekend and has a great relationship with them. They understand that their dad works hard to provide a good life for them.'

'Yes, but I'm sure his children would have liked to see more of him,' I pointed out. I didn't want to have a row about it, but I had to be honest.

'Well, he was busy working and earning so they could go to the top schools and have the best opportunities possible. You can't have it every way.'

'But maybe if he worked less and they went to normal schools, they'd be happier. Kids love having their parents around.'

'Do they? I hated my mother being around all the time, and I only saw my dad twice a year when he was home from Chicago.'

I thought about it. My parents had been home all the time. Dad had had a nine-to-five job and they were always at home for dinner and at weekends. I'd liked having them there. I'd felt very secure, growing up with two parents who were present. 'But, Lucy, they're only small for a short time. When they're thirteen they won't want to know us. It's nice to see them grow up and do things for the first time. You don't want to miss that.'

Lucy was quiet for a few moments. Then she said, 'That stuff doesn't really bother me. I missed Serge's first step. But I saw him taking two steps the next day. He's not going to remember that I wasn't there for the first and I still got to see his almost-first step, so I don't see it as a big deal. I've seen him learning to walk. Does it really matter that I didn't see his first exact wobbly step? I think women who don't work make a big hoo-ha out of these things to make working mothers feel guilty and themselves feel more important or needed.'

Was she serious? Women didn't make a big deal about the first step: it just *was* a big deal, a huge milestone and a precious memory.

'Hang on, Lucy. Stay-at-home mums don't spend all day thinking up ways to make working mums feel guilty. A baby's first step *is* a big deal. Just like the first tooth and the first word.'

'So you can tell me what day Lara's first tooth appeared, can you?' Lucy challenged me.

I hesitated. I had no idea what date it was, but I do remember her smiling one day and seeing a little white flash in her gum. I'd been so excited. 'No, I can't. But I remember how I felt when I saw it.'

'Would you have felt any differently if you'd seen it two days later?'

'No, but you're missing the point.'

'What is the point?' she asked, sounding exasperated.

I began to feel a bit angry. It was difficult to explain why these moments were so precious. They just were. Mothers knew that. It was instinctive to want to be there for the milestones. I tried to put it into words. 'Lucy, it's not about dates and times. It's about emotion, it's about connection, it's about being present and cherishing memories. I missed Yuri's first tooth, I missed his first smile, and I feel really sad about that because I'm sure no one in the orphanage paid the slightest bit of attention to either. So when he took his first step in our house, I was ecstatic to be there to see it. As he wobbled about, I cheered and clapped and whooped, and he beamed up at me. He won't remember the day or the time, but he'll remember the feeling he had when his mother was there to cheer him on. He'll remember being loved and made to feel like the most important person in the world for those few minutes.'

Silence.

'Lucy?'

'For God's sake, you've just gone and made me cry.' I could hear her sniffing. 'Maybe the reason I'm cold is because neither of my parents were present for any of my milestones. It was the nanny who must have clapped when I walked.'

'You're not cold,' I assured her. 'You're just not a gushing mother and that's OK. And you're right. What difference does it make if you witness Serge's accomplishments a day later? None. The important thing is to show up and cheer. So tomorrow set your alarm for seven p.m., pop out of whatever meeting you're in and Skype him. It's vital that you don't forget.'

'What would I do without you? You're a rock of sense. Now, all we've done is talk about me. How are you?'

'Fine, thanks. All good.' I yawned. It was half past eleven and I was exhausted. I decided there was no point in opening the can of worms that was Babs at this time of night.

'Come on, we both need sleep. You especially after getting up at four. I'll talk to you soon. Good luck tomorrow and don't forget to set your alarm for Skyping.'

'I won't. Thanks, Emma. Night, then. Sweet dreams.'
There was a click and she was gone.

Sweet dreams? Not likely, given the nightmarish scenario
Babs had landed herself in. I took a deep breath and willed
myself not to think about it. When I'd had some sleep, I'd be
in a much better position to consider it sensibly.

11

I spent the whole tube journey to work trying to figure out what to do about Babs. James had asked me at breakfast what I was going to say to her and I was stumped. I had no idea. Was Babs capable of raising a child? She was so selfish and irresponsible, would a child be safe with her? Or maybe it would be the making of her. Perhaps a baby would bring out a nicer side, a softer side. Being forced to think about and look after someone else for a change might be the best thing for Babs. But then again, what about Gary? Would he even acknowledge the child? I was annoyed with her for being so stupid. It was bad enough to sleep with married men, but why the hell could she not have used protection?

As I was walking up the steps of Manor House station on my way to work, mulling over how I was going to handle my sister when I saw her, my phone rang. Thinking it was Babs, I grabbed it and answered on the first ring.

'Hello, is that Emma?'

Damn. It was Mum. I mustn't let on that anything was wrong.

'Hello? Hello there? It's your mother calling. Can you hear me?'

'Yes, Mum, perfectly. I'm in London, not Kabul.' I turned left and walked towards work.

'I see you haven't lost your sarcasm. I'm not sure that'll go down too well over there. You might want to rein it in, Emma. You need to make friends, not alienate people.'

'So far people haven't run screaming in the opposite direction, so I think it's all right.'

'What has you in such a sunny mood?'

I counted to five. 'I'm not in a mood, I'm fine. How are you?' I walked past Starbucks and, even though I could have murdered a coffee, I didn't go in. I needed to be on full alert for this conversation, no distractions.

'All right, I suppose, a bit lonely without my grandchildren. How are my little pets? How's that lovely husband of yours? I hope you're minding him. It's not easy starting a new job. It can be very stressful. He'll need a good dinner on the table every night and a lot of encouragement. Apparently all that coaching is very bad for the blood pressure. Remember Alex Ferguson's purple face.'

'Alex Ferguson was a pensioner, Mum.'

'He'd looked that way since he was forty. I'm warning you, make sure James has no stress when he comes home. Don't be annoying him with your worries. He needs a nice smile and a warm welcome.'

'I don't *annoy* him with my worries. We share our concerns with each other. It's called communicating.'

'Some women communicate too much. Nuala was over this morning.'

Oh, God, not Nuala! Whenever my mother's best friend/ worst enemy, Nuala, called over, Mum always got completely wound up. What the hell had she said this time?

'Nuala said her niece, Hayley Johnson – you were in the same ballet class as Hayley, you used to be pals. Remember?'

'No, I don't.'

Mum clicked her tongue. 'Of course you do. The two of you were great pals. Her sister married that fella, what's his name . . .?'

I crossed the road, almost getting run over by a cyclist who shouted at me.

'You know – that fella who worked in the bank. He had some big job and then they transferred him off to Argentina or Colombia or one of those places. Oh, actually, maybe it was Russia. Anyway, I think his name was Brian or Brendan.'

'What has any of this got to do with me?' I was getting exasperated.

'Nuala said that Hayley's marriage is gone, over, kaput. And he left her because she was always moaning.'

'Well, it sounds like a lucky escape for her. He's obviously a bit of an idiot.'

'That's not the point, Emma.'

'No? What is the point, then?' I hoped there wasn't much more to this tale of woe.

'The point is, Hayley was a moaner, just like you are, and it cost her her marriage.'

There really was nothing like a pep talk with my mother to put a spring in my step. I gritted my teeth. 'I do not moan.'

'Emma, you have a great capacity for complaining. You're a glass-half-empty kind of person. I saw a programme the other day about positive thinking. They had this woman on – she was an American psychologist or psychiatrist or psychoanalyst. I can never make out which is which. Anyway, she said that when you wake up in the morning, it's up to you to decide if today is going to be a glass-half-empty day or a glass-half-full day. So I'm telling you, Emma, you need to concentrate on being a glass-half-full girl. No man likes a sulky face. You're at a dangerous stage – men tend to go a bit funny in their forties. I saw it with your father. At forty he suddenly realized half his life was over and he went out and bought a sports car and a leather jacket. He looked ridiculous.

He could barely get in or out of the car because of his bad knees and the jacket was too small for him.'

I remembered the sports car. I must have been about nine at the time and I thought it was very cool. 'Well, so far we're OK. James gets the train to work. I don't see any sign of his mid-life crisis yet.'

'Don't be flippant, Emma. It happens to the best of us. Now, the other thing the woman on the TV said was that the better you feel about yourself, the nicer you'll be to others. There was something else about the universe and your conscious mind but that part was a bit complicated. I think it's time you went on a diet and got rid of that baby weight you're still carrying. If you don't shift it now, you'll never get rid of it. Once the menopause hits you, your metabolism shuts down. I've barely lost a pound in twenty years and I've drunk all those awful milkshakes and cabbage soups and none of them works. Lose the weight now, Emma, before it's too late.'

Right, that was it. I needed a comforting latte. I stopped at the little coffee cart opposite the studio and mouthed, 'Full-fat latte,' to the man. As my mother continued to talk, I poured two sachets of sugar into it and took a long, soothing gulp.

'Emma?' Mum barked. 'Are you listening to me?'

'Yes! I'm going to lose the weight. It'll be easier now I'm working. When I'm at home, I'm constantly grazing.'

'Good. Now, tell me, did you find a good nanny? Are you happy with her?'

'Yes. A really sweet girl called Claire – she's originally from Leitrim.'

'I don't believe it! That's wonderful. A nice Irish country girl. It'll be good for the children. You don't want some foreign girl with no English. It would hamper their development, and poor Yuri's already had ten months of Russian. He needs consistency now. A nice Irish girl sounds perfect. Well, kiss their little faces for me.'

My mother's love for her grandchildren was a very redeeming feature. She adored them. 'OK, Mum, I will. I'd better go now – I've just arrived at work.'

'Hold on a minute. How is your bold sister? She never returns my calls. She just texts me, "I'm busy." I'm delighted you're working with her. You can keep an eye on her and make sure she's not getting up to mischief. I worry about that girl. She's going to end up in trouble, I can feel it.'

If only she knew!

I pushed the door open and came face to face with Babs. I held my hand up and whispered, 'Mum.' Babs waved her arms, meaning she didn't want to speak to her.

'I'll tell Babs to call you, Mum.' I glared at my sister. 'I'll be seeing lots of her now we're working together so I'll make sure she stays in touch.'

Babs glared back at me.

'Make sure you do, and keep an eye on her. If only she could meet a nice man like James. Is there any nice fellow in work?'

Staring directly at my sister, I said, 'I can assure you, Mum, that there are no suitable men in work for Babs. Now I really have to go. 'Bye.'

Before she could say anything else, I hung up and put my phone into my pocket. 'Well, are you all right?' I asked Babs.

'I'm fine.'

'What the hell –'

Babs grabbed my arm. 'Not here,' she hissed, pulling me through the studio doors and into the makeup room.

I locked the door and turned to her. 'Have you told him?'

She avoided my eyes. 'Not yet. I only found out a week ago.'

'How pregnant are you?'

Babs shrugged. 'I dunno – not very. A few weeks?'

'How did it happen? Didn't you use protection?'

She turned away. 'We usually use condoms, but one night we were really drunk and he didn't have any and I thought it would be fine. I mean, it took you years to get pregnant, so I didn't think it would happen to me after one unprotected shag.'

'OK, that could happen to anyone. So, what are you going to do?' I asked, determined to make her face up to this responsibility.

Babs stiffened. 'What do you mean, what am I going to do? I'm going to have a baby with Gary.'

Was she completely delusional? 'He's married, remember? With two children already. He might not be too thrilled about this.' Gary was going to go mad.

Babs flicked back her hair. 'I know him and he'll be fine about it. He's mad about me and, besides, he hates his wife so this'll give him a good excuse to leave her.'

'Oh, Babs, are you really that naïve? Gary doesn't want another wife, he wants guilt-free sex with a hot twenty-seven-year-old TV presenter.'

Babs flinched and I felt bad for saying that to her, but it was the truth.

'You haven't a clue about my relationship with Gary.'

She was angry with me, but I had to make her understand that Gary was never going to play happy families with her. He was in it for the illicit thrills, not alimony payments and custody battles. 'Well, if it's so wonderful, why haven't you told him yet?'

'I haven't had the opportunity.'

'You see him every day.'

'I want to find the right time. And, besides, he's going on

some stupid holiday tomorrow – to Disney World in Florida for two weeks. I didn't want to tell him before he went. I'll tell him when he gets back.'

'OK, so after two weeks in a Disneyland paradise for families, hanging out with his wife and kids and Mickey Mouse, you're going to land this on him and you think he's going to be thrilled? Come on, Babs, listen to yourself. Can you honestly tell me you believe what you're saying?'

Babs began to chew a nail and I suddenly noticed that all of her nails were down to the quick. She hadn't bitten them since she was a kid. I could see how upset she was although, being Babs, she'd rather have died than admit it.

It was obvious that, deep down, Babs knew Gary wasn't going to be happy with her news. I could see now that she was afraid to tell him, and my heart ached for her. God, what a mess.

I decided to try a gentler approach. Putting my hand on her arm, I asked, 'Babs, what will you do if Gary doesn't want the baby?'

'He will, I know he will.' For a second I saw her lip tremble, but she held herself in check.

'OK, but what if he doesn't? It's helpful to have a plan B.'

She pushed me away. 'Shut up, Emma. I don't need your negativity.'

'Babs, you've got a baby growing inside you. You have to be realistic about this.'

Babs stepped towards me, her face cold with fury. 'I swear, Emma, if you bring this up again, I'll have you fired. I do not want to talk about it. This is between me and Gary. I'll tell him when he gets home from his trip, so back off.'

She strode out, slamming the door so hard that the walls of the tiny makeup room nearly rattled. I'd lost her now. I knew she'd refuse to talk to me for days after that exit. I'd been too hard, too honest. But then again, she was pregnant and she had to face up to reality. Still, early pregnancy is no fun for anyone: you feel dreadful and you're worried. I should have trodden more carefully. I'd have to pull back for a bit now. Maybe it was no harm. She'd think about what I'd said and hopefully she'd realize that I was right about Gary and then we could talk again. In the meantime I'd have to staple my mouth shut and avoid my mother at all costs. Neither was going to be easy . . .

12

For the next week things at home continued to go smoothly as we all settled into our new life. I was bringing the children to school twice a week and James dropped them on the other days. Yuri had made a friend, a boy called Jackson, and he was much happier. Lara had a list of girls who were now her 'best friend' and skipped into her classroom every day. Claire continued to get them to eat vegetables and fruit. James and I were constantly praising her for that alone. When I came home from work, the house was always tidy and the children were happy.

It wasn't all plain sailing, though. Work wasn't much fun because Babs refused to talk to me and was avoiding me. But I knew my sister and that she'd crack eventually. I had to wait it out. Usually I'd talk to James about it, but he worked late every night. I hardly saw him. He was devoting all of his time and energy to the club and none to his family. I was putting the kids to bed every night and then going up early to read my book because there was no one to talk to. I felt very alone.

Finally, it was Friday again – a break from work and from Babs stonewalling me. I stopped at the little delicatessen on the corner on the way home and spent more than I should have on a really nice bottle of red and some beef bourguignon. James had promised to be home to put the children to bed, so I decided it was a good chance for some quality time together.

I pushed open the front door and heard the children laughing. I smiled to myself. Claire didn't seem to lose patience towards the end of the day – like I did whenever I had them on my own for long stretches. She really had a calling for this work.

I crept into the kitchen and unpacked the shopping. Then I tiptoed to the door of the lounge. Inside, the three of them were sitting on the floor, playing a raucous game of Snap. They were completely absorbed in it, and I watched them for a few minutes. Then the urge to hug Yuri and Lara became too great and I walked in to join them.

As soon as she saw me, Claire jumped up. 'Hey, you two, Mum's home.' Yuri and Lara leapt to their feet and ran to me. Claire smiled. 'I'll give you a minute,' she said. 'Can I get you a cup of tea?'

'I'd love one,' I said, flopping down into the couch. It had been a long day. The lady we had made over had taken a huge dislike to Babs and there had been a lot of arguing and storming off the set. Babs had been really uptight and more obnoxious than usual. As a result, filming had run over.

'So, guys, how was your day?'

'Fine,' Yuri said, sitting back down. His mind was obviously on the game.

'Just fine? Come on, tell me about it.'

'*Muuuum*, it was the same.'

I kept smiling, but I felt a stab of guilt mixed with regret. This was the horrible part of being a working mum – Claire knew more about their day than I did. No doubt they had run out of school and spilt their tales to her on the walk home – they always told their news in the first hour after school ended. But I was never there to hear it. Claire came back in and handed me a cup of tea.

'Thanks, you're an angel. Sorry for being late. It was one of those days.'

'Don't worry, it's fine. I'm in no hurry to go home.'

Yuri tugged at Claire's sweatshirt. 'Come on, Claire, we want to play.'

Claire sat down and continued the game. I kicked off my shoes and watched them. It was a very peaceful scene. I relaxed into the couch and looked forward to my nice bottle of wine later with James. It would be good to catch up.

My phone beeped. James: *Sorry darling – have to stay on bit longer – see you in couple of hours – text if we need anything from shop and will pick it up on way. Xx*

'Damn.'

'Is everything OK?' Claire asked, looking round.

I threw my phone onto the cushion and dropped my head back against the couch. 'Fine. It was just James saying he'll be late. Again. It's the fifth night in a row.' I knew I was over-sharing, but I was too ticked off to care.

Claire was gazing at me anxiously. 'I can stay and help you put them to bed, Emma, it's no problem.'

I was going to say no, but then I thought, Why not? I wanted some adult company and putting the kids to bed every night on my own wasn't much fun. A second pair of hands made it so much easier.

'You know what, Claire? That would be great. Thanks a million.' I decided I'd add another twenty to her envelope to thank her.

We bathed the children together. It was nice having her there. We sang silly songs and chatted to the kids as they played with the bubbles. It was all very relaxed. Then, while I dried the children's hair, Claire cleaned the bath.

I read them a story and kissed them goodnight. When I came downstairs, Claire had tidied the living room and the kitchen.

I opened the fridge and took out the beef. My phone beeped again. James: *Sorry darling, won't be home for dinner. Tied up here.*

I cursed under my breath.

'Is everything all right?' Claire asked.

'James isn't going to be back for dinner. I've got all this food.' I looked at Claire. What the hell? I'd ask her to join me. 'Do you fancy beef bourguignon?'

'Are you sure?'

'Yes, otherwise it'll go to waste. I've already opened the wine to let it breathe, so we might as well tuck into that too.'

She giggled nervously, like a naughty schoolgirl. 'OK, wow, cool.' She seemed so young for a nineteen-year-old. She must have led a very sheltered life.

I poured her a glass of wine. She clearly wasn't used to it – her nose wrinkled as she sipped. That was a good thing, though: I didn't want some secret wino looking after the children.

'Cheers to you,' I said, clinking her glass. 'You've really been a Godsend.'

'Thanks.' Claire blushed. 'I love working here. It's so nice.'

I patted her hand. 'Well, we love having you. It's such a relief for me to know the children are happy and safe while I'm at work.'

'I'm mad about them,' she gushed. 'They're really amazing kids.'

'I agree!' I laughed.

I served up the beef, which turned out to be delicious. 'So, any plans for the weekend?' I asked her.

'Not really, probably just chill out.'

Claire seemed like a loner. I wondered if she had any friends. She was probably wary of other teenagers because of being bullied. 'Have you made any friends since you moved here? I know it's not easy in a new city.'

Claire looked down at her plate. 'One or two, I suppose, but I'm not very sociable. I prefer to be working or listening to music. I don't like noisy places full of people. They freak me out.'

'Do you ever go out with your mum, to the movies or for dinner?'

'Not really. She doesn't like going out either.'

I had been curious to know about Claire's father. Was he in the picture at all? 'Do you have any other family here? Like your dad or siblings or anything?'

Claire's face darkened. 'No, it's just me and Mum.' She hesitated, then looked at me. 'My father walked out when I was two. He wasn't interested in us. He left my mum with nothing and never paid her a penny in child support.'

I could see the hurt in her eyes. 'That's terrible. Your poor mum.'

'She did her best, but it was really hard.'

'It must have been difficult for you, too.'

Claire nodded. 'Yuri and Lara are lucky to have a dad around. Kids need a dad.'

'James is a great father.'

'And you're a good mother,' Claire added quickly.

'Thanks.' I loved hearing that. 'I'm sorry about your dad.'

She shrugged. 'I'm fine about it now. The hard part was when he moved to the next village with his new family.'

I topped up our glasses. 'He had more children?'

'Two girls. One is sixteen and the other is fourteen.'

'God, that sounds tough on you.'

'I saw him with them once, in the cinema. He was buying them popcorn.'

'Did you go over to him?'

She shook her head. 'No way. I hate him.'

It was clear that her emotions about her dad were still raw, even after all these years. She hadn't dealt with him abandoning her. The anger and grief were still simmering beneath the surface. 'I'm sorry, Claire, it must have been awful to see him with his two daughters like that.'

She bit a nail. 'It was no big deal.'

It clearly was, judging by her nails, which were bitten down to the quick, just like Babs's. Men could cause a whole world of trouble.

'Well, you're safe here from bullying and bumping into your father or anything bad like that. James and I think you're fantastic. Honestly, I don't know what I'd do without you. You really are a treasure.'

She blushed, and smiled shyly at me. 'Really? Do you really think that? Does James too?'

'He's always saying how wonderful you are.' I laid the praise on thick. The poor girl had had very negative experiences with men. She could do with some positive affirmation from father figures like James.

'I never really see him because he works late so much,' she said.

I sighed. 'I know, and it's a pain. I haven't seen him much myself. He's working like a maniac to prove to his club that he's the right man for the job. I'm hoping he might calm down a bit after their first match and we can get some time together. God knows we need a night out.'

'Would you like me to babysit for you some night? I'd be delighted to do it.'

I laughed. 'I hadn't actually thought of that. But you're here so much already you'd hardly want to stay on for hours in the evening as well.'

'Honestly, I don't mind. I'd bring a good book and you'd be able to go out knowing the kids were safe.'

I could have kissed her. 'Well, if you're really sure, then, yes, I'd be thrilled to have you babysit. We'll pay you the going rate, of course.' I beamed at her, already planning which restaurant James and I would try first. 'Thanks so much, Claire. I'll talk to James, see what night suits and let you know.'

'Great. I'm always available.'

Claire stood up to clear the plates, but I insisted she sit down. 'You're not working now, feet up.'

'I feel like I'm in a restaurant.'

'Now, I don't really have any dessert.' I rummaged around in the freezer for ice-cream.

Claire's phone rang. 'I'm fine, Mum . . . No . . . I'm just here with Emma . . . I'll be home soon . . . I know that . . . I'll be back in twenty minutes . . . Chill out, I'm fine.'

Claire hung up and threw her phone into her backpack. 'She's always checking up on me.'

I smiled at her. 'We mothers worry. Look, why don't you head off? I don't want to cause your mum any concern. Thanks for staying. You were a great help.' I walked her to the door and handed her her wages. She went down the path, her hands deep in the pockets of her hoodie.

I closed the door, took the remainder of the bottle of red wine to the couch and curled up. Poor thing, I thought. She seemed to have had a terrible life. She was so awkward and unsure of herself. I decided to try to boost Claire's confidence and bring her out of herself. She was young. With a bit of makeup and some decent clothes, she'd be pretty. She couldn't spend her life sitting in with her mother. She needed to get out and have some fun.

13

Claire ended up babysitting for us a lot sooner than I had expected. James came home very late that Friday night with news that Henry and Imogen had invited us to a lawyers' charity dinner in aid of animal protection on Sunday night. I thought it sounded incredibly boring and Sunday night was a ridiculous night to hold a party, but it was a chance to dress up and go out with my husband, whom I was barely seeing these days, so I agreed to go.

I got James to call Henry and see if he could get two more tickets. I thought it would be a good idea to invite Lucy and Donal. Sunday night would be perfect for them but Lucy said that unfortunately they couldn't come because Donal was going to be in France until late Sunday night at some match. She sounded stressed so I made her promise to meet me on Monday for a quick lunch and a chat.

I was dreading seeing Imogen and having to listen to her caustic remarks, but hopefully I'd be sitting beside Henry, and I planned to drink lots of wine and let my hair down. Between worrying about Babs and Lucy, getting the children settled and starting a new job, the move to London had been exhausting. I was in need of a good night out.

I put on my Spanx and squeezed into my favourite black dress. It was covered with black beads that shimmered when I moved. I knew I looked good – it was a fail-safe dress. By the time I'd done my makeup, fixed my hair and slipped my feet into my high heels, I felt great.

When I came downstairs, James was talking to Claire

about football. She supported the same team he did – Liverpool. I think he was relieved to have something to talk to her
about because she was so quiet. 'Who's your favourite player?'
he was asking, as I walked in.

'Gerrard,' she said.

James high-fived her. 'That's my girl, the one and only Stevie
Gerrard.'

Claire blushed.

'If he's annoying you, Claire, tell him where to go,' I joked.

James whistled. 'Look at you!'

'Great dress, Emma,' Claire said.

'Oooooh, Mummy, you're all sparkly.' Lara came over to
touch the beads. 'Will you wear this when you bring me to
school on Monday?'

I laughed and rubbed her cheek. 'I think it might be a bit
too much for nine o'clock in the morning. Or, as your auntie
Imogen would say, "a bit too jazzy".'

'I think it's beautiful, Mummy. If I had a sparkly dress, I'd
wear it all the time, even in bed.'

James walked over to hug me, and whispered in my ear,
'I'm hoping the dress will be long gone by the time we get to
bed.'

I kissed his cheek and winked at him. Yes, this dress was a
sure-fire winner every time.

We kissed the children goodnight, then I put on my long
black satin coat with the diamond bow clasp, made sure
Claire had everything she needed and headed outside to
where the cab was waiting to take us to the Gotham Club in
Mayfair.

When we got there, we were greeted at the door with
champagne – a very promising start. The dining room was to
the left, and a waiter ushered us in. It was lit with candles and
beautifully decorated, with about twelve round tables. It

would be a big night, by the look of things. Some people were already seated, while others milled about the room. There was a huge amount of air-kissing going on. We checked the room plan and headed for table nine. In the middle of each table there was an ice sculpture of an animal – ours was a horse, but its tail was already melting. James and I took our seats and kept an eye out for Henry and Imogen – in Henry's case, because we wanted to see him; in Imogen's case, to have advance warning of her imminent arrival.

I looked around the room, interested to see what London ladies wore to a 'cocktail wear' event. I have to say it was a mixed bag. I was worried I'd look drab and not chic enough, but the women were in all kinds of everything. Some were dressed up, like me, others were wearing plain shift dresses in various shades of beige, and one looked like a really trashy WAG. She had the fakest boobs I've ever seen, lips like pillows and a tan that would have given an orangutan a run for his money. She was wearing a skin-tight silver dress with a slit way too far up her thigh.

As I checked out the room, I caught sight of Imogen. She was standing next to an ice sculpture of a bull, chewing the ear off some poor man. She was wearing a navy silk jacket and matching navy dress. She had a scarf with horses on it around her neck and navy pumps with a one-inch heel. It was the most dressed-up I'd ever seen her.

'Cheers, darling,' James said, clinking his glass with mine. 'Here's to a good night. At last.'

'I'll drink to that!' It was so lovely to be out with him and have his undivided attention – no kids, no mobile phone, no TV, no laptop, just the two of us . . . and a hundred strangers, but I was going to forget about them.

'Hello!' Henry bounded over to us. He was six foot four and very gangly. He gave James a handshake/hug, the way men do, which I always think looks really awkward, and kissed me on both cheeks. 'Thanks awfully for coming. I know animals aren't really your thing, Emma.'

'I'll have you know I had two goldfish when I was six. They were called Tom and Jerry and they lasted five whole weeks before dying of starvation because we went on holiday and forgot about them. We came home to see two floaters in the bowl.'

James and Henry laughed. 'You might not want to tell that story to anyone else tonight,' Henry said, in a low voice. 'Some people are passionate about animals, to the point of extremism.'

'And there I was, thinking you lawyers were a boring old lot.'

'Oh, no!' Henry feigned shock. 'We're a crazy bunch when we want to be. If I'm not mistaken, someone stayed until one a.m. at last year's event.'

We all laughed. Then Imogen came over. 'Hello, James,' she said, air-kissing him, 'don't you look marvellous?' Then she looked me up and down. 'And Emma, always so jazzy.'

I was determined not to let her ruin my two-glasses-of-champagne-on-an-empty-stomach buzz. 'This old thing? You should have seen what I was going to wear.'

'I had to talk her out of tight leather hot pants,' James said, managing to keep a straight face.

'He was worried one of the old lawyers might have a heart-attack, so I opted for this instead.' I cackled.

Henry laughed and slapped James playfully on the arm, but Imogen was clearly appalled.

We were asked to take our seats and I found myself beside Henry. On my other side was the guest of honour, Paul Aldridge, a philosopher and author, who informed me that he was going to be talking to us after dinner about Animals, Ethics and the Law.

'Excellent.' I beamed at him as I knocked back my wine. I'd need to be anaesthetized by alcohol when he got up to speak.

Imogen was sitting on Paul's other side and kept him in a headlock about horses for most of the meal, leaving me free to catch up with Henry.

'How's London been treating you so far?' he asked.

I paused, chewing a piece of beef. I was surprised the dinner wasn't green and vegetarian, seeing as we were all about animals and ethics. I swallowed. 'It's been hectic, to be honest. It all happened so quickly. James found out about the job and four weeks later we had moved country. I'm only really getting my head around it now.'

'It can't be easy, particularly with small children.'

The children were causing the least problems, I thought. It was my sister and my best friend who had me awake all night worrying. 'They weren't happy about it at first – well, Yuri wasn't. He hates change. But he's actually settled quite well, and Lara is really enjoying her new school.'

'And what about James?' Henry asked, glancing at his brother. 'How do you think he's finding it?'

The wine was threatening to loosen my tongue a bit too much. I tried to rein myself in. 'He's definitely feeling huge pressure to succeed. He's in work almost twenty-four/seven, proving himself to everyone at the club.'

Henry nodded thoughtfully. 'I got that impression from talking to him. He seems very stressed about their first game. I'm sure it's tough on you, keeping the show on the road at home, but it's very important James gets a win to boost his confidence and keep the owners and fans happy. It's a difficult career, very high stress levels.'

I glanced at James, who was sitting almost opposite us and chatting to a couple on his left. I caught snippets of their

148

conversation – they were discussing rugby. I appreciated Henry's grasp of both sides of the argument, and his tact. He was a decent man. The Hamilton boys came from good stock. I decided I could be honest with him. 'The truth is, Henry, I'm worried,' I admitted. 'I'm scared that if this doesn't work out, he'll fall apart. He was so upset about the Ireland job. I've never seen him so down.'

The waiter dipped between us to clear our plates and when he had moved on Henry said, 'James is a fighter. He'll be all right – he'll make this work. He's very good at what he does and he has such a passion for it. I admire him for following that passion. There's a lot to be said for branching out and doing something different.'

'Yes, but it's risky,' I pointed out. 'Being a lawyer is a job for life. A rugby coach is only ever a temporary job. Who knows where we'll end up next, even if this does work out for him? I only realized the lack of security in James's profession this year. There are no long-term jobs in this game. I Googled "rugby coaches" the other night, and four years seems to be about the average length of time for a good one to stay with a club. That means, in the best-case scenario, with everything going right for James and London Irish, we'll have to move again when Yuri's eight and Lara's seven.'

Dessert arrived: chocolate cake. Large slices were placed in front of us.

'Some very good coaches stay on longer,' Henry said, 'but I see your point. It is an uncertain future. But then again, Emma, no jobs are safe any longer. There is no such thing as a job for life now. We're all at risk.'

The global economic crisis had meant that people in 'jobs for life' had found themselves out on the street. But, still, if Henry was laid off, he would be able to get a new job in London with another firm. Rugby coaches moved around all the time, different countries and continents. I hated to think of Yuri having to be the new boy all over again, just when he'd become comfortable here.

Henry interrupted my thoughts. 'I did say to James recently that it was very important for him to try to have a good work/life balance. The problem with doing something you feel so passionately about and being desperate to prove yourself is that you can lose perspective.'

'Thanks, Henry, he needs to hear that from you. I've been nagging him for weeks about working late, so I'm glad you said it.' I popped the last piece of chocolate cake into my mouth and savoured it.

Henry smiled and offered me his helping.

'Are you mad? If I eat that – and, believe me, I'd love to – my dress will explode and my Spanx are really not attractive.' Unfortunately, just at that moment Paul turned to us. Obviously Imogen had bored him long enough about her children and her horses.

'What are Spanx?' both men asked at the same time. I put down my wine glass and picked up my water. What was wrong with me? This was not the time or place to be discussing my iron underwear with my brother-in-law and a total stranger who was a fanatic about animals. For all I knew, Spanx could be made of raccoon skin, and if my dress did explode, I'd be carted off in chains by the animal police.

'They're just, uhm, these things that kind of suck it all in.'

'Suck what in?' Paul asked. He obviously wasn't married.

'Your flab,' I explained, pointing to my stomach.

'How do they do that?' Henry chuckled mischievously.

Was he serious? Didn't Imogen have Spanx to suck in her big arse? Clearly not. Maybe I should buy her some for Christmas.

I threw my hands dramatically into the air. 'Isn't it obvious? By cutting off the circulation between your collarbone and your knees.'

Henry threw back his head and laughed, but Paul looked at me as if I was definitely mad, possibly dangerous – a species to be handled with care. I flashed him a smile to show I was joking, but he continued to stare at me in shocked silence.

Thankfully, before I could regale him with any more secrets about my undergarments, he was called upon to give his speech. He proceeded to talk at length about his book, *Animals Have Rights Too*. I tuned out as he banged on about animal welfare and ethics.

James moved over to sit beside me in Paul's now empty chair, while Paul droned on about equality beyond humanity. 'What about the rights of the dinner guests not to have to listen to this torturously long speech?' James whispered. I giggled.

'Why don't we go and find the bar?' I whispered back. 'I'll pretend I'm going to the toilet and then you follow me out.'

Three minutes later we were sitting on two high stools at the bar in the back of the club. We had left our wine glasses behind, so James ordered two mojitos and we toasted our escape.

'This is more like it,' James said. 'A cocktail with my lovely wife – just perfect.'

'Really?' I said, raising an eyebrow. 'I thought you'd forgotten you had a wife, let alone a lovely one.'

He put down his glass and looked at me. Then he kissed me lightly. 'I'm sorry I've been so busy. It's just . . .'

'I know,' I said gently. 'I want you to do well, so I'm not going to get at you now about it. But we need to do more of this. We should try to go out once a week, James. It's important.'

He held my hand. 'I agree wholeheartedly. I've been

spending too much time at the club, I know that. Once this first match is out of the way, I'll be able to relax a bit. I just need to win this one.'

'Well, Claire said she'll babysit anytime. So we just need to plan ahead.'

'Good idea.' He seemed relieved that I wasn't giving him a hard time.

'I find Claire a bit easier now, don't you? She used to be so shy it was like dragging blood from a stone trying to talk to her. She seems to be coming out of herself. Thank God for Liverpool – it gives us common ground. She's very enthusiastic about football. I said I'd try to get her tickets for a game. She doesn't seem to have much of a life.'

'I'm delighted to hear that,' I said. 'She told me about her childhood and it was a bit grim. I think she could do with some confidence-building.'

'Well, the children adore her, which is fantastic.'

I didn't want to end up talking about Yuri and Lara. I knew that if we started we'd still be on that subject going home in the taxi. I changed tack. 'How is everything going with your training?' I asked.

'Overall, fine, but I'm having trouble with one of the assistant coaches. He went for my job, didn't get it and resents me. He's been difficult to manage, but Harriet says he's always been a tricky character.'

'Who's Harriet?' I asked, my another-woman radar perking up immediately.

'She looks after the administration of the club.'

'You've never mentioned her before.'

'Yes, I have.'

'No, you have not. I'd remember if you had. Is she young?'

James thought for a second. 'I don't know what age she is. I suppose a bit younger than you.'

Younger than me? I didn't like the sound of that. 'Married?'

He grinned. 'Engaged.'

'Good.' Engaged women were in the throes of love. They still thought their other half was marvellous. They hadn't got to the stage where they wanted to stab him for chewing too loudly or buying full-fat milk when they'd specifically asked for skimmed.

James kissed me again – I'd forgotten just how good it felt to inhale his aftershave while his face was close to mine. 'And how are you finding it all? You seem to be adapting really well.'

I put my glass on the bar. 'It's been fine, partly because I've been so busy. I do find the evenings lonely, though, with you working late so much. I miss being able to pop into Mum and Dad's or meet Lucy for a drink. I thought I'd see her now that she's based in London, but she's busy with meetings and trips to Eastern Europe. Although she's pencilled me in for a quick lunch tomorrow.'

James grimaced. 'I was talking to Donal yesterday. He is not a happy man. He says they never see each other. She comes home on a Friday night and he works all day Saturday and a lot of Sundays, too. He sounded really fed up. Plus he was talking again about having another child. He really wants one.'

'I'm telling you now, Lucy doesn't. She can barely cope with Serge. Donal needs to drop it or he'll push her further away.'

James shook his head. 'But that's not really fair. It's a huge sacrifice for him to give up his dream of having another child. I understand why he wants Serge to have a sibling. To be honest, I think Lucy's being selfish.'

I felt torn between the two sides, but I felt I had to defend my friend. 'Hold on a minute. She didn't want to have *any* children, but she gave in and had Serge because Donal wanted kids so badly. She's done her bit.'

James could see that I was being defensive. 'Well, it's complicated, I grant you, but hearing the way Donal was talking, well, I'd worry about their relationship. And I know you're really anxious about Lucy. Which, on top of Babs, is a lot for you to take on.'

I sighed. 'The Babs thing's keeping me up at night,' I admitted. 'She's still not talking to me – she's polite in front of the others and completely silent if we're ever alone. That tosser Gary gets back soon so it'll be out in the open one way or another.'

James nodded sympathetically. 'Unfortunately, from what you've told me, I can't see it ending well.'

I rubbed my forehead. 'She hasn't got a clue what she's in for. He's going to dump her and probably find a way to fire her. It's a complete mess.' I began to get emotional and struggled to compose myself.

James squeezed my hand and I held on to him gratefully. This was silly. I needed to get the conversation back on safe ground or I'd end up tipsy and emotional – never a good mix. James was about to say something else, when his phone beeped in his pocket. He took it out and his eyes widened. 'What the hell?'

'What? Is something wrong with the kids?' I asked.

'No, nothing like that. Sorry. I've just received a very strange text.'

I leant over and read it: *I think ur hot.* 'Who's it from?'

'I don't recognize the number.'

'Call it.'

James began to smile. 'Oh, hang on, I know what this is. It's the guys joking around. They do this to each other all the time on their Facebook pages.

'Watch this.' James texted back: *You're barking up the wrong tree, mate.*

No I'm not. Ur hot and so am I.

I giggled.

'I bet it's Jamie. He's the joker on the squad,' James said.

I grabbed his phone and typed, *Hands off my husband.*

Another text came straight back: *I plan to have my hands all over him.*

'Don't respond, Emma.' James was beginning to look annoyed. 'I do not want to encourage this. I'm their manager, not their friend.'

We could hear applause from the dining room. Clearly the longest speech in history was finally over.

James took my hand. 'Right, then, Mrs Hamilton. Let's say a quick goodbye and get you home and out of that dress.'

I beamed at James as I swayed back into the room, feeling young and carefree for the first time in ages.

14

I had a very sore head in work the next day, but I didn't mind because I also had that lovely post-sex feeling of closeness with James. We really did need to go out on our own more often. We had definitely drifted lately. I was feeling very loved up as I walked into the studio.

When I got Babs alone to do her makeup, I decided to continue with my more subtle approach.

'How are you feeling?' I asked her.

'Fine,' she said, nibbling on a Rich Tea biscuit.

'Morning sickness can be tough.'

'I'm fine.' She was clearly determined not to enter any conversation with me.

I looked down at her hands. She had put red stick-on nails over her own chewed ones. 'Look, Babs, I know this is hard for you and I know, despite your bravado, that you're worried about Gary's reaction. So all I want to say is that I'm here for you. Whenever you need a shoulder to cry on or advice about pregnancy or just someone to talk or rant to, I'm here.'

She didn't say anything. I finished applying her blusher, and as she went to open the door to walk onto the set, she said quietly, 'Thanks, Emma.'

As I watched her thin frame leave, I felt really emotional. My ballsy, brassy little sister was really struggling. Damn you, Gary, I thought. I hope you get flung out of a roller-coaster and die a painful death.

At lunchtime, I raced out to meet Lucy. She had booked a table in a posh café called Sophia's near where she worked.

She was typing furiously on her BlackBerry when I arrived. She looked tired.

We hugged, then I took off my jacket and sat down. 'How are you?' I asked.

'Exhausted,' she replied.

'You look a bit peaky. Work?'

Lucy put her phone down. 'Serge has been awake the last two nights with an ear infection.'

'Was Donal not around?'

She looked out of the window. 'He's still in the spare room.'

'Oh, Lucy, I thought things were better.'

'He was beginning to thaw a little bit, but then I told him I had to go to a meeting in Prague this Saturday and he freaked. He said weekends were supposed to be sacrosanct. They usually are, but this is a really important meeting. The investors are big hitters and I need to be there.'

I ordered a latte and Lucy a double espresso.

'You need a rest, Lucy. Don't burn yourself out.'

She sighed. 'It's been insane. I'm working fourteen-hour days. I've hardly been in our London office. I've spent most of the last few weeks flying to Eastern Europe to get clients to lease our private planes. I've never worked so hard in my life.'

I stirred my coffee. 'Is it going well?'

'We've had a lot of clients signing on, which is a relief because we've had to borrow eighty million euro from the German banks.'

'How do you sleep at night? The stress of borrowing that much would kill me.'

'I know it's a huge amount, but I really believe this business is going to fly – no pun intended! We've committed the first sixty million already to buy planes.'

'So when do you start making money? Won't it take for ever to pay that loan back?'

'Don't worry. You know me, I've done the figures. The big bucks will come rolling in soon enough.' Lucy stifled a yawn.

Sticking with my new softer approach, I decided to ask Lucy about Serge. 'How are you coping with being away from home so much?'

Lucy replied to a text and I ordered two bowls of soup. 'Sorry.' She looked up again. 'What did you ask?'

I tried not to get annoyed. I had just sprinted across London to meet her in a place near her office for lunch and she wasn't even listening to me. I took a deep breath. 'How are you coping with being away from home so much?'

'I'm fine about it. It's Donal that's the problem. The weird thing is that we still have good sex. The only way we communicate these days is physically. Except that afterwards he goes and sleeps in the spare room. It's as if he wants to dominate me and prove he's still the man of the house or something, then remembers he's annoyed with me and walks away. It's ridiculous and sad. I'm lonely, Emma, lonely in my marriage and I know Donal is too.'

I reached out and held her hand. I felt bad for being cross with her when her marriage was in crisis. 'I'm sorry you guys are having a tough time, but you'll sort it out.'

'I hope so,' Lucy said. 'No man would have turned down the opportunity I've been given, so why am I the bad guy? Where's the crime in what I've done?'

'There's no crime,' I chose my words carefully, 'but you're married and you're mum to a small boy so it's not straightforward.'

Lucy didn't like what I'd said. 'And that same boy will grow up and leave home. I don't want to look back and regret not having grasped a golden opportunity.'

I felt I had to be honest with her. I wanted to make her see the other side. 'Yes, but the reality of your being away five days a week is tough on Donal and Serge. They miss you.'

'OK, well, let's say Donal was offered a job presenting sports on Sky TV. It's an incredible contract, huge opportunity, but it means being away in London four nights a week. Should he take it?'

'It depends.'

Lucy was getting frustrated. 'Come on, Emma, I thought you were on my side.'

'I am, but you're sacrificing a lot for this job and Donal will probably get more fed up as time passes.'

'For goodness' sake, it's not as if Donal's landed with looking after Serge all day long. I told you, I have a brilliant nanny who does most of it, and the babysitter comes every Wednesday so Donal can go out with his friends. And when I come home on Friday, I look after Serge all weekend while Donal works.'

'But, Lucy,' I said, 'it's not just about childcare. It's about being together as a family and spending time with Serge and Donal. I have to be honest, since James started working late all the time, it's really affected our relationship. We're like ships passing in the night and it's causing friction. I know you love your job, but maybe when things calm down a bit you could try to travel less.'

Lucy sank back in her chair. 'I think I'm more like my mother than I realized,' she admitted sadly.

This again, I thought. I could no longer tell if that was guilt talking or just her way of justifying her actions – as if she was driven because it was in her genes. 'You're nothing like your awful mother,' I assured her.

She answered another email. 'Sorry. Actually, Emma, in a way I am. My mother doesn't like small children. She has no interest in Serge and he's her only grandchild. She only became interested in me when I was about eight. Before that she left me with nannies all the time. She found the baby-and-small-child phase boring. And I do too. Going to the park and pushing Serge on a swing for an hour drives me nuts. It's mind-numbing. I don't want to sing stupid songs over and over again. I hate feeding him because he spits most of his food out. I like him when he's fed, bathed and in his pyjamas.' She covered her face in her hands. 'I know I'm a wretched human being with no motherly instincts, but that is honestly how I feel.'

I pulled her hands down. 'You're not a wretched human being. You're a warm, lovely, generous person, who is struggling with motherhood. We all do.' I tried to reassure her.

'No.' Lucy was firm. 'I see the way you look at your kids – it's different. I love Serge, but I don't need him the way you need your kids. When I'm in work, I don't miss him. I don't feel the need to run home to see him. If he's asleep when I get home, that's fine. I like watching him sleeping – he looks cute and I can relax. I'm hoping as he gets older that I'll feel more of an umbilical attachment, but I do *not* find this stage easy or fun.'

'Lucy, lots of women feel the way you do, they just don't admit it. But I think you need to be very careful not to spend too much time away,' I warned her.

'I know, but if I'd turned down this amazing offer, I'd be sitting at home now resenting Donal and Serge, and that would be worse.'

Lucy's phone rang. 'I'm on my way,' she said into it. Then, looking at me, she said, 'God, I'm so sorry, Emma, I have to go, some problem with one of our investors. Talk soon.' She gave me a quick kiss and rushed out of the door into the cool autumn afternoon.

I watched her go, her shoulders hunched. Life was so much more complicated now. Everything that happened had serious repercussions. Every decision you made affected lots of people and the responsibility for that was sometimes crippling.

Our soup arrived as the door closed behind her. I asked for mine to be put into a take-away cup. I'd drink it on the tube on the way back to work. No one could maintain the pace of life Lucy was currently living. Something would have to give. Would it be work, her marriage or her health?

15

By the end of the week, I was exhausted. I'd been putting the kids to bed on my own every night and trying to tiptoe around Babs at work. I was thrilled when Karen said on Thursday evening that we were done for the week and could take Friday off.

I gave Claire the day off and brought the kids to school. It was lovely to see them running in the gate. Well, Lara ran and Yuri walked, still a little tentative, but definitely happier. They were settling in so well and I was really proud of them. I decided to use my time wisely and organize a play-date for Yuri. He seemed very keen on this boy called Jackson. I glanced around and spotted a stick-thin woman in Lycra: Jackson's mum. She was standing with a group of other gym bunnies.

They stopped talking as I approached them. I went up to Jackson's mum and proffered a hand. 'Hi there, sorry to interrupt. I'm Emma, Yuri's mum.'

She looked me up and down. 'Who?'

'Yuri – he's new to the class this term.'

She stared blankly at me. Clearly she was not one of those warm, fuzzy earth-mothers. All of the Lycra gang were staring at me. I could feel perspiration on my back. 'Right, well, Yuri was saying that he'd like to have Jackson over for a play some day, so I wondered if this afternoon suited.'

'This afternoon?' She looked as if I'd just asked her to eat a cream pie. The others tittered.

I willed myself to stay calm. 'Yes, this afternoon.'

'I'm sorry, what's your name?'

'Emma.'

'You're not from here, are you, sweetie?'

'No, I'm not.'

'Well, Emma, Jackson has a very full after-school schedule. Yurgi will need to book him a couple of weeks in advance at least.' Then, adding to my humiliation, she placed a manicured hand on my shoulder. 'I'm sure you'll get the hang of it soon.'

Fearing that I might rip her manicured hand off her toned arm, I turned on my heel and walked briskly away from the school gate and my public mortification. I was furious. How dare she be so rude and condescending? How dare she mispronounce my son's name and pretend she hadn't heard of him? Her snot-nosed kid would be lucky to have a friend like Yuri. I felt so alone. I fought back tears. Why was it so difficult to make friends? Why were the mothers so unfriendly? Was I a freak? Did I stand out as weird? All I wanted to do was fit in.

As I turned the corner to walk up my road, muttering to myself like a mad woman, I bumped into Poppy. She was wearing a fuchsia pink Juicy Couture tracksuit and was carrying a large box from Chez Florence, the patisserie at the end of our road.

'Hello, Emma – on the way to work?'

I was very glad to see her friendly face. 'Actually, no, I've got the day off.'

'But that's marvellous! Now you can come to my coffee morning.'

I was in no mood for small-talk with Poppy and her *über*-glamorous friends. I wanted to go home and punch a cushion. 'Thanks, Poppy, but I'm not sure I'm up for meeting a whole new bunch of people today. I'm finding it hard to fit in, to be honest.'

Poppy linked my arm. 'It took me ages to make friends when I moved to Putney. Rome wasn't built in a day. Now, the only way you're going to make friends is to say yes to everything. Accept every invitation and soon you'll have a few ladies you can talk to and trust. Staying at home feeling homesick will do you no good. I'm not taking no for an answer. I'll see you at ten thirty, sharp. Carol's coming, so you'll know at least one person.' Poppy went up her driveway, waving at me over her shoulder.

I smiled. Poppy was a tonic. And she was right, I did need to get out and about. Maybe her friends could help me work out how to fit in at the school gate.

I decided to check if Carol had been to a coffee morning at Poppy's before and therefore could tell me if it would be casual or dressy, and whether I should bring something. I didn't want to make any more social *faux-pas* this morning.

I went into the garden and looked over the fence to where Carol was, as always, working on her vegetable patch.

'Hi, Carol, sorry to interrupt. It's just about Poppy's coffee morning later. Should I go in jeans, or will everyone be dressed up?'

Carol pulled a stray hair out of her face. 'You know Poppy. She'll be dressed to the nines. The last time I went to one of her coffees, the women all looked as if they were off to Ascot.'

'Oh, God!' I groaned. 'I'm not sure I can fit into any of my nice clothes.'

'I'll be casual. I don't own a dress.'

'Yes, but you do the whole casual thing really well,' I lied.

Carol made her own clothes, and I had no doubt she'd be wearing one of her home-made shirts to Poppy's house.

They were made up of scraps of material she found in haberdasheries. She'd sew the scraps together, regardless of colour or pattern, and create a shirt out of them. Her outfits were completely bonkers, but she got away with it because she wore them with confidence. Carol felt fantastic in her clothes because she had created something from recycled goods and was doing her bit to save the planet. I, on the other hand, would have looked like a homeless person in her stuff.

'Will you call in for me on your way?' I asked her.

'Sure. See you at ten thirty.'

I went into the house and tried on everything I owned. I eventually opted for a white shirt and a high-waisted black pencil skirt, which was made with some kind of reinforced elastic that sucked in my stomach. I paired it with black, wedge-heeled, strappy sandals. When I looked in the mirror, I was pleased with the result.

I spent ages on my makeup, trying to camouflage my tired eyes and dehydrated skin, the result of all the wine I'd drunk last night. James had promised to be home for dinner, but as usual had called to say he was stuck in work, so I had finished an entire bottle on my own. At this rate, I'd be a lush in no time. Maybe that was why Jackson's mother hadn't given me the time of day: she'd smelt alcohol on my breath. I gave my teeth a good scrub. I didn't want Poppy's friends getting the wrong idea – the boozy Irish neighbour was such a cliché.

An hour later, Carol picked me up to walk next door to Poppy's. She was wearing a shirt that had blue pin-stripe sleeves, a red paisley front, a flowery purple back and a white collar. She had combined it with khaki combats, open-toed sandals . . . and looked radiant. She beamed from ear to ear. In her hand she had a basket of vegetables, freshly picked from the garden. I knew Poppy would just throw them into the bin. I reckoned anything with mud on it was a no-no to Poppy. I'd have said the only vegetables she allowed into her house were in Marks & Spencer's packaging.

I had a box of chocolates I'd found in the cupboard. I knew Poppy wouldn't eat them, but at least I wasn't arriving empty-handed. I was sure she hadn't eaten anything since the nineties.

Carol pointed to the three large SUVs parked on the road outside Poppy's house. 'It's a bloody disgrace,' she fumed. 'Why can't those women cycle, use public transport or at least buy hybrid cars? Don't they care about global warming?'

I said nothing, but somehow I doubted that Poppy and her friends cared about anything but the latest Prada handbag or Victoria Beckham dress. Carol was wasting her breath. She rang the doorbell. Sophie answered it, wearing her perfect Parisian pout and little else.

''Ello, come in,' the au pair mumbled, strutting ahead of us in her micro mini skirt. 'Ze ladies are in zere in zeir ridiculous shoes zat zey cannot walk in.'

We followed her into the lounge where Poppy jumped up to greet us. She was dressed to the nines in a tight Roland Mouret ice-blue dress and nude, sky-high Louboutin heels.

'You look fantastic,' I said, as Poppy air-kissed me. She did look fantastic for a woman going to a wedding or a very posh lunch. It was all a bit much for not-even-eleven-a.m., but maybe that was how they did it in London. If so, I'd have to take out a bank loan for my next coffee morning.

'All these clothes are remnants of the good old days when I had a black American Express card,' Poppy said, with an exaggerated sigh.

I'd never heard of a black credit card. Obviously it was the really fancy kind. This was a whole new world. I decided to concentrate, try to understand these women and fit in. I needed friends.

Carol sat down on the chair nearest the door and I sat opposite her, on the couch, where I took up about three times as much space as the model-thin women who were already perched there.

Poppy introduced us. 'Girls, these are my neighbours. Carol, the eco-warrior, and Emma, who's just moved over from Ireland. And these are my friends, Holly, Jo and Sasha.'

I smiled and nodded at them. Each one was wearing a figure-hugging dress and stiletto heels. They all had coiffed blonde hair and Botoxed faces. Sasha and Jo also had collagen lips and put-your-eye-out boob jobs, as Mum called them. None of them ate any of the dainty food. I sucked my stomach in and sipped my coffee.

'Emma's a makeup artist,' Poppy told them.

'Really?' Sasha looked surprised.

'Any tips?' Jo asked.

'Don't drink too much wine at night because you'll wake up with dehydrated skin,' I said, pointing to my own face and smiling.

'Oh, that explains it,' Poppy said. 'I thought you were a bit pale.'

'Sweetie, you should only ever drink vodka and soda water. It's very low in calories, and the soda hydrates you,' Sasha informed me, as if she were passing on the meaning of life.

'Excellent. Thanks.'

'We were just talking about Annabelle's birthday,' Poppy explained. 'She'll be eight next week and Jo is throwing the most incredible party for her. Tell them, Jo.'

Jo smiled widely, revealing a perfect set of dazzling white veneers. 'Well, Annabelle loves Nobu.'

'Who doesn't?' Holly chuckled.

Hang on, wasn't Nobu the restaurant all the celebrities went to?

'So she asked if she could have her party there. Well, what could I say?'

'How about "no"?' The words were out of my big mouth before I realized it. Oops.

Silence. They all stared at me, except Carol, who looked at the floor.

'Just kidding,' I lied. I mean, Nobu, really? One of the top restaurants in the world and they think it's perfect for a kid's birthday party? I could have done with one of those vodka-and-sodas right then and there.

'The Irish sense of humour always gets me,' Jo said. 'Anyway, I called Christophe, the manager – he knows me well because we eat there at least once a week. He said it was an unusual request, but that of course he'd arrange it.'

'It's so exciting. My Diana can't wait,' Sasha said, through her puffed-up lips.

'How many girls have you invited?' Poppy asked.

'Fourteen. We're having dinner at Nobu and then a sleep-over at our house. I've hired a magician, a fire-eater and a juggler, and then we're having a disco. I've converted the playroom into a nightclub, with mirror balls and a dance-floor, and we've hired a DJ and some professional dancers to teach the girls some new moves.'

The urge to laugh vanished and I felt acutely lonely. I'd never fit in. These women were on a different planet from me. Nobu? Fire-eaters? It was nonsense. I wished Lucy was there, so I could catch her eye and giggle. This was insane. The woman was talking about having a party for an eight-year-old that was going to cost thousands of pounds. Was I the only one who thought it was ridiculous? I glanced at Carol, who was listening intently, blank-faced. It was impossible to tell what she was thinking.

'I wish I'd had girls.' Poppy groaned. 'Boys are so boisterous and energetic. I find them exhausting. All they want to do is fight and eat and talk about poo. I should have had two girls I could dress up and take shopping with me.'

'There's no guarantee that a girl will love shopping, though,' I said, deciding to be honest and not try to fit in. It was pointless anyway: I never would. 'My friend Jess's daughter refuses to wear anything but the Manchester United football kit.'

The women looked shocked – or as shocked as their Botox would allow.

'But that's crazy! The mother needs to put her foot down,' Holly exclaimed.

'She's tried, but every time she hides the jersey, Sally has a nervous breakdown and refuses to leave the house. Her life isn't worth living when Sally doesn't have the jersey on. She's got two younger children, so she can't spend all day fighting with her daughter.'

'A bit more discipline is required,' Holly said. 'Your friend is the one in control.'

'She tried that. She told Sally if she didn't take the jersey off, she'd have to go and live somewhere else.'

'And?' Poppy asked.

'Sally packed her bags and left. So Jess followed her. Sally went into the local police station and told them her mother was abusing her mentally and she wanted to be adopted by a new family, but they had to be Manchester United fans.'

While the other women stared at me in horror, Carol laughed.

'What did your friend do?' Poppy asked.

I grinned at the memory. 'She had to explain to the police what had happened and drag Sally home. Since then, she lets her wear what she wants.'

'That girl needs to go to boarding school,' Jo said.

I gave in to my rumbling stomach and tucked into one of the cup cakes. 'It's not that serious. It's just a phase.'

Sasha put her coffee cup on the table. 'Diana is going through a ballet phase. She can't stop dancing. Her teacher says she's very talented. She's started extra classes on Tuesdays and Thursdays. It's a nightmare to juggle because she has music appreciation on Tuesdays and tennis on Thursdays as well.'

So now we all know your daughter is amazing at ballet! Didn't Sasha know how transparent she was?

'Tell me about it!' Jo exclaimed. 'Annabelle has Pony Club on Mondays, straight after her deportment class.'

I almost choked on my cup cake – *deportment class*? What could that possibly entail? Walking around with books on your head to improve your posture? Learning to drink from a teacup with your little finger sticking up in the air? Come on! Was this for real?

I had a feeling I'd regret it, but I had to ask: 'What exactly happens during a deportment class?'

Jo put one perfectly manicured hand over the other. 'They're marvellous, Emma. They teach the girls how to walk and sit and behave in public. Miss Herrington-Brown is very strict on manners and etiquette. Annabelle's come on so much since she started going – people always comment on how poised and graceful she is.'

Maybe I should send Yuri and Lara to deportment classes. Maybe Miss Herrington-Brown could get them to stop shouting, spitting out their vegetables and screaming like banshees when they heard the word 'bath'.

I wondered if French children did deportment classes. When we went to France on holidays last year, Yuri and Lara had wriggled and writhed, roared and shrieked in every restaurant we entered. Yuri had a full-scale meltdown when the waiter served his pizza with a sprinkling of chives on it. He kept shouting, 'Get the green things off.' Meanwhile, the French children sat calmly and quietly, eating frogs' legs and squid while their parents had interesting and stimulating conversations about Proust and existentialism.

James and I, on the other hand, had spent our mealtimes whisper-shouting at the children, scooping large amounts of food off the floor and shoving ice-cream down their throats to shut them up for five minutes. Our 'adult' conversations consisted of blaming each other for being too lenient with Yuri and Lara, swearing to be stricter in future and getting as much wine down our necks as we could before going home and facing bath- and bedtime.

When we'd got back from the holiday, I'd asked my mother how Babs, Sean and I had behaved when we were taken out to restaurants as children. Mum had looked at me as if I had three heads. 'Restaurants? Are you mad? Do you honestly think your father and I would have paid good money to listen to you lot moaning, watch you run wild and waste food?'

I was brought back to the present when I heard Sasha ask Jo, 'What gift should I buy for Annabelle? I was thinking an iPod touch?'

'She has one,' Jo said.

Of course she does. She probably had it before any normal grown-up. She probably has a pony, an LCD TV and a Kindle Fire too, I thought.

'How about a little outfit from Chloé, or would you prefer Prada?' Sasha persisted.

Jo thought for a moment. 'I think I'd rather Prada. They

have some really nice colours this season. Burgundy is particularly stunning on Annabelle.'

You'd need a bank loan to go to this kid's party. I sincerely hoped none of the children in Yuri and Lara's classes had parents with as much cash to burn. Clearly the global recession hadn't affected these women. Whatever happened to colouring books and jigsaws as good birthday presents? I sighed. In Dublin I could spot one of these ladies-who-lunch a mile away and avoid them, but in London I was so grateful to be invited anywhere, I had to put up with it.

I placed my cup on the coffee-table and picked up another cake. I knew they were staring at me as if I was some kind of savage. Apparently eating was not the done thing in London either, but I needed the sugar to cheer me up and get me through this conversation. As I took a large bite, I caught Carol's eye. She discreetly rolled her eyes. Thank God! I was so relieved that someone else in the room thought Prada outfits and dinner at Nobu for eight-year-olds was nuts. I wasn't alone. Hurrah!

'I can't help wondering where you got your shirt, Carol? Is it new season Tibi or Peter Pilotto?' Jo enquired.

I disguised my laughter with a coughing fit.

Carol gave Jo a dazzling smile. 'It's neither actually. It's an original Carol Richards.'

Jo's brow tried to frown, but it was frozen in place. 'I haven't heard of her. Has she just left design college? It does look a bit . . . well . . . uhm . . . raw.'

Poppy clicked her tongue. 'Carol makes her own clothes. And grows all her own vegetables and cycles everywhere. She thinks I'm a disgrace to the human race for driving an SUV.'

Emboldened by the sugar rush from the second cup cake, I announced, 'My outfit is last season's spring/summer collection from Primark.'

Sasha squealed. I thought I'd pushed her over the edge with my Primark comment. 'OMG, it's eleven thirty! I have to go! I've got an appointment with my stylist at twelve.' She stood up and was followed by Jo, who had a hair appointment even though her hair was absolutely perfect, and Holly had to run to get her immaculate nails redone.

We all said polite goodbyes. I picked up my bag to go, but Poppy told me to put it down. Kicking off her sky-high shoes, she linked her arm through mine and Carol's. 'You're going nowhere. I need a drink after that. Is it too early for gin?'

Carol grinned. 'Probably.'

'You could have a brandy coffee, though,' I suggested.

'Emma, you're a genius.' Poppy led us into her kitchen and we sat down at the table while she made us coffee. Mine was laced with brandy but she left Carol's plain. Her own was really just brandy with a dash of coffee. Clearly she was feeling stressed.

'How do you know those women?' I wondered.

Poppy took a glug of her coffee. 'We grew up together. We were good pals for years but when I ended up divorced and living in Putney, we drifted. They're nice girls, they still invite me to lunches and things, but we have less in common. I'm on a budget now and they have husbands with very, very deep pockets. God, I miss the good old days.' Poppy sighed and drank deeply from her brandy coffee.

'Is Nigel keeping up his payments?' Carol asked.

Poppy nodded. 'He missed last month, but I sent him a solicitor's letter so he's paid up now. Hopefully that's the end of him shirking his responsibility. Bastard keeps telling me things are not going well at work and then I find out he's going to St Lucia for Christmas with that bitch Georgina.'

'You'll be all right, Poppy. You're made of stern stuff,' Carol said.

'I'm tired, Carol. I'm sick of being on my own. I hate having to pay bills and put the bloody bins out and deal with the boys on my own. I wasn't made for singledom. I've always had a man in my life. I know we're all supposed to be modern women who can do everything for themselves, but I hate it. I need to meet a millionaire who'll look after me.'

'Well, you look amazing, so I'm sure you will,' I said, trying to make her feel better.

Poppy patted my arm. 'Thank you, darling, but London is cut-throat. There are a million stunning young women out there looking for men with money. I'm positively ancient compared to them and I have the baggage of two young boys. If only Daddy hadn't gambled all the money away, at least I'd be rich and lonely.'

'Money isn't everything,' Carol pointed out. 'Happiness comes from inside, not out.'

'Christ, Carol, spare me your hippie-dippy crap today. I can't take it.'

'You know I'm right,' Carol said good-humouredly.

'Happiness is a black American Express card and a bottomless bank account.'

'Rubbish,' Carol said. 'Happiness is being content with what you have. Living in the present, not the past.'

'Well, I'm not content.' Poppy rubbed her eyes, and mascara smudged onto her cheeks. 'I'm bloody miserable. I want to be looked after. I want to be secure.'

'Do you think marriage brings security?' I asked, emboldened by the brandy coffee.

Poppy snorted. 'It didn't bring me much security. Nigel was unfaithful after only a few years. And I was a good wife to him. I really tried because I wanted it to work. But it wasn't enough for him.'

'So what is the secret to a happy marriage, then?' I asked.

'Communication and respect,' Carol answered, without hesitating.

'Really?'

'Yes, I know from experience. Keith isn't my first husband. I had a disastrous first marriage that ended after three years.'

'I had no idea. I'm sorry.' Everyone on this road had a story to tell. I felt positively boring.

'I'm glad it happened. I learnt a lot from that relationship. I think I'm a better wife this time around.'

'You're a bloody saint, Carol,' Poppy said. 'Keith's a lucky man.'

'In what way are you a better wife?'

'I listen, I talk honestly and I don't take Keith for granted.'

'But don't you occasionally want to punch his nose? Like when he does something really irritating?' I asked, thinking about how annoyed I was with James for standing me up again last night.

Carol laughed. 'When I feel like that, I go out and start digging. Physical exertion takes the edge off.'

'I need to buy a spade.' I grinned.

'I have a shed full of them.' Poppy giggled.

'It takes work, though, doesn't it?' I mused. 'When kids come along and other stresses, you really have to work at your relationship.'

'Of course you do,' Carol said. 'Marriage is a job, like any other. You need to work hard to keep it alive.'

'And keep the sex going,' Poppy added. 'I made that mistake. I thought Nigel was just too old and tired to have sex with me, so I let it go. I should have guessed something was up. It was only when I found the texts that I finally realized what was going on. I should have seen it a mile away. A man not wanting sex is a cheater.'

'James has been getting saucy texts.'

'What?' Both women were shocked.

'No! It's OK – they're from the players on his rugby team. They're just trying to wind him up.' James had had another late last night, saying, *I no u fancy me, I can c it in ur eyes. Im here waiting 4 u.*

Poppy took my hand. 'Darling, are you sure that's who they're from?'

I smiled. 'Positive. I think they're kind of funny, but James is getting very het up about it. He thinks it shows a lack of respect for him as a manager.'

'I can see his point. I doubt the Manchester United players ever sent sexy texts to Alex Ferguson,' Carol put in.

'That's exactly what James said. He tried to trace the number last night, to find out which player it is, but you can't reverse-search a mobile phone in the UK. He's gone to work today to sort it out. He was pretty angry. I'd say the players ever are going to get a roasting.'

Poppy looked at me. 'I'm sure it is the boys being silly, but I'd keep a close eye on it. Check his phone regularly.'

I finished my coffee. 'Honestly, Poppy, I'm not being stupid or naïve. I know from James's reaction that this is just one of the guys messing about. He's really annoyed about it.'

'Hopefully he'll sort it out with the players today and it'll stop,' Carol said.

'Good old Carol, always looking on the bright side.' Poppy put an arm around her. 'I'm sure it's nothing, darling, but I'd keep an eye on his phone anyway, just as an extra precaution.'

'Don't listen to Poppy,' Carol said. 'She doesn't trust anyone.'

'In my sad and sorry experience, men are pigs,' Poppy slurred. The brandy was taking effect.

I glanced at my watch. 'Oh, God, I'm late to pick up the

kids. Sorry, guys, I have to dash.' I kissed Poppy and Carol, ran out of the door and all the way to the school gates, where a very grumpy Yuri and Lara were waiting for me with their teachers. They were the last children to be collected. I felt terrible, but at least none of the other mothers had been there to smell my brandy breath.

16

James tossed and turned all that night, then got up at six and began pacing up and down like a caged tiger. At half past I told him to go to the club. There was no point in him being at home: he needed to be at work, near the pitch, near his players and staff. Today was the first Heineken Cup match of the season, the first opportunity for James to prove himself as the new coach. I'd never seen him so nervous. I couldn't wait for the damn match to be over.

Minutes after he'd left, I fell asleep again, but was woken at nine when Yuri climbed into bed beside me and tugged at me. 'Mummy, I'm starving. I need Cheerios or I'll die.'

I hugged him tightly.

'Ouch, you're hurting me.' He wriggled away.

'I need a hug. Please, Yuri, just give Mummy a big one.'

'Will you give me a treat if I do?' he bargained.

I nodded.

Yuri grudgingly obliged and let me hug him, while his hands hung limply by his sides. I inhaled the scent of his hair. How I loved this child.

'Get off me now,' he said. 'Where's my treat?'

'I want a treat, I want a treat!' Lara padded into the room in her Minnie Mouse pyjamas, looking adorable. I picked her up and squeezed her.

'Mummy! Squashy,' she squealed.

'She squashed me too,' Yuri complained.

I kissed them both. 'Sometimes mummies need hugs.'

'Treat!' Yuri demanded.

We went down to the kitchen where I handed them both, as a special treat, a chocolate chip cookie. While they were happily dropping crumbs all over the place, the doorbell rang. I peeped out of the window. It was Mum and Dad!

Christ, they were due at eleven! They'd come over for James's first match, but I'd thought I had a couple of hours to set things straight. The house was a mess and so was I. With James's constant tossing and turning, I'd had a terrible night. I had huge black shadows under my eyes and my hair was sticking up.

'Mummy, there's someone at the door!' Yuri shouted.

'Yes, I know. Guess what? It's Granny and Granddad.'

'Hurrah!' Yuri and Lara jumped down from their chairs and ran to the door.

'About bloody time! We've been standing out here for ten minutes.' Dad swept past me. 'We've been up since four this morning. Your mother insisted on getting an early flight.'

Dad patted the children on the head, marched into the kitchen, sat down, opened his newspaper and began to read it.

'Don't mind him. He's very grumpy.' Mum kissed the children, then took in the mess in the kitchen. 'I would have thought you'd put on a bit of breakfast for us. I texted you to say we'd be here at about nine thirty.'

'I'm sorry. It's been a bit crazy and my phone is on silent.'

Mum took her coat off. 'Well, I'll put the kettle on and you can tidy up a bit.' She looked around. 'It's not bad, Emma. It's a nice family house. It needs cleaning and tidying, but it's got a nice feel to it. We passed some lovely shops in the taxi. It seems to be a very pleasant area. You did well, pet.'

Lara waved her cookie in her granny's face. 'Look what we got for breakfast.'

Mum glared at me. 'What on earth are you filling them

with rubbish for at this hour? Porridge is what you should be feeding them, especially Yuri. All that sugar will stunt his growth.'

'Do you think I'm bigger since you saw me, Granny?' Yuri's brown eyes begged his grandmother to say yes.

Mum squeezed his cheek. 'The minute I saw you, I knew you'd grown. Sure you're flying up. But you need to eat healthy food.'

Lara hopped from one foot to the other. 'Guess what? I can count to twenty. Claire teached me.'

'Taught you,' Mum corrected her. 'Good for Claire.'

'And she teached me how to do a jigsaw with twenty pieces all by myself,' Lara added.

'Claire sounds like a gem,' Mum noted.

'Why don't you go and do your jigsaw now and show it to us when you've finished?' I suggested. Lara ran out, keen to impress her grandparents.

'Take your time, Lara, no need to rush it.' Dad put his paper down and poured milk into the coffee Mum had made for him.

'I can do a fifty-piece one,' Yuri told his granddad.

'Even better,' Dad said. 'Off you go.'

Yuri galloped after his sister.

I quickly tidied up the kitchen counter and wiped the table free of crumbs. 'Sorry about the terrible welcome. We'll go for a nice lunch later.'

'What time is the match?' Dad asked.

'I think it's a three o'clock kick-off, but I'll call James and double check.'

'Don't be bothering him. I'm sure he's in the middle of pre-match training. I'll Google it here.'

Mum sniffed. 'Google this and Google that. Since he got that annoying iPhone, he never has a conversation with me any more. He's got his nose stuck in it from morning till night. And, of course, there's no mention of the ozone layer when he's charging it every night.'

I nibbled absentmindedly on a biscuit.

Mum looked at me closely. 'You're exhausted and a bit rounder about the waist. Lord, Emma! Don't tell me you're pregnant. You're far too old to be having more children.'

'First of all, I am not pregnant. Second, you're one to talk – you had Babs at forty.'

Mum pursed her lips. 'And look how well that turned out! I didn't have the energy to discipline her and she's wild.'

She had a point there. If only she knew how wild. I concentrated on sipping my coffee and steered the conversation away from Babs. 'You can relax, Mum. I'm not planning on having any more children.'

'Good. I don't think you'd be able for any more. You seem to find two difficult enough.'

'No, I don't. I just –'

Mum cut across me: 'Why do you look so shattered? Were you out gallivanting last night?'

'No, I just slept badly.'

'Two o'clock kick-off,' Dad announced, waving his phone.

'Plenty of time to smarten yourself up for your husband,' Mum said to me. 'Now, why don't you go off and get your hair done? We'll mind the children.'

'Really?' I was thrilled at the prospect of an hour to myself.

'What?' Dad didn't like this plan. If I was gone, he'd have to do some actual childminding rather than being Grumpy Granddad in the corner.

'Oh, for goodness' sake, we haven't seen the little dotes in ages. Get your nose out of that paper and turn your phone off,' Mum snapped.

Before they could change their minds I ran upstairs, flung

on tracksuit bottoms and a fleece jacket and sprinted out of the house.

When I got back from the salon, I found Dad watching *Tangled*, with Lara howling the songs into his ear. Mum was in the kitchen with Yuri, reading him stories from his *Batman* comic.

'Much better,' Mum said, when she saw me. 'Now you just need to find something smart to wear. I see the diet hasn't started yet.'

I sat down and stroked Yuri's hair. 'It's been stressful settling in.'

'Fair enough, but you'd need to get on with it. Be nice to lose it before Christmas – and it's not that far away.'

I was tempted to tell Mum I was lonely but I didn't want to worry her, especially as she was soon going to find out that her younger daughter was pregnant with a married man's child.

'How is James getting on in his new job?' Mum asked. Yuri climbed down from her lap and carried his comic to his granddad.

'Well, I think. He spends all of his time there – he's always working late. He's really uptight about this match, but maybe if they win today he'll relax a bit.'

'I can understand him being stressed. It can't be easy training all those lads and managing all the personalities.'

'They seem to like him. One of the players has been sending him texts saying "I really fancy you" and "You have a great bum", that kind of thing. He's going to nip it in the bud. You can't be too friendly with the players – you need distance.'

'That sounds very odd,' Mum said. 'Whoever is sending them needs to be told off. James is the boss. He should be treated with respect. Does he know which player it is?'

'None of them owned up when he asked them. They all denied it.'

'And you say the texts are about fancying him?'

I nodded.

Mum shook her head. 'I don't like the sound of that, Emma. I think someone else could be sending them.'

I looked at her in surprise. 'What do you mean?'

Mum sipped her tea. 'James is a very handsome, charming man. I'm sure there's many a lady whose head would be turned by him. I'd keep an eye on that texting if I was you.'

'Do you think James is lying to me?'

'Of course not, but it's possible that those messages could be from a woman who likes him.'

'But he said –'

Mum shook her finger in front of my face. 'Now don't go off on one of your tangents and start dreaming up all sorts of problems for yourself. It's probably nothing, but I'm just saying you need to mind your husband. A lot of women out there would gladly run off with him.'

'I do mind him, Mum. I'm a very good wife, actually. Haven't I just moved country for him?'

'That's what wives do, Emma. They support their husbands – and they don't get medals for it,' she said pointedly.

'Not all wives, Mum. Lucy's moved here to start a new job that's going to make her millions. Donal didn't follow her.'

Mum looked unconvinced. 'Lucy would need to be careful, too. No man likes to be alone. Men are no good on their own – they always seek out a woman. They like to be minded.'

'What about us? Don't we women get a say? I'd like to be minded. I'd like to come home to a clean house and a cooked dinner every night after work.'

Mum shrugged. 'You can say what you want about the

world changing and equality and all of that, but it comes down to human nature, Emma. Men do not like being alone, and a wife who doesn't look after her husband will lose him. Mark my words, I've seen it happen. And your forties are the most dangerous time of all.'

I hadn't heard anyone say that before. 'Really? Why?'

'Mid-life crisis, I suppose. Your children aren't babies any more so they don't need you as much. You're getting more sleep, you've got energy again and you know that the next big birthday is fifty, and fifty is old. People see their forties as the last hurrah. And not just men, women too. A lot of marriages go awry during your forties.'

I thought about my own friends. So far most of them seemed to be holding it together, except Lucy and Donal. No one had ever told me my forties would be a dangerous decade. 'Did many of your friends have affairs, Mum?'

'Some.' She was being deliberately vague. I knew she'd never tell me who.

'Did the partners forgive them or did they break up?'

'About half and half, I'd say. Marriage isn't easy, Emma. It's a long, bumpy road and it's not for the faint-hearted.'

So far my marriage had been quite smooth. We'd struggled to have children, but that had brought us closer. We'd fought, like most couples, and when the children came along and we were up all night, we'd snapped at each other because we were tired. But I had always felt loved and secure. James came from a solid background, his parents had been together for almost fifty years, and he believed in marriage and family. I knew there were times when I drove him nuts, but I had never felt for a second that he'd leave me. When I heard stories of women finding out their husbands were cheating, I always assumed their marriages must have been in crisis, or the husbands were the cheating kind. James was so solid and steady. I had always trusted him . . . until the day I'd seen him with Mandy, but I was pretty sure that had been just a little flirtation. Hadn't it? Now I was worried. I could hear Poppy warning me to be careful, too, just like Mum. Could those texts have been from a woman?

Mum patted my arm. 'Don't worry, Emma. I'm just saying that marriages need work. But keep an eye on those texts. Now, upstairs with you, and we'll find you something decent to wear. I want you to give me that tracksuit. It's going straight in the bin.'

We went up to my bedroom, where Mum riffled through my wardrobe.

'Mum, I'm forty years old. I know what to wear,' I objected.

Mum spun around, holding a pair of beige leather shorts I had bought in the sales the year before. 'Clearly not!'

'I've never worn them. They were a mistake.'

'You can say that again.' Mum kept rummaging. 'Emma, there comes a stage in a woman's life where anything above the knee just looks cheap.' She turned again, holding a midnight blue wrap dress this time. 'Here we go. This colour is good on you. It doesn't clash with your hair.'

She was right. 'Now I know where Babs gets her talent for styling from.' We laughed.

'She should be here soon,' Mum said, looking at her watch.

'What?' There was no way Babs would be anywhere near Mum at the moment. 'She isn't coming, Mum.'

'Oh yes she is. I sent her a text last night and told her to be here at twelve sharp or I'd go over to her flat and drag her out. I want to see her. I'm worried about her. She's been avoiding me. She said she'd come.'

God, I hoped Babs would be able to hold it together and not give anything away. I'd been texting her every night after work to see if she was OK and had been getting the usual

'I'm fine' answers back. But that wouldn't cut it with our mother, certainly not in the flesh.

I tried the dress on. It was a bit tight around the waist.

'Have you got those suck-you-in pants?' Mum asked.

'Yes, lots of them.' Sighing, I opened a drawer and pulled out a pair of flesh-coloured Spanx. I went into the bathroom and wrestled them on. When I caught sight of myself in the mirror, I stopped dead. I looked an utter fright.

Mum barged in. 'Come on, we haven't got all day. Your father's complaining about being hungry. Lord, those are awful-looking things. Mind you, they do suck you in. My advice to you is to take them off privately. Men don't need to know our secrets. A bit of mystery is no harm at all.'

I thought back to the day I'd bought them. When I'd got home, I'd put them on and stuck one of James's gum shields in my mouth. When he arrived home, I had jumped out and paraded up and down in front of him, doing Sumo wrestler poses and laughing hysterically. He had laughed, too. But maybe he'd been thinking, My God, she looks a state. Maybe Mum was right: perhaps I needed to keep a bit of mystery.

Mum tied the belt on the dress and took a step back. 'Much better. You look very nice. Now go and do your makeup. I'll get the children ready.'

I layered my makeup, hiding the dark circles with concealer, giving colour to my pasty cheeks with a light pink blusher and opening up my tired eyes with mascara and eye-shadow.

Twenty minutes later, we were in the hall with our coats on. As we opened the front door to head out to a pre-match early lunch, Babs walked up the garden path.

'About time you turned up to say hello to your parents,' Mum huffed.

Babs was wearing her trademark dark glasses and a white fur jacket with skinny jeans and thigh-high black leather boots.

'Interesting get-up.' Dad took in the outfit. 'Bit much for the side-lines, I would have thought.'

Babs patted his cheek. 'Coming from a man wearing a brown duffel coat he bought in the 1970s, I'll take that as a compliment.'

'Apparently these are very trendy now,' Dad said.

'In whose world? The golf-club gang's?' Babs snorted.

'The boots are ludicrous. Take them off – you look like a street-walker,' Mum ordered Babs. 'Emma can lend you shoes.'

'Emma wears granny-shoes. I wouldn't be seen dead in flat boots.'

I was relieved to hear Babs sounding more like her usual self. I gave her a smile, and she smiled back. Then she grasped my arm and murmured, 'Please don't leave me on my own with Mum.'

'Forget about the bloody shoes,' Dad snapped. 'For the love of God, can we go and get something to eat before I start gnawing my own arm off?'

We walked to the high street, aiming for a little restaurant called Cinnamon. On the way we bumped into Poppy, whose clothes would have given Babs a run for her money. She was wearing tight black leather trousers, high wedge-heeled ankle boots and a black fur gilet over a white shirt. She looked overdressed, but very sexy. I felt frumpy beside her. I introduced her to my parents and sister.

'Very nice to meet you all,' Poppy said, in her beautiful cut-glass accent. 'I'm afraid I can't shake your hands, I've just had my nails done.' She wiggled her red nails. 'Hot date tonight.' She winked at me.

'Good for you,' I said, with a grin.

'Lovely to meet you, but we must be off,' Dad said, determined not to let anything or anyone sidetrack us from getting to the restaurant.

'Excuse my husband.' Mum was embarrassed. 'He's hungry, and you know what men are like when they want food.'

'Of course I do.' Poppy smiled. 'Nigel would have stepped on my head to get to the fridge.'

Mum laughed.

'Where's James?' Poppy asked.

'London Irish play their first Heineken Cup match today and we're going to watch it after lunch,' I explained.

'No wonder he looked so serious when I saw him this morning,' Poppy said. 'He's usually so friendly.'

'Come on, ladies, enough nattering.' Dad ushered us away.

'Seriously!' Babs looked at me. 'That MILF lives next door?'

'MILF?' Mum asked. 'I thought her name was Poppy?'

'MILF stands for Mother I'd Like to Fu—'

'Babs!' I stopped her.

Mum's cheeks reddened. 'Well, I never.'

'It's just an expression,' Babs said, with a wicked gleam in her eye.

'A crude one.' Mum was unimpressed.

'Poppy looks good for an older woman,' Babs commented.

'She's much the same age as me,' I pointed out.

'Really? God, she looks years younger.'

Thank you, sister.

'She seems nice,' Mum said. 'But I wouldn't get too friendly with her, Emma. She's a bit, well . . .'

'Sexy?' Babs said.

'Available,' Mum said. 'You can see she's dissatisfied with her life.'

I stared at Mum. 'From a ten-second meeting you can tell all that?'

'Of course. She's completely overdressed for a Saturday afternoon, in clothes that are too young for her. There's an air of desperation about that. She's obviously craving male attention. The only reason a woman craves attention is when she isn't getting enough at home and she's bored with her life. She's looking for excitement.'

'I have to say, Mum, I'm actually impressed,' Babs admitted.

I was too. Mum had completely summed up Poppy. She smiled. 'When you've been around as long as I have, you notice things.'

'Stop talking!' Dad roared. 'I don't care if that woman is humping David Cameron in her spare time, I need food.'

'Calm down or you'll have a heart-attack,' Mum remonstrated.

'What's "humping" mean?' Yuri asked.

'Walking like a camel,' Babs told him, as Dad stormed into the restaurant and threw himself down at a table.

'Why is Granddad grumpy?' Lara asked.

'Because he's old, and when you get old, you get mean and nasty and grumpy,' Babs said.

'Granny's old and she's not grumpy,' Lara pointed out.

Babs and I burst out laughing.

17

We had to eat quickly as Dad wanted to be at the rugby ground well before kick-off. We hustled the children onto the train, scurried from the station and got there twenty minutes early – a long time to keep two young children occupied. I'd have much preferred to spend those twenty minutes in the comfort of the restaurant.

The stadium was packed with London Irish fans, wearing dark green jerseys, and Gloucester fans, in red and white stripes. The atmosphere was fantastic. I looked for James and eventually made him out: he was sitting down in his warm black jacket and tracksuit bottoms, surrounded by men all wearing identical kit. He had an earpiece and was talking to the guy beside him, who had a laptop that he was furiously pointing to.

'I see James is coaching from the pitch,' Dad said. 'It's great the way he stays down near the players.'

I waved at James, but he didn't see me: he was too busy concentrating.

He really was handsome, I found myself thinking. Even though he looked tired and older, he wore it well. If anything, he was even more attractive in that older-guy way. My James, my lovely James. I wondered about what Mum had said. Were we entering a dangerous decade? I'd have to keep a closer eye on him. With me working all day and looking after the kids, I really didn't know much about his day-to-day life or the people in it. We needed to go out more together and talk. Communication was the key to a happy marriage. I wanted this handsome man to stick with me. God, I hoped Mum was wrong: I hoped someone out there didn't fancy him.

I'd had no idea about Mandy until I'd caught James flirting with her. He could have met someone new at work. He could be flirting with someone all day long. I'd have to look into it further. I'd have to be more vigilant. I didn't want to end up on my own in London with two kids after James had left me for some hot London babe.

I examined all the people around him, looking for suspects, but they were all male.

'I'm bored, Mummy,' Lara complained.

Dad clapped a hand to his forehead. 'Tell me she's not going to complain for the next eighty minutes!'

'She's three, Dad, give her a break.' I was fed up with Dad bossing us around. He was a nightmare to go to matches with. He got completely wound up and spent the entire time shouting at the players.

'Here, take my phone. I've got some cool games on it.' Babs quickly deleted some messages and handed Lara her mobile.

'I want to play!' Yuri grabbed the phone. Lara let out a blood-curdling shriek.

'Jesus Christ!' Dad exclaimed.

Babs grabbed her phone back. 'Hey, Stumpy, take it easy. And you, Miss, stop trying to burst everyone's eardrums. You can take it in turns to play. But if you fight, I'll make you be my slaves for a week. You'll have to clean and wash all day long. But if you're good, I'll buy you crisps at half-time.'

They immediately stopped fighting and began to play on the phone together.

Mum and Dad were looking at the match programme, so

I took the opportunity to have a quiet word with Babs. I'd been dying to talk to her since she'd arrived. 'Have you been on to Gary?' I whispered.

Babs gritted her teeth. 'He gets back tomorrow – I told you already.'

'When are you meeting him?'

'I don't know. I'll see him in work on Monday and make an arrangement.'

'How are you feeling?'

'Fine.'

'Are you worried about telling him?'

'Jesus, Emma, Mum and Dad are beside us! I'm not getting into this now. Drop it.'

Her earlier good mood had evaporated and I could see the tension in her body again. I wished she could talk to me without clamming up. James was right: this really wasn't going to end well. I looked down at my husband again, then decided to ask Babs about the texts. It would distract us from Gary and, since Mum had planted that seed of doubt, I badly needed to talk to someone about it. I was hoping Babs would tell me that Mum's theory was ridiculous.

'Have you ever got texts from people saying they fancy you and stuff like that?' I asked.

Babs looked at me as if I was mad. 'I think you're talking about sextexts and, yes, of course I have. Millions of them. I send loads, too. Welcome to the twenty-first century, Emma. It's a bit more advanced than when you were dating. People don't write letters with feathers any more and send them by pigeon.'

I chose to ignore the sarcasm. 'But do you always know the people who send you the messages?'

'Of course I do. I don't give my number out to strangers. I have to protect myself from psycho fans.'

'OK. Have you ever received a text from a number you didn't recognize?'

Babs nodded. 'Yeah, a few from crazy fans. But rarely.'

'What kind of things would they say?'

'The usual stuff – "You're so hot, I want to screw you", blah blah blah.'

'What did you do?'

'I ignored them.'

'Did they stop?'

Babs popped a mint into her mouth. 'Some went on for a few weeks, but got bored when they got no reaction. Why are you so interested all of a sudden? Are you trying to spice up your marriage by sending sextexts to James?'

I chewed my lower lip. 'No. James has been getting texts from an unknown number.'

Babs let out a whoop. 'James! Come on, Emma, it's obviously one of the rugby guys winding him up.'

'That's what I thought too, but then Mum said she thought it was suspicious. She reckons the players wouldn't mess around with the coach.'

'What did the texts say?' Babs was curious.

'Stuff like "I fancy you" and "You've got a great arse."'

Babs rolled her eyes. 'That sounds so lame. James works all day with a bunch of testosterone-fuelled young men. I guarantee you it's one of them winding him up.'

I frowned. 'It's kind of an odd trick to play on your boss, though, especially if you want to get picked for the team.'

'Half those guys have been concussed so many times their brains are fried. Mum always goes for the dramatic or the negative, you know that. She shouldn't have suggested it to you. He works in a business where practical jokes are the norm – he's the new guy so he's fair game.'

I began to calm down. She was probably right. It must have been the players messing about.

'Besides,' Babs continued, 'James isn't the type to have an affair. He's too boring and conservative.'

'Thank God for that!' I said, and we smiled at each other.

When the final whistle blew the score was twelve–three to London Irish and the home crowd went wild. They sang and cheered and gave the players a standing ovation. The mood was electric – even Yuri and Lara got caught up in it. They jumped up and down like maniacs – although a large part of that was due to sugar overload.

After the match, I sent James a text saying I was proud of him and that we had all come to support him. He sent one back saying he was thrilled we'd been there and he was so relieved about the win. We arranged to meet in the clubhouse and head home together.

When we got back to Putney, I found a package, addressed to me, on the doorstep. I didn't remember ordering anything. 'Did you buy me something?' I asked James.

He shook his head. 'Sorry, darling, no.'

I shook the parcel. Something rattled inside. Maybe it was a present from Lucy, or my other friend Jess back in Dublin. I was dying to open it.

While everyone took off their coats and went into the kitchen, I got a pair of scissors from a kitchen drawer and opened the package. Inside, something was heavily bound in bubble wrap.

'Hurry, Mummy, open it. I want to see the present,' Lara said.

When I finally cut through the Sellotape, a box fell out onto the floor. It was pink and had 'RAMPANT RABBIT' written down the side. What the hell? As Lara reached to grab it, I tried to stuff it back into the box, but the bottom was ripped and the object fell onto the floor. Lara picked it up and put it on the table.

'What is it?' she asked.

I was speechless. I tried desperately to think of an appropriate answer to fob her off.

'It looks like an alien,' Yuri said, scrunching his nose up.

'Is it one of those little Hoovers for the car?' Mum asked.

Dad took out his handkerchief and began to blow his nose furiously.

Babs looked up from her phone and burst out laughing. 'Emma, you dirtbag.'

James, who was making coffee, turned around. 'What is it, darling?' Seeing the object now sitting on the kitchen table, he stopped dead in his tracks. 'What on earth?' He looked at me. 'Emma?'

'I did not order this,' I hissed.

I grabbed it and began to stuff it back into the bubble wrap. Dad's face was now purple.

'Don't hold it in, Dad. Let it out.' Babs giggled as Dad began to shake with laughter.

Mum grabbed it. 'What has you all laughing?' She examined it.

'Mum!' I tried to snatch it back.

'I want a go!' Lara reached for it, but her grandmother held it at arm's length, frowning as she examined it.

'Let me have that.' James tried to take it out of Mum's hand, but she held firm.

'Dan?' Mum eyeballed her husband, waving the Rabbit about. 'What is it?'

Dad shook his head, unable to speak.

'It's a Rampant Rabbit,' Babs told her.

'BABS!' I shouted.

'What's so funny about that?' Mum asked.

'It's a vibrator,' Babs informed her.

My face was hot and I could feel tears forming behind my eyes. This was just unbelievable. I didn't know what to do.

'Christ,' James cursed.

Mum gasped and dropped it. The Rabbit hit the floor with a thud and began to vibrate. Yuri and Lara squealed with delight and tried to pick it up.

I lunged, seized it and stuffed it back into the box, still vibrating. I was trying not to cry. What the hell was going on?

'I'm speechless.' Mum was shocked.

'Well, there's a first time for everything,' Dad said, as he wiped the tears from his eyes.

'I'm dreadfully sorry. I can't apologize enough. It's . . . I . . .' James struggled to explain the mortifying incident.

'The children will be traumatized,' Mum muttered.

'No, they won't. It's just a toy to them,' Babs said.

'I want to play with the shaky rabbit,' Lara whinged.

'You are not to go near that dirty thing,' Mum warned her grandchildren. 'Do you hear me? NEVER!'

The children's eyes widened, and they nodded their little heads.

'Now you see how scary Granny can be,' Babs said.

James crouched down. 'Hey, guys, why don't you two pop into the lounge and play? I'll come in and give you a biscuit in a minute.'

Yuri and Lara reluctantly left the room.

'Who sent it, James?' Babs grinned at him.

'I did not!' James spluttered.

'That's enough. I don't want to know any more about it.' Mum went to put the kettle on. Then, turning to Dad, she added, 'And how do you know about this . . . thing? Is that what you're doing all the time on that iPhone? Pornography sites, is it? I'm disgusted.'

I was still too shocked to speak. I wanted them all to leave. I wanted the floor to swallow me. I picked up the box to hide it under the sink when I noticed a small card. I opened it: *You can use this when he leaves you for me.* I stood there, staring at it, unable to form a coherent thought.

Babs read the card over my shoulder. She frowned. 'Now that's a step too far,' she said. 'This guy needs to be kicked off the team for a few weeks.'

If it is a guy, I thought.

James came over to me and grabbed the card. 'I don't believe this,' he said. 'I'm going to kill whoever sent it.'

'It seems most peculiar that a player would send something so revolting to his coach's wife on match day. It doesn't add up to me,' Mum said, shooting me a meaningful look.

I hadn't thought I could feel any worse, but now I did. She was right: something weird was going on.

Dad stood up. 'It's been a very interesting day, but we must be off. Plane to catch. Well done, James, great win. Best of luck with the next game. I'll be watching.' Dad kissed me goodbye, then he and Mum walked to the door.

'Hang on, I'll come with you.' Babs grabbed her coat and followed them out.

As Mum hugged me, she said, 'Be careful, Emma. Something isn't right about this.'

I waved them off, feeling confused and embarrassed. The implications of what had just happened were sinking in. Someone had sent me, James's wife, a vibrator. This person knew our address and my name. Judging by the note, they wanted me out of the picture.

James and I went through the motions of putting the kids

to bed and then, when they were settled, we sat down to talk. Now my mind was clearer. I knew exactly what I wanted to ask and what I needed to know.

I took a deep breath. 'James, I'm only going to ask you this once. Are you having an affair?' My voice trembled.

James immediately took me in his arms. 'No! Of course not. Emma, I'm as shocked as you are about all of this. I cannot believe that one of the guys would do such a thing. But I promise you I'll hunt him down and he'll be kicked out of the club. There's no way I'm letting this go.'

I pulled back from him. 'James, I really don't think one of your players would do this unless he has a death wish. I think a woman sent it.'

'Who?'

'You tell me. Have you been flirting with anyone?'

'Emma, I've barely had time to breathe since we moved here. I eat, sleep and work. It has to be one of the players. Maybe it was Ken – I dropped him from the team for the game and he was really furious. He has a very high opinion of himself. It could have been his way of getting back at me, although admittedly it does seem very extreme.'

Maybe it had been Ken. I hoped so. I really hoped it was some stupid prank and not something more sinister or threatening. I decided to trust James and give him the benefit of the doubt. He genuinely seemed as upset as I was.

'Well, you go in there on Monday and sort the guy out. I never, ever want anything sent to this house again. It's totally out of order.'

James gently pushed my hair off my face. 'I promise you I'll make whoever did this pay for it.'

James headed for bed early, exhausted from the highs and lows of the day, but I was too agitated to sleep. I decided to call Lucy to run it by her. She always gave really good, measured advice.

'Hi, Emma, I was just thinking about you. I heard London Irish won. Brilliant news,' Lucy said, when she answered her phone.

'James is thrilled. Listen, Lucy, I –'

Lucy's phone began to beep. Another call was coming in.

'Damn! Sorry, Emma, I have to take this – it's a big client. I'll call you back.'

I waited up for an hour, alone on the sofa in the dark, but she never rang.

18

I arrived into work on Monday and found Babs waiting to have her makeup done. I began to apply moisturizer while she bit into a croissant. 'I thought the vibrator was priceless. Did you see Mum's face? She'll *never* get over it.'

'Yeah, it was a real riot for me.' I rubbed a base coat of foundation into Babs's cheeks.

'Ouch! There's no need to scrub my bloody face off,' she complained.

'Sorry. I'm just really annoyed about what happened and worried that maybe someone fancies James or he's having an affair or . . . something.'

'Who would fancy James? He's so obviously married with kids. He has no sex appeal whatsoever.'

I stopped mid-application. 'James has lots of sex appeal. Loads of women think he's gorgeous, he's great fun and has a very cool job. He's not an accountant with thick glasses who watches *University Challenge* for kicks and thinks a glass of shandy is living on the edge.'

Babs polished off her croissant. 'Relax, I'm just saying he's not exactly a player.'

I rummaged around for an eye-shadow brush. 'Of course he isn't. I wouldn't have married him if he were. I've no interest in being with someone who flirts with other women and makes me feel insecure. I don't understand relationships like that. What's the point in being with a man who needs constant attention? You'll always come second to his ego and you'll never be able to trust him.'

As if on cue, Gary stuck his head around the door. 'Are you nearly ready? We're all set up now.'

'One minute. I want to look my best today.' Babs grinned.

'You look good to me.' Gary winked and left the room.

'I see you haven't told him yet.' I brushed on some blusher.

'He's only just back and I'm hardly going to announce it at work,' Babs snapped. 'We're going for dinner tomorrow and I'll tell him then.'

'How far along are you now?' I asked quietly.

'I don't know exactly – and that's the last time I want you to ask questions like that here. I mean it.'

'Don't you feel even a little bit guilty about sleeping with a married man? Do you ever think about his wife and children?'

Babs shrugged. 'I'm not married. He's the one with the baggage, Emma. He's the one with the family.'

'I know, but I feel for his wife. I'd die if I found out James was cheating on me with a much younger woman.'

'If he wasn't sleeping with me, he'd be shagging someone else. It's not his first time. Gary's not a great family man who suddenly decided to sleep with someone. He's got a reputation as a cheat.'

'So why cheapen yourself by being another notch on his bedpost?'

'Keep your voice down,' Babs hissed. 'You should have seen the texts he was sending me when he was away. He said the holiday was incredibly boring. I'm not just some other girl. He wants to leave his wife for me. We'll be amazing together and he can really help me grow my career.'

I had to clench my fists tightly so I wouldn't grab her by the shoulders and shake her. 'And what about the baby? Is it going to slot into your plans?' I added some bronzer.

'Why not? Look at Angelina Jolie. She has millions of kids and they haven't held her back.'

I stared at my sister. Could she really be so stupid and shallow? 'Babs, I love you, which is why I'm trying to save you from being badly hurt. Listen to me. Gary will not leave his wife for you.'

Babs laughed. 'Oh, Emma, you really don't have a clue. Gary's mad about me.'

Karen knocked on the door. 'We need you on set now, Babs.'

I applied her lipstick, then Babs got up and stomped out. I watched her go. She seemed completely oblivious to the crash that was coming her way. How could she be so blind? She was usually so strong when it came to men. She had always had men falling over her, but she'd never had a proper relationship. She never allowed anyone in. Not friends or boyfriends. Once a relationship got past about two months and the guy started getting serious, she'd dump him. She was incapable of intimacy. I'd never really understood why. Was it because she had been spoilt? Being so much younger than me and my brother, she had been raised like an only child. Mum and Dad had showered her with attention and, of course, they'd been older and much less strict than they were with us. Babs had had them wrapped around her little finger from the word go and that hadn't changed.

Sean, my brother, and I had talked about it a lot. Neither of us really knew where Babs had come from. She was so different from us in so many ways. But somehow Gary had got to her. It was the first time I'd ever seen her fall for someone. I was really worried how she'd cope when he dumped her. She was so impulsive and bolshie that she was likely to smash a bottle over his head or call up his wife. I needed to keep a close eye on her and catch her when she fell.

While Babs was filming, I called James to ask if he'd found out who had sent the vibrator.

'I'm working on it,' he said, sounding cross. 'I've had a meeting with all the players and the staff and told them how appalled I was about the texts and the package that had been sent to my house. I didn't say what it was, but I implied it was something unsavoury. But none of the players would admit to it. And the captain, Johnny, just came into my office to tell me that he had personally asked each player and they had all strenuously denied knowing anything about it. He was quite upset. He said they were very happy with me as a coach and he really felt none of them would do anything stupid to wind me up.'

'Did you ask Ken, the guy you'd dropped?'

'Yes, but he swore he hadn't done anything.'

'Well, then, who was it?'

'Honestly, Emma, I don't know what to think.'

I smacked the wall with my palm. 'God, James, this is beginning to creep me out.'

'I know, but for now I have no other leads. I'll keep at it, though. I'll keep asking questions and see if I can figure it out.'

'OK. 'Bye.' I felt deflated. I'd been really hoping James would say that Ken was the guilty party and that he had fired him. Damn.

I really needed to talk to someone, so I sent Lucy a text. *Do u want to make up for not calling back on Sat?*

Yes please! So sorry.

I need to talk to you about smthg. U free for cuppa this avo? I'm finishing early.

Call around to the office. I can show u where I spend my life!

I got the tube to Cannon Street and walked up the road to number twenty-five. I went through the glass doors of Image Leasing into the plush reception area. It had a luxurious slate grey carpet and the walls were covered with big canvases of modern art. It was very impressive.

Lucy's door was open and she was sitting back in her chair, talking animatedly to a man of about fifty. 'Nice place you've got here,' I said.

She jumped up and came over to hug me, then introduced me to Paul, one of her partners. 'Lovely to meet you.' He shook my hand. 'Lucy tells me your husband is James Hamilton.'

'Yes.'

'Well, he's had a fantastic start at London Irish. I'm a big fan of the club and I can tell you we were relieved when we heard he was taking over. The last fellow was a disaster.'

Lucy handed me coffee in a delicate china cup. Everything about the office was stylish and spoke of success.

I smiled at Paul. 'Well, let's hope they continue to win. It makes my life a whole lot easier.'

He laughed. 'I can imagine. Now, Emma, I need to ask you, do you play golf?'

'No, there aren't enough hours in my day for that.'

'Ah, but you see that's the wrong way of looking at it. It's a fantastic de-stresser. You're out and about in the fresh air and you're thinking of nothing but your next shot. It's also excellent for networking. I play every Saturday morning. I was just trying to persuade Lucy to take it up.'

Lucy rolled her eyes. 'Can you imagine Donal's face if I announced I was going to play eighteen holes of golf on Saturday mornings?'

Paul came over to top up my coffee. 'Donal has to understand that Lucy works fourteen-hour days and she needs to decompress. We all do. I had heart problems a few years ago and the specialist said it's very important to have your fresh air and exercise and switch off for a few hours.'

Lucy patted his shoulder. 'That's all very well, Paul. You have a wife who will look after your children while you swan around the golf course for five hours. I have a husband who is waiting at the front door when I arrive back on Friday and literally throws my child into my arms and goes out to work.'

'No offence, Paul, but men just don't get it,' I said. 'James comes home late most nights. He can do that because I'm there to look after the children. But what if I had to work late? Who would look after the kids? A married man always has back-up – his wife. A married woman doesn't.'

Paul smiled. 'The solution is very simple – hire a nanny.'

'You can't leave your kids with a nanny twenty-four/seven. At some point they want to see a parent,' I replied.

'I'm always saying that working women need wives,' Lucy said. 'Donal's great and he looks after Serge when I'm away, but he resents it and disappears all weekend, which means I never get any time to myself. If I had a wife, she'd just accept I had to work away and would be happy to see me when I got home.'

I frowned. 'Hold on a minute, Lucy. If you had a wife and you worked away all week, I'm sure she would mind. No one wants to be alone all the time with the kids. It's hard work and it's lonely.'

There was a silence that lasted a fraction too long. Paul spoke up again. 'I commuted to Berlin for years. I wouldn't say my wife loved it, but she was able to afford a lot of help and she certainly enjoyed spending the money I was making. I don't think it's as difficult as you women make out.'

I put my hands up. 'Have you dealt with two simultaneous tantrums in a supermarket? Have you spent hours cooking a nutritious dinner only to have it spat out? Have you spent three hours freezing your arse off in the park, catatonic with boredom, while your kids go up and down a slide? Have you tried to scoop poo out of bathwater?'

Paul laughed. 'No, but nor has my wife. Like I said, she's always had help around the house.'

I was annoyed by his persistence. 'No matter how much help you have, your children still want you in the middle of the night when they have a bad dream. They still want you when they wet the bed, when they're sick or tired or when they've had a bad day at school. I understand that having a husband who earns a big salary would make your life easier, but it's still no picnic. I've stayed at home and I've worked and, I can tell you, working is a lot easier.'

Before Paul could respond, the receptionist came in and told him his conference call was about to begin.

Lucy went over and closed her door. 'So, what's up? You sounded very serious on the phone. Are you OK?'

I filled her in on all the recent drama. 'The thing is, Lucy, if it's not this guy Ken, who the hell is it? I'm beginning to think James might be cheating on me.'

'No! James wouldn't do that. He's mad about you.'

'Really? What about Mandy?'

Lucy paused. 'OK, he had a flirtation with someone, but that's all it was. Come on, haven't you flirted with someone since you've been married?'

I thought about it for a minute. Had I? A guest on *Afternoon with Amanda*, the show I used to work on, had caught my eye. He was the resident doctor on the show and advised callers on their medical problems. He was good-looking and very charismatic, and we had flirted a bit while I did his makeup, but it had been innocent enough. He had asked me out for coffee once and I'd said no. I'd been tempted to go, but it would have taken things in a direction I might have regretted.

'I suppose I did with one guy.'

'You see?' Lucy waved her hand in my direction. 'You're

not innocent either. But flirting is nothing. It's just reminding yourself that you're still a sexual being, that you're not just a boring mother and wife. It's a national pastime in Italy, so it really means nothing. You have to stop obsessing about Mandy. James didn't sleep with her. It was a passing fancy.'

It was easy for Lucy to say. She hadn't seen the way James had looked at Mandy. I knew that look. It was the way he'd looked at me when we'd first met. I still wondered whether, if he hadn't got fired, he would have had an affair with her. I'd never seen him like that with anyone else. It had frightened me.

'You're right, I do obsess about it. But the texts and the vibrator are real. I mean, they sent the vibrator to our house. Don't you think that's really weird?'

'That's one way of putting it. I think it's positively bizarre and a bit sick. The guy must be brain damaged.'

'What if it isn't a guy?'

Lucy frowned. 'OK, for the sake of argument, let's say James is sleeping with someone. What woman would send a vibrator to the wife of the man she's having an affair with? It just doesn't add up. It's too odd. It has to be some moron at the rugby club. You know what some of those rugby guys are like. They can be so immature, like hormonal teenagers.'

'I suppose so.' I wasn't sure what to think any more. The vibrator had blind-sided me. My head throbbed.

Paul popped his head round the door. 'Sorry to interrupt, Lucy, but we need you on this call.'

Lucy headed for the conference room and I headed home.

19

When I got home, I found Lara, Yuri and Claire sitting around the kitchen table making puppets from paper plates and coloured paper. The children were thrilled with their new toys.

'Look, Mummy, it's a ladybird,' Lara said.

'Mine's a scary spider,' Yuri said, waving it in my face.

'Wow, they're really brilliant,' I enthused. I was delighted that Claire was doing arts and crafts with the kids. It was something I rarely did. For some reason, whenever I planned something like that, the result was invariably dreadful and the kids lost interest. *Blue Peter* was never going to be knocking on my door, that was for sure.

'And we went to the shop and boughted blackberries and made a cake,' Yuri added.

'It's not a cake, it's a rumble,' Lara corrected him.

'Crumble? Yum! I love blackberry crumble and it's Daddy's favourite.'

'You seemed a bit hassled this morning, so we wanted to make something nice for you,' Claire said.

'That was so sweet of you.'

'Is everything OK? Can I help at all?' she asked.

I looked at my beautiful children, so happy and sweet and adorable. 'Everything's fine. I have something on my mind, but it's not a big deal.'

'Would you like me to heat up the crumble now, or would you prefer to wait and have it with James when he gets home?'

'I'll heat it up later. If I start it now, there'll be none left for him!'

Claire started tidying the kitchen table, putting the craft things away. 'I heard James's team won on Saturday. That's great. I guess it means he'll be working late a lot, preparing for the next game?'

'I hope not. The deal was that he'd get through that game, then start keeping more regular hours.'

'Well, if you need me to do extra to help you out, I'd be happy to. By the way, I made a lasagne for your dinner. It's in the fridge.'

'Thanks, Claire. I honestly don't know what I'd do without you.' She really was fantastic. I was too tired to cook anything and now it was all done.

'It was easy to do. I also finished the ironing.'

I smiled at her. 'Brilliant. James says you're by far the best ironer we've ever had.'

Claire blushed. 'I actually like ironing,' she said. 'I find it very soothing.'

Soothing? I found it really frustrating. Just when you got one side of a shirt crease-free, another crease would appear on the other. It drove me nuts.

'How are things with you?' I asked. 'Were you out this weekend at all?'

She stacked the children's dinner plates in the dishwasher. 'I'm kind of seeing a guy actually,' she said shyly.

'Oh, my God, that's fantastic! Is he nice?' I was thrilled for her.

'Well, I'm taking it slowly. We're still getting to know each other.'

'I'm so pleased for you.' I noticed she was wearing new red trainers. It was a start: maybe she'd begin making more of an effort with her appearance now she had a boyfriend. 'If you ever want me to make you up for a date or anything, just ask. I'd be happy to do it.'

'Thanks so much,' she said.

The doorbell rang and I went to answer it. An oddly familiar woman was standing outside in a raincoat.

'Emma?' she said, holding out a hand.

'Yes.'

'I'm Maggie, Claire's mum.'

'Oh, right. Hello, nice to meet you.' I ushered her in out of the rain. She was an older version of Claire.

'I was working late at Poppy's and I thought I'd call in and walk home with Claire.'

'No problem. I must say we're so happy with Claire – she's just wonderful.'

'Oh, that's good.' She looked pleased. 'So, everything's going well, then?'

'Couldn't be better.'

'Poppy tells me your husband is a rugby coach. That's exciting.'

'He's with London Irish.' I didn't think it was so exciting any more.

'Does that mean he's around much during the day?'

'What?' I looked at Maggie, and then I understood. She was worried about Claire being around an older man after her bad experience with the teacher.

'My husband is hardly ever here, to be honest. He works very long hours. I did notice that Claire was terribly shy around him in the beginning, but she's coming out of her shell a little more each week. James thinks she's great too.'

When we walked into the kitchen and Claire saw her mother, she frowned. 'What are you doing here?' she asked, in a not too friendly tone.

'I thought we could go home together,' Maggie said. 'It's getting dark earlier and I don't like you being alone.'

'I don't need a chaperone, Mum. You're like a stalker,' Claire snapped.

I could see that Claire found her mother overbearing and I felt for her – my own mother drove me to drink sometimes. But I also understood why Maggie felt protective of her. I thought it was sweet that she had come round to walk her home. Claire's reaction reminded me that she was still a teenager – we'd all gone through that phase of being embarrassed by our mothers.

'Are you Claire's mummy?' Lara asked.

'Yes, pet, I am.' Maggie leant down to talk to her.

'You looks just like her,' Lara said.

'And you look like your mummy,' Maggie pointed out.

'Yes, but Babs said I'm lucky cos I don't have Mummy's yucky hair. I have beautifuller yellow hair like Babs.'

Maggie seemed taken aback.

'My sister's a bit mad,' I explained.

'I doesn't look like Mummy or Daddy cos I comed from an orf'nage, but I'm the same as them in all the other ways,' Yuri said.

Maggie went over to him. 'I've heard all about you. Claire is always telling me what great children you are.'

'I love Claire,' Lara said, going over to hug her.

'Would you like a cup of tea, Maggie?' I offered.

'No, thank you. We'll be off now and leave you in peace.' Maggie picked up Claire's coat and bag and ushered her out.

Claire whispered to me, as Maggie left the room, 'Don't say anything about my boyfriend. I don't want her to find out.'

I winked at her. 'Your secret is safe with me.'

20

I woke up on Wednesday morning feeling rested for the first time in days. Until last night I hadn't slept properly since the vibrator incident on Saturday. Apart from a brief nightmare, when I'd dreamt Babs had killed Gary with an axe and gone to prison, I'd had a good night.

By this evening, Gary would know about the baby and I suspected my sister would have discovered what a scumbag he really was.

I turned to James. 'Don't forget I need you home early. Babs is telling Gary and we both know what his reaction is going to be.'

James rolled out of bed and headed for the shower. 'It's not going to be pretty. I wouldn't be surprised if Babs stabbed him in the face with her fork or something.'

'Jesus, James, don't say that. I'm worried enough as it is.'

'Sorry!' He closed the bathroom door and I could hear the shower running.

His phone beeped. I checked the message: *I am H4Y. IWS*.

Christ, what was this? I had no idea what the texts even meant, so I called the one person who would be able to decipher them: Babs.

'It's eight o'clock in the bloody morning so this'd better be an emergency,' Babs croaked. 'You know we don't have to be in until eleven today.'

'I need help. James just got another text and I don't understand it. It's all coded and I need to know what it means.' I read the text out.

Babs sighed. '"H4Y" is obviously "Hot for You". And "IWS" is "I Want Sex". I'm going back to sleep now. Do not call me unless someone is dying. In fact, don't call unless someone is actually dead.' Babs hung up and I sat in bed, waiting for James to come in from the bathroom.

As I was waiting the door burst open and Yuri came in with a pile of post. He was waving something around.

'What have you got there? I asked, still distracted by the text.

'It's a present, Mummy.' He put the post on the bed and concentrated on the package. He ripped the paper off the 'present'. Something fell out. 'Wow!' He sounded thrilled. 'Come on, Mummy, play with me. You be the bad guy and I'll be the policeman and I'll put these clickies on you.'

I peered at his hand. Jesus Christ, he was holding a pair of leather handcuffs. I grabbed them, but he refused to let go. 'No! I founded them, they're mine.'

I ripped them out of his hand and grabbed the paper. There was a printed label, addressed to Mrs Emma Hamilton and a card that said: *J loves using these on me.*

A sob escaped from my mouth, but it was drowned by Yuri wailing, 'Give them back to *meeeeeeee.*'

The bathroom door burst open. 'What in the name of God is going on?' James demanded.

I threw the handcuffs at him. 'These, James! And this text!' I shouted, shoving his phone up to his nose.

'I hate you, Mummy! You're so mean!' Yuri roared, as he tried to snatch the handcuffs from James.

James read the message and clung firmly to the handcuffs, despite Yuri's best efforts to take them from him. He looked gobsmacked. 'Emma . . . I don't . . . What the hell is this?'

Yuri was winding up for a full tantrum. I needed to get him out of the room. 'Yuri,' I said firmly, 'go downstairs and get yourself some crisps.'

'Really?' He was so shocked to be getting crisps before school that he forgot about the tantrum.

'Yes.'

'*Cooooooool!*' He ran out of the room.

To James, I said, 'Would you like to explain to me what this means? Filthy texts and now handcuffs! Jesus Christ, what the bloody hell is going on?' My heart was pounding in my chest.

James sat down heavily on the bed and stared at the card. 'I haven't got a clue. I don't understand any of this. It's completely insane. Who is doing this?'

I stood up. I didn't want to be near James. I was so angry with him. He had brought this on us. It was clear now that it wasn't one of the rugby guys, unless they were insane, so it must be a woman. It had to be someone who was in love with James and wanted to get rid of me. She had our address, she knew my name. She was sending porn to our house in front of our children. What the bloody hell had James done? Whatever it was, it was now invading all of our lives.

'You must have some idea who this is,' I yelled. 'You have *got* to know who this nutter could be. Who have you been talking to? Who have you been flirting with? Who have you been having sex with?'

James threw his hands into the air. 'I have no idea. I swear to you, I haven't even looked at another woman. I don't speak to other women. All I've bloody done since we moved here is work, eat and sleep. I've been one hundred per cent focused on proving myself to the management so I get to keep my job.'

I grabbed his arm. 'You *must* have led someone on. A woman doesn't do something crazy like this without being provoked. This is *Fatal Attraction* stuff. You've brought this on yourself and me and your family.' I began to cry.

James tried to put his arm around me, but I shook it off. 'Emma, I swear on our children's lives I have no idea who this is. I'm just as shocked and furious as you are.'

My whole body was shaking with rage and fear and confusion. 'Figure out who the hell it is and then tell the lunatic to *stop*. And if you've had sex with someone and are trying to pretend you didn't, I swear to you, I will kill you. Confess now, because if I find out you're lying, I will NEVER forgive you. Are you having an affair?'

'No, I bloody am not,' James barked. 'I'm as much in the dark as you are. I'm horrified. Do you think I'd knowingly allow someone to do this to you, or our children? I have no idea how any of it happened. I don't understand why someone would do this.'

'Really, James? Are all those late nights just about rugby?'

'YES! I need to make this work. I can't lose another job. I'm trying to provide for my family. Since when did that become a crime?'

'So who the hell is doing this?' I screamed at him.

James grabbed me by the shoulders and forced me to look at him. His voice was low and urgent. 'I swear to you I have no idea who this person is. I can't even think of a woman I've had a five-minute chat with since we moved to London. There is no one.'

'What about Harriet in the club?'

'I barely see her and she's a very normal person, happily engaged *and* she's pregnant. I don't see her as being capable of something like this. Emma, you have to believe me, I just don't know.'

He let go of me and stood back. I looked at my husband, the man I loved, the man I had agreed to spend the rest of my life with. I felt only doubt and anger. This was the first time in my marriage that I had ever felt so vulnerable. I could feel a tightness in my chest. 'The problem is, James, I don't believe you. This cannot have come from nowhere. There's something you're not telling me.'

'I don't know what else to say to you, Emma. I'm as confused as you are. I have no idea why someone would send sextexts to me and crazy stuff like this to you.'

'I don't believe you,' I said, tears pouring down my cheeks now.

The door burst open. 'I want crisps too,' Lara demanded.

I quickly wiped my face and stuck on a smile. I was glad of the interruption. I needed to get away from James. I needed to think.

Somehow we managed to get the children fed and ready for the day. I was taking them to school as I was starting work late. James tried to kiss me goodbye but I pulled away from him.

'I'll call you later. I love you, Emma, and we'll figure this out,' he said, as he left. I didn't answer.

As we walked to school, Yuri brought up the 'present' again. 'Mummy, when I come home I want to play with the clickies.' Damn, I was hoping he'd forgotten about the bloody handcuffs.

'What clickies?' Lara asked.

'The things that the police put on bad guys. Like the sheriff in *Scooby-Doo*.'

'I want to play with them.' Lara pouted.

'Forget about them. They're not for kids,' I said.

'Who gaved them to you?' Yuri asked. 'It's not your birthday, is it, Mummy?'

'No, pet, it isn't.'

'Why did you get a present, then?'

I sighed. 'It wasn't a present, it was kind of a joke. A really stupid joke. Now just forget about them.'

'I didn't see them. It's not fair. I want to see them and play with them.' Lara was relentless.

'Lara, I'm warning you. I do not want to hear another word about those stupid things. Just drop it,' I shouted.

Lara's eyes welled. 'You're a meanie. I hate you. You're always grumpy. I love Claire. She's nice and she never shouts. I wish she was my mummy.'

I felt as if I'd been stabbed. Lara knew exactly how to hurt me.

'I'm not always grumpy,' I said, feebly defending myself.

'You are grumpy, Mummy, and you're very grumpy to Daddy,' Yuri joined in. 'I hearded you shouting at him. Claire never shouts and she likes playing Lego with me and you never do.'

I willed myself not to cry. I felt really guilty for snapping at the children and upsetting them. But I was angry too – furious with James for bringing all this weirdness into our lives.

Taking a deep breath, I forced myself to sound calm. I crouched down. 'I'm sorry I was snappy and I'm sorry I was grumpy too.'

'Why are you cross with Daddy?' Lara asked. 'He looked sad today.'

'Because he . . .' I hesitated. I needed to tread carefully. Despite my anger towards my husband, these two little people thought their father was perfect. It wasn't fair to criticize him in front of them. 'Because he's working too hard and I think he should come home and spend more time with us.'

Yuri's smooth, pale brow creased. 'But, Mummy, he has to work hard. He has to make his team the bestest so they can win the big prize.'

I opened my arms and pulled my two precious babies into a bear hug. 'I love you, guys.'

Thankfully, Lara and Yuri hugged me back. 'I love you too, Mummy, but I love Claire best.' Lara drove the knife further into my heart.

'I love Daddy the most,' Yuri told me, twisting it.

I wanted to cry. What a morning! I dropped them off at the gate and headed straight for the tube. I wanted to get away from the school and sit down in a coffee shop to gather my thoughts before work. I was in a state. I needed to get a grip on my emotions.

As I sat in Caffè Nero, near Putney Bridge tube station, I went over the morning's events. Although my initial reaction was that James must be having an affair, Lucy was right: why would someone he was sleeping with send stuff to my house? Unless she was a complete nutter, of course, but then, I couldn't imagine James having sex with a crazy person. Besides that, he seemed genuinely shocked and upset by it all. Should I trust him? He wasn't acting like a man having an affair: he always left his phone on the table for me to read his texts if I felt like it. But he was working late a lot . . . Then again, so did a lot of people.

I rubbed my eyes. I felt exhausted and it was only ten a.m. I decided to give James the benefit of the doubt. I wouldn't jump to conclusions. I wouldn't let this deranged joker ruin our lives. Whoever it was, he or she was obviously trying to frighten me. I wouldn't let them win. I straightened my shoulders, and picked up my bag. Onwards and upwards . . .

21

I wanted to talk to Babs about it, but when I got to work and saw how pale and stressed she looked, I decided not to say anything. She was clearly dreading telling Gary later. I tiptoed around her all day, glad of the distraction of work. I pushed my problems to the back of my mind and focused on doing a good job.

When it was time to go home, I went over and hugged her. 'Good luck tonight,' I whispered in her ear.

Babs shrugged me off. 'I don't need luck.'

I took her by the shoulders and forced her to look at me. 'Babs, he might not take it well. If he doesn't, call me. OK? I'm here for you. We can sort this out with or without Gary.'

My delusional little sister took a step back from me. 'For the millionth time, Emma, it's all going to be fine. He adores me.'

As she turned to pick up her coat, I saw that her hands were shaking.

I was walking towards Manor House tube station, feeling worn out from the whole sorry day, when I heard someone calling my name. I spun around and saw, with surprise, Henry pushing his way through the rush-hour crowds, waving at me. I realized I was trembling. The strange voice had frightened me. God, I was a nervous wreck.

'I thought it was you,' he said breathlessly, when he reached me.

'Is this where you work?' I asked.

'My office is on Devonshire Square. I'm just coming from a meeting with a client.'

'Oh, right.'

'So, how are you?'

'Uhm . . . OK, I guess.' To my absolute horror, I began to cry.

'Gosh, Emma, are you all right?' Henry put a comforting arm around my shoulders.

'I'm fine – I'm so sorry.'

Henry handed me a linen handkerchief. I think he was the only forty-five-year-old man who still carried them.

'I'm so sorry,' I said, wiping my face and ruining his clean handkerchief with mascara. 'I've just had a bad day.'

'When I have bad days, I always find a brandy helps. How does that sound?' he asked gently.

I gave him a watery smile. 'It sounds perfect, but can I have wine instead?'

'Absolutely.' Henry steered me into a pub across the road, settled me into a comfy corner seat and got the drinks.

He handed me a large glass of white wine. 'Can I help in any way? I hate to see you so upset.'

I took a deep sip. 'It's silly, really,' I said, willing myself to stop blubbing. 'It's just this thing with James. He's been getting these texts.' I looked down, embarrassed. 'Sextexts, quite explicit, actually. And then a vibrator and handcuffs were sent to our house, addressed to me. I don't understand what's going on. At first we thought it was one of the London Irish players messing around, but now I think it's someone else and . . . and I don't know what to think.'

Henry was taken aback. 'Sounds very odd indeed. What does James think?'

'He says he has no idea but . . .' I hesitated, took another sip of my wine and decided to be honest. 'Henry, I'm beginning to wonder if he's having an affair.'

Henry shook his head. 'I doubt that very much. James is devoted to you and the children. He's certainly never mentioned anything to me. I know men can stray, but I also know my little brother. He's just not that kind of a man. Now, about those texts and parcels. Having spent years at boarding school, I've seen how utterly moronic men can be, especially when they wind each other up. Perhaps one of the younger players has just taken the joke too far.'

'James has asked them repeatedly. He even called a special meeting to confront them and demand that it stop. But they all denied it and the captain says he thinks they're telling the truth. I'd been telling myself that was all it was, even after the vibrator appeared, but after this morning . . . it just doesn't add up. It has to be a woman.'

Henry nodded thoughtfully. 'It does happen, I suppose. I had a case a few years back of a woman who became obsessed with and stalked a married man.'

'Was he having an affair with her?' I asked immediately.

'Not at all. In fact, John barely knew her. She worked in the local shop where he bought his newspaper every day. She was in her fifties and seemed perfectly nice and normal. John would have a little chat with her in the mornings about the weather or what-have-you, but that was it. Suddenly he was receiving text messages of a sexual nature and emails. She sent love letters to his house. She sent flowers and chocolates to his office. She then began sending emails to his boss describing their sexual exploits in graphic detail.'

I couldn't see how this story was supposed to help cheer me up. 'What did he do?' I asked, almost afraid to hear the answer.

'The poor fellow became paranoid and began to suspect

all the women in his office. He accused his secretary, who went straight to HR and John was in very hot water at work. He almost lost his job. He never imagined it was this older lady from the corner shop.'

'But what happened? How did he find out it was her?'

'She eventually called in to John's wife and told her she was having an affair with her husband and that she was pregnant with their lovechild. Thankfully, due to the stalker's advanced years, the wife knew this couldn't be possible and she called the police.'

'She actually confronted his wife in person?' I felt nauseous. 'Did she go to jail?'

'No, there wasn't enough evidence. Unfortunately, John had thrown away the letters and deleted most of the emails and texts, so we were only able to get a barring order.'

'And then did she stop? Did she stay away?'

Henry lowered his voice. 'She was fired from her job. The owner of the shop was appalled when he found out what she'd been doing. When he fired her, she flew into a terrible rage and tried to stab him with a pair of scissors. After that we had a stronger case and she was sent to a psychiatric hospital.'

'Bloody hell, Henry! How is this reassuring?'

Henry smiled ruefully. 'Probably a little too much detail. But the reason I'm telling you, Emma, is to show you that there are lonely women out there who can become fixated on nice friendly men, of which James is one. I would bet my life on him not having an affair, and the fact that this person has been posting things addressed to you is most peculiar. If it is a woman, she has to be unhinged in some way and living out a fantasy through James. And, like John, it could be something as simple as the fact that he buys his newspaper or his coffee from her.'

I looked at him in despair. 'Then how do we figure it out?'

'Get James to think of all the women – even the much older ones – he speaks to or even waves at during the week. It doesn't matter how unlikely a woman seems, think it through and see if it fits. But don't accuse anyone until you're absolutely sure or you could find yourselves in a lot of trouble. The best thing to do is keep the evidence – and do *not* respond to any of the messages.'

'We responded in the beginning because we thought it was a joke.'

'Well, don't respond any more. In most cases the individual will get bored when they receive no reaction and stop.'

Henry's phone rang. He looked at the number and sighed. 'It's the War Office.' He answered, and Imogen's booming voice bellowed into the earpiece so loudly that even I could hear her.

'I'll be at the stables until six thirty. I need you to pick up some fillet steaks on the way home. Don't go to Hardy's for them, go to Kavanagh's, and make sure you tell him they're for me. Under no circumstances are you to bring home small ones. Get medium to large. Don't forget Thomas's recital is tonight. We must be there at eight sharp. We also need . . .'

When she finally paused for breath, Henry said, 'Imogen, can I call you back? I'm just having a quick drink with Emma.'

'Emma who?' she barked.

'My sister-in-law.'

'What on earth . . .?'

'We bumped into each other at the tube,' he explained.

'Why are you drinking with her?'

I tried to pretend I couldn't hear her foghorn voice. Poor Henry looked embarrassed. 'I'll call you back in five minutes.'

'What are you two talking about?' she demanded.

223

'SEX!' I wanted to shout, just to wind her up. But out of respect for Henry, I kept my mouth shut.

'Just this and that. I'll call you back,' he said, for the third time.

'Don't bother, Henry. Unlike you and Emma, I don't have time to sit around chit-chatting. I'm far too busy.'

Busy sitting on horses and driving everyone within a mile radius mad, I thought grumpily.

'All right. We can chat later. I'll send Emma your best.' Henry tried to cover his wife's rudeness.

'I hope I didn't get you into trouble,' I said.

'Not at all, Emma. Imogen can be a little, ah . . . abrupt at times.'

'Abrupt' was the nicest word I could think of to describe Imogen. Henry really was a saint. 'Thanks for being so nice to me. I'm so sorry about offloading all of this on you. I'm afraid you caught me at just the wrong moment.'

Henry squeezed my hand. 'Emma, my dear, it's always a pleasure to see you. I'm delighted we bumped into each other and had this chat. Now, please do remember that James is the best of men. You know you can trust him. He would never do anything to hurt you or the children, of that I'm sure.'

'I'll try, Henry, but marriages do get stale and husbands and wives do wander. Even my mother admitted that your forties are a difficult time and affairs happen.'

Henry polished off his brandy. 'The way I see it, marriage is a contract where you commit to being with someone. Then when you have children it's your responsibility to give them the best life possible.'

He was old-fashioned in his ways, but he was a true gentleman. It was such a pity he hadn't married someone nicer. He deserved a sweet wife who loved him, not a sergeant major who bossed him around.

'You and James have something very special,' Henry said, looking into his glass. 'You don't just have a marriage, you have a true friendship. It's worth protecting and fighting for. Don't let some unhinged individual ruin that.'

He was right: James wasn't just my husband, he was my best friend. We talked about everything. I trusted him and valued his opinion above all others. I'd be lost without James, completely lost. I was going to give him the benefit of the doubt, go home and work this out.

We stood up and walked out of the pub. As we parted ways at the tube station, I reached up and kissed Henry on the cheek. 'Thank you, Henry. You have no idea how much this conversation's helped me. I owe you one.'

'My dear girl,' he said, with a grin, 'that's what family is for.'

22

At home the house was tidy, the children fed and happy, as usual. I could have cried with relief. I felt utterly weary and was dying to have a hot bath and a glass of wine. Once I had the children in bed, I would do just that.

Yuri and Lara ran over and hugged me. Thankfully, they had forgotten they hated me. That was the wonderful thing about kids: they were endlessly forgiving. I could learn something from them. I held them close and told them I loved them. They were like my very own Valium. I felt calmer and happier once I'd hugged them.

Claire was wearing a pair of skinny jeans. I realized I'd never seen her legs before – they were always hidden inside oversized tracksuit bottoms. She had great legs, long and slim. I also noticed she was wearing mascara. Oh, to be young and in love, I thought, looking at her radiant face.

'Are you seeing your boyfriend tonight? How's it going?' I asked her.

Claire smiled. 'Yes, I am. It's going well, thanks. I think he really likes me.'

'Of course he does. What's not to like? You're great,' I enthused.

I heard the front door bang. The next moment James came into the room and dropped his bag on the floor.

'You're home early.' I didn't look directly at him. I felt awkward after this morning.

He approached me. 'I decided to come home and give the children their bath so that you can have a break.'

He was trying to catch my eye. I remembered what Henry had said and looked up at him. He had black circles under his eyes and his shoulders were hunched. I willed myself to be nice. 'That's great, thanks.'

'No problem. I'm happy to help.'

We were like two strangers. I didn't want Claire to sense the tension so I tried to act normally. 'Guess what? Claire has a boyfriend,' I said. 'And it's going really well.'

Claire went as red as her new runners.

'I presume he's a Liverpool fan?' James said, with a half-grin. He was trying too.

'Of course he is,' she said, and smiled.

'Did you see the game this weekend? They were robbed.'

'I was gutted,' Claire agreed.

'Hopefully they'll beat Newcastle this weekend.'

'If Gerrard is back from injury, I reckon they'll beat them easily.'

'That's the spirit.' James slapped her on the shoulder. He was being overly jovial, but Claire didn't seem to notice. 'By the way, your lasagne the other night was fantastic, best I've ever had. If you ever tire of childcare, you could open a restaurant.'

'Don't even think of encouraging her into another profession,' I said. 'She has to stay right here and keep us all in order.'

Claire smiled at me. 'There's no worry of me leaving this house,' she said. 'I love it here.'

'Well, thank you so much for your work today,' I said. 'The house looks great and the children are as happy as ever.'

As Claire was picking up her bag to go, she turned to me. 'Oh, I almost forgot, Emma. When we got back from school there was something on the doorstep for you.' She pointed to a small parcel on the side-table. It was addressed to Emma Hamilton. I felt sick.

'Who delivered it?' James asked tersely.

Claire looked surprised by the change in his tone. 'I didn't see. It was just here when I got back with the children.' She looked from James to me and back again. 'Is everything all right?'

'We've been getting deliveries from some fruit-cake lately and they're very upsetting for Emma,' James replied.

'Who's sending them?'

'We don't know.' James's jaw was set.

Claire looked puzzled. 'That sounds a bit weird,' she said.

I opened the parcel with trembling hands. Inside, in pink wrapping paper, there was a whip. The card read: *James loves to tie me up and whip me. He's a naughty boy.* I let it fall to the floor and began to cry.

James swore and Claire looked startled. She came over to me. 'Are you all right?'

I pushed back my shoulders and wiped my eyes with a hand. 'I'm fine, thanks. Look, Claire, you head off home. I'm just a bit upset, but I'll be fine.'

I ran upstairs and locked myself into the bathroom. I sat on the floor and stared into space. I could hear Claire saying goodbye to James and the front door closing. I rested my head on the side of the bath. James came up and asked me to open the door, but I didn't answer him. He talked through the door: he kept saying he didn't understand . . . and why . . . and who . . . I wanted so much to believe him, but my head was aching with all the possibilities. Was he innocent? Was I being a fool?

As I soaked in a hot bath, I could hear James putting the children to bed. I heard him reading *Goldilocks* to Lara and *The Gruffalo* to Yuri. When the house was quiet, I dragged myself out of the bath and put on my dressing-gown. I opened the door and found James sitting on the floor with a bottle of wine and two glasses.

'Drink?' He offered me a glass. I gulped it down. At this rate I'd be an alcoholic by the end of the week.

James spoke quietly but firmly. 'Emma, I need you to believe me. I do not know what is going on and who is doing this. When I find out, I'm going to kill them.'

I decided to tell him about Henry. 'I bumped into Henry today. I was upset and ended up telling him everything. He said he had a client who was stalked by this older woman who sold him the newspaper every day. He said she seemed nice and normal but it turned out she was obsessed with this guy and stalked him. She ended up being violent.'

'I read the newspaper online,' James attempted a joke.

'I'm scared, James. This person knows where we live and she wants to get rid of me. What if she attacks me – or, worse, the kids?' I shuddered. 'She could throw acid in my face or something. It's really scary, James.'

He reached over and hugged me to him. A phone buzzed. We looked down at his, but it was mine. *I hope u liked my gift. Go back to Ireland u stupid cow. James is mine.*

I held my hand to my mouth to stop myself screaming. Now she had my mobile number as well! 'James!' I cried.

James had turned green, but he was trying to look composed. 'Don't worry, darling. Don't panic. I'll call Henry and see if he knows a police officer we can talk to or a detective. I'll stop this, I promise. I won't let anyone hurt you or the children. We will not let this person ruin our lives. We just have to figure out who the hell it is.'

I knew I wasn't supposed to reply. Henry had specifically said not to, but I didn't care, I texted back: *Fuck off you psycho.*

Another message came back: *I'll never go away. NEVER.*

23

As I turned the corner to go into the studio, I heard my name being called. I spun around and saw Babs frantically waving at me from a taxi. She was wearing dark glasses, even though it was raining.

'Where the hell have you been?' she shouted. 'I've been calling you all night and you never bothered to answer me. What happened to "I'll be there for you, Babs, I'll look after you, Babs"?'

Oh, God. James had made me turn my phone off after the text so I wouldn't be tempted to reply again. I felt terrible. 'I'm so sorry. Are you OK?' I could see she wasn't. Babs was wearing a tracksuit and had no makeup on. I hadn't even known she owned a tracksuit. I strongly suspected that behind the sunglasses were puffy red eyes. Things with Gary must have gone very badly.

'Get in, for God's sake,' she ordered. 'I don't want anyone to see me.'

I climbed into the taxi and turned to look at her properly. Even with the glasses on, she looked terrible. Her face was drained of any colour. I reached over and pulled her glasses down.

'Jesus! That bad?' I asked. Her eyes were completely swollen from crying.

She snapped them back up. 'The bastard doesn't want the baby. He told me to get rid of it.'

'The shit!'

'I know, but I'm not doing it. I told him I was having the baby with or without him.'

'What did he say to that?'

'He said if I ever told anyone it was his, he'd deny it. He said people in the industry think I'm a slut and no one will believe me.'

God, he was a real low-life.

'I told him I could force him to have a paternity test, like Liz Hurley did to that millionaire guy who tried to deny her kid.'

'Good for you. How did he react to that?'

'He told me that if I did he'd make sure I never worked in TV again. That I'd end up in a council house with a screaming kid and no money.'

'How dare he?' I was shocked. I wanted to kill the bastard.

Babs bit her lip. 'Well, you were right, Emma. Gary is an arsehole. He had no intention of leaving his wife and I was just another notch in his belt. Here's your big chance to say, "I told you so."' She gazed at me anxiously.

'I'd never say that. I'm sick for you.'

She tried to look defiant, but her voice shook. 'There is no way in hell I'm going to let him ruin my life.'

I took her hands in mine. 'Babs, I promise I'll help you through all of this. He is a despicable human being, but what he doesn't know is that you have a supportive family who love you and who'll look after you.'

Babs then did something she had never done before – she threw her arms around my neck and hugged me. I was so shocked that at first I froze, and then I hugged her back.

'You can't go to work today. I'll call in sick for you. You need some rest,' I said.

'I already called. I told Karen that both you and I have food poisoning.'

'What?'

'I don't want to be on my own today, Emma. Last night was the longest night of my life. I couldn't sleep or even sit still. I tried your phone a zillion times and then I tried James, but his phone was switched off too. I almost cracked and called Mum.'

I gasped. 'You didn't, though, did you?'

She rolled her eyes. 'I haven't completely lost my mind.'

I was relieved. We needed to think this through and come up with a plan of how and when to tell Mum about the baby. It had to be managed with an incredible degree of delicacy. Mum was not going to react well to the news that her youngest child was pregnant with a married man's baby and that said married man was denying the child was his.

'OK, well, let's get you home and tucked up in bed. You're exhausted. After you've had a sleep we can talk about how to deal with Gary . . . and everything.'

Babs crossed her arms. 'I know exactly how I'd like to deal with Gary. I'd like to cut his penis off and feed it to a pack of hungry wolves.'

I smiled. It was good to see that her spirit hadn't been totally crushed. 'Well, let's try and think of legal ways to make his life miserable. I don't think prison is the best place to bring up a child.'

Babs smiled wanly. 'Let's go.'

When we arrived at Babs's apartment, I sat her on the couch with a cup of sugary tea and some chocolate biscuits while I changed her bed. I always think that fresh sheets are one of life's great comforts. Then I tucked her in and closed the curtains.

'Now, have a good sleep and we'll talk when you wake up,' I said, closing the door softly.

'Emma?' she called.

'Yes?'

'Will you stay with me until I nod off?'

That was what Lara often asked me to do. 'Of course,' I said, going over to her bed and lying down beside her.

She looked so young and vulnerable, tucked under her duvet. For all her bluster, she was just a twenty-seven-year-old girl who had fallen in love with the wrong man and was now going to be a single mother. Her life would change for ever. I stroked her brow and she was asleep within minutes, exhausted physically and emotionally from the horror of finding out her beloved Gary was actually a total scumbag.

While Babs slept, I tidied up her messy apartment. Clothes were strewn everywhere. Her fridge contained only bottles of Prosecco and Corona Light, and chocolate bars. Her cupboards were almost bare, save for a few packets of biscuits and a box of Cheerios. Suddenly my diet didn't seem so bad.

She'd have to learn to cook for the baby. It was all very well for her to eat out most nights or order takeaways, but a baby needed proper food. I'd have to buy her some books and get her to practise a few basic recipes.

Among her post, most of which was stuffed into an overflowing drawer, I found an open bank statement. Babs was six thousand pounds in debt on her Visa card. She'd need to start looking after her finances, too. I'd get Sean to talk to her about how to manage her money. I wasn't the best at it myself, but I'd never run up Visa bills like that.

As I went around the small apartment – estate agents would describe it as *bijou* – I realized Babs had a lot of work ahead of her if she was to become a responsible parent. But it would do her good to grow up and have to think about someone other than herself. Maybe it would be the making of her. But I was worried about her career. Gary could cause a lot of problems for her if he wanted to play nasty. She'd have to be very careful with him. She didn't want him bad-mouthing her about town.

It was all so complicated. Both of our lives were a mess. Maybe we'd end up moving in together and raising our children side by side. Or even living back home with Mum and Dad in Dublin, in a kind of commune-type environment, sharing child-rearing and chores. No! That definitely wouldn't work. I could never live with Babs. We'd kill each other.

While Babs slept, I poured myself a large glass of Prosecco. Drinking at ten in the morning was not something I normally did, but today I needed something to take the edge off. My emotions were dangerously close to the surface and I wanted to calm down.

I had never seen my sister like this before, so vulnerable and upset. Gary was some jerk. I hated him. But I was glad to hear Babs talking about going back to work. She'd need to keep busy. It was all that was keeping me going these days.

I went to her bedroom and peeped inside – she was fast asleep. Good. She'd be able to think more clearly after a rest. I sat on the couch and finished my Prosecco. Babs's laptop was on the coffee-table. I decided to go to the *Daily Mail* showbiz website, one of my guilty pleasures. I found looking at the photos of celebrities mind-numbing in a good way.

I was flicking through the pictures, marvelling at Heidi Klum's body, when I saw the word 'stalker' out of the corner of my eye. I sat up and clicked on the link. It was a story about some country singer I'd never heard of being stalked by a crazy fan. She had just got a restraining order to stop him following her.

I wondered if there were other articles on the same theme and typed 'stalker' into Google. Oh, my God, seventy-four million results! I decided to narrow it down to 'being stalked'. More than three million. Apparently stalking was an epidemic. How had I not known it was such a problem?

I clicked on some of the stories and found one in the *Guardian* about a man who was stalked by a woman he'd only met twice. I read on . . . Oh, he'd slept with her on the second meeting and then she'd told him she loved him and stalked him for months. Had James done that? Had he slept with someone and then she'd gone crazy? I clicked on another article that said, 'Are you being stalked?' and gave a list of eight things that meant you were. Five matched my experience.

My chest was tightening again as the realization that I was being stalked sank in. These people were dangerous. Some of the stories said that the victim ended up as an alcoholic – I immediately vowed to stop using alcohol as a crutch – depressed, or harmed. Some stalkers attacked their victims, some of whom ended up dead. My heart was pounding. What was I going to do? How was I going to stop this?

I decided that information was key. I kept searching and found a website that linked into a chat room. It was all about how to get rid of your lover's wife. The women suggested sending sextexts to drive a wedge between the couple. I gasped. That was exactly what was happening to me! I wondered if she was on this chat room. She must be, chatting away to all the nutters and finding ways to get rid of me. It was terrifying.

I forced myself to read on. Another suggestion was to send things to the wife's workplace or home to freak her out. I was reading about my own life! Maybe this was our stalker, telling all the other freaks how to get rid of other wives. They all agreed that men with children were harder to push into leaving their families. They said you had to be more aggressive with those wives to get rid of them. How much more aggressive? I held my breath and read on. One woman suggested slashing the wife's tyres, another recommended sending hard-core porn to her work, and another said you should harm her.

I tried not to cry. I'd had the texts, the parcels. All that was left was for her to harm me. I had never felt so terrified.

'What are you looking at?'

I jumped. I hadn't heard Babs come out of her bedroom. I snapped the laptop shut. 'Just googling the *Daily Mail* showbiz page,' I lied. 'How are you feeling? Did you sleep well?'

She nodded. 'Better, thanks.'

She flopped down beside me, pulled a chocolate bar from her bag and began to eat it.

'Babs, you need to make some changes,' I said. 'You've probably only got about seven months until the baby is born so you need to eat more healthily and look after yourself properly. The baby needs less sugar and more vegetables and fruit. You drink about ten cups of coffee a day and you'll have to cut down on that too. Maybe you could switch to decaf and try green tea.'

Babs said nothing as she shovelled another square of chocolate into her mouth.

'You'll need to start saving, too. Babies are expensive. I can help you out with buggies, cots and clothes, but you need to get your finances in order. You're going to have to stop buying clothes and shoes and put money aside for the baby.'

Babs got up from the couch. 'I'm going to have a shower.'

She clearly wasn't ready to face the realities of being a mother. I'd leave her for now, but sooner or later she was going to have to accept the stark fact that babies need minding.

She closed the bathroom door and I logged out of the stalker sites on her laptop. As I switched it off, my hands were shaking from the shock of what I had seen and read. I'd have to watch my back. Someone was out to get me.

24

By the time I got home that night, I had calmed down a bit. But I was still extremely jumpy. I kept looking over my shoulder as I was walking home from the tube to make sure no one was following me. I had taken a knife from Babs's kitchen and was holding it in my coat pocket. I closed the door and put the chain on. I was so happy to be home and to see the children.

Claire offered to give them their bath, but I wanted to. I needed to be with them. I bathed them and put them to bed. We had lovely cuddles before I turned their lights out. I felt much less shaky by the time I came downstairs. Claire was still there because she was babysitting for me. James was working late and I was going to Carol's. She'd invited Poppy and me over to taste her new batch of home-made wine. Before I left, I sat Claire down and told her that someone was potentially stalking us. I didn't want to worry her or involve her too much, but I felt she should have an idea of what was going on so that she could be extra careful with the children. I wanted her to be really vigilant. I explained it as briefly and succinctly as I could, playing it down so as not to frighten her.

She was shocked. 'How awful! I knew you were rattled by that package the other day, but I had no idea things were so bad. You must be so stressed.'

'I am,' I admitted.

'What does James think? Does he have any idea who it could be?'

I was uncomfortable discussing James and his possible unfaithfulness, so I was deliberately vague. 'Well, he thinks it might be someone at the club playing a very unfunny joke on us. We really don't know, to be honest. So if you can just keep the kids close to you at all times and don't answer the door to anyone, except your mother, obviously, if she's calling in from Poppy's.'

Claire's face darkened at the mention of her mother. 'I'd be glad not to open the door to her. She's such a control freak. It drives me mad. You'd think I was nine, not nineteen.'

'Well, I'm sure she's just protective of you because you had a tough time in the past.'

'She needs to back off,' Claire said, biting her nail.

I smiled. 'All mothers can be a bit overbearing at times. She'll probably ease off when she sees that you're happy and in a good place.' I put my coat on. 'I won't be long and if there are any problems, I'm just next door.'

Carol answered the door in a dress that looked as if she'd made it out of old curtains.

'Do you like my dress?' She twirled around. 'I've just finished sewing it. I made it from some old curtains I found in a second-hand shop.'

'It's very floral and cheerful,' I said, trying to be as honest as possible without hurting her feelings.

Poppy arrived up the path, behind me. 'Christ, Carol, what's *that*?'

'My new dress.'

'It's beyond hideous. Please take yourself down to Putney High Street and buy yourself something decent. You're a lovely-looking woman, so why do you insist on hiding behind these appalling outfits?'

'I love it,' Carol beamed, 'and it only cost three quid.'

Poppy laid her hand on Carol's shoulder. 'Darling, it looks as if it cost fifty pence. I admire your attempts to save the planet and be frugal, but really and truly there is a limit.'

Carol seemed completely unfazed by Poppy's brutal honesty. I would have taken the criticism so personally, but she was so happy in her own skin that Poppy's comments slid away, like water off a duck's back. She was amazing, really.

Carol showed us into her 'good' room. I'd never been into it before. It was filled with the strangest mish-mash of furniture I'd ever seen. The coffee-table was a tree trunk. One chair was made from steel rods and cable wire. Poppy sat on another that was made of four branches nailed together, with a skateboard on top for the seat. She looked hilarious, perched there with her Louboutins skimming the wooden floor. I sat in a third made entirely from coils of thick rope, with a hard cushion in the middle.

'Did you make the furniture yourself too?' I asked, as Carol poured us a glass of muddy-looking red wine.

'Yes,' she said proudly. 'The boys helped me. Almost everything in the house is home-made.'

'You'd never guess,' Poppy said, with a raised eyebrow, and I bit my lip to stop myself laughing.

Carol grinned. 'I'm thinking of our children's future.'

'By the time my kids are grown-up, I'll be too tired or Xanaxed to care,' Poppy drawled. I burst out laughing. These two women were the original chalk and cheese. 'Now, Carol, can you please explain what this foggy-looking drink is? Tell me there's alcohol in it.' Poppy looked suspiciously at her glass.

Carol nodded. 'Yes, there is.'

I took a small sip and tried not to gag. It was awful, really vile. I managed to swallow it and put my glass down.

Poppy spat hers back into her glass. 'Are you trying to kill us? This is poison.'

Carol sipped hers. 'I think it's lovely.'

'It's probably an acquired taste,' I said diplomatically.

'The only thing you'll acquire drinking that is hair on your chest. Sod this. I'm sorry, Carol, but I suspected the home-made wine would taste like old socks, so I came prepared.' Poppy pulled two bottles out of her large Louis Vuitton tote. I could have kissed her. I wanted a glass of proper wine, not gloopy muddy water. She waved them at Carol. 'There's a reason that we leave wine-making to the professionals. Now get me a corkscrew and let's have a drink.'

'I'll stick to my own,' Carol said, handing Poppy a cork-screw.

I felt bad about abandoning Carol's wine, but it was really awful. As Poppy poured, I remembered what Mum had said about not getting too friendly with her. Could she be stalking us? I thought it was very unlikely, but then again, she could easily leave parcels on our doorstep, and she bumped into James sometimes on the street. He thought she was abso-lutely mad, but that didn't mean she didn't fancy him.

As if reading my thoughts, Poppy said, 'Darlings, I have some news. I've met someone and he's stinking rich.'

That ruled James out.

'Is he a nice person?' Carol asked.

Poppy waved her glass. 'He's a bit of a bore, actually, but the private jet more than makes up for it.' She grinned delightedly at us. 'He took me to lunch yesterday . . . in Paris! We went to the divine Sur Mesure on the rue St Honoré. The food is so good there, I actually ate it. Anyway, Jasper started banging on about some merger he's working on. Obviously I had to stop him before I keeled over with bore-dom, so I said, "Look, Jasper, I haven't eaten a meal since I turned thirty-five and my metabolism shut down. This body is the result of starvation and yoga. All that boring chat about your merger is ruining my appetite."

'Well, he looked at me for a few seconds, then he said, "You are the rudest person I've ever been to lunch with. All of my previous dates found me very interesting."'

'Did you think you'd blown it?' I asked, thoroughly enjoying this wonderfully distracting saga.

Poppy smiled. 'I said to him, "Jasper, for a man who has clearly made millions in business, you are incredibly stupid. I can assure you that no woman who has been out to lunch with you has ever found your mergers and acquisitions conversations interesting. The only thing they're interested in is your bank balance."'

Carol and I burst out laughing.

'So he said, "I find that offensive." That was when I decided to give it to him straight between the eyes. I'm too old for pussy-footing about.'

'What did you say?' Carol asked, her eyes wide.

'I said, "Let's be honest here. You are a short, round, fifty-five-year-old man. Any woman younger than thirty-nine is only interested in your cash. I'm actually interested in it too, but I'm also looking for company. I'm lonely, Jasper. I don't like being divorced. I want someone to go to dinner, the theatre and cinema with. I want someone to talk to who isn't under six and who doesn't think that poo is the most fascinating topic in the world. I wouldn't have looked at you twice ten years ago, but I'm older, wiser and more realistic now. I'm not going to meet a Bradley Cooper lookalike with deep pockets."'

'You never!' Carol gasped.

'That's not the end of it.' Poppy was enjoying our rapt attention. 'I told him, "I'm too old for games. I want a companion. I want someone to have a laugh with and talk to. I no longer look particularly attractive in the morning. It takes a while to put this face on. If you're not great in bed, that's OK. Half the time I'm too damn tired for sex anyway. I have two small boys who I'm very fond of, but don't really understand. I hate football and the opera. I have an ex-husband who just told me he's expecting a baby with his new young beautiful wife, who has a pert bum and breasts that defy gravity. I know that some of my clothes are too young for me and that really depresses me. I know I should do charity work, but I don't want to. I hate all animals, even goldfish, and I have a secret crush on Justin Bieber, which is very worrying."'

I shook my head in disbelief. 'Poppy, you are some woman. I like a straight talker, but that takes it to a whole new level.'

Poppy smiled. 'Sometimes honesty is the only way, ladies. Anyway, thankfully, Jasper wasn't one to be scared away so easily. He laughed and then said, "You're something else, Poppy. I can honestly say I've never had a lunch quite like this before. But I appreciate your honesty. So here's the thing. I got divorced ten years ago and I'm used to my own space now. I like eating toast lathered with honey in bed while watching old war movies. I hate exercise. I find it boring and tiring. I enjoy sex, but my sex drive is definitely not what it used to be. I find lately that I have a tendency to fall asleep in the cinema. I don't understand Twitter. I think most modern music is loud and noisy. I have a house full of gadgets that I have no idea how to use. I have a teenage daughter who is a nightmare and an ex-wife with a cocaine problem." I just clinked my glass against his and said, "Then we're a match made in heaven." He winked at me then and said, "How do you fancy flying back to London, coming to my house and having average sex?"'

Carol and I squealed like schoolgirls.

'Well, ladies, I looked that wealthy average man in the eye and said, "Best offer I've had in years."' She held her glass up to us and took a big gulp of wine.

Carol and I cheered.

'That has to be the best date story I've ever heard,' I told her, and we laughed. 'So . . . how was the sex?' I asked, curiosity getting the better of me.

'Average,' Poppy admitted, 'but in a nice way.'

'He sounds lovely,' Carol said. 'A nice, decent man, just what you need.'

'Yes, with the added bonus of the private plane and a mansion in Holland Park.'

'So, have you arranged another date?' Carol asked.

'I'm seeing him tomorrow. We're going to the cinema. Let's hope he can stay awake for the whole film. I suggested he drink a double espresso beforehand.' Poppy glowed. It was lovely to see.

'Romance is alive and well in Putney,' Carol noted.

Poppy held up the bottle to me to suggest another glass and I checked my watch. 'I'd better not,' I said. 'I told Claire I'd only be an hour. She's spending too much time at our house as it is – the poor girl practically lives with us.'

'How's it going? Are you still finding her good?' Poppy asked.

'Gosh, yes, absolutely brilliant.'

'Good. Her mother, Maggie, is wonderful. But she does worry about Claire a lot – too much, probably. If I was her, I'd be thinking my job was done and I'd be off living the high life.'

'She does seem very protective,' I agreed. 'Claire's a bit fed up with it, actually. You can see the tension between them.'

'Claire was at my house the other day while your children were at school. When I walked into the kitchen, I saw Maggie trying to grab her phone. Claire was going crazy and pulling it back.'

'Oh, I know what that's about,' I said, 'but you must swear not to breathe a word. Claire has a new boyfriend and she doesn't want her mother to know about it because she won't approve.'

'I'm glad to hear it,' Poppy said, with a grin. 'She seems so mousy and quiet. A boyfriend will do her good.'

I reached for my bag and coat. 'I'd really better go. Thanks so much, Carol, for a lovely night.' I tried to climb out of my chair, but my bum was stuck in the rope. I gave myself a tug, lost my balance and fell out sideways. Poppy jumped up to help me, but her jeans got stuck in the edge of her skateboard chair and ripped.

'Carol!' she exclaimed. 'Will you please buy some normal chairs? These jeans are my brand new Hudsons.'

'I'm sure I could patch them for you.' Carol examined the large hole in the side of Poppy's jeans. 'I've got some curtain material left over.' Poppy looked utterly horrified. Carol burst out laughing. 'I'm joking, but you should see your face.'

I went home smiling. Having a laugh with those two was the perfect antidote to all the crazy stuff going on at the moment. I needed all the 'normality' and fun I could find if I was to have any chance of staying sane.

25

Babs didn't come to work the next day. I had called her the night before, when I'd got back from Carol's, but she hadn't answered the phone. She had texted, though: *I'm fine, talk tomorrow.*

Thankfully, Gary was at a meeting so I didn't have to face him. I knew I wouldn't be able to stop myself saying something – I was so angry with him for crushing my sister like this.

I tried calling Babs, but again, no answer. I tried every hour, but she never picked up. We spent the morning shooting the part where I do the guest's makeup. They filmed me going through the process step by step, describing what I'm doing to the camera and showing what products I'm using. When we finished the segment at noon, I told Karen I was worried about Babs and wanted to pop over at lunchtime to check on her. She said that as they'd done the makeup shots I could leave for the day.

I rang Babs again. Still no answer. I sent a text telling her I was on my way. I was really beginning to worry.

As my taxi was heading towards her apartment I received a reply: *I'm not at home. Meet me 127 Harley Street.*

I was relieved. Babs had obviously decided to see an obstetrician. She was clearly taking control of the situation. Maybe I'd make it in time for her first scan. It would be lovely to be there with her to see the tiny baby. I wanted to be as big a support as I could. She'd need me. Having a baby on your own must be the loneliest thing in the world. I felt emotional just thinking about it. James had been with me every step of the way with Yuri's adoption and Lara's early arrival and I had needed him. Babs would need me and, no matter what was going on in my crazy life, I was determined to be there for her.

The taxi pulled up beside a building with a small, discreet plaque that said 'Westgate Clinic'. It was tucked away in a little courtyard off Harley Street. I pushed the door open and looked around the reception room. It was dimly lit and had a very sombre feel. I peered about the waiting area for Babs, but I couldn't see her.

There was a woman who looked about the same age as me and had her eyes closed, listening to music on her earphones. Opposite her, a young girl was sitting beside an older woman, who I guessed was her mother. The girl, who couldn't have been more than sixteen, was sobbing quietly. She looked terrified. The poor thing: having a baby at sixteen would be very difficult. She was practically a baby herself. To the girl's right there were two women of about thirty. One was holding the other's hand and kept whispering, 'It's for the best.'

I looked around the room and my eyes fell on a notice board. I moved closer to it and suddenly the penny dropped.

A door to the left opened and Babs walked out.

'NO!' I shouted. 'NO WAY.'

Babs grabbed my arm and dragged me into a chair beside her. 'Shut up,' she hissed.

I stood straight back up and pulled her to her feet. 'You're not doing this.'

She yanked her hand away. 'Yes, I am. Now sit the hell down and listen to me, or else leave.'

I sat down shakily.

'Emma, I need you to listen and not speak. I spent all of last night thinking about having a child on my own. And the bottom line is, I can't do it. I don't want to bring up a kid by

247

myself. I stupidly thought Gary would leave his wife and we'd play happy families. I can't believe I was so moronic and naïve.' She sighed and twisted her hands together tightly. 'Anyway, the thing is, I can barely look after myself. What the hell am I going to do with a baby? I was all gung-ho about it yesterday because in a way I wanted to have the baby to spite Gary, to throw it in his face. But that's not a reason to give birth. I'm ambitious, I want a big career in TV, and a kid now is just not going to fit into my life. I'd be a shitty mother. We both know I don't like kids, only yours, and even then I'm always glad to get home to my own space.'

'I'll help you,' I interrupted. 'I'll look after the baby for you when you're working. You'll probably be a great mother. Yuri and Lara adore you.'

'Yeah, because I'm the cool aunt who gives them junk food and huge presents. That's who I am, Emma. I'm the aunt, not the mother. I don't want the responsibility of motherhood. I started having a panic attack last night thinking about nappies and bottles and prams and schools and –'

I cut across her – I had to make her see that an abortion was not the answer: 'That's normal! All first-time mothers panic.'

Babs gripped my arm. 'Emma, come on, we both know I'd be a disaster. I like my freedom. I'm selfish and egocentric and very ambitious. A baby will not fit into my life. I see how much you give to your kids and I admire you for it. But I am not going to bring a child into this world whose father doesn't want to know it and whose mother can't look after it.'

I was touched. Babs had never told me she admired me for anything.

'I don't want to sit at home with a baby. I don't want to give up my life and live in the suburbs and become one of those boring school mums. I feel sorry for them.'

And in one fell swoop she was back to insulting me.

'It's not boring. OK, sometimes it is, but it's also magical and fulfilling and joyful and precious. This baby is Yuri and Lara's cousin. Think of the lovely times we'll have together with our kids.'

'I'd hate it. I could think of nothing worse than being on a beach or in a restaurant with screaming kids. After an hour in your house I want to run out the door – and, as I say, I like your kids. Emma, I know myself. I cannot do this.'

I paused and then I spoke all in a rush, not even knowing exactly what I was saying. 'OK, I'll raise it. We can pretend I adopted another child. Then no one needs to know. You can say you've put on weight, then take a little sabbatical and I'll just arrive home and say I adopted another baby. No one will ever find out.'

Babs stared at me. 'Are you mental? There is no way I'm going to have a child, hand it over to you and pretend it's not mine. Forget it, Emma. Nothing, and I mean nothing, you can say will change my mind. When I made this appointment, the only thing I felt was relief. I know this is the right decision.'

I could see that she was absolutely determined to go through with it, but I gave it one last shot. 'I'm begging you, please just come out with me and have a coffee and talk about it some more. Please don't do it today. It could be a gorgeous little girl, a mini you. Please, just reconsider.'

Babs shook her head sadly. 'Stop it, Emma. Just stop.'

Before I could say anything else, Babs's name was called. I stood up and followed her through the door.

She turned back to me. 'I'll do this bit alone. I just need you to be here after, to help me get home. They said I might be a bit shaky after.'

I glared at her. 'I am not sitting out here while you go in there alone. No way. I said I'd be here for you and I will.'

Babs nodded. 'OK, but no more talking.'

Babs was taken to change into a gown and I met her in the ultrasound room. The doctor explained that they had to confirm the pregnancy, check the size of the foetus and rule out any potential problems or pitfalls. I tried to hold her hand as we stared at the screen, but she swatted me away.

'You look about ten weeks gone,' the doctor said, as we watched the little black shadow on the screen.

I stifled a sob.

The doctor asked Babs if she still wanted to go ahead with the procedure. In a very firm voice, she said, 'Yes.'

I gave it one last shot. 'Please don't do this.'

She glared at me.

The doctor looked at his notes. 'I see you've opted for a surgical termination with a local anaesthetic.'

'What does that mean?' I asked. 'How long will it take? Well . . . How does it happen? What do I need to do? Can I stay with her?'

Babs sat up and wiped the ultrasound gel from her stomach. 'No. I'm doing this bit alone. You can wait for me outside.'

The doctor asked the nurse to show me back to the waiting room and told me they'd call me when Babs was ready to go home. I kissed my sister on the cheek. She felt ice cold.

I hesitated. 'Babs, I –'

'Go.' She pushed me away.

As the nurse escorted me out of the room, I asked her what the procedure would involve. She explained that a speculum is inserted into the vagina and then a local anaesthetic is administered to the cervix. Then a narrow tube, attached to an aspirator device, is inserted into the uterus and the contents are emptied using suction.

I put my hands over my mouth to stop the cry escaping.

The nurse patted me on the back. 'The procedure takes about ten minutes. Your friend?'

'Sister.'

'Your sister will experience cramps and bleeding afterwards. We'll keep her in the recovery room for about forty minutes to check her blood pressure and heart rate, and then, all being well, you can take her home.'

Exactly forty-five minutes later a nurse escorted Babs into the waiting room. She was bent over and shuffling. I jumped up and ran to help her. The nurse handed me a bottle of antibiotics. 'Make sure your sister takes them,' she instructed.

'Are you all right?' I asked. 'You're really pale.'

'I just want to get out of here,' she muttered.

'Come back to my house. I'll look after you,' I said. 'You shouldn't be on your own.'

Babs nodded silently. She was shivering. I wrapped my coat around her shoulders. There were no words left to say. The whole way home in the taxi, she stared out of the window, bending over every now and then as the cramps stabbed at her. When we got back to my house, she had a shower and put on a pair of my pyjamas. I tucked her up in the spare bedroom and pumped her full of painkillers.

'Thanks,' she whispered. 'I know you don't approve of what I did, but thanks for being there for me.'

Tears slid down my cheeks. 'I'm glad I could be. It's just a pity it had to end this way.'

Babs rolled away from me and began to cry softly. I rubbed her back as she sobbed. It broke my heart to see my ballsy, confident sister so crushed.

After a few minutes she stopped crying. She said, 'I don't ever want to talk about this again. I never want it mentioned. I'm going to block it out and move past it. I have to.' Her voice began to break. Gathering her composure, she added, 'As far as I'm concerned, it never happened.'

'Maybe you should think about counselling,' I suggested.

'Emma, I don't need counselling. I need you to promise me that you'll forget this and never bring it up with me again.'

'I can't promise to forget it, but I promise not to raise the subject if you really don't want me to. But I want you to know that you can talk to me about it any time you feel like it.'

'I will never discuss it again.'

'Fine.' I wasn't going to argue with her now. 'Look, you're not going to feel very well for a few days. What do you want me to say to work?'

'Tell them I have the flu and I'll be back on Monday. I'll be fine after the weekend. I need work to distract me. I'm going to show that bastard he can't ruin my career. I'm going back to work with a vengeance.' She pulled the duvet up and buried her head under it.

'OK – but, Babs, you need to look after yourself. Only go in on Monday if you feel up to it. Why don't you stay here for the weekend?'

'I'd like that,' she said wearily. 'Now can you go?'

I kissed her head and left her to sleep away her memories and block out her pain.

26

It was nice having Babs with us. She seemed to like having the children around and was very affectionate with them. She was still tired and crampy, but I didn't see anything to suggest that she regretted her decision or was depressed. It wouldn't have been my choice, but I understood that it just hadn't been the right time for her – or the right man. That was for sure.

On Saturday night, James and I were due to go to his parents' fiftieth wedding anniversary party. I didn't want to leave Babs alone, but she insisted that I go and offered to babysit. When she woke up late on Saturday morning, though, she announced that she was feeling much better and asked if she could come to the dinner with us.

'Seriously?' I was shocked that she'd want to be there. 'It won't be a lot of fun. James's family are very reserved.'

'I'm bored. I need to get out and have a few drinks,' Babs said.

'OK. I'm glad you're feeling better.'

'I feel fine, Emma. I need to get out of the house and blow this off.'

'Well, don't drink too much and watch what you say. James's parents are easily shocked,' I warned her.

She rolled her eyes. 'Don't worry, I won't make a show of you. I'll just sit in a corner, drink and smile.'

I somehow doubted that.

James was out getting the team ready for their game that afternoon, so I took it upon myself to call my mother-in-law, Anne. I explained that my sister was staying with me for a few days and asked if it would be all right for her to come along to the dinner. She was very sweet and said, yes, of course, she'd be delighted to get reacquainted with Babs.

As I was talking to Anne on the house phone, I heard my mobile pinging in my bag. I froze, thinking it might be another crazy text. After I'd said goodbye to James's mother, I pulled it out, then breathed a sigh of relief. It was from Lucy, asking if I was free for dinner on Monday night. I texted her quickly and we arranged a time and place.

Babs had no clothes with her, apart from her tracksuit, so she had to wear one of my dresses, with a big belt to hold it up because she was two sizes smaller than me. At least she looked respectable. I put on a plain navy dress, which Babs insisted I accessorize with a bright green scarf, which made it look much better.

I did my sister's makeup. She needed a lot of concealer to hide the black circles under her eyes and extra blusher as she was still very pale. When she asked me for bright red lipstick, I didn't argue. It gave her ghostly face a lift.

That day James's team had won their second cup match, thank God. He had sounded very jubilant when he'd called. At least it meant he'd be in good form for the evening. He was doing some post-match analysis, so we agreed to meet him at the restaurant. Claire arrived to babysit the children.

'Wow,' Babs said, as Claire took off her coat to reveal a figure-hugging red top.

'You look great!' I exclaimed. 'Were you out with your boyfriend?'

She shook her head. 'No, but I'll be seeing him later on.'

'How long have you been dating?' Babs asked.

Claire looked at the floor. 'A few weeks.'

'Well, you look a million times better. I never would have thought you had such a hot body under all those baggy clothes you used to wear. You're quite a dark horse, aren't you, Claire? I bet we don't know the half of what you get up to in your time off.'

Claire blushed and hurried out to find the children, who were in the lounge.

'Be nice!' I muttered. 'You'll make her really uncomfortable. She can't cope with too much attention. She's very shy.'

Babs snorted. 'If she's so shy, why is she walking around in a low-cut top and skin-tight jeans?'

'It's the first time she's ever worn anything remotely revealing. It's great to see – it shows she's growing in confidence. This boyfriend is working wonders. She's so much happier in herself and looks so much better.'

Babs shook her head. 'She's weird.'

'She's great. Now, come on, let's go. James's parents are sticklers for punctuality.'

'It's only six! Are we going for the early-bird special?'

'Anne is seventy-eight and Jonathan is eighty-two. They like to eat early. No rude comments and no cursing. They don't do bad language.'

'Well, I look like a granny in this dress you lent me, so I'll just act like one too.'

'Perfect.'

We arrived at Rules, the oldest restaurant in London, at exactly seven o'clock. It was decorated in red velvet and the subtle lighting gave it a warm, cosy feel. The walls were covered with beautifully framed paintings, cartoons and sketches.

Anne and Jonathan Hamilton were waiting for us, with Imogen, Henry and James.

The Hamiltons were always on time. They almost had a nervous breakdown when they came to Dublin to visit me and James when we got engaged. Mum and Dad had invited them for dinner. They'd said, 'Come at eight-ish.' In Irish terms that meant under no circumstance should you even think about coming near the house before nine. But, true to form, they had arrived at eight sharp. Thinking it was the man from the wine shop delivering the bottles they had ordered, my mum answered the door in her dressing-gown and rollers. She was so shocked to see James's parents that she slammed the door and ran upstairs to get dressed. Whereupon Dad reopened the door and invited the bewildered pair into the lounge. He proceeded to fling newspapers, magazines and stray slippers under the couch. Then he gave them a large glass of wine each and left them alone while he went to shave and put on a clean shirt.

They'd spent the next hour sitting alone in the lounge, with occasional visits from Dad to refill their glasses and from Mum to apologize for slamming the door in their faces. At nine, everyone else arrived, and proceeded to drink and chat until ten. As the food was about to be served, the neighbours called in – they'd seen the light on and decided to pop in for one drink. Mum didn't have enough food for the four neighbours, so she put the dinner back in the oven until they'd left. By the time the neighbours did leave, it was close to eleven and Anne and Jonathan were both fast asleep on the couch – drunk, starving and exhausted.

When they came back to Dublin, it was for our wedding. The invitation said three, so they turned up at four and missed the entire ceremony.

Babs and I walked over to say hello to everyone. Henry

jumped up first to give us a kiss. 'Good to see you, Emma. You look super as always. Hello, Barbara, what a nice surprise to have you with us.'

Imogen remained seated, looked us up and down slowly, then air-kissed us. Anne and Jonathan welcomed us warmly and James ordered us drinks.

'Vodka and slimline tonic. Make it a double,' Babs said. This did not bode well. Mixing alcohol with antibiotics was never a good idea.

'Well done on the game today,' Henry said to a radiant James.

'Thanks. Bloody relieved, I can tell you. It was a close call.'

'Fantastic try in the last five minutes. Marvellous winger that Gordonson,' Jonathan enthused.

'He's really stepped it up this season,' James agreed.

While the men dissected the match, Anne leant over to me. 'We can't believe we've seen so little of you since you moved here,' she said. 'Between James's work and our travels, it's been a very busy time. You must come down for Sunday lunch next week. I insist.'

'That'd be lovely,' I said. I'd been a bit hurt that James's parents hadn't made more of an effort. We had seen them twice in the first month. Then they'd gone away on a six-week cruise and we hadn't seen them since their return.

'How was the holiday?' I asked.

'Marvellous,' Jonathan enthused. The rugby analysis had ended.

'Really?' Babs said, draining her vodka and ordering another. 'I always thought cruises would be incredibly boring. Full of really old people shuffling around complaining about piles and bunions.'

There was silence, then Henry burst out laughing. 'I'd forgotten how funny you are,' he said.

'A few more vodkas and I'll be a riot!' Babs winked at him.

'How are you finding London life, Emma?' Imogen cut across her husband's laughter.

I caught James's eye. 'To be honest, it's been more difficult than I'd thought. It was a big upheaval for all of us.'

Imogen rearranged her velvet headband. 'I think it's fair to say, Emma, that you don't make things easy for yourself. You should have rented a house in a smarter area and sent the children to a decent school. Has Lara started talking yet? My goodness, the day I was there all the poor child could say was "Ribbit" – it was most disturbing. I said to Henry when I got home, "You must call James and have that child seen by a psychologist."'

Henry squirmed. 'I obviously chose not to call you. I'm sure it's just a phase.'

'Good decision,' James said. His face was blank but he was staring hard at Imogen. Yes! Finally he was seeing her for the witch she was.

I clasped my hands to stop myself slapping Imogen's fat face. Through gritted teeth, I said, 'Lara never stops talking. She was pretending to be a frog that day. It was no big deal.'

'She does that all the time,' Babs put in. 'You should see her cow impression – it's hilarious. I think she's going to be a brilliant actress. I bet you she wins an Oscar one day.'

Anne laid a hand gently on my arm. 'I'm sure she's as bright as a little button, but we were concerned when Imogen told us about the incident. You see, I had an aunt who was a little . . . ah . . . different, so I'm afraid Lara's behaviour could be genetic.'

I glared at James, but he had reverted to his rugby conversation with his father and hadn't heard his mother's comment.

'There is nothing wrong with Lara. She's actually one of

the cleverest kids in her class. Her teacher told me she's a joy to teach.' This was a big fat lie. The only thing Miss Timmons had said was that Lara was very spirited, which had sounded more like a negative than a positive.

Anne looked relieved. 'Wonderful! I'm so pleased to hear that.'

Out of the corner of my eye I saw Babs ordering another vodka. She was drinking way too fast.

Imogen fiddled with her pearl necklace. 'Has your son grown at all? My goodness, I couldn't get over how tiny he still is. I said to Anne, "He's the same size Thomas was when he was two." He'll be a midget if he doesn't grow. Have you thought about growth hormones?'

'There was a fellow in school with me who was small. He became the most fantastic jockey.' Henry tried to be helpful.

'Yuri is growing at a normal and healthy pace.' I was furious with Imogen. I could feel sweaty patches forming under my arms. At this rate, I wouldn't make it to the starter without throwing something at her.

'Normal!' Imogen snorted. 'He's the smallest four-year-old I've ever seen. Of course, his mother was probably a drug-addicted prostitute. I saw a documentary on those Russian orphanages. They showed the mothers abandoning their children on the doorstep. They were utterly appalling women. I'd say most of the children are completely damaged and will end up addicted to drugs, too.'

There was a silence and everyone looked uncomfortable. I didn't trust myself to open my mouth – I'd either start screaming or crying. It was Babs who reacted first: 'Does that mean your mother looked like the back of a horse, had a voice like a foghorn and insulted everyone she ever met?'

I loved my sister.

'How dare you –'

Babs drained yet another drink. 'How dare I what? Insult you? If you can dish it out, you should be able to take it. You've just been rude about my niece and nephew and I'm not having it. They're amazing kids.'

'Henry,' Imogen snapped, 'are you going to let her insult me?'

'You were a tad harsh,' Henry noted, as his wife glared at him.

James addressed Imogen: 'Emma is Yuri's mother and the person he loves most in the world. The woman who gave birth to him may have been a prostitute or she may have been a sweet young girl who was unable to look after him. It doesn't matter, because we are his parents and he is our son. He may never grow to be six feet tall, but he is a giant in our eyes.'

'Well said.' Babs patted him on the back.

I blinked furiously to stop the tears falling down my cheeks. This was the James I knew and loved. This was the man I had married.

Jonathan cleared his throat. 'Shall we take our seats and order?'

'I'll keep my mouth shut, shall I? Apparently I'm not allowed to have an opinion this evening,' Imogen grumbled, as we headed to the table.

The rest of the meal went relatively smoothly. We kept the conversation on safe ground – sport, books and theatre. Babs, however, continued to drink at a fast pace and kept telling us that her favourite book was *Fifty Shades of Grey* and winking at Jonathan, who didn't know where to look. I kept pouring her water and trying to get her to drink some.

At coffee, James politely asked how Thomas was getting on at boarding school.

'Marvellously,' Imogen barked.

'Not well,' Henry said, at the same time.

My ears pricked up. I wasn't letting this one go. 'I'm so sorry to hear that, Henry. What's going on?'

Henry put his coffee cup down. 'I'm afraid he's on a final warning.'

'What?' Anne, Jonathan and James looked shocked. Clearly this was bad.

'What does that mean?' Babs asked. 'Is he getting expelled?'

'Henry!' Imogen's face was purple. 'Stop this nonsense. Thomas is fine.'

I was enjoying every minute of her discomfort.

'Imogen, this is our family. We can be honest with them.' Henry turned to Babs. 'Final warning means that if he misbehaves again, he'll be expelled, yes.'

'Expelled!' I gasped loudly for effect. 'Wow, that really is serious. What did he do?'

'I had no idea.' Anne frowned and looked upset. 'We thought Thomas was thriving at St David's. Imogen told us so.'

'Apparently not,' Babs said, grinning.

'He's been bullying one of the other boys. Tormenting the poor chap on a daily basis apparently.' Henry was clearly crestfallen that his ten-year-old son was such a tosser.

'Are you sure?' James asked. 'Could the boy be exaggerating or maybe out to get Thomas?'

'Fat chance.' Babs snorted. 'That kid needs a firm hand.'

'My Thomas wouldn't hurt a fly,' Imogen spluttered. 'What the hell would you know about children anyway?'

I held my breath and watched Babs carefully, ready to pounce if she lost her cool.

'I may not have children,' Babs said, slowly and deliberately, 'but I know that they need boundaries and discipline. That kid of yours was wild from a young age and you never said no to him. Now he's obviously turning into a horrible person. If you don't deal with it, he'll end up in big trouble. Why don't you get your head out of your arse and face the fact that your son is out of order and needs discipline? Stop criticizing everyone else and get your own house in order.'

'How dare you speak to me like that? Who the hell do you think you are, coming into my family and insulting me?'

'Emma, Yuri and Lara are my family and you've insulted them all.'

'Now, ladies, let's not argue. This is, after all, Mother and Father's anniversary dinner,' Henry reminded us.

Imogen looked as if she was going to explode. Anne quietly told her to keep her cool.

'What exactly has Thomas been doing?' I asked Henry, determined to hear the full story.

'Oh, the usual bully stuff, calling the other child names, giving him wedgies, kicking him, stealing all the food from his tuck box . . . But last week Thomas tripped him on the stairs and the poor fellow broke two ribs. We've had a terrible time with his parents. They're threatening to sue us.'

'Thomas said it was an accident. It was *not* his fault,' Imogen snapped.

'Do they have a case?' James asked. 'Witnesses?'

'Thankfully, no,' Henry said. 'It was just the two of them. So it's the boy's word against Thomas's. But I know he did it.'

'Henry!' Imogen was apoplectic.

'He's a brat,' Henry admitted.

'Now, now, Henry, let's not be too harsh.' Jonathan defended his grandson. 'Thomas is a lively boy, I'll grant you that, but he's not a bad chap.'

'No, he's just a little boisterous. But all boys are energetic at that age,' Anne added.

I jumped in. 'What are you going to do?' I wasn't in the least surprised that Thomas was a bully. Babs was right: he had been a brat since the day he was born and Imogen never gave out to him or told him to stop. I was surprised at Henry, but he worked long hours so it was Imogen who spent most time with the kids.

'He's been told in no uncertain terms that unless he pulls his socks up and is nice to this boy and all the other boys, he'll be expelled. If that happens, I've threatened to send him to Scotland to a boarding school for young offenders.'

'Really?' That sounded a bit harsh.

'Sounds perfect. Sign him up.'

'Babs, zip it,' James said. Then he smiled at his brother. 'Is it the school Father was going to send us to?'

Henry smiled. 'The very same.'

James explained, 'Whenever we misbehaved, Father told us he'd send us to a special boarding school in the wilds of Scotland. It was only in later life that we discovered it didn't exist.'

Jonathan laughed. 'Well, it worked. You never gave me any trouble. And I dare say it will work on young Thomas, too.'

I glanced at Imogen. She was sitting with her arms folded, glowering at Henry. He'd get an earful when they got home.

'Well, I hope it all sorts itself out,' I said, trying to be kind, for Henry's sake.

'It already has,' Imogen snapped. 'The whole affair is behind us. I really don't know why Henry felt the need to bring it up. Thomas was wrongly accused and he knows now that he has to be careful. This nasty boy is clearly out to cause trouble. He's jealous of Thomas because he's so popular and good at sports. That's what happens when you're a star pupil. Other students envy you and want to drag you down.'

Babs shook her head. 'Delusional,' she said.

Henry looked sad. 'That's simply not the case, Imogen. Thomas is a spoilt boy who needs discipline.'

Imogen's fist slammed onto the table, making us all jump. 'You lay one hand on that child and I will divorce you.'

'Imogen!' It was Anne's turn to be shocked.

'Lucky escape, if you ask me. Go home and wallop the kid,' Babs muttered.

I realized that my marriage wasn't the only one with problems. Imogen glowered at Henry. The tension at the table was horrible.

'Why don't we change the subject? Children are a very emotive topic,' Anne said lightly. She couldn't cope with anger or confrontation.

'Quite right,' Jonathan said. 'Tell me, James, who do you think they'll pick to play scrum-half for England this year?'

While the others talked about rugby and Imogen stomped off to the Ladies, Henry leant in to me. 'How are things?' he asked.

'Not great. More texts and parcels, and now she's texting my phone too. It's frightening, to be honest.'

'James called me about getting in touch with the police. I asked around, but everyone I spoke to said you'll probably need more evidence before the police will get involved.'

'I'm scared she's going to attack me.'

'I got the name of a private detective I'm trying to track down. It might be the best route. If he can find out who it is, we could stop them.'

I squeezed his hand. 'That would be great.'

'I must say, James is very upset. He was really most distressed on the phone. I can assure you, Emma, this is no affair. James is innocent, but for some reason a woman, or indeed a man, has become fixated on him.'

I was so glad Henry had said that. It made it easier for me

to believe James. 'Thanks, Henry. Listen, I'm sorry about my sister. She's drunk and she's had a bad week. I hope Imogen is all right.'

Henry smiled ruefully. 'Emma, we both know that my wife has skin as thick as an elephant's. I find your sister most entertaining.'

'Well, it's getting late, we really should be going,' Anne said, clearly dying to get away from us all. It had been a fairly unusual anniversary dinner, that was for sure.

Babs looked at her watch. 'Ah, come on, Mrs H, I know you're old, but it's only ten. Live a little, stay up until ten thirty.'

Anne gave Babs one of her tight, disapproving smiles. 'Goodnight, Barbara.' To me, she said, 'I'll call you soon, Emma dear.'

Imogen stood up, too.

'Let's have a nightcap and then we'll go,' Henry suggested hopefully.

'Nightcap? Come on, guys, what age are you? It's only ten.' Babs giggled.

'Henry,' Imogen hissed, 'we're leaving. Now.'

Henry sighed and got up. He said his goodbyes and followed his wife out of the door.

'That poor guy is so bitch-slapped,' Babs said.

'Interesting evening,' James noted. 'Nice of you to come and mix it up a bit, Babs.'

'Your family are the dullest people ever. At least Imogen has a bit of spark about her. Your parents are –'

'James doesn't need his family to be insulted. Drop it,' I warned her.

'Fine. Order me another drink,' she said.

'OK, but then we're going home, I'm tired.' I stifled a yawn.

'Me too,' James said.

Babs slapped her forehead. 'Oh, my God, you guys are killing me. Have some self-respect. Go crazy and stay out until eleven. It won't kill you.'

At ten thirty, Babs fell asleep on the table . . .

27

On Monday morning Babs was up early, banging on my bedroom door to have her makeup done. She wanted to look really good so she could face Gary with confidence. She'd gone shopping on Sunday afternoon and bought herself an indigo jumpsuit that looked incredible on her.

'I want smoky eyes,' she demanded. 'I'm going to strut into that studio and own it. To hell with Gary! He's just a slimy git. I must have been mad to sleep with him.'

'How do you think you'll react when you see him?' I asked.

Babs flicked back her hair. 'Don't worry, I know exactly how to handle him.'

When we got to work, Gary came straight up to Babs. He pulled her to one side and I heard him whisper, 'Did you make a decision?'

Babs looked at him quizzically. 'What decision?'

Gary gripped her arm. 'You know what I mean.'

Babs prised her arm out of his grip and smiled brightly at him. 'Sorry, Gary, I have no idea what you're talking about. You must be mixing me up with someone else.' With that she sauntered off to talk to Karen, leaving Gary clearly worried.

He caught my eye. I looked away and smiled to myself. Babs was playing it so well. She was going to let him sweat it out until he eventually realized, when her stomach didn't expand, that the pregnancy was over. I was very proud of my little sister.

*

That night, Babs offered to babysit to thank me for looking after her, and I went to meet Lucy for an early dinner at a tapas bar in Fulham. As I was leaving the house, Lucy sent a text: *Sod tapas, am treating u to posh drinks in Berkeley hotel. See u in 20 mins.* That sounded good to me. As I was walking to the tube I received another text: *I said go back to Ireland. Now go!* I spun around, looking to see if anyone was following me. Then I ran all the way to the tube, trembling.

In Knightsbridge, I walked quickly to the Berkeley. On the way I decided to try hard not to let that text ruin my night. I had to be strong. I arrived into the Blue Bar, which was very blue and full of gorgeous people. Lucy was waiting for me, looking stylish, as always, in a black shift dress.

'It's so good to see you.' I hugged her tightly.

'You too. You've lost weight.'

'Have I?' I hadn't noticed. 'It must be the stalker diet.' I sighed. 'Come on, let's order some cocktails. We need to blow off steam.' Lucy ordered two mojitos.

'Make mine a really strong one,' I told the barman.

Lucy raised an eyebrow. 'So, more texts?'

I nodded. 'And that's the least of it. She's still sending me things.'

'You're saying "she" now?'

'Has to be,' I said, shaking my head. 'I've received the vibrator *and* a set of handcuffs delivered to the house. And I'm now getting texts to my own mobile, which means some-how this person has that number as well.'

Lucy looked very concerned. 'God, Emma, that's kind of . . . creepy,' she said. 'Have you thought about reporting it?'

I sighed. 'Henry's helping us. He's getting in touch with a private detective. We're hoping he'll help us track this nutter down.'

'Oh, Emma . . .' Lucy's voice was full of sympathy, and it

was hard for me not to start crying on her shoulder. 'How is James reacting to it?'

The waiter delivered our drinks. I twirled the mint leaves around my mojito. 'He seems very angry. But I just don't know what to believe any more. I keep lurching from believing he's innocent to feeling paranoid about him cheating on me. I feel like I'm going a bit mad. I'm looking over my shoulder every time I leave the house. I don't know what this woman is going to do next. It's sex toys now, but what will it be next month? Knives? Acid? You should see the stuff on the Internet about stalkers. It's really frightening.'

Lucy wagged a finger at me. 'Emma, stay away from the Internet.'

'I just don't know who or what to believe. I'm second-guessing myself all the time. I feel very alone actually.' I took a drink to stop the lump forming in my throat.

'I'm here for you,' Lucy said. 'And don't you see your sister in work every day?'

I nodded, but the truth was that I felt alone. Everyone was so busy and under so much pressure. The person I usually talked to about everything – James – was the cause of all this stress. Lucy and Babs had their own problems and worries. And my other close friend, Jess, was under huge financial pressure so I didn't want to burden her either.

'Well, Babs has a lot going on at the moment.' I didn't want to tell Lucy about the pregnancy, although I felt she'd probably agree with Babs's decision. 'I just don't know what to do about the stalker. It's beginning to cause a rift between James and me.'

Lucy ordered some wine and the waiter brought it over and poured us a small glass each.

'We have to think logically about it, Emma. This woman has to be someone you or James knows. Have you checked out the woman he mentioned in work?'

'Not yet.'

'Emma!' Lucy threw her hands into the air. 'I told you to suss her out. She has to be prime suspect number one until you know otherwise.'

'I know, but James said Harriet is pregnant, so I counted her out.'

Lucy was incredulous. '*Pregnant?* Emma, pregnant women can be totally nuts. With all the hormones flying around, it could easily be her.'

'I don't think a pregnant woman would be stalking us,' I said doubtfully.

'Why not? Just because she's pregnant doesn't mean she wouldn't fancy James. You have to go and see this Harriet. You need to see her for yourself to decide if she's a suspect or not. Get all dressed up and just "pop by" the training ground.'

'All right,' I said, nodding. 'You're probably right. I'll do that this week.'

Lucy topped up our glasses. I fiddled with the cocktail napkin. 'Lucy, be completely honest. Do you think James is shagging someone else and wants to get rid of me, but hasn't got the balls to do it so he's asked his mistress to frighten me off?'

Lucy considered this. 'Why would he do that?'

'I don't know. Look, just answer quickly – give me your gut response.'

Lucy leant back in her chair. 'OK. It seems to me that James *may* have flirted or perhaps even slept with someone who unfortunately happens to be really unstable. Now that she realizes he's actually happily married, she's annoyed and seeking some kind of perverse revenge.'

'Do you think he did have sex with her?'

Lucy stared into her glass, then looked up at me again.

'I'm not sure, but he certainly doesn't seem to be behaving like a guilty man. You said he's as fed up and angry as you are, which would suggest he hasn't been unfaithful. Knowing James, he'd be riddled with guilt if he'd slept with someone else. I think you'd see it all over his face.'

'It's terrible but I don't trust him any more. I'm constantly checking his phone and his emails now.'

Lucy patted my arm. 'This is just a bump in the road, a glitch.'

'It's not a bump, Lucy, it's becoming a crater. I hardly ever see him. We haven't had sex in weeks because I'm angry and upset. We still have occasional moments of the old us, but they're increasingly rare. Soon we'll be too far apart to find our way back again.'

Lucy tied her hair back in a knot. 'Marriage is a lot harder than we're led to believe.'

'Are things still bad with Donal?'

'Extremely.'

'Do you think you can do it, Lucy? Do you think you can be away every week and keep up a happy home life?' Seeing her face cloud, I added, 'I'm not judging you, I'm just worried that you'll become disengaged from Donal and Serge with all the travelling.'

'How many times do I have to say it? I couldn't turn down this opportunity. The offer was just too good.'

'I know. I understand.'

'I wish Donal did. We had the worst fight ever last week.'

'I'm so sorry. I was really hoping you guys would be able to sort things out.'

Lucy closed her eyes. 'He said some pretty low things.'

'Like?'

'Like that I'm not a "normal" woman because I have no maternal instincts and I'd rather be in work than at home.

That I'm cold and selfish and don't give a damn about him or Serge. That I'm a spoilt only child who only cares about herself.'

'He's just lashing out because he's scared of losing you,' I said.

Lucy shook her head. 'He'll lose me if he tries to tie me to the kitchen sink. If I'd turned down this job, I'd never have forgiven him. I know what I'm like. So I took it and now he hates me. You see, Emma, there *is* no solution. There is no black and white in any marriage. It's all bloody grey.'

I poured more wine into our glasses. 'God, I miss my twenties. I miss rolling out of bed and only having to think about my needs for the day. I miss only worrying about what I want to eat and drink and do. Now, it's always about the kids or James or bloody psychos who want to steal my husband. It's as if, somewhere along the way, I became a non-person. I don't count. What I want is of no interest to anyone in my family. How did that happen?'

Lucy nodded vigorously. 'That's exactly what I'm talking about. Traditionally, women disappear in marriages, and I refuse to do that. If I gave Donal the cold shoulder because he took a promotion, everyone would say I was a thundering bitch. But it's fine for him to freeze me out because I'm a heartless cow for accepting a better job. There are still different rules for men and women. When a man takes his child to the park, everyone tells him what a great dad he is. If a woman takes her child to the park, it's expected. Despite all the giant steps towards equality, it's still a man's world.'

I rested my head against the back of my chair. 'When I married James, I really thought it would be for ever. I never in my wildest dreams would have imagined that we could split up. But now I can see that it's possible. It's so frightening.'

'Me too. Because of my parents' disastrous marriage, I didn't think I'd ever marry, and then Donal came along and made me want to marry him. I still love him. We used to have such good times, but Serge has changed the dynamic. It's all about him and not about us any more and I find that really hard. I miss the fun we used to have going out together and just having a really good laugh. I can tell you one thing this new job has made very clear, though – I will never be having another child. As Donal pointed out, I'm not very maternal, so I need to use the little bit I have to focus on Serge. I love him, but I can't really relate to him.' Lucy put her hand up to stop me interrupting her. 'I know what you're going to say and it's OK, I know it'll get better as he gets older. In fact he said, "I dove you, Nunny," the other day and my cold, hard heart did melt.'

My eyes filled with tears. The wine was beginning to have an effect. 'Oh, Lucy, that's a huge deal. The first time they tell you they love you is really special.'

She nodded. 'It *was* special and I felt really emotional. I gave him a huge hug and then he wiped his snotty nose on my silk blouse and I was really cheesed off. You see, I'm not a nice person. Donal's right, I'm abnormal.' Now Lucy's eyes welled. 'It was such a huge moment, my little boy telling me he loved me, and then I ruined it by letting the snot bother me. I'm awful.'

'No, you're not. You're one of my favourite people in the whole world, and you'll get better at the mother thing as he gets older. You were never into small kids. Remember when Yuri dribbled all over your suede Prada bag?'

Lucy smiled. 'It was a brand-new powder-blue clutch that I'd treated myself to after getting a promotion! I should have known then that children were not for me.'

I picked up a handful of fancy nuts from the silver bowl on

the table and popped them into my mouth. 'I don't want to break up with James. I'd hate to be on my own. I'd even forgive him a one-night stand, if that was all it was.' I was surprised to hear myself say this, but it was true. I'd thought about it a lot, and if he had had a one-night stand that meant nothing and he was really sorry and grovelled at my feet for weeks, I probably would forgive him. I knew how broken and shattered Yuri and Lara would be if we split up. But if he was lying to me and he was having an affair, our marriage would be over.

'You guys won't break up,' Lucy said. 'You're strong and you'll get through this, I know you will. Obviously the stalking business is very upsetting – you really need to figure out who the person is and get them locked up, scare them off, run them over in your car or something.'

I laughed at her gallows humour. 'I wish we'd never moved. Everything's gone wrong since we got here.'

Lucy put down her wine glass. 'No, it hasn't. James's job is going well, and yours is too. The kids are happy and you've got a great nanny. London's a brilliant place to live. I mean, look at us tonight – you don't get the Blue Bar in Dublin. You've just had bad luck with this crazy stalker thing. But that could have happened anywhere.'

'There are eight million people in this city. That's eight times more than there are in Dublin, which means eight times more nutters.'

Lucy laughed. 'There are plenty of nutters in Dublin.'

I looked at my best friend and thought of the things that were happening to us both that we could never have imagined. 'Do you think we'll end up single again?'

Lucy shrugged. 'Who knows? But at least we'd have each other.'

'I don't want to bring up the kids on my own. I'd hate to see James swanning around with some young English rose called Phoebe, while I'm at all the school plays alone, pretending I don't mind. And Phoebe will be fun and give the kids sweets, and I'll be strict and bring them to the dentist and they'll hate me because I'm bitter and twisted and I hate their father and his stupid girlfriend. And then Phoebe will give birth to a perfect baby boy, in a paddling pool in the kitchen at sunset, and he will be sweet and good and the image of James and sleep all night from the day he's born. Phoebe and the baby will keep James young and I'll be wrinkly and fat because I'm misery-eating and I'll die alone with my two cats.'

Lucy stared at me, then threw back her head and laughed.

'It's not funny, Lucy. I can actually see it happening.'

'OK. Well, while you're doing that, I'll be a bitter divorcee, working nineteen-hour days. Donal will be with some tall country bumpkin called Kathleen, who wears wellies and fleeces and loves being outdoors. They'll have six big strapping boys, whom Kathleen will push out without breaking a sweat because she has big child-bearing hips. Serge will adore his new family and hate me. I'll probably only get to see him every fourth weekend, which he'll spend sulking. I'll shower him with gifts to try to make him like me, but it won't work because he'd rather be watching dog-racing in a field with his brothers than playing on his iPad. I'll get a full facelift at fifty and have lots of meaningless affairs with colleagues. I'll be forced to retire at sixty and spend the next twenty years sitting in my perfect house watching Donal's six sons playing rugby for Ireland, while he and Kathleen hold hands and cheer from the sidelines. Serge will marry a girl who is the complete opposite of me and visit me once a year out of guilt.'

I burst out laughing. Lucy joined in and soon we were hysterical with alcohol-fuelled mirth. People began to look at us, which made us laugh even louder.

'What are we like?' I dabbed my face with a napkin.

'You have to laugh or you'd cry,' Lucy said.

Two men approached our table. 'Hi, Lucy, we don't mean to interrupt you, but you seemed to be having so much fun, we wondered if we could buy you a drink and join you.'

Lucy looked up. 'Hi, I didn't see you in here.' I knew by her voice that she wasn't particularly thrilled to see them. She introduced them to me. The small one was Harry and he worked for Barclay's Bank and the tall one was John and he was a management consultant or something, I was too drunk to care. They sat down. Harry was not very attractive. John was quite good-looking.

'I hear you jumped ship,' Harry said to Lucy.

'Yes.' Lucy nodded.

'Sounds good. There's a lot of money to be made in aircraft leasing, if you get it right. Where did you get the funding?'

'Germany, AABA Bank. We shopped around, but they gave us the best terms.'

'So, how's it going?' John asked.

'Really well, thanks. We've sourced the planes and we're signing clients all over Eastern Europe.'

'Looks like you hit the jackpot.'

I waved my arm at them and, slurring, said, 'No work chat. Keep it light and fluffy. I need a break from my life.'

Three bottles of wine later, I was feeling no pain. At about eleven, the men suggested we go to another bar. It seemed like a good idea at the time. It was dark and had loud music. Lucy went to the Ladies, leaving me dancing to Rihanna while Harry and John went to the bar.

When Lucy came back, I was flinging myself energetically around the dance-floor. It was fantastic – I was having great fun. John came over and joined me. He was a good dancer. We swayed to the music, dancing closer and closer. Suddenly, I toppled over. John reached out to catch me. His face was very close to mine. I could feel his breath on my neck and then, without thinking at all, acting on impulse alone, I leant in and kissed him. His mouth opened in response and we began to kiss passionately.

Lucy charged over and pulled us apart. 'Emma! What the hell are you doing?'

'Having some bloody fun for a change,' I snapped.

'We're going home.' Lucy grabbed my arm and yanked me through the crowd to the door. When we got out onto the street, she handed me my coat and bag. I put my coat on in silence.

Lucy laid a hand on my shoulder. 'Emma, this is really not the way to solve your problems.'

I looked at Lucy, tears streaming down my cheeks. 'Well, please tell me what is.'

28

I peeled my eyes open. It was still dark. My head was pounding and my mouth felt like sandpaper. I rolled over and realized I was lying on the couch, fully clothed. I hadn't even managed to take off my coat or shoes.

I gingerly swung my feet to the floor, padded upstairs and tiptoed past a sleeping James to the bathroom. Every step was like a mini bomb going off in my head. I leant against the sink and looked at my reflection in the mirror. My face was streaked with mascara, my hair was a tangled, knotty mess and I looked pale and drawn. What a night! I hadn't felt this rough in years. How much had I drunk? I splashed cold water on my face and tried to rub off my makeup with a flannel. Then it hit me . . .

OH, MY GOD. I had snogged John in the middle of the dance-floor. I began to shake. How could I? I'm not the type of person who gets blind drunk and kisses strange men in nightclubs. I'm a wife and a mum and I'm happy with my lot. Well . . . I used to be happy. But now . . . now I was confused and paranoid. I buried my face in a towel. If this was what it felt like to be unfaithful, it wasn't worth it. I was so ashamed. My face burnt as the memories flashed back. I had been the one who had initiated it, too. I'd wanted to kiss John. I had really wanted to kiss another man, to just let go, misbehave, do something crazy. If I'm being totally honest, the kiss was actually pretty great, very passionate. If Lucy hadn't dragged me away, would I have let it go further? Would I have slept with him? I could suddenly see how it was possible to get carried away in the moment, in spite of your best intentions, in spite of your real feelings, even. Was that what James was doing?

I wiped mascara from my eyelashes and looked into my bloodshot eyes. I'd made a complete fool of myself, throwing myself at John. From now on, I'd have to avoid drinking. Alcohol was not my friend.

I sat down on the edge of the bath. My phone buzzed in my coat pocket. It was Lucy. *U OK? Worried about you.*

I texted straight back. *Fine. Sry bout last night. Mortified. Can we never mention incident?*

Lucy's reply was instant: *What incident?*

I smiled. Good old Lucy. I knew my secret would go to the grave with her.

Suddenly the bathroom was flooded with light. I winced as the brightness pierced my eyes. James stood looking at me, in his boxer shorts, scratching his head. 'What are you doing in the dark in your coat? Have you only come home now?' He looked at his watch. 'It's half six.'

I stood up. 'No, I got home ages ago. I fell asleep on the couch.'

'Judging by the alcohol fumes emanating from you, I'd say you had a good night,' James mumbled. He walked past me and reached for his toothbrush.

'Too much wine.' I decided to keep it short and as close to the truth as possible.

'I'm glad you had a good time. You needed a night out. How's Lucy?'

'Fine, but things with Donal aren't great.'

James stopped brushing his teeth. 'Hardly surprising. She's never there. He's practically raising Serge alone.'

'Well, it's a big opportunity for her.' I didn't want to get into a debate about the pros and cons of Lucy's new job. I needed sleep. All I wanted to do was crawl into bed and put the duvet over my head.

'That's all very well, but she has a husband and a child she barely sees.'

'Well, she's home every Friday and spends all weekend with them.'

James scratched his stubbly chin. 'It's not a good idea to spend so much time apart.'

'I know, James,' I snapped. 'I'm all too aware of how one person working late all the time affects a relationship. I live with it every day.'

James put his hands on the washbasin and sighed. 'Once I prove myself at the club, I can start leaving earlier. A few more wins and I'll have shown them I'm the man for the job. You'll see, things will settle down.'

I slammed my hand against the edge of the bath. 'You said all that would happen after you won the first match, but very little has changed. Oh, apart from the lunatic out there stalking us because of you.'

'Emma, calm down. You know I wouldn't cheat on you. And I really think that if we continue to ignore her, she'll go away and we can get back to normal.'

Normal? I didn't even know what normal was any more.

I decided to change the subject. I was too hung-over to get into an argument about our messed-up life. 'Why are you up so early anyway?'

'I couldn't sleep so I thought I'd go for a run before work.'

'It's pitch dark outside.'

'I know. I had a horrible dream and I need to shake it off.'

'What was it about?' I asked.

James rinsed his toothbrush slowly. 'It was about you leaving me and taking the children.'

'Oh.' I didn't know where to look. Did he suspect me? Had he guessed what I'd got up to last night?

James caught my eye in the mirror. 'We're all right, aren't we, darling? I know things have been horribly difficult lately, but we'll get through it, won't we?' He sounded genuinely worried.

I really looked at my husband for the first time in ages. His eyes were puffy from lack of sleep and he had lost more weight, which didn't suit him. He had the air of a man under huge pressure. I suddenly felt sorry for him.

'As long as you never lie to me, James, we'll be fine. But if I find out you've lied to me about the stalker, we won't be.' I felt a little guilty taking the moral high ground, having just kissed someone else, but then, what was a kiss compared to sex toys?

James turned and bent to kiss me on the lips. 'I haven't lied to you and I never will,' he assured me. He tasted of mint toothpaste: nice. He handed me his toothbrush. 'I think you might need to freshen up your breath.'

'Charming!'

He grinned. 'You know me. I can't lie!'

While I crawled into bed, James went for a run. I closed my eyes and waited for sleep to wash away my guilt.

An hour and a half later, Yuri and Lara were bouncing on me.

'Wake up, sleepy-head,' Yuri shouted.

'Mummy, you smell yucky,' Lara told me.

I actually felt worse after the sleep. I dragged myself out of bed and shakily poured their cereal into bowls. Thankfully, Claire arrived soon after. It was one of the days she came in early to do laundry and light housework. I almost kissed her when I saw her. I asked her to dress the children and take them to school, then went upstairs and tried, in vain, to make myself presentable for work.

*

Today we were filming the scenes where Babs takes the make-over volunteer shopping for some new clothes, which meant I could spend most of the day standing to one side, feeling sick without being noticed. We headed to a shopping centre near the studio, which had Topshop, New Look and Next. Babs had one hundred pounds to spend on each guest's clothes. This time, she was making over Sandra, a single mother of seven children from Liverpool who worked part-time as a dinner lady. She was very overweight, but had a pretty face and lovely thick chestnut hair.

We headed to Topshop first, Sandra wearing tracksuit bottoms and an oversized sweatshirt. Babs was wearing a bright yellow bodycon dress, which looked sensational. She was still being very breezy with Gary and you could see he didn't know what to think. I caught him staring at her stomach for signs of a bump. I shot filthy looks at him whenever he came in range of me, so he knew better than to try talking to me about it.

As the camera crew were setting up, Babs handed me an extra strong mint. 'You absolutely reek of booze and you look like you slept under a bridge. Where were you last night?'

'I met Lucy and things got a bit crazy. Too much white wine.'

'Are you sober?'

'I think so.'

'I'll do my own mascara today, thanks. I'm not having you poking me in the eye with your shaky hands.'

'Probably a good idea,' I whispered.

They began to shoot. Babs took Sandra by the arm and whisked her around the shop, picking up bundles of items from different rails as she went. Then she ushered her into the changing room and handed her the first outfit. It was a strapless black maxi dress, which Babs was matching with a short denim jacket.

'I'm not wearing tha',' Sandra said firmly.

Babs waved the hangers at her. 'Just put it on. It'll work.'

'Are you deaf, luv? I said I'm not putting tha' on.'

'Oh, shit, here we go,' Karen muttered. The cameraman grinned at the soundman.

'Excuse me?' Babs glared at Sandra, who had the changing-room curtain draped around her to hide her underwear.

'You need to get them ears seen to,' Sandra said.

'Oh, I heard you correctly. I'm just in shock. Do you not understand the show, Sandra? You come on looking like crap and I make you over.'

'I understand perfectly, luv, but I'm not wearing no long dress. Me mates tell me I've got dead good legs, so I'm not hiding them under tha' big tent of a thing.'

I watched as Babs rapped her blue fingernails on the hanger. 'OK, Sandra, let's be clear here. This is my show. You are a guest. When I tell you to try something on, you try it on. That's how the show works.'

'I'm not being bossed around by some jumped-up tart from Ireland.'

Everyone gasped. 'Get a close-up of Babs's face,' Karen hissed at the cameraman. 'This is dynamite TV.'

Babs smiled sweetly and brought her face closer to Sandra's. 'Your friends are a bunch of lying wenches. Your legs are like two tree trunks. Your only hope of ever looking in any way normal is if you get help from someone like me, who actually knows how to dress. So you can either shag off back to Liverpool in your saggy-arse tracksuit and have chips for dinner, or you can listen to me and go home looking like a human being.'

Babs was on fire. The crew were all trying not to laugh.

Sandra's mouth opened and closed like a fish's. Then she gathered herself. 'I'll stay, but not because I think you're good at your job, but because I want the free clothes.'

Babs handed her the outfit. 'Fine, whatever. Just put these on.'

Sandra snatched the hangers and snapped the curtain shut.

'The cheeky cow,' Babs hissed.

'Keep your cool,' Karen said. 'The viewers are going to lap this up. It'll be good for ratings.'

Babs flicked her hair back and smoothed down her dress. I watched her composing herself. The word 'ratings' was like a drug to Babs. Now she was even more obsessed with getting better ones, because that meant she'd get more attention from other channels. Then she could leave this show and, more importantly, Gary behind.

Five minutes later, Sandra came out of the changing room, looking, it has to be said, a lot better. She stood in front of the mirror, swinging left and right.

'Well?' Babs glared at her, arms crossed. 'What do you think?'

Sandra wrinkled her nose. 'It's all right, but it's a bit grannyish.'

'You're forty-seven and a size twenty. What do you want to wear? Mini dresses?'

Sandra pouted. 'Just because I'm older don't mean I have to dress all frumpy, like.'

Babs adjusted the jacket on Sandra's shoulder. 'This outfit is not frumpy. It's cool, it's flattering and it makes you look five stone lighter.'

'What else have you got?' Sandra was unimpressed.

Babs handed her a pair of streamlined charcoal grey trousers and a floaty pale grey chiffon top that was cut quite low at the front and had little cap sleeves. 'The trousers are free of pockets and anything that will add to your bulk. The top will just land at the bottom of your stomach, hiding the worst part, and the cap sleeves will broaden your shoulders and cover the fattest part of your arms.'

'Looks like something a secretary would wear to work,' Sandra complained.

Babs's eyes narrowed. 'What exactly are you looking for? Smart-casual clothes or something to wear clubbing?'

Sandra rounded on her. 'What I'm looking for, luv, is something to wear to the pub on a Friday night. I wouldn't be seen dead in them boring trousers.'

'Fine. Well, why don't you go and choose yourself an outfit and we'll see how you get on? Go on, Sandra, knock yourself out.' Babs led her out to the shop floor and gave her a not-so-gentle nudge.

Sandra didn't need to be asked twice. She raced around and came back with a white vest-top with big red sparkly lips painted across the chest and a denim mini skirt. She put them on and came strutting out of the dressing room like a model on a catwalk.

There was complete silence from the crew.

Babs pursed her lips. 'Tell me, Sandra, how do you think this outfit enhances your shape? How are you hiding the flabby bits and showing off the best bits with these clothes?'

Sandra grinned. 'Well, luv, I've got my tits on show, which is always a good thing as far as men are concerned. I look like a woman who wants to have a laugh and not like a woman who wants to look at spreadsheets. The only sheets I want to look at are bedsheets.' She cackled.

Babs started laughing too. 'You know what, Sandra? I have to tell you as a professional that you look an absolute state. But if you think you look good and you're happy to go to the pub like that and have a laugh, well, off you go. I'm not going to dress you in clothes that flatter you because you won't wear them. It's clear you're a woman who likes to party and I appreciate that. So, I'm going to get you some party clothes that are a bit less tarty than what you have on, but I'm not going to try to change you or make you over because you're having fun and I like a woman who knows how to have a good time.'

Everyone laughed. By the end of the day Babs and Sandra were the best of pals and Sandra went home with a bagful of sparkly clothes for her Friday nights in the pub.

Gary came back into the shop for the last part of filming and witnessed the fantastic dynamic between Babs and Sandra. Karen filled him in on the brilliant scenes they had shot earlier. I hovered near my sister when I saw him approaching her.

'Well done, Babs. I hear the earlier footage is even better,' he said.

Babs looked him directly in the eyes. 'Yes, it is. I was on fire.'

'So . . . you're good? You're back on track?'

Babs shrugged. 'When was I ever off-track, Gary?'

'Well, you know, what I mean is . . . that whole other drama is over. Right?'

'What drama?'

'Come on,' he hissed.

Babs patted him on the cheek. 'Chill out, Gary, you're becoming paranoid.'

He grabbed her arm. 'Don't play games with me. Did you sort it out?'

Babs yanked her arm away. 'I guess you'll just have to wait and see.' She strutted out of the shop, swinging her hips as she went.

29

That Wednesday, filming was cancelled due to some technical hitch, so Babs spent the day with me. Although she'd never admit it, she still didn't like being on her own.

I was making coffee for us when my phone buzzed. Babs picked it up. 'Bloody hell!' she exclaimed.

I snatched the phone: *I had hot sex with James yesterday. Now dont u think its time to bugger off back to Ireland.* I let out a scream of pure frustration.

'Jesus, my eardrums!' Babs complained.

I was devastated. James and I had been getting on quite well since my illicit snog. We hadn't received any parcels or messages and I was beginning to think maybe the ignoring tactic had worked and the stalker had stopped.

'I can't take much more of this.' I was crying. 'He must be cheating on me.'

'Oh, God, don't start wailing.' Babs placed a cup of coffee in front of me. 'You need to stay calm. Don't jump to conclusions. None of this is proof that he's shagging anyone, although I'll admit it doesn't look good.'

I tried to slow my breathing. My heart was racing. It was time I acted. I needed to get down to the rugby club and see the pregnant Harriet and any other women who worked there. 'Lucy says I should call into James in the rugby club and see if the stalker works there.'

Babs took a large bite of a chocolate biscuit. 'She's right, but you can't go looking like you normally do. You have to make an impression. You must turn up looking amazing and totally in control. Then if it is one of them, they'll see you're not a wimpy woman who's going to just let her husband go. They'll see you as a force to be reckoned with.'

'I was going to get something new and fabulous to wear and have my hair done so I look my best.'

'You'll need a lot of help. But, luckily for you, I'm here.'

'Great. I can't think straight at the moment.'

As we put our coats and scarves on to protect us from an icy wind, Babs said, 'By the way, I'm not styling you for free.'

'I'm your sister!' I pulled on my gloves.

'You can cook me dinner later as payment.'

'I'll buy you a takeaway.'

'Deal.'

We got a taxi to Fenwick's in Bond Street. I'd never been there before, but Babs assured me that it was the best place to go for quick, stylish results. It was a very smart department store. Babs swished through the front door and headed straight for the escalator. On the first floor she walked straight to the L. K. Bennett concession.

I looked around. 'Isn't it a bit expensive here?'

Babs looked me up and down. 'Emma, you're not exactly young any more. You need to spend more money to look good.' She handed me a dark purple, figure-hugging wrap dress. 'Try this on. It's long enough to cover your saggy knees, it's tapered here on the stomach, which will hide your belly, and it has little sleeves that will camouflage your chunky upper arms. On top of all that, the colour will look good with your ginger mop.'

'I don't like the colour. It's too dark.'

Ignoring me completely, Babs pushed me into a changing room and stood outside waiting.

I tried on the dress and was pleasantly surprised at how

good I looked. The deep purple went surprisingly well with my hair and the shape did camouflage my lumpy bits. Best of all, the size twelve fitted me perfectly. I was thrilled.

As I was admiring myself in the mirror, I heard Babs's voice outside: 'I'm sorry, but I can't let you buy that.'

I peeped out from behind the curtain. A woman of about fifty was standing in front of the shop mirror in a blue dress that was very tight and unflattering on her.

'Excuse me?' The woman turned to Babs.

Babs went over to stand beside her. 'I'm a stylist, and as a professional I cannot allow you to spend money on that dress. It's hideous on you. What are you buying for? A wedding?'

'No, it's for my son's graduation.'

'Well, he will not be happy to see you turning up in that. You look like Moby-Dick. Now, what you need for your shape – which is pear by the way – is this.' Babs handed the woman a fifties style dress that went in at the waist and then kicked out.

'Excuse me, madam, I am dealing with this customer.' The shop assistant bustled over, carrying a pair of shoes.

Babs spun around to face her. 'You obviously work on commission and have no conscience. How could you let this woman go home with this horrendous dress and be the laughing stock of her son's big day?'

'My customer looks wonderful.' The shop assistant wasn't giving an inch.

'She looks like a whale.'

The woman puffed out her chest, put her hands on her hips and bellowed, 'Excuse me, I'm not deaf. I'm standing right here and you are being very insulting.'

Babs thrust the other dress into her hand. 'No, I am not. I'm just being honest. If you want to look good, in a dress that flatters all your good bits and hides the bad, then you'll put this one on. When you see your reflection, you'll realize I'm a genius and buy it. Otherwise, buy the blue one and look hideous. It's up to you.'

'Madam, if you do not stop harassing my customer, I'll have to call security.'

'I'm right and you know it,' Babs replied. Then, to the woman, she said, 'Good luck with the graduation. Take my advice and don't embarrass yourself or your son.'

I didn't want Babs being arrested before I'd had the chance to pay for my dress. I frantically waved my arms to catch her attention. She came over to the dressing room and looked inside. I did a little twirl.

'Told you.'

'OK, you were right, it does suit me. Now can you please stop harassing customers and staff? Let's pay for this and get the hell out of here before you have us in trouble.'

Babs rolled her eyes. 'Relax, that woman is going to thank me when she sees how flattering that dress is on her. Now, back to you, we need to get some shoes for the dress. Don't move.'

Babs swished off and came back a minute later with a pair of very high black heels. I put them on. They looked great, but were so high that my body was pitched forward. They were extremely difficult to walk in.

'I can't get these. Too high.'

Babs wagged a finger at me. 'No, they're not. They're perfect. They make you look taller and thinner, both very important for someone who is small and round, although you do seem to have lost weight. Stop being such a granny and get the shoes. You'll get loads of wear out of black heels.'

'I'm not buying shoes I can't walk in.'

'Fine.' She sighed. 'I had a feeling you'd say that. Try these.'

Babs handed me a pair of shoes half the height of the previous ones. They were still high, but I was able to walk normally in them.

Next she handed me a chunky silver necklace that sat perfectly at the curve of the neckline of the dress. It immediately made the dress look edgier. 'Perfect,' she said, nodding her approval.

Babs had found me a great outfit. I would feel confident, attractive and good about myself turning up to the club in these clothes. I bought the lot.

As I was paying, Babs got a tap on the shoulder. It was the other customer.

'You were right, dear. This dress is much nicer. Thank you for the advice. Might I say, however, that you need to work on your approach? It's a little assertive.'

I turned to her, laughing. 'I'm afraid my sister is unfamiliar with the word "subtle".'

Babs shrugged. 'Why waste time beating around the bush? Are you both happy? Properly styled? Buying dresses that will make you feel and look good?'

We nodded.

'Well, then, what are you complaining about?'

When we got back to my house, the children were playing cards with Claire. They seemed to be having great fun. Whenever I played cards with the kids, Lara's attention span was all of one minute, Yuri got into a rage if he didn't win and the 'game' inevitably ended in tears. Claire certainly had a knack with children – she had them playing properly, without any tantrums.

They jumped up and, as I put my arms out to hug them, they pushed past me to Babs.

'STOP! Hands where I can see them,' Babs roared.

Yuri and Lara skidded to a halt and put their hands up. Babs inspected them, front and back. 'All right, they're clean. You can hug me now.'

The children hugged her. I saw her wince as Yuri squeezed her stomach. She must still be feeling sore. They asked if Babs had any treats for them. 'What do you think I am? A travelling shop?'

'Look in your big bag,' Yuri begged her.

'*Pleeeeeeeeease*, Babs,' Lara added, giving her puppy-dog eyes.

Babs made a big show of rooting about in her bag before producing a Galaxy bar. 'This is actually mine, but I'll share it with you,' she said, as they whooped with delight. 'Now, go and sit down and I'll give you three squares each. Don't give any to your mother. She's just bought a new dress and there's no room for any extra inches on her waist.'

'What did you buyed, Mummy?' Lara asked.

'A lovely dress.' I pulled it out of the bag and held it up.

'*Oooooooh*, I love purple.' Lara was enthusiastic. That was something. Yuri was far too busy stuffing his face with chocolate to comment.

While the children were eating, Babs asked Claire if she was still seeing her boyfriend.

Claire blushed and looked at the floor. 'Yes.'

'Wow, you have that loved-up glow,' Babs said. 'Is it serious?'

Claire nodded. 'Yes, it is. I'm hoping to move in with him soon.'

'Really?' It was my turn to be surprised. Claire hadn't been going out with him long.

'Yes,' she said, smiling. 'He has a really nice place, but we just need his housemate to move out before I can move in.'

'It seems very quick.' I was worried Claire was rushing into this. She was very innocent. 'Are you sure you're ready for a big move like that?'

'I'm positive. This guy is really special.'

'So, what's he like? Tall, dark and handsome?' Babs asked.

'Yes.'

'I hope he treats you well and appreciates you,' I said.

Claire fidgeted with her backpack. 'He does. He especially loves my cooking.'

'I'm not surprised, so do the kids. And you know James adores your lasagne,' I enthused.

'What does your boyfriend do?' Babs asked, but before Claire could reply, Lara fell off her chair and started bawling.

I ran over to her, but Claire got there first. She picked up Lara and cuddled her. I know it shouldn't have bothered me, but it did. I wanted to comfort my child. Lara nestled her head into Claire's shoulder.

When Lara had calmed down and Claire had left, Babs put her feet up on the chair in front of her and shook her head. 'I'm telling you, Emma, there's something not right about her. I know she's great with the kids and all that, but I just don't trust her.'

'We love Claire,' Yuri defended his nanny.

'Do you love her more than your mummy?' Babs asked.

They paused. 'The same.'

'Brilliant. Thanks for that.' I glared at Babs, feeling really hurt that my children loved their nanny as much as, and probably more than, me.

'You should get rid of her,' Babs said.

I asked the children to go and watch cartoons for a minute while I prepared dinner. I closed the kitchen door and turned to my sister. 'Don't you dare come in here and start harassing my nanny and insulting her in front of my kids. Claire is the only reason I'm still sane. She's brilliant with the kids – as you can see, they like her more than they do me.'

'I wouldn't have anyone in my house that my kids preferred to me. I'd get rid of her, if I were you. They like her way too much.'

'I know they do and I find it hard sometimes, but I'd be lost without the help. I'm serious, Babs, back off. My life is complicated enough as it is without you stirring things up.'

I pulled the Indian takeaway menu from the drawer under the kettle. 'Let's order.'

As I took my phone out of my bag, it buzzed. A new message: *U r 2 old n ugly 4 James. He is way too hot 4 u.*

I covered my eyes with my hands. Babs grabbed the phone from me and threw it on the counter. She pulled out a chair and sat me down. Then she poured me a glass of wine, which, despite my recent decision never to drink again, I gulped down.

Babs read the message. 'This is all way too strange. This woman is completely delusional. No matter how much I liked a man, I'd never stalk his wife! She's unhinged. Even her texts feel very forced and unnatural. I wonder if it's someone who has serious mental issues. She could be dangerous, Emma.'

My hands shook as I put the glass down. 'It looks like James has been sleeping with a younger woman.'

'Well, he's hardly likely to shag an older one,' Babs pointed out.

I began to cry. 'I am old and I am ugly and I am past my best. James looks great. Everyone's always telling me how handsome he is and how charming and nice. Maybe he just woke up one day and looked at me and thought, What the hell am doing settling for her?'

'Come on, drama queen, you're not that bad. And he's not

that good-looking. You look great for forty, and now that you've lost some weight, you look better than you have since you had the kids. James looks good too, but please, he's not exactly Ed Westwick.'

I sniffed. 'Mum said your forties is a really dangerous time and that lots of people have affairs.'

Babs popped a piece of chocolate into her mouth. 'I'm sure they do, but it doesn't mean James is. Look, I reckon the worst-case scenario here is that he had a one-night stand and is now paying for it. And you know what, Emma, a one-night stand is nothing. It means nothing. It was probably just a drunken ten-minute shag.'

'It's not nothing! It's a very big deal, actually. It's a break of trust and commitment, not to mind the hurt of knowing he wanted to have sex with someone else. What if he's in love with her?'

Babs pointed to the phone. 'I can tell you now, no man is in love with this nutter. She's obviously deranged, and if James was stupid enough to shag her, you can be sure he regrets it *soooooo* badly. He'll never go offside again after this experience. And if the poor guy didn't do anything and the stalker is just a freak who became obsessed with him because she sees him in work, then I really feel sorry for him.'

'What do I do?' I cried.

'Get your arse down to that club and find out who the hell it is. Be strong, Emma. Take back control. Sitting around crying isn't going to solve anything. Go down there and show the bitch you're not going anywhere.'

The kitchen door swung open. '*Muuuuummy*, we're *huuuu-ungry*.'

Babs pulled one child onto each of her knees. 'We're ordering food from a restaurant. What do you want?'

'I want chicken nuggets and chips,' Yuri said.

Babs turned his face to hers. 'Listen, Shorty, fried food is not going to make you grow, OK? You need to be eating sirloin steak, roast potatoes and broccoli.'

'Yuck, yuck, yuck.'

'Do you want to be the smallest kid in your class for ever? Do you want to miss out on all the hot tall girls when you're older? Do you want to be the last kid picked for every team?'

'Steady on!' I didn't want Yuri's confidence knocked. I spent my whole life building him up and telling him it didn't matter that he was small. I constantly assured him that the best things came in small packages.

'Why are the tall girls hot? Will they burn me?'

Babs chuckled. 'Probably.'

'Am I a hot tall girl?' Lara wanted to know.

'Not yet, but your prospects are good.'

'Is Mummy?' she asked.

Babs burst out laughing. 'You must be joking.'

'Are you?' Yuri asked his aunt.

'Hell, yes.' Babs winked at them. 'The hottest.'

'Do you burn boys with your hotness?' Yuri was keen to find out if Babs was a fire hazard.

'Every day.' She grinned.

'OK, hot stuff, you can stop filling my children's heads with rubbish.' I rolled my eyes. Babs was incorrigible but it was good to see her spark back. Now I just had to scrape my crushed ego off the floor for long enough for me to suss out the women at the club and show them that I wasn't backing down.

30

Babs had said she'd cover for me in work the next day as the only makeup I had to do was hers. They were just filming her pieces to camera, so she could get away with doing her own face. So, the next morning, after taking the kids to school in my tracksuit, I dashed home and set about making myself look as attractive as possible. I showered with my Jo Malone gel – used only on very special occasions – then wrestled myself into my Spanx. I put on my new purple dress and necklace, black tights and my high heels. I felt over-dressed for the daytime, but it was vital that I was at my best.

I applied my makeup slowly and meticulously, going for a glowy, fresh-faced look with strong eyes. I wanted to look really good when I confronted this Harriet person. I had decided during yet another sleepless night that the stalker must be Harriet. She saw James every day, she had obviously become obsessed with him and pregnant women often behaved very strangely. I was determined to find her and give her a piece of my mind.

I walked gingerly down the stairs, put on my coat and picked up my bag. The shoes were already killing me – I could feel a blister forming on my heel. There was no way I was going to be able to walk to the hairdresser in them, then get the train to the London Irish ground. I took them off and put them into my bag, then slipped on a pair of flat ballet pumps and headed to get my unruly mane tamed into silky waves.

I left the hairdresser an hour later, having assured the girl that I had no holiday plans, was not going anywhere nice tonight and did not need a supersize bottle of Moroccan oil. I caught my reflection in a shop window and smiled. I looked as good as I possibly could. But then, just as I boarded the train to Sunbury, it began to rain. Not little drizzly rain but big, sheeting rain. Damn, I hadn't brought an umbrella with me. I gazed at the dark clouds overhead and prayed that by the time I got to Sunbury it would have stopped.

I rested my head against the train window and watched the scenery whiz by. I tried to practise what I was going to say to Harriet. I wanted to be calm, cool and cutting. I wanted to be like one of those heroines of Second World War movies, those women who parachuted into occupied territory carrying vital messages. When they were captured by the Germans they held their heads high and refused to name names. Even when the big fat Gestapo captain threatened to pull their nails out, they still didn't cave. They looked straight at their captors and smirked at them. Brave, stoic and superior.

By the time the train pulled into the station, I felt invincible. Watch out, Psycho Woman, here I come . . .

I stepped onto the platform into the kind of rain that comes at you sideways, so even if you did have an umbrella, you'd still get wet. Every taxi that went by was full. There was nothing for it, I was here now, and I had to get to the training ground. I walked up Staines Road East and The Avenue, trying to hold my coat over my head to protect my blow-dry. But by the time I reached the London Irish stadium, I was drenched and my lovely bouncy, silky hair was ruined. My tights were soaking, as was the lower half of my dress. I staggered inside the building and took off my dripping coat. I switched from my flat shoes into my high heels and tried to get my hair into some kind of controlled shape. But it was a lost cause – only the very back was still dry, the front was soggy and limp.

Taking a deep breath to try to control my nerves and frustration, I attempted to stride confidently down the hallway. As I tottered around a corner, I saw a young guy dressed in a London Irish tracksuit. I asked him if he knew where James Hamilton's office was. He pointed to a door at the end of the corridor.

I clip-clopped on, feeling blisters forming on both heels now. When I reached James's office, I flung the door open, tripped on the threshold and stumbled, landing on my hands and knees.

Thank God, the office was empty. I picked myself up and examined the damage. Great! My tights were ripped at both knees and had ladders running down to my ankles. So far nothing was going according to plan. Stoic heroines didn't fall about in ripped tights and wet hair. I turned to leave, and bumped straight into one of the players. He was about seven feet tall and had white-blond hair. I recognized him from the match I'd gone to see. He was covered with mud.

'Are you all right?' he asked, taking in my dishevelled state.

'Fine, thank you. I'm looking for my husband, James Hamilton. Do you happen to know where he is?'

'Sure. He's just finishing a training session. Go out of that exit door and turn right.'

I nodded and carefully clunked towards the exit. When I stepped outside, my new shoes sank into the muddy grass. I yanked my feet out and sploshed along the side of the pitch, where the players were practising. I saw James on the sideline, deep in discussion with a young, sporty blonde woman. She was talking very intensely, and when she'd finished, James put his arms around her and gave her a hug.

What the . . . ?

I completely lost it. My cool, calm plan went right out of the window. How dare he? How dare he carry on a full-blown affair in front of everyone? He wasn't even hiding her in his office. He was blatantly flaunting his floozy in front of everyone. Did he have no respect for me? Was he really such a cold-hearted bastard that he could carry on this affair and come home every night and pretend nothing was going on?

I could feel my heart pounding in my chest. I could hear nothing and see nothing but James's smug face. I started to run over, but my left shoe got stuck in the mud. I tried to pull it out, but the heel was firmly entrenched. To hell with it, I kicked it off and hobbled the last twenty yards on one shoe.

As I got closer, James looked round and saw me. His face dropped. He went pale and his arms fell away from the blonde girl's shoulders.

'YOU BASTARD!' I screamed. I was less stiff-upper-lipped POW and more screeching fishwife. Much more.

I turned to the blonde, who was staring at me, open-mouthed. 'You dirty slut. Do you think you can screw my husband and stalk me? Do you have any idea what you've done to me?'

I turned to wallop her with my bag, but James reached and grabbed it. I let go of it and slapped the woman across her smug face with my hand.

She looked positively frightened. 'Who the hell are you?'

'I'm his *wife*, you whore.' I went to slap her again, but this time she was prepared. She grabbed hold of my arm and twisted it behind my back.

'OW!' I cried.

'STOP!' James pulled us apart. Then, to the blonde, he said, 'Paula, I'm so sorry about all this.'

'SORRY!' I shouted. 'Sorry for what? For being the biggest prick in England?'

Paula glared at me. 'I don't know what your problem is,

but you need help.' She turned to James. 'I'll leave you to your domestic.' She jogged off across the pitch.

I was suddenly aware of an eerie silence. All of the players had stopped what they were doing and were staring at me. An older man shouted to James, 'Everything all right, Mr Hamilton?'

James glared at me and, in a strangled voice, said, 'Fine. Carry on, lads. Sorry about the interruption.' Before I could protest, he grabbed my right arm and dragged me across the pitch, jaw clenched.

'Let go of me this instant.' I struggled to get free, but he tightened his grip.

When we got inside, James pushed me into his office and slammed the door. I threw my bag onto the floor and massaged my arm. 'How dare you do that to me?' I screamed. 'You're a monster. You're a horrible human being. How could you humiliate me like that?'

James put his face right up to mine. 'HUMILIATE YOU?' he bellowed. 'Have you lost your mind? Have you finally gone completely insane? How dare *you* come to my workplace and embarrass me like that?'

I poked him hard in the chest. 'Embarrass you? Oh, I'm sorry, James, did I make you and your whore feel uncomfortable? How awful of me. Imagine a wife being upset about her husband having an affair and lying about it for weeks while he allowed his psychotic mistress to send her texts and sex toys. Poor you. Poor little James.'

James put his hands on my shoulders and shook me. 'STOP IT. Stop jumping to conclusions and going off the deep end. Can you for once in your bloody life listen to me? Paula is not my mistress.'

'Oh, really? Well, you looked very cosy to me, you lying toad.'

'I am not sleeping with her.'

'Why the hell would I believe a word that comes out of your mouth?'

'Because, Emma, she's a lesbian.'

I pushed him away roughly. 'You're pathetic. Is that the best you can come up with? Pretending your mistress is gay? You are such an arsehole.'

James pulled me over to his desk and made me sit down. He clicked a few buttons on his laptop and a photo appeared. 'Now do you believe me?'

The picture was of the blonde, Paula, in a white dress on a beach. She was holding hands with a dark-haired woman in a navy dress, who was heavily pregnant. In front of them was a minister with an open Bible in his hands, and they were surrounded by guests.

I felt an awful sense of foreboding in the pit of my stomach, but I pushed it down and ploughed on. 'You could easily have made that up in Photoshop, or whatever it's called, to trick me.'

James sat on the edge of his desk, facing me. His arms were folded and he was breathing deeply. 'Emma, as I have told you over and over again, I am not having an affair. Paula is gay. She got married a week ago in Barbados. She came back from honeymoon today and I was very glad to see her. She's the junior physio, but she's way ahead of Tommy, the older guy. The players love her and she's brilliant at her job.'

I examined the photo again. It did look authentic. Maybe he was telling the truth. 'Why were you hugging her out there? Do you hug everyone who works for you?'

'No. I put my arms around her because she'd just told me that her father had finally accepted that she's gay. I was happy for her because I know how upset she was that he refused to go to the wedding.'

My heart had stopped racing and I was beginning to feel slightly calmer. He did seem to be telling the truth. But then I remembered Harriet. She was the person I had come to see. This Paula person had distracted me. 'Where's Harriet? I want to see her now.'

James marched out of his door and knocked on the one opposite. He stuck his head in. I heard him say, 'Harriet, could you come here for a minute? I'd like you to meet my wife.'

James stood back and held the door for Harriet. She waddled towards me, her arm outstretched. Shaking my hand, she said, 'How nice to meet you. My goodness, you're soaked through, you poor thing.'

I knew immediately that Harriet was not the stalker. She was the woman in the wedding picture. She was Paula's partner.

'When are you due?' I asked, pointing to her protruding stomach.

'Fifteen weeks to go.' She beamed.

'Congratulations,' I said flatly.

James led Harriet back to her office. 'Sorry to interrupt you.'

I heard Harriet whisper, 'It's fine, but is she all right? She looks . . . very distressed.'

'She's fine. She's just having a bad morning.'

Paula came flying around the corner. 'Harriet, you're not going to believe what just –' She stopped when she saw James.

'I'm so sorry, Paula. Emma's a bit upset at the moment, but she does have good reason, even though she was completely out of order.'

Paula glared at me, went into Harriet's office and shut the door.

I laid my head back on the chair. I was exhausted, damp,

shoeless, miserable and confused. Tears flowed steadily down my cheeks.

James closed the door. 'So, you can now strike Harriet and Paula off your list of possible mistresses.'

'Why didn't you tell me she was gay?'

'I didn't know until a week ago. They never said they were a couple. They're very private about it because they aren't sure how people will react, especially in such a male-dominated environment.'

'I think I'm going mad.' I wiped my eyes.

Normally if I was really upset, James would hug me and try to console me. But he did nothing. He sat opposite me and glowered.

Looking at his feet, he said, 'I know it's been difficult for you lately. But you cannot come to my workplace and start accusing people of sleeping with me. Nor can you physically assault my colleagues. You have made a complete fool of me in front of all my players and the coaching staff. I am trying to build up a reputation for being utterly professional and now you have stormed into the middle of training and accused me of infidelity. Everyone now thinks my wife is insane and my private life is a mess.'

James's hands were bunched into tight fists. I'd never seen him so incensed. He couldn't even look at me he was so furious. I had completely misjudged the situation. I had made a complete show of myself, and of James.

I took a deep breath and tried to reason with him. 'I'm sorry, James. I'm really sorry that I caused a scene, but I don't know what to think any more. I don't know who to trust or who to suspect or what I'm doing or where we're going or if you're being unfaithful or . . . or . . . or if you want to leave me. I've never been so confused or miserable in my life. I hate this, I hate our life here.'

'I know you're unhappy, Emma, but what goes on at home is private. I do not want it aired in my workplace. I'm in the middle of running a training session, so I need you to go home, calm down and we'll talk about it later. And, please, don't ever come down here again and cause a scene. I'll be home early tonight and we can talk then.'

James picked up the phone and called a taxi. He walked me out to the front gate and held the door while I climbed in. He didn't say goodbye, he didn't kiss me or touch my hand, nothing. He turned around and walked away, shoulders slumped.

31

I stood in the shower, trying to wash away my shame and misery. As the water cascaded over me, I tried to calm down. I didn't know if it was anger, embarrassment or stress, or perhaps it was a combination of all three, but I couldn't stop shaking.

Shivering, I stepped out and wrapped myself in my towelling robe. I crawled under my duvet and rang Lucy. I needed my friend. I needed to talk to her and tell her what a mess I'd made and ask her for advice and have her soothe me with her wise words.

Her phone rang into voicemail. As I hung up, my mobile rang. It was Babs's number. I answered it.

'Well?'

'Not good.'

'What did you do?'

I covered my face with my hands. 'I don't want to talk about it.'

'Did you stab her?'

'What?'

'Did you stab Harriet? Did you find them having sex over the desk and stab her?'

'No!'

'Did you stab James?'

'No, stop. There is no affair.'

'How do you know? How pregnant is she? Have you done the maths?'

I sighed. 'It's not James's baby.'

'So . . . what? You went down there and shouted at a pregnant woman?'

'Not quite.' I cringed at the memory. 'When I got to the club James was hugging this blonde woman, so I smacked her and accused her of having an affair with him. But it turns out she's a lesbian and she married Harriet last week and they're having a baby together.'

'Did James give them his sperm?' Babs gasped.

'No. This is my life, not a soap opera.'

'FYI, Emma, your life *is* a soap opera.'

She had a point. At the moment it felt like a really bad, twisted TV show.

'Well, at least you looked good while you were making a fool of yourself.'

I cringed. 'Not so much. I got caught in the rain and arrived soaking wet and then my shoe got stuck in the mud and I fell over and ripped my tights.'

Babs began to laugh hysterically.

'It's not funny,' I snapped.

'Come on! You couldn't make this stuff up. They must all think you're off your rocker. I bet they feel really sorry for James now, married to a mad Irish woman with mental problems.'

I lay back on the pillow. 'James is livid with me. I don't think I've ever seen him so angry.'

'Hardly surprising.'

'*You* told me to do it. *You* said it was a good idea.'

'Hold on. I said it was a good idea to turn up looking great and coolly threaten Harriet. I did not suggest that you rock up looking like a drowned rat and do a Frank Spencer impression by falling all over the place and then accuse random strangers of shagging your husband.'

'Stop. I feel bad enough as it is.'

'Right. Well, I'll leave you and your split personality alone. Good luck with James. If I was you, I'd get some kinky lingerie on and distract him with sex.'

A little later, I heard the children coming in from school. I rushed down, still in my robe, to see them. I needed a hug. I needed them close to me. I craved the comfort of their little arms around my neck. I ran in and scooped Lara, then Yuri into a big bear hug. They squirmed.

'Mummy, too tight,' they objected.

'Are you ill?' Claire asked.

'Filming's been cancelled so I've got the day off. I just got drowned in the rain.' Turning to the children, I said, 'I was thinking we could do something fun together.'

'Like what?' Yuri asked.

Claire moved over beside me. 'You're very pale, Emma. Are you sure you're not coming down with something? You look exhausted. You should go back to bed.'

My brief elation at seeing the children faded. I did feel tired and I had a terrible headache. But I wanted to spend time with Yuri and Lara and do something nice to distract myself from the horror of this morning.

'I'm fine, it's just a headache.'

'What fun stuff will we do, Mummy?' Yuri asked again.

'Well, we could go to the library and then for a hot chocolate.' A combination of educational and treat.

Claire fixed Lara's ponytail. 'Actually, Emma, I'd planned to take them to the cinema today. They really want to see the new *Happy Feet* movie.'

'Yeah, *Happy Feet*.' Yuri and Lara jumped up and down with excitement.

I frowned. 'Well, can't you do that on a day when I'm working?'

308

'I booked the tickets already,' she said, as the children continued to whoop. 'I don't want to let them down.'

'Oh.' I was disappointed.

'If you really want to take them, I suppose I could give you the tickets,' she muttered.

I was a bit taken aback by her attitude. It felt as if our roles had been reversed: she was the mother and I was the nanny trying to butt in.

'No, I want Claire to bringed us,' Lara said, clinging to Claire's leg.

'Yeah, we want Claire.' Yuri ran around in circles.

I felt completely marginalized. No one in my family wanted to be with me. My husband hated me and my children preferred their nanny. If I disappeared, would any of them care? Maybe I should just pack up and leave. Clearly I was superfluous in this house. No one even seemed to like me any more.

I forced myself to smile. 'OK, well, have fun. I'll see you later.' I scurried out of the kitchen before I started to cry.

I spent the next few hours in bed under the covers, feeling sorry for myself. I cried about my children choosing to spend time with their nanny instead of their own mother. When I stopped crying about that, I relived the horror of the scene I'd caused that morning at the London Irish club. Every time I thought of slapping the physiotherapist, I blushed from my toes to my hairline. I was mortified. I really had made a complete fool of myself.

Even so, I thought James should have been more understanding. After all, my paranoia was due to the stalker he had brought into our lives. I wished I could rewind the clock and things go back to the way they had been when our life was quiet and boring. I hated my new reality. I'd never felt so miserable or alone in my life.

I received a text from Lucy. *Sry can't talk, meetings all day. Call later.* Everyone was busy working and I was alone.

I went downstairs to get something to eat and saw the post on the hall table. There was a letter addressed to me.

I opened it, and something fell out. I reached down to pick it up. It was a printout of the photo of our family that had been taken on the day of James's interview when we'd first moved to London. James and the children were smiling out at the camera, but my face had been blackened out. I turned the photo over: *You no longer exist.*

Jesus! This was getting really frightening. Before I could take it in, I heard Claire and the children coming up the path, so I shoved the photo into a drawer and took a deep, calming breath.

The kids burst through the door, laughing with Claire about something funny that had happened in the movie.

'Did you have a nice time?' I asked.

'The best ever,' Yuri enthused.

'Good,' I lied.

'Do you want me to stay and cook them dinner?' Claire asked. 'You still look terrible.'

I'd had enough of being told I looked like crap and I wanted to be on my own with the children. 'No, it's fine. I can manage, thanks. You head off home.'

'I'm happy to stay.'

'No,' I said firmly. 'I'll look after my children. You can go and see your boyfriend. Have you moved in with him yet?'

Claire smiled at me. 'Not yet, but very soon. I reckon by the end of next week I'll be sharing his house.'

'Wow! Well, good luck with all that. It can be tricky when you first move in with someone. It takes a while to get used to it.'

She shook her head. 'I know it'll be brilliant. He's a really amazing person and he adores me.'

'Have you introduced him to Maggie yet?' I asked.

'No,' she said, sounding defensive. 'He's in love with me. He's not interested in my mother. Besides, she probably won't think he's right for me – she never thinks anyone's right for me.'

Well, Claire had certainly grown in confidence. The shy little mouse who had first come to us suddenly seemed so sure of herself. She was like a different person. She looked so much better and she was happy now. She seemed so in love, and I envied her that. When I'd first met James, I was exactly the same, radiating happiness and full of confidence . . . but it all seemed very far away now.

Claire left and I tried to be 'fun Mum'. The children were becoming too attached to Claire. I needed to focus on them more. I'd been so distracted lately and short-tempered, I wasn't surprised that they preferred Claire. But I couldn't let it continue indefinitely.

I cooked them sausages and mashed potato and let them drown it with ketchup. As they were playing with their food, I asked them about the movie and what parts were funny.

'The best bit was when Claire buyed us loads of sweeties,' Lara said.

'What?' I had specifically told Claire no sweets were allowed, unless it was a special occasion.

'Lara! It's supposed to be a secret, you idiot,' Yuri reminded her.

'Hey, don't call your sister names, and I've told you, we have no secrets in this house. I don't like secrets. Now tell me about the sweets.'

Yuri and Lara looked down at their food.

'Come on, guys, I promise I won't be cross. Just tell me.'

'Claire buyed us loads of sweets,' Yuri admitted.

'How many?' I wanted details.

311

'Loads of jellies and she buyed us Coke for a drink,' Lara said.

'Coke!' I was furious.

'You said you wouldn't get cross,' Yuri reminded me.

'I know, but fizzy drinks are really bad for your teeth. Claire knows you're not allowed to have them.'

'Well, Claire is super-nice and she lets us,' Yuri said.

I was really annoyed. What the hell was she doing? I had very clearly said no fizzy drinks. I wondered if this was a one-off or a regular thing. 'Does she buy you sweets on other days?'

'Yes.' Lara was in full confession mode.

'Like what?'

'Crisps and chocolate buttons,' Lara listed.

'She said not to tell you because you'd be cross with her and with us. But you're not cross, are you, Mummy?' Yuri asked.

'No,' I lied. I was extremely cross. 'I'm just a bit surprised, that's all. I told Claire that you were only to have treats on special days.' I'd have to have a stern talk with her in the morning. She couldn't start changing rules like this.

Yuri pushed his barely touched dinner aside. 'I'm full, Mummy.'

'Come on, love, have some more.'

'There's no more room in my tummy.'

'Me too.' Lara pushed her plate away.

I put the plates back in front of the children. 'Now hold on a minute. You can't go and stuff yourselves with sweets and then not eat your dinner. Come on, eat up.'

'I'm not hungry,' Lara whinged.

'I don't want this,' Yuri complained.

'It's your favourite! Eat a bit more,' I said.

'No!' Yuri jumped down from his chair and headed for the kitchen door.

'YURI!' I bellowed. 'Sit down and eat your dinner.'

'*Nonononononononono!*' He opened the door, but I grabbed him by the arm before he could run away.

I picked him up and sat him on his chair. 'I said eat.'

'I don't want to,' Yuri shouted.

'It's yucky,' Lara moaned.

'Jesus Christ, just eat your BLOODY dinner!' I roared.

The two children stared at me. Lara's lip began to wobble. 'You saided you wouldn't get cross. I hate you, Mummy.'

'You're a big meanie.' Yuri backed his sister up. 'I hate you too. I want Daddy.'

'Yeah, well, Daddy isn't here as usual,' I snarled.

'I want Claire,' Lara sobbed.

I grabbed the plates and flung them into the sink. 'I want a new life,' I wailed.

Although James had said he would be home early to talk to me, he was very late. He eventually walked through the door at half past ten. He came into the lounge, threw his kitbag onto the floor and stood in front of me, arms folded. He still looked very angry.

'One of the owners of London Irish called in to see me this evening. He wanted to know if everything was all right. He'd heard there had been a commotion at the club and wanted to know if I needed to take some time off to sort out my personal life.'

This was bad, very bad. I shrank back, holding a cushion protectively across my stomach.

James was breathing deeply, desperately trying not to shout. 'I'm working my bollocks off to make a good impression so I can keep this job and provide a stable, secure home for my family, and then *you* behave like some kind of raving lunatic and sabotage my career.'

Hold on a minute, I wasn't taking this. I stood up. 'I did not go down there to make your life difficult. I went because I'm demented and paranoid and I don't know who or what to believe. I can't take much more of this, James. It's eating me up inside. I don't know if I can trust you, I don't know if you're cheating on me or not. I suspect everyone of sleeping with you. Why are we being stalked? Why am I being tormented? You must have done SOMETHING!'

James threw his hands into the air. 'I'm sick and tired of being accused of something I haven't done. This is not my fault, so stop blaming me. We've been over this a million times. I am not having an affair. I can't have this bloody conversation again.'

'I'm sorry you're tired of having this conversation, because I haven't finished. I got the nicest letter in the post today. You might want to have a peek.' I flung the photo at him.

He picked it up. His face fell. Wearily, he placed the photo down. 'Emma, I don't know what's going on. I'm as confused and fed up as you are. I think we'll have to get the police involved. This is out of control. I want it stopped. But right now, I need to take a bath and just be on my own for a while. I've got a splitting headache and I need some peace and quiet.'

'No problem, James. You can have all the peace and quiet you want in the spare room.' I walked out, slamming the door as I went, hoping it would make his headache worse. Then I crawled into bed and cried myself to sleep.

32

I tossed and turned all night, eventually falling into a fitful sleep at four. I woke up on Friday morning to my phone buzzing. I picked it up. It was a text from a new number. *We look so hot 2gthr.* There was an attachment. It was a photo of two people having sex. It was taken from the neck down and was very grainy. I peered closely to see if I recognized James, but it was impossible to tell.

Rage took over rationality. Ignoring Henry's voice in my head telling me not to respond, I typed back: *Why don't you crawl back under the rock you came from you sick cow?*

A message came straight back: *Give up Emma, he loves me. Go back to Ireland where u belong.*

James loves his family, you're wasting your time you lunatic. Go to hell and leave us alone.

Wake up u stupid bitch. James wants me & only me. U r past it. U can't satisfy him. I can. And do.

U better watch out, we're going to the police. They'll track u down and put u in the mental institution where u belong.

U r so stupid & blind. Why dont u look in the bedside drawer & c what James bought for me? Maybe then ull believe me.

What?

I looked over at James's bedside locker. Unlike my messy one, which was covered with books, magazines, sweet wrappers and tissues, James's was very neat. He had only one book placed on the top. It was about rugby, *Winning!* by Clive Woodward.

I slid across the bed. With trembling hands, I pulled open

the top drawer. Inside was James's good watch, some cuff-links, his passport and cheque book. No sign of anything else. I pulled open the bottom drawer. Lying there was the Father's Day card the children and I had made for him last year. 'We love you, Daddy' was written across the top and Yuri had drawn a picture of four stick people with big smiling faces . . . our little family. Underneath the card were some photos of the children when they were very small and one of us on our wedding day, looking so young and happy. I lifted the photos out, and that was when I saw them.

The red crotchless knickers were in a corner of the drawer, underneath the photos and the card. James had hidden this disgusting thing under our happy family pictures. I stared at it in disbelief. I felt a cold chill down my spine. I didn't scream, cry, shout or freak out. I just sat there, staring at the knickers. I felt weirdly calm and clear-headed, as if all the emotions had been drained out of me in a split second.

James came into the room wrapped in a towel. He stopped dead when he saw my face.

'What?' He looked at my hand and saw the underwear. 'Christ, not another delivery?'

I shook my head. 'No, James. These were in the bottom drawer of your bedside table. She texted me to let me know where to find them.'

'What? How the hell –'

'– could they have got there?' I finished his sentence. 'I can think of only one way.'

'Emma, they –'

I raised my hand. 'Stop,' I said quietly. 'Stop talking. Stop lying. Stop making up excuses. I have the proof now. I know what I need to do.'

'What do you mean?' James looked stricken.

My mind had been made up for me. I had only one option.

There was only one path for me now. 'I'm leaving you.'

'WHAT?' James's mouth hung open. 'You can't be serious.'

'I'm deadly serious.'

'Emma, come on, don't do this. You can't walk out now. We'll fix this. I'll fix this. Henry's calling me today with the name of that detective. I'm going to pay him whatever it takes to hunt down this crazy woman.'

'Too little too late,' I said, somehow still calm and in control.

James grabbed my arm. His voice was breaking as he said, 'Emma, I'm begging you. Don't do this. We'll work it out.'

I pulled away from him. It was as if ice was running through my veins. I felt nothing for him. I was completely numb. 'So you keep saying, but the problem is, James, I don't believe a word you say any more. You've been lying to me for weeks. I've been a blind fool and I've had enough.'

'You can't leave me,' James said faintly.

'Yes, I can, and I am. I'm going to take the kids home to Dublin for a while. I need to get away from this house and you, and figure out what to do.'

'You can't take my children away.' He was so horrified that I almost cracked. I had to steel myself so I wouldn't cave in to him.

'I'm hardly going to leave them here with a father who's never around.'

'I'll work less. I'll come home for dinner. I'll find out who this lunatic is. We'll track her down and put her in prison.'

I shook my head. I couldn't believe how calm I was being. My voice wasn't even shaking. Was this what happened when you went into shock?

'Too late, James. I've given you so many chances and you lied and lied. I've been an idiot and I'm not going to be made a fool of any more. I don't know what happened, but since we've moved here, you've changed.'

'I haven't changed, I've just been working hard, maybe too hard, and then some lunatic started stalking us. How am I to blame for someone else's psychosis? I have done nothing wrong. You have to believe me.'

'I don't.'

James looked at me in shock. I was appalled by my own coldness, but I had just reached the end of my tolerance. I couldn't do it any more. It was as simple as that.

He kept pleading and claiming his innocence. He asked me to go with him to Toulouse that afternoon, for his away game. I refused. He told me he'd book the Eurostar to Paris for us the following weekend. I refused. He begged me to wait until he got back from his match in Toulouse on Sunday to sort everything out. I refused.

'Please, Emma, please. When I get back, we'll go to the police together and get them to stop this nonsense. Come on, darling, we can sort this out. But we must stay strong and we must stay together.'

Finally, I agreed to stay and wait for him to come back from Toulouse . . . but I had no intention of waiting for him. I was going as soon as he was out of the door.

Once he had gone, I dialled my parents' number. It rang ten times before Dad answered. He sounded out of breath and very grumpy. 'What?' he snapped.

'Hi, Dad, how are you?'

'Who is it?'

'Your daughter.'

'Barbara, you can shag off if you think I'm sending you any more money.'

'No, Dad, it's Emma.'

'Oh, what's up?'

'Well, the thing is, I need to come back for a bit.'

'Back where?'

'To Dublin.'

'Why?' He sounded suspicious.

'Because . . . well . . . because I need to get away from here for a while.'

'Where are you going to stay?'

'With you and Mum, I hope.'

'Are you bringing the children?'

'Yes.'

'What's a while? A day or two?' he asked optimistically.

I hesitated. 'No, Dad. I was thinking more like a couple of weeks.'

'Weeks!' Dad sounded shocked. 'Why? Why do you need to stay here for a couple of weeks?'

'Because . . . well, the thing is –'

'Jesus, Emma, will you spit it out? I'm in the middle of watching the golf. Rory McIlroy is four up on the thirteenth. He birdied the last two holes.'

My composure crumbled and I began to sob. 'Because James is having an affair and I'm being stalked and if I don't get out of here I'm going to have a nervous breakdown.'

Silence.

Then, 'UNAAAAAAA!'

Dad had rushed off to get Mum. I could hear him roaring, 'Una, get down here! Emma's having a breakdown. Hurry up, she's bawling. She wants to move back in with us, kids and all. Sort her out.'

I could hear Mum's feet running along the hall. 'Emma? What's going on?'

'I need to come home, Mum. I uh . . . uh . . . need to get out of here for a bit.'

'Why, pet? What's happened?'

Hearing Mum call me 'pet' was the final straw. My composure went right out of the window. I wailed into the phone, 'It's awful, Mum. James is having an affair and I found knickers and I'm being stalked and the kids hate me and they love Claire and I'm all paranoid and I made a fool of myself and I can't *sleeeeeeep*.'

'There, there, Emma,' Mum soothed. 'You sound a bit hysterical. Now I need you to take three deep breaths and try to talk coherently. All I can hear is screeching. I hope the children aren't there to see you in this state. It's not good for children to see their parents upset.'

I tried to calm down, gulping in air so I could speak. 'Mum, I need to come home. James is having an affair.'

'I don't believe it. James wouldn't do that.'

Typical! My own mother wouldn't believe wonderful James could possibly behave badly. 'Well, he is,' I barked, anger taking over from tears.

'How do you know? You're inclined to be dramatic, Emma. Don't jump to silly conclusions.'

'Well, Mum, let me see. He's been getting tons of sextexts, he works late every night and . . . oh, yes, I happened to come across the whore's knickers in his bedside drawer.'

'Are you sure they're not yours?'

I screamed silently and, in a strangled voice, said, 'Yes, Mum, quite sure.'

'I still don't believe it. James is devoted to you and the children. Maybe the pants were left there by the people who rented before you.'

'No, Mum, they do not belong to the previous tenant. They are his mistress's red satin crotchless knickers, OK?'

There was a moment's silence. 'You can't run home every time you have a problem in your marriage, Emma.

All marriages go through ups and downs. You need to stay there and work it out.'

I willed myself to remain calm, but it was impossible. 'Mum, if I stay here, we'll break up for good. If I come back to Dublin, get some space and clear my head, then maybe we can work it out. I am not running away at the first hurdle. I've put up with so much stress and I've given him the benefit of the doubt a million times. But right now I need to get out of this house before I go insane.'

'How long are you planning on staying?'

'I don't know. A couple of weeks, maybe.' How long did it take to get over an affair, stalking and humiliation?

'What about the children?'

'They're coming with me.'

'What about their schooling?'

I was getting exasperated. 'They're four and three. A couple of weeks won't make any difference. They're not going to miss out on trigonometry and bloody Yeats.'

Mum sniffed. 'What does James think about all this?'

'I don't give a damn what James thinks about all this. This is what *I* need. Believe it or not, Mum, I actually matter, you know. I am a real person with feelings who has been put through hell and, if it isn't too much trouble, I'd like you to take my feelings into consideration for once.'

'I'm sorry, Emma, but it's out of the question that you take those children away from their father. You need to stay there and try to work this out. Now, if you want some space, go and stay with your sister. I'll get the first flight to London tomorrow and I'll mind the children while you go off with James somewhere nice and try to sort this mess out. Marriages require lots of hard work and compromise.'

'James is working this weekend. He always works at the

weekends so we can't go somewhere nice and, besides, I want to kill him, not spend more time with him.'

Mum tutted. 'Don't you think there have been many times when I've wanted to drive a stake through your father's heart? I've lost count of how many occasions I've wanted to smack him over the head with a golf club, but I just got on with it.'

Crikey, poor Dad. Did he have any idea how close he'd been to death?

'Now, calm yourself down. Don't let the children see you in a state. Get dressed and go about your day. I'll see you in the morning. What you need is time with your husband to rekindle the romance. Every marriage needs that.'

'What about the small detail of his mistress, Mum?'

She coughed. 'Nonsense. I don't believe he has one, and if he does, she can be got rid of, I assure you. Many's the wife who saw off a mistress. Now, lipstick on, Emma, and best foot forward.'

'We're not in *Downton Abbey*, Mum!' I was exasperated beyond belief.

'Maybe not, but those upper-crust Brits had the right attitude in times of stress – stiff upper lip and carry on.'

I needed to get off the phone before I lost my temper and said something I would regret. 'Fine. Me and my stiff upper lip will see you tomorrow.'

I rang in sick to work and then went in to talk to the children. I told them they weren't going to school today and that we were going for a little stay with Auntie Babs. They were thrilled.

'How many sleepies will we have in her house?' Lara asked.

'Well, I'm not sure. A few,' I fudged. I had no idea how long it would be, plus I hadn't even asked her yet.

'Is Daddy coming with us or will he come after work?'

I tried to sound breezy. 'Well, sweetheart, Daddy has to work, so he won't be coming with us.'

'Is Claire coming?' Lara asked.

'No, just Mummy.'

'Oh.' They both looked disappointed.

Once more, I saw I needed to spend more time with them. Mind you, now that I was going to be a single parent, I'd see plenty of them.

'Come on, let's pack a suitcase for our adventure.' I tried to pack, aided and abetted by the children. They were more of a hindrance than a help. Yuri kept putting his football in and Lara insisted on packing her whole army of cuddly toys and dolls.

'Lara, darling, you can't put all of your toys into the suitcase. They won't fit.'

'But I can't leave any of them here. They'll be lonely.'

'But Mr Hippo is almost the same size as the suitcase. We can't bring him.'

Lara crossed her arms and pursed her lips. 'Well, then, I'm not coming.'

Mr Hippo was enormous. James had won him at some rugby club quiz a year ago. Lara had taken a huge shine to him. I was going to have to be persuasive. 'All right, why don't we leave him with Daddy? Then Daddy and Mr Hippo can keep each other company so neither of them gets lonely.'

Lara thought about this for a minute, then nodded.

'I'm not leaving my football with Daddy,' Yuri announced.

'Babs doesn't have a garden,' I said. 'You won't need it.'

'But it's my Liverpool one. I love it.' Yuri hugged it.

I crouched down. 'Yuri, pet, why don't you leave it in your bedroom so it's safe? When we come back we'll play with it.'

He shook his head vehemently. There was no getting around him and I didn't have time for intricate arguments. 'OK, put the ball in.'

'What about Mr Hippo?' Lara complained.

'He's just too big.'

'It's not fair, Mummy.' She burst into tears.

I grabbed Mr Hippo and flung him into the suitcase. 'Fine, he can bloody well come.'

'You said a bad word and you're grumpy again,' Yuri noted.

'Hello?' Claire's voice called from downstairs.

Yuri and Lara ran down. 'We're going on holidays,' they told her.

I followed them, lugging the suitcase.

'What's going on?' Claire asked, puzzled.

Seeing her reminded me that I wanted to talk to her about buying the kids sweets and fizzy drinks, but I didn't have the energy. I couldn't face a confrontation. Not now, not with everything that was going on.

'We're going on a little trip.' I decided to be vague. I didn't want Claire to know my marriage was in tatters. 'But don't worry, I'll pay you while I'm gone.'

'It's kind of sudden. Is everything all right?'

I busied myself with the locks on the suitcase. 'Yes, I just fancy a break.'

'Is James going too – a family holiday?'

'Uhm, no. He's away at a match in Toulouse. He'll be back on Sunday.' I felt my resolve breaking and I began to cry.

Claire ushered the children into the lounge. She came back and put her arm around me. 'What's wrong?' she asked gently.

I wiped my eyes. 'It's this stalker person. She's ruining our lives. I need a break from it all. I need to get away and clear my head. Everything is such a mess. I just don't understand any of it. Who is this person? Why is she trying to ruin my marriage?'

Claire looked a bit sheepish. 'Actually, Emma, I didn't tell you this because you've been so stressed, but there is a woman at the school who's been asking me questions about James.'

My head snapped up. 'Which woman?'

'The one with the long blonde hair and the really tight jeans and she always wears high heels, even when it's raining.'

I racked my brains. There were quite a few mothers who fitted that description. 'What did she ask you?'

'Just what James did and where he worked and stuff.'

I stared at her. 'Why didn't you tell me? It must be her. How long ago was this?'

Claire looked uncomfortable. 'A couple of weeks.'

'Do you know what her kids are called?' I wanted to find out her name.

She shook her head. 'She has one boy, but he's in the baby class.'

'Oh, my God, it must be her.' I was annoyed with Claire for not telling me. This was the woman. It had to be. I'd be able to confront her on Monday at the school gate. I'd get Claire to come with me and point her out. I'd give that bitch a piece of my mind.

Claire was worried now. 'Emma, it might not be her. She could have been interested in James because of his London Irish jacket.'

'No, it's definitely her, it has to be.'

Yuri and Lara came out. 'Are we going?' Lara asked.

I bent down to her. 'Yes, pet.'

'Would you like me to do a grocery shop for James while you're gone and keep the place tidy and do some laundry?' Claire asked.

That was a great idea. I beckoned her to the side of the hall. 'Actually, Claire, that would be great. Can you keep an eye out and let me know if anything or anyone arrives to the house? I'd really appreciate it.'

Claire put a hand on my arm. 'I'd be happy to. Don't worry, I'll be here to look after everything. You go and try to relax. You deserve a break, you look exhausted.'

I hugged her. 'Thanks, Claire, you're a rock.'

33

I rang Babs from the car to tell her about the knickers and to let her know that we were moving in with her. She said we could stay for a few days but no more because her apartment was small and she didn't want the kids breaking her things. She sounded very stressed at the idea of it and, really, I couldn't blame her.

When we arrived, she showed the children her tiny spare room, then got snappy when they jumped on the bed.

'Could you try to be a bit nicer?' I asked.

'I don't want my stuff getting wrecked,' she barked.

'Fine. I'll tie them to a chair. Will that make you happy?'

'Don't be stupid.'

'Sorry, I'm just freaking out here.' I went into the spare bedroom and told the kids to unpack the suitcase in the hope that it would keep them busy and out of trouble for ten minutes.

When I came out, Babs was sitting on the sofa, her feet curled under her. 'Emma, there's something weird about this supposed affair. It doesn't add up. The whole thing is so wacky. Who the hell would have an affair with a nut-job? If it is this school mum, why would she ask your nanny questions about your husband? Surely she knew Claire would tell you.'

'She's obviously deranged, so maybe she doesn't care.'

Babs shrugged. 'I suppose so. Anyway, I have to go to work. I told them I'd be late, but I have to be in for eleven. Please try and stop the kids from trashing my apartment.'

Yuri and Lara were soon causing havoc in Babs's shoebox

home, so I decided to take them out for a few hours to tire them. We spent the afternoon in Hyde Park, feeding the ducks and going for tea and scones in the coffee shop. Then I walked them down Oxford Street and we went for pizza in a little restaurant off Marylebone Lane. By the time we got back to Babs's that evening, the children were exhausted. They collapsed into bed and were fast asleep before their heads hit the pillows.

I closed the bedroom door and sank into the couch. Babs was watching Gok Wan's show, where he was doing a make-over. She kept muttering about how much better she was. Her face was very pale and she had black rings under her eyes. 'I saw you arguing with Gary at work on Tuesday. What happened? Did you tell him about the abortion?'

Babs put her hands over her face and groaned. 'He is the biggest prick that ever lived,' she fumed.

'What happened?'

'It was later, when I was packing up to leave for the day. He came into the makeup room and shut the door. He asked me why I was avoiding him and said he was sorry about "the other thing", as he so brilliantly put it.'

'He's such a dickhead,' I said, feeling my blood boiling at the mere thought of him.

'So he says, "Look, Babs, we have to work together and everyone's noticed how icy the atmosphere has been. Can we just put this behind us and be professional about it? I can see you're angry and I get that. But it's over now, we need to move on."'

'It's all about Gary,' I observed.

'So I told him exactly how angry I was and why. "You filled me with bullshit about your unhappy marriage and your bitch of a wife and when I got pregnant you didn't want to know me. You're such a great guy, Gary. A real gem."'

328

'Good for you.' I was delighted she had stood up to him. 'What did he say?'

'He sneered at me, "And you're such a lovely girl with such a pure reputation. No one in the industry thinks you're a slut. No one thinks you're an easy shag. Do you know what they call you? The Irish greyhound. You're like a dog in heat. Every man knows you'll shag him if it'll help your career. You think you're so hot. Wake up, babe, this is TV. There's always someone better-looking, smarter and more ambitious coming up behind you."'

My mouth fell open. 'What? How dare he? That's – that's horrible.'

'Yeah, I was pretty shocked myself, but I just told him he was full of crap and that I'm a brilliant presenter, and then he really stuck his boot in.' Babs looked upset. 'He told me that the ratings went down after I shouted at that guest last week who was colour-blind and that people are sick of my arrogance and my bluntness. He says he'll have me replaced within six weeks.'

I was outraged. 'That's rubbish. People love it that you're so honest. It's your thing, your trademark. It's what makes you different. Don't let him threaten you like that. He has no right. I bet you he's bluffing so you'll leave.'

'The problem is, Emma, that if I get fired from a crappy show on a TV channel that has mediocre viewing figures at the best of times, I'm screwed. This show was supposed to be a stepping stone. I was using it as a launching pad to showcase my talent. But now they're going to replace me and it won't be easy to get another presenting job.'

'But he can't get away with that! It's outrageous! He's trying to fire you because of the pregnancy.'

Babs sighed. 'What can I do? If my ratings are down, he's entitled to fire me.'

'You could threaten to tell his wife,' I suggested.

'I did,' Babs admitted. 'But he said I'd never work in TV again. He could ruin my career. The producers are the ones with all the power in TV.'

'Oh, Babs, I could strangle him. He is such a scumbag.'

Babs clasped her hands together. 'I know, but unless my agent can find me something really quickly, my career could be over.' Her eyes were filling. This was Babs: she never cried. She was absolutely devastated: first the abortion, then being dumped and now her job . . .

I needed to boost her confidence. 'Don't you dare let that snake knock you down. Get onto your agent and start auditioning for other jobs. You're brilliant at what you do. OK, you can be harsh at times, but your honesty is what makes you stand out. Don't let this stop you. It's just a bump in the road. Come on, stiff upper lip, onwards and upwards!' I'd morphed into our mother.

'I rang my agent first thing this morning. She's going to look around for me.'

'Good for you.'

'I just can't believe I was so stupid. I actually believed him. Me! The most cynical person alive! I believed a total tosser when he said he loved me. Christ, I can't even bear to think of him. How did I ever fancy him? He is so gross. I hope he gets syphilis from his next fling and that his dick falls off.'

'I hope James gets it too.'

We smiled, despite our situations.

Babs's phone beeped and she showed it to me. It was a text from James: *Have you heard from Emma?*

She replied: *Yes she fine no thks 2 u!!!!*

Her phone rang. It was James.

'Answer it and put it on loudspeaker,' I urged her, rushing over to close the bedroom door so the children wouldn't wake up.

'I did not have an affair!' James sounded furious.

'Really? Well, how the hell did those red knickers end up in your drawer?'

Go, Babs! I gave her the thumbs-up.

'I have absolutely no idea, but I swear to you, I did not put them there. Come on, Babs, you know me. I love Emma, I love my kids and all I do is work. I haven't got time for an affair.'

'It doesn't take much time for a quick shag.'

'I have no interest in other women. I love my wife.'

My hardened heart softened a tiny bit.

'Have you heard from Emma? She won't answer my calls.'

'She's staying here with me for a few days. Give her some space. You can't rush her on this.'

'I swear on my children's lives I have not been unfaithful. I've been racking my brains, but I just don't see who could be doing this. I'm hiring a detective to get to the bottom of it. It's destroying my life.' James's voice wobbled.

My heart melted a little more.

Babs was having none of it. 'Oh, God, don't start getting emotional. Where's that stiff upper lip you Brits are born with? Come on, James, pull it together. I think a detective is a good idea. You need to prove to Emma that you're not a cheating scumbag.'

'Will you please talk to her for me?'

Babs smiled at me. 'Look, I'll tell her I think you're inno-cent, but you need to get the proof.'

'I will, thanks.'

Babs hung up. 'Well?'

I had a lump in my throat. He had sounded so upset, so genuine, so . . . like the old James. My head throbbed.

Babs fished in her bag and handed me a tablet.

'What is it?'

'Xanax.'

'Are you nuts? I'm not taking this.'

'Emma, there are times in your life when prescribed medication is vital. I've been living on these since . . . well, since the baby thing.' Babs popped one into her mouth. 'They take the edge off.'

What the hell? Taking the edge off sounded great. I held out my hand.

34

Mum and Dad arrived the next morning. Mum hugged me tightly, then examined my face. 'You look exhausted. We need to spruce you up.'

Babs was not happy. 'You can't stay. I can't fit you all in. It's too crowded in here already,' she grumbled.

'Stay here?' Dad said, looking around the shoebox apartment. 'You must be joking. We're booked into a B-and-B around the corner.'

Yuri and Lara were thrilled to see their grandparents. They ran to them and wrapped their arms around their legs.

'Come here to me, my little angels.' Mum pulled them into a bear hug. 'Now, I have a little treat for you.' She pulled two Kinder eggs out of her bag.

Lara threw her arms around her grandmother. 'I love you, Granny.'

Mum picked her up and cuddled her. 'I've missed you so much,' she said, kissing Lara's nose.

'What about me?' Yuri tugged at her jumper. 'Did you miss me?'

Mum put Lara down and bent low to Yuri. 'Yes, I did, desperately. I'm so happy to see you.'

As the three of them sat on the couch, Dad shuffled uncomfortably beside me. With his hands buried deep in his trouser pockets, he said, 'So, James has been . . . ah . . . uhm . . . that is to say . . . playing the field, as it were?'

'If by that you mean sleeping with another woman, the evidence certainly makes it look that way.'

Dad shook his head, still avoiding eye contact. 'I just don't see it. James isn't the type.'

I shrugged. 'Well, apparently, he is the type. But the woman is a total nutter. She's been stalking me and sending awful things to me at the house.'

'Like the ah . . . uhm . . . other thing.'

Babs snorted behind me.

I no longer had any shame or anything to hide. They had all seen the vibrator and they now suspected James was a philanderer, so I decided to give Dad a full account of the parcels. 'The vibrator, yes, and handcuffs and a whip and –'

Dad's eyes bulged and he coughed loudly. 'Right, yes, well . . . I see.' He grabbed his newspaper and tapped the front page. 'Have you seen this? Bloody government,' he huffed. 'Disgrace. More charges, more taxes – they're bleeding us dry.'

'Nice change of subject, Dad.' Babs smirked.

'Who's bleeding?' Lara was alarmed.

'Everyone in Ireland,' Dad said.

Lara's eyes widened. I went over and placed a reassuring hand on her little head. 'No one is actually bleeding. It's just an expression.'

'Don't mind your granddad. He's very grumpy,' Mum told her granddaughter.

'Why are you grumpy, Granddad?' Yuri asked.

'Because I cancelled his Sky Sports,' Mum explained.

'Sports in the sky?' Yuri giggled.

'Why did you do that?' Babs asked. 'He's obsessed with sports.'

'It was an unnecessary expense, and there are plenty of sports on the normal TV channels. Besides, I came in the other day and found your father watching curling.'

'Curling hair?' Lara was confused.

'Is curling the one where they throw the big round stone thing and the other two players brush the ice with brooms?' I asked.

'Exactly,' Mum said.

'Ah, Dad, come on.' Babs laughed. 'It's the most boring sport ever invented.'

Dad bristled. 'It's actually very skilful, but Philistines like you and your mother wouldn't understand.'

'Skill? In brushing ice?' I grinned.

'I want to play that,' Lara said. 'I'm a good brusher, aren't I, Mummy?'

'Yes, you are, pet,' I agreed.

'Maybe Granddad could train you for the 2028 Olympics,' Babs suggested.

'I want to be in the 'Lympics, too.' Yuri was not going to be left out. 'But I'm not brushing anything, no way. What can I do?'

'Not basketball anyway,' Dad mumbled.

I glared at him. 'You can do anything you want,' I told Yuri.

'I want to be a rugby player and for Daddy to be my coach.'

'That's an excellent idea,' Dad said, clearly feeling guilty about his quip.

Yuri ate some of his Kinder egg. 'Daddy said it doesn't matter if you're small in rugby. He said the only thing that matters is if I'm strong, and I am. He said the bestest rugby players are the small strong ones. He said small is brilliant because you can zip around the pitch and score tries between big players' legs.' Yuri's face was glowing. 'Daddy said when I'm eight he'll teach me rugby. My daddy is the best rugby coach in the world. Did you know that, Granddad?'

'Of course I did,' Dad said. 'Your dad is a brilliant coach.'

'Daddy says he's proud of me all the time, but I'm super-proud of him,' Yuri announced.

I rushed out of the room and locked myself into the bathroom. I tried to stifle my sobs in a towel. Why had James put me in this awful position? Why did he have to go and ruin everything? Yuri would be completely heartbroken if we split up. Oh, God, what was I going to do?

There was a knock on the door. 'Emma?' Mum called.

'Just a second,' I mumbled.

'Open up. I want to talk to you.'

I opened the door. Mum came in, closed it behind her and sat on the rim of the bath. 'What are you going to do, Emma?'

I sat down beside her. 'I don't know.'

'Are you sure he was unfaithful?'

'Ninety-nine point nine per cent. How else do you explain the texts and the stalking and the sex toys?'

'It could have been a woman who was obsessed with him.'

'Mum, I found knickers in his drawer.'

Mum pursed her lips. 'That's a bad sign, all right. Look, Emma, in a marriage you have to take the rough with the smooth.'

'So what are you saying? I should pretend it never happened and go running back to him?'

'I'm saying that there are two people in a marriage. If one of them strays, maybe the other needs to look at the reasons why.'

My jaw dropped. 'Are you suggesting it's my fault that James is sleeping with someone else?'

'No, but you can be difficult at times, and you went to London with a bit of a puss on your face. Every time I spoke to you, you were giving out about how much James was working. I don't think you did yourself any favours.'

I could not believe that my mother was blaming *me*. I felt anger rising. 'First of all, I've been bloody brilliant since we moved here. I got myself a job, I found a great nanny, I set the kids up in a nice school, I made friends with my neighbours and I put the kids to bed almost every night on my own. James makes brief appearances on Sundays. I've encouraged him in his job but, yes, his late nights do bother me – they'd bother anyone. I'm lonely, Mum. I'm on my own a lot. It's not easy being alone in a strange city with two small kids. Do I get any credit for that? Is there any chance that someone would say, "Well done, Emma, you're doing your best, but your husband is an ungrateful, cheating bastard"?'

Mum sighed. 'There's no need to get angry. Relationships are a work in progress. You have to put a lot of effort in and oftentimes you have to bite your tongue and put a smile on your face, even when you don't feel like it.'

Was she serious? Mum had never in her life bitten her tongue. She had always said exactly what she thought about everything. And as for smiling when she didn't want to? Mum had probably smiled three times since the menopause had hit her.

'Mum, I'm a good wife and a good mother. I'm not the best, I'm not perfect, but I'm good. I do not deserve this shit in my life.'

'There's no need for bad language.'

I gritted my teeth. 'I do not deserve my husband to cheat on me. I do not deserve to have sex toys sent to my house and to be stalked. I've done nothing wrong.'

'Do you think the poor Africans deserve famine? Do you think the poor indigital people of Brazil deserve to have the Amazonian forest cut down?'

'It's "indigenous".'

Mum wagged her finger at me. 'Don't try to distract me. The point is, Emma, it's not about deserving or not deserving. It's about life not being smooth sailing.'

'We're not talking about a few ripples here, Mum,' I said. 'It's about a bloody great wave crashing down on me. Are you saying I should just forgive James and forget about it all?'

Mum stood up and folded a towel. 'I think you should consider it. He is a wonderful father and those children adore him. He has been a very good husband to you, Emma. Not many men would have been so strong and loyal through all that pregnancy struggle.'

'He wanted a baby too, Mum. I didn't force him into it.' I was really getting upset now. Was James allowed to walk all over me because he had been supportive through the adoption of *our* child?

'Not all men would have been open to adoption. Not all men would have taken to a child the way James took to Yuri. He's a good man, Emma. And you wouldn't do well on your own. You need a steady man in your life. It stops you going off on your tangents.'

'What tangents?' I huffed.

'You get very het up about things.'

'I think I'm entitled to get het up about my husband's infidelity, Mum!'

Mum put the towel down. 'All I'm saying is, don't be too hasty in making any decisions. Those children love their father, and being on your own would not suit you. Now, put on some makeup. You'll upset them going about looking like that.'

With her pearls of wisdom handed out, Mum left the bathroom. My mother never ceased to amaze me. Here I was, the victim of stalking and a husband who was likely cheating on me, but somehow, some way, by some means, it appeared to be my fault. I must have been mad to think of moving in with her for a couple of weeks. This crazy situation really was making me lose my mind.

35

That night as I tucked the children into the bed in the spare room – which was really a glorified wardrobe – I hugged them tightly. 'I love you guys so much. From now on we're going to do more fun things together, like go to the zoo and Legoland and lots of other things.'

'Yeah!' Lara clapped her hands together. 'I love the zoo.'

I kissed her nose. 'Me too. I love being with you guys. I'm sorry I've been so busy lately.'

'And grumpy,' Lara reminded me.

'Yes, and grumpy,' I admitted.

'And shouty,' Yuri added.

'Yes, and shouty.'

'And –'

'OK.' I drowned out their further complaints. 'I'm sorry for all of it, and I promise to try to be happy Mummy now.'

'And super-nice like Claire?' Lara said.

'And fun like Daddy?' Yuri said.

I switched off the light, so they wouldn't see my tears. 'Sleep tight.'

I wiped a hand across my eyes and went back into the lounge, where Babs was lying on the couch shouting at the TV. Mum and Dad had gone to meet friends for dinner, which was a good thing as I was definitely on the verge of having a blazing argument with Mum about my 'role' in James's lying and cheating.

'She's useless,' Babs roared at the TV.

I looked at the screen. It was *The X Factor*. A young girl was singing 'Light My Fire' out of tune.

'She must be sleeping with the producer. There's no way she's getting votes – she's tone deaf,' Babs grumbled.

I decided not to point out that she herself was a producer-shagger.

'That's the job I want,' she said.

'Singing on *X Factor*?' Was she completely delusional? Babs hadn't got a note in her head. It didn't matter who she slept with, she'd never make it.

She rolled her eyes. 'No, although I think I'd do very well. I want Dermot's job. I want to present the show. I'd be brilliant at it.'

'Well, he's pretty good at it himself,' I pointed out. I'd always had a bit of a crush on Dermot O'Leary.

'He's all right, but I could do better.' She bit her nail. 'I have to do something. I have to jump before Gary pushes me. I've told my agent to hurry up and find me a new job. I can't be fired. I have to go first.'

'I'm sure your agent will find something. You're very good,' I soothed.

'Well, I know that, but talent isn't everything. You need luck and timing and the right connections.'

My phone buzzed – *Just home. U on way?* It was Lucy. She'd called me when she'd heard my message and asked me over to her apartment for wine and a full debriefing.

I texted back: *Leaving now. See you soon.*

I left Babs complaining about having to sit in with the children yet again and got a taxi to Lucy's apartment in the City, around the corner from her office. She had to stay in London for some important meeting, so we had arranged to spend Saturday night together, drinking and talking about our failing marriages.

Her apartment was in a big block on the fifth floor. I hadn't been in it before. The building was soulless. From the outside, all the apartments looked the same. It seemed more like a hotel than a collection of homes.

I knocked and she opened immediately, handing me a huge glass of wine. I followed her into the living room. It was small and bare, but functional. There were no paintings, no photos, no cushions or throws. It felt very unlived-in. No wonder Lucy worked late: this place was so impersonal, you wouldn't want to go back to it. In fact, a hotel room would have been a whole lot nicer.

Before I even sat down, I received another text from James: *Pls call me. We need to talk. Ill b home tomorrow at 8. Come over 4 dinner. Pls Emma, I love u.*

Lucy read it over my shoulder. 'You should go,' she said.

'Why? Until he comes clean and tells me exactly what's going on, I don't want to see him.'

'Well, maybe he's ready to explain it all. Look, Emma, you need to find out what's going on.'

'I'm not ready yet. I need another day or two to clear my head.' I put down the wine and curled my feet under me. 'I cannot believe this is my life. One minute I'm getting married, the next I'm walking out on my cheating husband.'

'Tell me about it.' Lucy drank deeply from her glass.

'You look almost as bad as I do,' I noted, taking in her tired eyes and stooped shoulders.

'My marriage is in tatters too.' She sighed. 'So what are you going to do?'

'No more questions about me,' I begged, holding up my hands. 'Tell me all about how you're doing. I don't want to think about my life tonight.'

'How I'm doing?' Lucy shook her head. 'Shit, if you want the truth.'

'Donal's still on the warpath?'

'You won't believe what he's been up to, Emma. He's a lying, conniving bastard.'

I looked at her, alarmed. This sounded serious.

'He's been hiding my pill. I mean, how bloody devious, not to mention immature, is that? Every Sunday night, when I'm asleep, he takes my packet of pills out of my washbag so I won't have them in London and therefore I won't be protected. Then when I come home on Friday, he insists on having sex at the weekend. He is actually deluded enough to believe that I'm going to fall pregnant and that will solve everything.'

'Christ, Lucy, I'm . . . I'm kind of lost for words. That's such a low thing to do to someone who has been clear about not wanting more children. I'm really surprised at him. What is he thinking?'

'Thankfully he's no Columbo. I figured it out pretty quickly, so I keep spare packets of the pill here in the apartment and leave one in my washbag for him to nick. But it really blew up last Sunday night.'

'But when I saw you on Monday night, you never said?'

'It was still too raw, Emma. I just couldn't talk about it – I was reeling.'

'Oh, Lucy . . . what happened?'

Lucy explained.

She had just put Serge to bed and was tidying up downstairs when Donal came back from commentating on some rugby match. She had barely seen him all weekend because he'd been busy working.

'Are you hungry?' she asked. 'I could order a takeaway?'

'No, I'm fine. I grabbed a burger with Finn on my way home.'

'God, I'd love a burger,' Lucy said, trying to remember the

last time she'd allowed herself to pig out on a juicy one instead of her usual lean fish or chicken.

Donal turned around. 'Are you craving a burger?' he asked.

Lucy decided to goad him. 'Yes, actually, I've been craving them for a few weeks now. It's weird.'

Donal came closer to her. His eyes were shining. 'Do you think you might be pregnant?'

'How could I be pregnant? I'm on the pill.'

Donal paced the room. 'You've forgotten it the last few weeks.'

'Yes, but then we used condoms, remember?'

Donal avoided her eyes. 'Well, they can burst or be faulty sometimes.'

'Really? I thought they were very reliable nowadays.'

'You never know. Will I nip out and get a test?'

'I wouldn't bother if I was you. It'd be a waste of time and money. Forty-year-old women who use contraception don't get pregnant.'

Donal shuffled about. 'Let's just check to be sure.'

'You seem very confident that I might be pregnant, Donal. Why is that? Why would you imagine I could be? Do you have something you'd like to tell me? A confession perhaps? Something you did behind my back, without my knowledge or consent?' Lucy spat the words out.

Donal's face flushed. 'Are you pregnant?'

'What do you think?'

'I think you are.'

'Well, then, would you like to explain how it happened?'

Donal looked down at his hands. 'Look, Lucy, I know you said you don't want another baby, but I do. There are two of us in this marriage and you just made the decision. It was as if I didn't count. I really want a sibling for Serge – he's lonely. And I think another baby would fix things.'

344

'How do you figure that?' Lucy's rage was beginning to boil over.

Donal sat on the stool at the opposite side of the counter to Lucy. 'We're drifting apart. I feel like I'm losing you. All you care about is work. We miss you, me and Serge. We hate you being away so much. I think another baby will bring you home. You'll come back to us. We can be a family again.'

Lucy gripped her hands together. 'What did you do, Donal?'

Silence.

'Let's see. Well, I know you've been hiding my pill and I'm guessing you cut holes in the condoms I've been asking you to use. Am I right?'

Donal nodded. 'Guilty as charged.'

Lucy lost her cool. 'You sneaky, sly, underhanded shit. I –'

Donal cut across her: 'We *need* another child, Lucy. We need a sibling for Serge and we need to live in the same house and behave like a family. The way we live now is a joke. I hate it. I did not get married to see my wife for ten minutes a week. I know you keep saying you couldn't handle another child, but I know you can. When you're here, you're great with Serge. He adores you.'

'Really, Donal? Because I remember you telling me recently that I was a cold, selfish cow and that I was a bad mother because I didn't spend enough time with him.'

Donal fidgeted with his tie. 'I was angry. I've been very frustrated lately. This job of yours has consumed you. Nothing else matters. Lucy, I was beginning to think we wouldn't make it. I honestly think a baby will fix things. I want to save our marriage. I want you back. You're never here and even when you are you're always on that bloody BlackBerry.'

As if on cue, Lucy's BlackBerry beeped. Instinctively she

reached out for it, then stopped herself. Donal rolled his eyes.

Lucy's anger bubbled over. 'I'm sorry you've been feeling abandoned, but I still don't think that gives you the right to deceive me! And a pregnancy will not save our marriage. It will sink it to the ground. What you did to me was the lowest of the low. You knew I didn't want another baby and you went right ahead and TRICKED ME!' Lucy shouted.

'I was trying to save our marriage,' he shouted back.

'Well, your dirty little scheme didn't work,' Lucy spat. 'I knew exactly what you were up to. I've got spare boxes of the pill in London. I will not be having another baby, so you need to get that into your thick skull.'

'When did you become so cold?' Donal hissed.

'When you became a sneak and a liar,' Lucy retorted. '*You* wanted another child and I *never* did. But you went ahead anyway and tricked me. I'll never be able to trust you again.'

Donal glared at her and, in a cold, calm voice, said, 'Well, that makes two of us.' He almost took the door off the hinge as he left . . .

I went over and sat beside Lucy on the couch. She was crying. 'I think it's over, Emma. We're both so angry and now we're lying and deceiving each other. How can a marriage last on that basis?'

I bit my lip. That was the exact question I was struggling with – how could you get past a deliberate deception? Donal might not have shagged some random crazy woman, but he was as guilty as James was of trampling over his marriage vows. Honesty is what anchors couples together. Without it, a relationship is doomed.

'Come on, Lucy,' I said gently, rubbing her back. 'He does

346

love you, even if he's behaved like a total moron. There are still things you could try, like maybe flying home early some weeks to surprise him.'

She stared coldly at me. 'He tried to trick me into getting pregnant, Emma. It's an appalling thing to do. I don't see how I can ever trust him again.'

'I know, I know. It was wrong and sneaky, but he did it because he wants you to come home to him.'

'Well, then, he doesn't know me at all, because that would never work.'

'Maybe you should try marriage counselling. I think you need a mediator to help you communicate,' I said.

Lucy smiled ruefully. 'We're booked in to see one tomorrow. I managed to persuade the counsellor to see us on a Sunday by offering to double his fee. I'm flying home first thing in the morning and meeting Donal in the counsellor's office . . . if he turns up. He didn't reply to my text reminding him.'

I squeezed her hand. 'Donal will turn up. That's great, Lucy. It'll get you back on track. You'd never forgive yourself if you threw in the towel and didn't try.'

She raised an eyebrow. 'And does that apply to you, too?'

'What do you mean?'

'Does that mean you'll go to see James tomorrow night?'

'We were talking about you,' I said defensively.

'I know, but what you just said makes sense for both of us.'

I sighed. 'It probably does, but I need more time. I'll decide tomorrow. Right now, I'm going to decide to have another glass of wine – that's the only decision I can make at the moment.'

Lucy lifted up the bottle.

36

On Sunday morning as I was giving the children breakfast, while Babs lay in bed with the door shut, her earplugs in and her eye mask on, my phone rang. It was Henry.

'Morning, Emma. Hope I'm not disturbing you,' he said, politeness itself.

I grabbed the heaped spoon of sugar Yuri was about to pour over his Rice Krispies. 'No, not at all. How are you?'

'Fine, thank you. So . . . uhm . . . well, I'm calling about James.'

I stood up to walk to the corner of the room for some privacy. As I got up, Yuri grabbed the spoon back and drowned his cereal in sugar.

'Emma?'

I turned my back on Yuri's sugar mountain and concentrated on my phone call. 'Sorry, I'm here.'

'Well, the thing is, I hope I'm not overstepping the mark, but James called yesterday and he said things had got a bit sticky with all this stalking business. He's very troubled by it.'

Henry sounded as if he was addressing a room full of lawyers. He was clearly very uncomfortable with this conversation. I thought it was sweet of him to try.

I lowered my voice so the children wouldn't hear me. 'I'm sure he is, Henry, but I now have proof of the affair. I know that James has been lying to me and cheating on me.'

'He claims he is totally innocent. I have to say he really sounded very upset. I'm inclined to believe him. James has never been the sort of chap to lie. He says he has no idea what's going on and that all of this is as shocking to him as it is to you.'

I sat down on the arm of Babs's couch. 'I found her knickers in his drawer,' I whispered. 'Even you would have to agree the evidence is pretty damning.' I used language Henry could relate to.

'Well, indeed.' He coughed. 'But James is adamant that he's innocent and as much a victim of this person as you are.'

'He's lying.'

'Why don't you go and talk to him? It's important that you meet up to discuss all of this. At least give him the chance to tell you his side of the story. It's only fair, Emma. He's a good man. Let him have his say. He'll be home from Toulouse at eight o'clock this evening. He really wants to see you. I think you should hear him out. Remember the stalker case I told you about? That man was innocent. I believe James is too.'

I chewed my lip. 'I'll think about it, Henry, OK? Right now, I really don't want to see him, but if I calm down later I might go over to the house. But I'm not promising anything.'

'Excellent.' Henry sounded relieved. His duty as mediator was over. He didn't have to listen to me ranting on about knickers in drawers any longer. 'Well, I'll be off. I have to take Thomas to his riding lesson.'

'Bye, Henry. And thanks for calling.'

I hung up and jumped when I saw Lara standing directly behind me. 'Don't sneak up on me like that. Have you been there long?'

'You saided, "He's lying." Who's lying, Mummy?'

'No one. You shouldn't be listening to my conversations anyway,' I scolded her.

'I'm bored. I want to go home.' Yuri threw himself onto the couch.

'Me too. Babs has no dolls,' Lara moaned.

'There's nothing to play with here,' Yuri grumbled.

Lara's voice rose: 'I want my Disco Barbie.'

'I want my Batman car,' Yuri shouted.

The door to Babs's bedroom flew open. 'I want sleep!' she shouted, shaking her sleep mask and earplugs at us. 'Can you stop shouting and go to the park or something?'

As she turned to go back to bed, her buzzer rang. It was Mum and Dad. I decided to get the children out of the apartment, so we took them to the zoo. As we walked around in the cold, staring at shivering tigers and miserable meerkats, I tried to decide what to do about James. He had sent twenty texts begging me to meet him and hear his side of the story.

'Penny for your thoughts,' Dad said.

'James wants to see me tonight to talk. I'm just not sure I want to see him.'

Dad linked his arm through mine. It felt nice, but a bit strange. We weren't arm-linkers. He had never done more than pat me on the back before. He was an old-fashioned man who felt that shaking hands was quite sufficient. He hated having to kiss his friends' wives on the cheek when he met them. He thought it was fake and that we should 'leave all that rubbish to the French'.

As we strolled on through the zoo, he said quietly, 'Marriage is like a business, Emma. You only get out of it what you put in. James is a decent man. He may have slipped up, in which case I'm very disappointed in him, but I don't think he's the type of man to do it twice. You didn't marry a philanderer, you married a solid man who values family.'

'That's who I thought I married,' I said. 'But it seems I was wrong.'

'I think you should go and talk to James. He's earned that

much after nine years with you. Let him explain what happened and then make a decision. You're a great girl, Emma. You've worked very hard to create your little family. Don't throw it all away unless you're absolutely sure you can't make it work. Hear the man out.'

I gulped back tears. Dad had never told me I was great before or acknowledged how much I had done to create my family. I was touched that he was telling me now. And I knew, deep down, that what he was saying was true – you couldn't be married to someone for nine years and then not listen to them about something like this. I knew that my indecision was really fear: I was afraid that I would go there, listen to James telling me about some steamy affair and have my heart completely broken.

'OK, Dad, I'll go and see him. But I tell you now, if I find out he was having an affair the whole time and lying to me, it's over.' I looked up at him. 'I may end up back living with you and Mum.'

He stopped dead in his tracks. His arm shot out of mine. 'Now let's not be hasty. You need to try to make your marriage work. You can't be running home to us. We don't really have the space for you and the kids anyway. I've an office in Sean's old bedroom now and your mother has turned your bedroom into a gym. We have an exercise bike and one of those big balls and we're getting a treadmill this Christmas.'

What? My bedroom turned into a gym? And I noticed that while my room and Sean's were being used for their entertainment, there had been no mention of Babs's being touched at all.

'What about Babs's bedroom?'

Dad rolled his eyes. 'I've no doubt we'll end up with her back home. This presenting thing won't last and, sure, what man would have her? She's pure mad.'

I felt a bit better. At least they weren't keeping her room as a shrine to their favourite child.

'Well, if I do need to come and stay for a bit, I suppose we'll all just have to sleep in Babs's room.'

Dad couldn't hide his alarm. 'Hopefully it won't come to that. Go and sort things out with James.'

Mum came over to us. 'I'm frozen. Really and truly, the zoo at this time of year is not a good idea. Come on, I can't watch another poor animal shivering. Let's find a coffee shop and defrost.'

We headed off in the direction of the café. Yuri and Lara put their little gloved hands in mine and, as I looked down at their sweet, innocent faces, I knew I had to try to save my marriage for their sakes. I'd go and hear what James had to say.

37

As eight o'clock drew closer, I began to get nervous. Babs poured me a huge glass of wine, then put me into a taxi. 'Good luck – and if he is guilty, give him hell.' My stomach lurched. I was about to have a conversation with my husband about his cheating. After tonight, I might be a single mother of two. I could be raising my kids on my own, sleeping alone every night, planning the future alone. Alone.

When the taxi pulled up outside, the lights were on in the house, so James was obviously back from Toulouse. I paid the driver and walked up to the front door, where I shakily put my key into the lock. I stepped inside and . . . What the hell? The hall was strewn with red rose petals that led all the way up the stairs. I could hear Céline Dion's 'My Heart Will Go On' playing loudly. James knew I hated that song. I suddenly felt overcome with anger. Did he really think rose petals leading to the bedroom and a stupid love song were going to solve our problems? Did he picture me coming here, being transported by Céline bloody Dion and falling into bed with him, everything forgotten?

I stomped up the stairs, crushing the rose petals as I went. I stormed across the landing and flung open the bedroom door, ready to give him a piece of my mind. I stepped inside, and stopped dead.

The room was lit entirely with candles and there was an overpowering smell of cheap perfume. In the dim lighting, I suddenly became aware of a person lying on the bed. I was about to shout at him, but then, with a cold shock, realized it was a half-naked woman. She was lying on her back, wearing nothing but a red see-through bra and crotchless knickers. The ones I'd found in the drawer. I was too stunned to say anything.

'James, at last!' she whispered. 'I've been waiting for you.' Then she saw me and froze. We stared at each other.

Slowly, I reached out my hand and felt along the wall. I flicked the switch and light flooded the room. I blinked.

Oh, my God!

'Emma!' she gasped, and sat up quickly, grabbing a pillow to cover herself.

'Claire!' I felt like I'd been punched in the stomach, as if every breath had been knocked out of me. My brain just kept repeating one phrase over and over: *This cannot be happening.*

Claire shook her hair, which was all wavy and bouncy. She was wearing bright red lipstick and, having recovered from her initial shock, a defiant pout. 'I'm waiting for James. Get out.'

'But how . . .' My mind was still trying to catch up with the reality of what I was seeing. Claire! Sweet, innocent, shy, retiring Claire was lying spread-eagled on my bed, in red lingerie, waiting to have sex with my husband.

'Get out,' she repeated.

I looked around the room. I thought I was going to vomit. Had my husband actually done the most clichéd thing in the world and had sex with the nanny?

'Was it all you? The texts, the sex toys, the photo?'

She smirked at me. 'Yes. You need to go now, Emma. James will be back soon and he'll be very angry if he finds you here spoiling things for us.'

I gazed at her, lovely little Claire. She looked like a hooker.

'Why would you do this to me?' I said, in a voice that didn't even sound like me. I felt as if I was swimming under water: everything was blurred.

'It's not about you, Emma. It's about James and me. He loves me, he wants me and you need to go.'

Did James love her? Had they been having sex behind my back the whole time? The thought of it sent a shot of pure rage through me. In that second, I hated both of them.

'How could you?' I screamed, my fists clenched.

Claire shrugged. 'James has been in love with me for ages. You don't deserve him. I do.'

'How dare you say that, you little bitch? I was so good to you. How long has this been going on?' I demanded, averting my eyes from Claire's boobs, which jiggled every time she moved.

'Ages. James loves me. It's Fate. We're meant to be together. I'm going to look after him so well. I'll be a way better wife than you. We'll go to the Liverpool matches together, we'll take the kids to Disneyland –'

Kids? Take my kids to Disneyland? Was that her plan – to slot in and take my place?

'Over my dead body,' I spat out. Then I lunged at her.

She was fast. She grabbed me by the hair and yanked me onto the bed. We wrestled. She punched me in the stomach. I twisted her arm. I screamed as her knee smashed into my cheekbone.

The door burst open and I felt a strong arm pulling me back. It was James. He pushed me behind him and looked down.

'Jesus Christ!' he exclaimed. 'Claire?' He looked utterly bewildered. 'What on earth is going on?'

'Why don't you tell me?' I shouted at him. 'Claire here says you've been at it for weeks, you bastard. How could you? The goddamn *nanny*? I mean, for Christ's sake, James.'

James looked at Claire. 'What in God's name are you doing? Have you lost your mind?'

Claire shuffled forward in her underwear and grabbed James's hand. 'Come on, baby, I know you love me.'

James recoiled from her touch.

'Tell her, James, tell her it's me you want.'

I was standing in the corner of the room, shaking. I watched as James leant down, his face bright red with rage. 'I have no idea why you think I have any interest in you. You must be mad. Now put some clothes on and get out of my sight before I call the police.'

Claire grabbed his hand. 'Why are you lying? I saw you looking at my body. I saw you watching me, wanting me. You said my cooking and my ironing were amazing. You fell for me because I look after you so well and because I'm so great with your kids. It's OK, James, you can admit it now. I want you too. We're soulmates.'

James yanked his hand away. 'Claire, listen to me very carefully. All of this is in your head. I am in love with my wife, Emma. I have never, ever looked at you in any kind of way. Now, put your clothes on and get out of our house.'

'How can you say that?' Claire looked like she was going to start crying. 'How can you stay with her? Is it because of the kids? You're such a good dad, I know you love them, but I'll be a great mum. Emma treats you like dirt, but I'll make you so happy. Our life will be so great, just you and me and the children . . .'

I felt as if my head was going to explode. I reached over and grabbed her by the arm, pulling her off the bed. 'You will not destroy this family.'

Claire wrenched herself free of my grasp and went over to James. She put her arm around his neck and tried to kiss him. He tried to push her away, but she clung to him.

'James, I love you and I know you love me too.'

'Get your hands off me, you freak. Do you have any idea

what you've done to us? I . . . I can't believe . . .' James prised her fingers from his neck and pushed her back.

Claire stood in front of him, eyes blazing. 'What about all the looks you gave me? All the conversations we had about football. How you told me my lasagne was amazing and my ironing. You do love me, I know you do. Just admit it. ADMIT IT!'

I grabbed her arm. 'GET OUT!' I screamed.

'But, James,' she pleaded, 'we're going to be happy. We're going to get married and have a baby boy.'

'What?' James was incredulous.

I looked into Claire's eyes. My God, she was completely insane. All this time I thought she was just shy and lacking in confidence, but she was actually dangerous. I had to get her out of our home. I couldn't stand the sight of her. I wanted to fling her out of the window.

'James,' I roared, 'just grab her and push her *out.*'

James dragged her down the stairs, kicking and screaming. I found her backpack beside the bed. As I leant down to pick it up, I suddenly noticed that none of my photos were on my bedside locker. None of my books were there either. My shoe rack was empty. I opened the wardrobe. It, too, was empty.

I ran down the stairs. James was struggling to get her to the front door and she was clinging to him, sobbing and demanding.

'Where are all my things?' I screamed at her. 'Every trace of me is gone, photos, clothes, books. Were you trying to erase me?'

'You don't exist any more. I'm the wife. I'm the mum.'

'Where are Emma's things?' James bellowed.

'In the Oxfam shop, where they belong,' Claire said, tri-umphant. 'Don't you see, James? We've got rid of her. She's gone, like she was never even here. We can be so happy now that she's not around.'

'Jesus Christ,' he breathed.

I opened the front door and James shoved her out. I threw her backpack and her coat after her and slammed the door shut. We stood staring at the door for a few seconds. Then I crumpled into a heap on the stairs. James double-locked the door and came over to sit beside me. 'Are you OK?' he whispered.

'Claire.' I shook my head. 'I never would have thought . . .'

'Neither did I,' James said, rubbing my back.

I was shaking badly. James clasped me to him. 'Emma, you're shivering. I think we need a drink.' He held out his hand. I took it. He pulled me up, walked me into the lounge and sat me down on the sofa. Adrenaline was still pumping through my veins.

'Claire?' I shook my head.

James handed me a large glass of brandy. 'I'm in too much shock to take this in.' He sat down heavily beside me and took a long drink of his brandy.

'But why would she think you were in love with her? You must have flirted with her. Did you?'

'Come on, Emma, you saw me with her – I barely spoke to her. Which was why I was pretty bloody surprised to see her laid bare on my bed.'

I drank half the brandy in one go, wincing as it fired down my throat and into my chest. 'So she sent all the texts and the sex toys,' I said, still unable to quite believe it. 'I never would have imagined she had that kind of a mind. She must be really messed up. Do you think she's dangerous?'

James ran his hands through his hair. 'I don't know. I hope not. She never threatened us with violence but, yeah, obviously she's very messed up.'

I felt my eyes welling with tears. 'God, James, the kids,' I said hoarsely.

James put his arm around me. 'I don't think we need to worry about that. I think she genuinely loved them. You can see she did them no harm. It was you, unfortunately, darling, that she wanted out of the way. Not the children.'

'I thought she was this poor, damaged girl who needed her confidence boosted. Could I have been any more of an idiot?' I felt ill at the thought that this was all my doing – I had hired her, having failed to pick up on what must be a serious mental illness. And I'd left her with the children. I sobbed into James's shoulder. 'Why did she want to destroy me like that?'

'I don't know,' James said, sounding tearful too. 'This has been the worst time of our lives together,' he said, pulling me tight to his chest. 'But it's over now, Emma. She's gone, and there will be no more texts or threats. I know it's hard to take in right now, but at least we know what's been happening. We can now put all this awfulness behind us and get on with our lives.'

I sobbed into his chest, but my mind was reeling. Could we just move past this whole episode and pretend it had never happened? Could we move on without a backward glance? I wasn't so sure. I wanted to believe we could, but I felt changed by it. I wasn't the same innocent Emma who had moved to London. Our marriage had been battered and bruised. Everything was different.

38

I woke up on the couch, fully clothed. James was beside me, snoring. I looked down at the bottle of brandy; it was almost empty. My head ached. I dragged myself off the couch and went to get a glass of water.

Out of the kitchen window I could see Carol digging in her garden. I checked my watch. It was eight in the morning and still almost dark. I suddenly had an urge to talk about last night, to say the words out loud, so I'd know it was real. I opened the back door and went over to her.

'Morning,' I said, over the fence.

She put down her shovel and smiled. 'Beautiful day, isn't it?'

I looked up at the sky. 'Uhm, yes, I suppose so. Can you even see what you're doing?'

Carol laughed. 'I know this garden like the back of my hand. I could tend it blindfolded. How are you? You look a bit peaky, if you don't mind my saying.'

I leant on the fence and sighed. 'The last few weeks have been nightmarish.'

She came rushing over. 'Is it that business with the texts and everything?'

I nodded. 'I'm fine now. But it turns out it was a stalker. You'll never believe who it was.'

She stared at me, frowning. 'Who?'

'Claire, our nanny.'

Carol's jaw dropped. 'The quiet mousy one who was great with the children?'

'It turns out she's not so mousy after all. She's been trying to get rid of me so she can have James and the kids to herself.'

Carol was visibly shocked. 'I never would have suspected her.'

I found that very comforting – if Carol, who didn't trust anyone with her children, had thought Claire trustworthy, then obviously it wasn't only me who'd been fooled.

'Where is she now?' Carol asked.

'I guess she's at home, I don't know. We had to throw her out of the house last night. She wouldn't leave – she clung to James and told him she wanted to have his child and that I was a terrible wife. It was an awful scene and the worst part is that I hired her and left her with my kids. I feel like vomiting every time I think about it.' Tears threatened again.

'Well, I can understand why,' Carol said, her face soft with sympathy, 'but I often saw her out in the garden with Yuri and Lara, and she was lovely with them. I would have told you straight away if I'd ever seen her being nasty to them. She never was.'

I felt huge relief at hearing this. 'Thanks, Carol, that makes me feel better. I've been so worried.'

Carol reached over and held my hand. 'You poor thing, what a fright.'

'I'm not sure we've seen the last of her. She still has keys to the house – I only thought of that after we'd chucked her out, so we'll have to change the locks. I'd like to get the police to call over and scare the life out of her for what she did, but I don't even know where she lives. She said she lived in Shepherd's Bush, but that's probably a lie too.'

'But wouldn't Poppy know?'

Of course! I'd forgotten about Maggie. 'Thanks, Carol, I'll go and ring her now.'

'Good luck. Let me know if I can help with anything.'

'I will. Thanks for listening.'

I went back inside and met James in the kitchen. 'Why did we drink so much brandy?' He groaned.

'We needed to numb the shock.'

'I think I numbed my brain.'

I told him about Poppy and Claire's mother, Maggie. James agreed that we should get in touch with Maggie and tell her what Claire had done. James wanted to go to the police immediately, but I felt we should talk to Maggie first – at least give her fair warning.

I dialled Poppy's number.

'Darling, what time is it?'

'Eight thirty.'

'I hope this is an emergency. I'm meeting Jasper later and I need my beauty sleep.'

I filled her in on Claire.

'Oh, darling, I am sorry. I'm astounded. My God, I feel responsible because I recommended her to you and then she turns out to be . . . I'm shocked. Maggie's so normal. I presumed her daughter would be too. Emma, how awful for you.'

Poppy gave me Maggie's mobile number and I promised to call her back later with an update.

When James got out of the shower, I rang Maggie and put her on loudspeaker. James introduced himself, then gave a brief outline of last night's events. His voice was cold and hard: he was furious. 'We're going to the police about this. Claire's behaviour was destructive and, quite frankly, sickening.'

Maggie said nothing until James had finished, and then she began to sob. We could hear her sniffling on the phone. When she had composed herself, she begged us not to call the police. She asked us to allow her to call over and talk to us, to explain some things. Somewhat reluctantly, we agreed.

Ten minutes later, the doorbell rang. I opened it. Maggie was standing on the step, with tears streaming down her face, absolutely distraught. I invited her in and led her into the lounge, where James was pacing. We stood facing each other in silence. There were no niceties, no small-talk.

'Did you call the police?' Maggie asked, clutching a tissue.

'Not yet,' James told her.

'Oh, thank God.' Maggie put her hand up to her heart. She seemed on the verge of collapse so I offered her a seat, which she gladly sank into.

'Why did Claire do this?' I demanded.

Maggie dabbed her eyes. 'I'm so sorry. I thought she was OK. I thought she was better and then, last night, she arrived home in a state and told me James was in love with her and wanted to marry her. I knew then that she must have stopped taking her tablets.'

'What tablets?' James asked.

'Anti-depressants. She goes very high and then very low. For years I just thought it was her hormones, until the incident in school.' Maggie took a deep breath. 'She became a bit obsessed with her history teacher, Mr Clancy. He was nice to her – he felt sorry for her because she didn't really have any friends. Claire's always found it hard to fit in. She was very badly affected by her dad leaving and she's no confidence. So she misunderstood Mr Clancy's kindness and thought he was in love with her. She started texting him and it all got a bit out of hand.'

Oh, my God, she'd done it before. Why had Maggie not warned us? How could she have let her daughter come into our home when she knew she was unhinged?

'What exactly do you mean by "out of hand"?' James's face was flushed with anger.

363

Maggie twisted her tissue between her hands. 'Well, she began to send him texts and emails, and then she started phoning him. When he refused to answer his mobile, she called his home phone and hung up if his wife answered. Sometimes she'd do it twenty times in a row.'

Now I had to sit down. She had actually stalked poor Mr Clancy's wife too. This was just too much to get my head around.

'What happened?' James asked quietly.

'Mr Clancy told her to stop. He said she was imagining he had feelings for her, that he was happily married. So Claire went to the headmistress and told her that Mr Clancy was in love with her and had been touching her and staring at her in class.'

James cursed under his breath.

'What did the headmistress do?' I asked.

'Well, Mr Clancy was suspended for a month while the school looked into it. They even got the police involved. They found the texts and emails and it was just awful. They came to the house and told Claire that if she didn't leave him alone she'd be in big trouble.'

'Did she?' James asked. 'Leave him alone?'

Maggie shook her head. She began to cry again. 'She kept contacting him. The police came back and said they were going to prosecute her, so I had to pack up everything and leave. We came to London. I had to get Claire away from him. She was so unhappy.' Maggie looked up at me. 'I know she's done wrong, but she's not a bad person. She's just a very lost young girl.'

James slapped his hand on the mantelpiece. 'I'm sorry, Maggie, but this is a lot more sinister than just a poor young girl thinking someone has a crush on her. She stalked me and Emma, sent sex toys to our home. We have small children. You have to see how threatening her behaviour is.'

'She doesn't mean it. She's always been looking for some-one to replace her father.'

'I'm sorry, but that's just not good enough,' James said. 'She's made our lives hell. She almost broke up our marriage. I don't give a damn whether her father left or not. She cannot do this to anyone else. Frankly, I'm appalled that you didn't tell us this when we hired her. How could you allow us to employ a clearly unstable person to look after our children?'

'I thought she was better. For the first six months we were in London, she was taking her tablets and she was much less down and she seemed back to the old Claire. I had no idea she'd stopped the medication. And I'd no idea she was stalk-ing you.' Maggie reached out her hands to James, as if imploring him to believe her. 'I even called over a good few times to see if you were here. I wanted to see how Claire behaved in your company. I'd have known straight away if I'd seen her with you, but you were always at work. Emma told me you worked late all the time and that you were hardly ever home. I was delighted because I thought Claire couldn't possibly become obsessed with someone she never saw.'

'It obviously doesn't take much for her to become obsessed,' I said drily. 'But it was wrong of you not to warn us.'

Maggie put her hands over her face for a moment, then looked at us again. Her voice was low and strained when she said, 'I never thought she'd do it again. I thought she'd learnt her lesson. I thought a new start would be good for her. She loved your children, adored them – they were all she talked about. She seemed so happy and content with you. I was thrilled. All a mother wants is for her child to be happy. It seems very black and white to you now because your chil-dren are small but, believe me, it gets very complicated as they grow older.'

'Claire's "complications" almost cost me my marriage,

and my sanity,' I snapped. 'I've been going out of my mind with worry and paranoia. This isn't some little mistake she's made. Her behaviour was incredibly destructive. Claire doesn't need pills, Maggie, she needs serious help. She's out of control.'

Maggie's mouth set in a tight line. 'She's a lovely girl, really. She's just confused is all. She's not mad and I won't have you saying she is. I brought her here for a new start. I thought it would work. She's my only child, my baby. You look at your children now and all you see is sweetness and innocence. But they will change. They'll challenge you in ways you never imagined. They won't stay sweet and innocent, but no matter what they do, you'll love them and mind them just the same.' Her voice caught, and she dissolved into tears, her shoulders shaking as she sobbed.

James came over and put his arm around me. 'If my children ever try to destroy someone's life, I can assure you that I'll make them face the consequences of their actions.'

'She's just a confused, lonely girl. Don't get the police involved, I'm begging you. I swear to you that I'll take her to a psychiatrist. I know I need to get proper help for her now. I know now this goes deeper than depression. But please don't let them send her to prison. She'll die in there. She's all I have – let me fix this.' Maggie buried her face in her hands.

Despite my rage at what had happened and my anger towards Claire, my heart went out to Maggie. Claire was her only child and you love your children unconditionally. I understood her feelings towards her daughter, of course I did. She had tried to protect and help her by taking her away from Ireland to start again. And Maggie had called into our house to check up on Claire and she had asked me about James working late. She had tried, in her own way, to protect us and make sure Claire wasn't up to anything. Unfortunately, she just didn't realize how delusional her daughter was.

James went over to Maggie and patted her shoulder. 'Please calm down. If you promise to send Claire to a psychiatrist and keep her far away from here, I won't go to the police. But if I see her again, near our home or my workplace, I'll contact the police immediately, no questions asked. I've kept records of everything she sent and all of her text messages. Do you understand?'

Maggie nodded. 'Thank you,' she whispered. 'I promise you'll never see either of us again. I'll hand in my notice to Poppy today. I'll find work somewhere else. I won't let Claire out of my sight until I'm sure she's well enough to handle things.'

I walked Maggie to the door. She handed me our house key on the Hello Kitty key-ring Claire had used. The poor woman seemed to have aged ten years overnight. I squeezed her arm. 'Good luck. I hope you can get her well.'

Maggie walked down the path to the gate, shoulders hunched. She was a weary woman with a long road ahead. I closed the door. It was over. Strangely, I didn't feel elated or happy. I was drained. I longed to lie down and sleep for a very long time.

39

James and I spent an hour straightening up the house, then headed over to Babs's apartment to see the children. I wanted to feel their little arms around me. But when we got there, Babs was on her own. She had phoned work and told them we weren't going to make it in. At this rate I'd probably be fired, but I didn't care. I had decided to hand in my notice. I wanted to spend more time with Yuri and Lara and I needed time to clear my head.

'Where are the kids?' I asked.

'Mum and Dad have taken them to the park. They said they'd meet me for lunch at Luella's on Fulham Road.' She cocked her head to one side. 'Are you going to tell me what happened between you two? I take it a sleepover is a positive thing?'

I sighed and sank onto the couch. 'You tell her, James, I haven't the energy.' I packed up the children's things while he filled Babs in on the night before and the meeting with Maggie this morning. It was the first time I'd seen Babs listen quietly for ten straight minutes in a row.

'So, I was right about her.' She shook her head. 'I knew from the beginning she was weird.'

'I should have listened to you.'

'But you chose to ignore me, like everyone else in the family,' Babs grumbled.

James picked up a suitcase. 'I'll pop this in the boot and we can head out to meet your parents, let them know everything's all right.'

I flopped down on the edge of the bed. 'I'm shattered. I can't believe this happened.'

Babs reapplied her lipstick in the mirror. 'It's over now, Emma. You can forget all about crazy Claire and being stalked and start being nice to James after all your accusations. The poor guy was totally innocent the whole time.'

I leant my head against the wall. Forget about it. Was that it? Was I just supposed to pretend it had never happened and move on? Was I supposed to be madly in love with James again just like that?

This must be what it's like coming back from war, I thought. After you've lived through hell, everyone just expects you to put your backpack away, change out of your uniform and be 'normal'. The fact that you got your leg blown off is irrelevant. The consensus is, 'It's over, move on. Forget about it – sure haven't you got your prosthetic now and sure you're grand. You were never very sporty anyway. It's not as if you were out running marathons. People live full lives with one leg. No point dwelling on it. Just put it behind you. One good leg is enough for anyone. Come on, let's all sit down and have a nice cup of tea.'

I wasn't comparing myself to a soldier with one leg, of course, but I did feel that a single night was not quite enough time for me to forget about the stress and hurt of the last couple of months. And I still felt sick about the kids being with someone so disturbed. I really needed to talk to the children, to make sure Claire hadn't said anything awful to them or done anything cruel.

When we got to the restaurant, I rushed over and hugged Yuri and Lara. For once, they didn't complain. They flung themselves at James, too. Mum and Dad looked at me expectantly.

'Please let me tell them,' Babs said.

I couldn't help smiling at her dramatics. 'Knock yourself out,' I said.

While James and I distracted the children, Babs gave Mum and Dad a detailed account of the whole thing.

Mum sat back. 'I told you James was no philanderer.'

James went bright red and mumbled, 'Thanks, Una.'

'Why is Daddy all red? What's a fladerer?' Lara asked.

Babs and Dad snorted behind their menus.

'Nothing, never mind. Now listen to me, both of you.' I turned in my seat so I was facing them. 'This is serious, so I want you to be really honest and I promise that, no matter what you say, I will not be cross, not even a tiny bit cross, so just tell Mummy the truth.'

'Not even a tweeny bit cross?' Lara asked.

'No.'

'Not even the tweensiest bit in the whole universe?' Yuri asked.

'No. Now just listen, OK? Daddy has found out that Claire was a bit naughty and we just want to make sure that she didn't say anything mean to you or do anything that wasn't nice.'

'I love Claire. She's super-nice,' Lara said.

'Claire's not naughty,' Yuri added.

'Well, now, there you are. She did them no harm. She was just a confused young girl. Don't make a big fuss, Emma. Leave the poor children alone,' Mum urged. 'Don't be making a mountain out of a molehill.'

I glared at her. 'She's a raving lunatic, and they spent more time with her than anyone else.'

'Darling, it might be best to do this later,' James suggested quietly.

'I need to know they're OK,' I said. 'This is about my sanity.'

'You said you wouldn't get cross,' Yuri said, pointing to my flushed face.

I fake-smiled at him. 'I'm not! Look!'

'That's a scary smile,' Lara said solemnly.

I took a deep breath. 'Mummy just wants to know if Claire was ever mean in any way or did anything a bit strange.'

They shook their heads.

'What did Claire do that was bold?' Yuri asked James.

James crouched down. 'She was mean to Mummy and we're cross with her for that.'

Lara's eyes widened. 'What did she do, Mummy? Did she scratch you? Did she bite you? Did she break your sparkly shoes?'

'No, sweetie, she didn't,' James reassured her. 'Claire was just . . . well, she was a bit nasty to Mummy and she said some mean things.'

'Did she say you're a big fat piggy?' Yuri asked.

'No.' I frowned.

'Did she say you're an ugly old witch?' Lara wondered.

'No. It wasn't –'

'I know!' Yuri jumped up and down. 'Did she say you're a grumpy old troll?'

'Jeez, guys, go easy on your mum. She's not *that* bad.' Babs grinned.

'Feel free to jump in and defend me anytime, James.'

'Sorry, darling. I thought you'd made it clear you wanted to handle this yourself.'

'Poor man was afraid of having his head ripped off,' Dad muttered, still behind his menu.

'Enough of this nonsense! Leave the poor children alone – can't you see they're perfectly fine?' Mum said.

'WHAT DID CLAIRE SAY?' Lara shouted.

'It was a grown-up thing and it doesn't matter, sweetheart,' James said.

'I need to go to the toilet,' Yuri announced.

'Any chance of a man getting a bite to eat around here?' Dad grumbled.

James took Yuri to the Gents and Lara insisted on going with them, probably to get away from me and my interrogation.

'That went well,' Babs remarked.

'Leave the children alone, Emma,' Mum said. 'That poor young girl was just looking for a father figure and took a shine to James. It's hardly surprising – he's so kind and handsome.'

'I was the one who hired Claire,' I snapped. 'I was the one who was nice to her. I was the one who boosted her ego. I was the one who tried to get her to come out of her shell and praised her all the time. Me. Not James, *me*. And yet somehow I still get trampled on. Somehow I'm the bad guy who gets stalked. I can't seem to catch a break.'

'Oh, boo-hoo,' Babs drawled. 'Next time hire a male nanny and maybe he'll fancy you if he's into bossy older women. And he can send James nasty texts.'

'That's not what I mean, I just feel . . . well . . .'

'Stupid? Guilty?' Babs suggested.

'Drained,' I admitted.

Mum unfolded her napkin. 'That's enough drama for one day. Put a smile on your face and be nice to your poor husband. Put this behind you and move forward. Don't be always looking back, Emma. Don't dwell on the past. Try to be more positive – remember, the glass is half full, not half empty. Now, let's talk about something else. Barbara, have you met a nice boy yet?'

I held my breath.

'Not yet.' Babs closed her menu. 'I met a real jerk recently, but don't worry, Mum, he's gone.'

'I'd love to see you settled with a nice man and some children.'

'Mum,' I tried to distract her.

'I think children would be the making of you,' Mum continued. 'They'd calm you down and stop you thinking only of yourself all the time.'

'Mum!' I barked.

'It's OK, Emma,' Babs said. 'Mum, I want you to listen to me. Really listen. I am going to focus on my career for the next few years. So don't ask me about kids, OK? I may or may not decide to have children in the future, but I really don't need to be nagged about it. I've had a crappy few months and I want you to back off. I'm going to concentrate on myself and my career.'

'So what's changed?' Dad smirked.

'I've changed,' Babs said.

'It's very subtle,' Dad retorted.

'It's internal,' Babs said, and thumped his arm.

Mum had narrowed her eyes and was staring hard at Babs. 'What's going on, Barbara? Did something happen?'

'Everything is fine, Mum.' Babs dipped her bread into the olive oil.

'Babs has been great to me since I moved here, really supportive.' I decided to change the subject.

'I'm glad to hear it. Family must stick together,' Mum said.

'Emma's been pretty good to me too,' Babs admitted.

'You all love each other, you're all great. Now, for the love of God, can we order some food?' Dad fumed.

James and the children came back and we ordered. Once the lunch arrived, Dad calmed down and became civil again. 'Well, Babs,' he began, 'how's your show going?'

'It's all right, but I'm going to move on. I've been talking to my agent and we've come up with a brilliant idea to move my career forward.'

'Good for you! What is it?' I asked.

'She's going to try and get me on *I'm A Celebrity . . . Get Me Out Of Here.*'

'WHAT?' Mum and I exclaimed.

Babs nodded. 'Myleene Klass went in with a low TV profile and now she's presenting almost everything. All I need is a couple of hot bikinis and I'm sorted.'

'Is that the show where they eat the insects?' Dad looked up from his steak.

'Yuck!' Lara squealed.

'*Cooooool.*' Yuri was impressed. 'Are you gonna eat bugs?'

'I might.' Babs winked at him.

Mum leant over and put her face right up to Babs's. 'Over my dead body will you be going on that appalling television show. How could I face the neighbours?'

Babs's phone beeped. She read the message and whooped. 'Well, Mum, it looks like you'll need to provide me with your dead body. That was my agent. I'm going into the jungle!'

40

That night, as I was looking forward to crawling into bed early and getting a good night's sleep for the first time in ages, I got a call from Lucy asking me to meet her urgently. She sounded very stressed on the phone. Although I was absolutely exhausted, I agreed immediately. I could tell she needed to talk.

James had some rugby meeting he had to go to, so I asked Babs to come over and babysit because I didn't trust anyone else. In fairness, she was nice about it. She'd been in fantastic form since she'd found out about *I'm A Celebrity*. She was going to hand in her notice next week and I knew she was working on the speech she was going to give Gary when she told him to shove his job. She was positively buoyant.

I hadn't been able to get my clothes back from the charity shop yet as it was closed on Mondays, so I wore my jeans and a top that Babs had lent me, which was surprisingly not too tight. I seemed to have lost a bit more weight in the last traumatic week.

When I arrived at the restaurant Lucy was on her Black-Berry. I sat down and ordered a drink while she talked furiously into her phone. After five minutes I began to get fed up. I looked at her and tapped my watch. She mouthed, 'Sorry,' spoke for another minute and hung up. 'There's a problem with one of our deals. It's been a crazy week.'

It was always a crazy week with Lucy. She'd always worked hard but since she'd gone out on her own she'd been twice as bad. We ordered food and she asked me to fill her in on Claire. I told her the whole saga. Towards the end, her phone beeped and she began to text back. I tried not to get annoyed.

'Sorry, go on.'

I finished telling her and she was as shocked as the rest of us.

'Emma, you poor thing. How absolutely horrendous. Thank God it's over now. You and James can get back to your lives and to normality.'

'It's been a real wake-up call. This whole Claire thing has made me take a step back and re-examine my life, my priorities and my relationship with James and the kids. I have to get a better balance.' I wanted to stress this point to Lucy because she also needed a better balance. 'To be honest, Lucy, I think you need to reassess too. Your schedule is crazy. You can't fix your marriage and spend time with Serge if you're always travelling or on the phone.'

Lucy's eyes brimmed with tears. 'Well, I'm going to have to make a lot of changes, actually. My life is going to be very different now. Donal's leaving me.'

I dropped my fork with a clatter. 'What?'

'We went to see that marriage counsellor yesterday. I really thought it would help, but all it did was prove that we're completely incompatible.' Lucy was struggling not to cry. 'All we did was shout at each other and blame each other. At the end of the session, Donal apologized for wasting the counsellor's time and stormed out.'

I leant over and held her hand. My heart was breaking for her.

'I followed him out and he said to me, "It's over. I can't do this any more. I don't like you, I don't respect you, I don't want to be married to you."'

God, that was harsh. I'd known Donal for more than

ten years, and I couldn't picture him saying such cruel things. The pressure of the situation must have taken its toll on him.

'I tried to reason with him,' Lucy said. 'I offered to come home earlier some weeks, like you'd suggested, but he just laughed in my face and told me not to make promises I wouldn't keep. He said it was clear that my job came first. He said I'd walked away from them when I'd taken it on, and now he was walking away.' Lucy dragged her hand across her eyes and took a few deep breaths. 'Then he said he'd found a two-bedroom town house to rent near our own house and he was going to move in there with Serge. He had it all organized, Emma. He'd made his decision before we'd even gone to the marriage counsellor.'

I grabbed her hand. 'Oh, Lucy, I just can't believe –'

Her phone beeped, and she was texting again.

'For God's sake, Lucy, you're in the middle of telling me your marriage is over and you're still texting?'

'If I don't answer this, a ten-million-euro deal could be lost,' she snapped. She put her phone down and rubbed her eyes. 'I'm sorry, Emma. I'm just sick of having to justify my job all the time. No one makes really big money without being on call day and night.'

'But your marriage is over because of it.' I was exasperated. 'Your family life is in tatters. Is any job worth that?'

Lucy shook her head. 'My marriage was over long before this. Donal and I have been limping along for a long time. You know it and so do I. Since he pushed me into having a baby we've been fighting and bickering non-stop. I resent him for forcing me to have a child and he resents me for not having more. We want different things in life. He wants a house full of children. One child is more than enough for me. I love Serge and I'm so glad I had him, but I'd hate to have any more.'

'But you and Donal were so good together. Think back to when you got married and how happy you were,' I reminded her.

'We *were* happy,' she said sadly, 'really happy, but it was a false happiness. We never really discussed children and family and careers. We just fell for each other and thought the rest of it would all fit neatly into place. But it didn't. Life gets more complicated as each year goes by, and if you don't have a rock-solid foundation, your relationship won't last. We're not like you and James.'

'I walked out on James three days ago. We're not bullet-proof either.'

'You've gone back. You guys are meant to be together.'

'I don't know, Lucy. I always thought so. I was very confident about my marriage, but this has really shaken me. I can see how stale we'd got and how we were taking each other for granted. James and I haven't had fun together in so long. Everything's been so serious and complicated and awful. When did the fun go out of our lives? Suddenly it's all about jobs and budgeting and bills and children and lying and suspicion and stress . . .' I chewed my lip. 'It's as if we woke up one day and life had ceased to be any fun at all.'

Lucy poured more wine into our glasses. 'I know – one minute we're having sex on the kitchen floor, licking whipped cream off each other, and the next we're sleeping in separate bedrooms.'

Whipped cream? Really? James and I had never done stuff like that.

'Do you think if you tried some really intense marriage counselling, you could make it work?' I asked.

Lucy shook her head. 'No, it's over. As I said, it'd been coming for ages. My new job just put another nail in the coffin, and Donal trying to trick me into getting pregnant made me realize we have no future. We want different things and we're just hurting each other and lying to each other now. The trust is gone.'

I sank back in my chair, completely weary. Our best friends were breaking up. It was just awful. They used to be so great together. 'Lucy, I'm so, so sorry.'

'I know, it sucks. I never wanted Serge to come from a broken home.' She was clearly fighting tears. 'But what can I do? He's better off living in a calm atmosphere rather than with two parents shouting at each other all the time. And I'll still see him the same amount. Donal said I can have him all weekend. So, in a way, Serge's life won't change.'

I set down my knife and fork. 'I've been so grumpy with the children because of all the stress. I want to spend more time with them and have them fall in love with me again. The whole Claire fiasco has shown me that it's not just about being physically there, it's about being there emotionally. They loved her because she played games with them, she cooked with them, she went to the park with them . . . She was fully present. When I'm with them, half the time I'm on the phone or reading a book or shouting at them to tidy up. I don't actually do things with them and that has to change.'

Lucy folded her napkin. 'Emma, please don't tell me I have to start crawling into sandpits with Serge.'

I laughed at the idea of Lucy with her Jimmy Choos full of wet sand. 'No, I draw the line at sandpits.'

'Thank God for that.' She smiled. 'But I do need to engage with Serge and take him to the park. Ignoring him while I catch up on emails isn't going to get me any Mum of the Year awards.'

'You might need to leave your BlackBerry at home,' I suggested.

Lucy looked horrified. 'How about if I only check it every hour?'

'Three hours.'

'Two,' she said, smiling.

We clinked glasses and toasted the future . . . whatever it held.

41

I sat in the lounge, surrounded by boxes. Inside were my clothes, shoes, bags, photos and accessories, all of which I had got back from the very nice lady in Oxfam on Putney High Street. When I explained to her that my belongings had been taken without my knowledge, she very kindly returned everything. James gave her a donation for the inconvenience.

'Here you go, darling.' James handed me a cup of tea.

'Thanks.' I gratefully took a sip. It was cold in the house, even with the heating on.

James sat on the floor beside me. I pulled out a framed photo of the two of us at a black-tie event. We were laughing, our arms entwined around each other.

'I remember this,' James said softly. 'It was a good night.'

I nodded, suddenly flooded with emotion. Despite my best efforts to stop myself, I began to cry.

'Hey now.' James put the photo down and put his arms around me.

'Sorry, I don't know why I'm crying, it's just all so . . .'

'Overwhelming.' He finished my sentence.

'Yes, overwhelmingly overwhelming.' I gave him a watery smile.

'Look at me,' he said, turning me to face him. 'I promise you that from now on things are going to be different. We're going to be happy. I'm not going to work past seven o'clock, and at least two nights a week, I'll be home by six. And we don't have to worry about Claire any more. Maggie called me to say she's booked her in to see a psychiatrist and she's not going to let her out of her sight.'

'I'm just scared.'

'Of what?'

I decided to be honest. 'Of the future. Of our life here in London.'

'It's going to be all right, darling. We're going to start with a clean slate. I'm going to work less and you're taking some time out from work to be with the children, which they're thrilled about. We'll do a family outing every Sunday, and things will be so much better, I promise. I know I've been obsessed with the club and that I neglected you.'

'I understand why you did it. I know you're just trying to prove yourself, but I find London lonely, James. I need you.'

'I know, I'm sorry.'

Things really would have to be different, I thought. I needed to carve out a life for myself here. I'd have to try to make friends. Good friends, women that I could be myself with. Carol was very different from me, but she was a lovely person, and although Poppy was a bit mad, she was nice too. I needed to work on those relationships and nurture them. The new Emma was going to host coffee mornings and force those mothers at the school gate to talk to her. I was going to break through their icy façades if it killed me.

'This whole Claire situation has made me realize we need to be more careful with each other,' I said.

'You mean not take each other for granted?'

'Yes.' I nodded. 'And make more time for ourselves. We need to be a couple again, James, like this.' I held up the photo.

'You're right. Lately it's been all about working and the children. We hardly ever go out on our own.'

It was simple, really. Life had got in the way: we had

382

neglected each other and our relationship. And, if I'm being honest, it wasn't just since we'd moved to London. Even before that we'd stopped making an effort. Even when we had gone out together, we'd usually been to the cinema and straight home. It had been a very long time since we'd had a really romantic night out, lingering over our wine until the restaurant staff begged us to leave. It had been a long time since we'd had fun together. We were stale, our marriage was stale. Yet beneath that James was still my James. Older, greyer, yes, but still the man I had fallen head over heels in love with, the man who had made me so happy. My rock. I reached over and kissed his cheek. It felt good.

'Why don't we have a weekly date-night?' I suggested. 'I know it's a really lame expression, but let's pick a night that's sacrosanct. Every week, on that night, we go out together, no matter what.'

'I like the sound of that.'

'But there's just one problem. Going out requires leaving our children with a babysitter.'

'We'll find a nice girl we can trust.'

'Claire was a nice girl we trusted.'

'Yes, but that was just very bad luck,' James said. 'We can't let it poison us against all babysitters and childminders.'

'I know, but it'll be difficult for me in the beginning.'

'We'll be very thorough in our research.'

'James?'

'Yes?'

'Let's be really nice to each other. Let's appreciate each other more from now on.'

'I think that's an excellent idea.'

'I know I can be a grumpy cow, but I do love you and I love our family.'

'Me too, darling. And, in a twisted kind of way, this whole

situation with Claire has made me appreciate what I have even more. To see my family unit threatened in that way and to realize that everything is breakable, well, it just makes me treasure you and the children. I have to be honest, losing my job with the Irish squad really threw me. My confidence was shattered.' James looked down at his hands. 'I consider myself the provider, the man of the house. I know it's old-fashioned, but that's the way I see things. I want to provide for my family. When I got this job with London Irish, I was so terrified of losing it that I really did block out everything else. I can see that now. I was obsessed with proving myself and making my position secure. I took my eye off the ball – excuse the pun. I put work first and I neglected you and the children.'

I kissed him again. 'You did it for all the right reasons. Look, James, I want you to be happy in your job. I want you to be secure and to do the best you possibly can because I know how important it is to you.'

'Thank you.' He tucked a strand of hair behind my ear. 'I know it's been difficult for you, moving to London and leaving your old life behind, but I do really believe that we can have a good life here. We just need to start again, slowly.'

'Well, it couldn't be worse than it has been.'

He smiled. 'That's true.'

We kissed deeply, longingly, hungrily. It felt so good. We stood up and looked at each other. I knew that glint in James's eye . . . I just hadn't seen it in a while.

'Hold that thought.' I grinned.

'Where are you going?' He tried to pull me back into a kiss.

'Don't worry, you'll like this.'

I ran into the kitchen and found it hiding at the back of the fridge. Rushing back into the lounge, where James was waiting for me on the couch, I shook it in his face.

'What on earth . . .?' He peered at it, trying to see what it was.

'Whipped cream!' I giggled. 'We've never tried it before. I've been told, by a reliable source, that it's very effective in the bedroom.'

James stood up and grabbed my hand. 'What the hell are we waiting for?'

Acknowledgements

I would especially like to thank the many people who told me their stories about stalking. I was shocked to find out how prevalent it is. A special thanks to Orla Tormey for being so generous with her time and for sharing her own incredible story with me.

Thanks also to, Rachel Pierce, my editor, whose help and advice were, as always, invaluable; Patricia Deevy, for all of her support and encouragement; Michael McLoughlin, Cliona Lewis, Patricia McVeigh, Brian Walker, and all the team at Penguin Ireland for making the publishing process so enjoyable; to all in the Penguin UK office, especially Tom Weldon, Joanna Prior and the fantastic sales, marketing and creative teams; to my agent Marianne Gunn O'Connor, thanks for believing in me; to Hazel Orme, as always, for her wonderful copy-editing; to Mum, Dad, Sue, Mike and my extended family for their unwavering support and loyalty, which mean so much; to my nephews, Mikey, James, Jack, Sam and Finn, and to my nieces, Cathy and Isabel; to Hugo, Geordy and Amy, you truly are the sunshine in my life. And as always, the biggest thank you to Troy.

Finally ... this book is dedicated to my girlfriends. Thank you for your love, loyalty and especially for all the laughs. Thanks for the late-night chats, for your honesty and for your support over all these years. Here's to many more.

If you enjoyed spending time with
Emma and James . . .

The events of *Mad about You* put Emma and James's
relationship under terrible life-altering pressure – the sort
of pressure that would break many couples. They had one
thing going for them, though – it wasn't the first time their
marriage had been tested. Read more of the Hamiltons'
story in *The Baby Trail* trilogy:

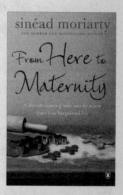

'Very funny,
with a cast
of wonderful
supporting
characters and
an unpredictable
ending. Marian
Keyes, you
have some
competition'
RTÉ Guide

'Will have readers
giggling and
sniffling in equal
measure'
Irish Independent

'Brilliantly
eccentric and
utterly charming –
we love this!'
OK!

Enjoy this exclusive extract from Sinéad's next novel,
The Secrets Sisters Keep, published in July 2014.

About *The Secrets Sisters Keep*

*The Devlin sisters rely on each other – but some things are just too
painful to share, even when your sisters are your best friends . . .*

*Mum-of-four Julie thought that if her family had more money, life
would be easier. But now that they've inherited a fortune, her problems
are just starting.*

*Lawyer Louise is used to having life go exactly as she wants it to.
So accepting that there are some things that even she can't control is
beyond her.*

*And former model Sophie can just about cope with getting older –
that's until her ex-husband finds a younger model.*

*All three women think that some battles are best fought alone.
Maybe they need to think again . . .*

Prologue

She switched off her electric toothbrush and listened. She could hear her husband shouting. He sounded panicked. Oh, my God, they were being robbed. She looked around the bathroom for a weapon. The only thing she could see was the toilet brush. She crept over to the door, opened it slowly and jumped out, shouting, 'Leave him alone!'

Instead of coming face to face with a balaclava-wearing thief, Anne found herself in front of a naked woman. She stared over at George, who was sitting bolt upright in bed, eyes wide with shock.

The young woman let out a bloodcurdling scream.

'What the hell is going on?' Anne shrieked.

'For the love of God, will you get her a towel or something?' George hissed.

'Who is she?' Anne snapped.

'I've no bloody idea. I woke up and found her stumbling around at the end of the bed.'

The bedroom door burst open and their son, Gavin, charged in, naked and dishevelled.

'Shit!' he exclaimed, rushing to the woman. 'She was looking for the loo.'

'Sorry!' the girl said, trying desperately to cover her breasts and nether regions with her hands.

'No problem, easy mistake to make,' George said. To his wife, he added, 'You can put that down now – we're not in any danger. Good thinking, though! A plastic toilet brush would have provided great protection.'

'This is Amelia,' Gavin said.

'Annalise,' she corrected him.

'Christ,' George muttered.

'Really?' Gavin frowned. 'I was sure it was Amelia.'

'No, Annalise.'

'Right, sorry.'

'When you two have finished having your little catch-up, perhaps you might consider putting some bloody clothes on!' Anne suggested.

'There's no need to be rude, Mum.' Gavin looked offended.

He pulled Annalise from the bedroom. As she left, she gave them a wave. 'Nice to meet you.'

'You too.' George smiled.

As they watched the naked lovebirds scamper across the landing, Anne turned to her husband. 'You can stop staring at her bottom now, George.'

'I was just keeping an eye on the poor girl to make sure she didn't get lost again.'

'Poor girl? She's the most brazen hussy I ever met. The cheek of her saying, "Nice to meet you," while she's bare-arsed in our bedroom!'

'How does Gavin get these girls? He's a complete gobshite.'

Anne bristled. 'He is not. He's handsome and charming and –'

George cut across her, 'Unemployed and penniless and going nowhere fast.'

'You're too hard on him. He's just finding his way.'

'He's not going to find it having sex with women whose names he can't remember.'

'Keep your voice down,' Anne said. 'The poor boy hasn't figured out what his path in life is yet.'

'How long is it going to take? He left university five years ago!'

'He'll get there soon enough.'

'You'll have him ruined,' George muttered. 'Spoilt rotten. The girls were never this lazy. It's ridiculous. I was running my own company at his age.'

'These are different times.'

'His sisters all had jobs at his age too!' George pointed out. 'He needs a kick up the arse.'

'Don't get all het up. If you have a heart attack you'll have to make your own way to hospital. I'm not missing Julie's lunch. I'm dying to see the new house. Apparently it's stunning.'

Three hours later

George parked beside the brand new Jaguar in the driveway.

'Is that Harry's new car?' Gavin asked.

'Yes.' Anne sniffed, 'It's very flashy. I think the money's gone a bit to his head.'

'It's awesome!' Gavin exclaimed.

They walked up the huge stone steps to Julie and Harry's new house. Gavin whistled. 'It's a bloody mansion.'

They rang the bell and heard a commotion inside. It was the triplets fighting over who would open the door. Losing patience, Anne bent down and shouted through the letterbox, 'Stop bickering and let us in.'

The door swung open as the three boys continued to wrestle. While Gavin and his father tried to prise them apart, Anne stepped over them and walked into the vast kitchen where her three daughters were sitting up at the marble counter.

Harry rushed over to greet his mother-in-law, then handed her a glass into which he made a big show of pouring Dom Pérignon.

'Oh, this is very decadent. Thank you, Harry.'

'Well, we're celebrating so I wanted to push the boat out.'

'I'd forgotten how good it tastes.' Sophie savoured it. 'I miss great champagne.'

'I don't see the difference. Prosecco would have been fine.' Julie looked cross.

Sophie placed a hand on her sister's arm. 'Relax and enjoy it, Julie.'

Gavin came in. 'Dude, this gaff is like something on *MTV Cribs*. I need an old aunt to die and leave me money. Harry, you are one lucky guy.'

George followed his son. 'Nice place, Julie. You'd need a map to find your way around.'

'A bit like Gavin's friend this morning, who got lost,' Anne said. Louise rolled her eyes. 'What's Gavin done now?'

'Unbeknown to your father and me, he brought a fast girl

home last night. This morning, she lost her way and ended up in our bedroom – naked.'

'Oh, my God! What did you do?' Julie tried not to laugh.

'Well, your mother thought it was a robber and came thundering out of the bathroom to fight him with a toilet brush.'

They all laughed.

'What did you do, Dad?' Louise asked.

'He stared a lot,' Anne huffed.

'Was she hot?' Sophie wondered.

'Well, I couldn't say. I tried to avert my eyes,' George protested.

'He was totally checking her out, the old perv.' Gavin chuckled.

'His eyes were out on sticks,' Anne added.

'Not a bad sight to wake up to.' Harry laughed. 'Better than Julie's fleecy pyjamas.'

'You don't actually wear those, do you?' Louise asked.

'They're comfortable.' Julie shrugged.

'You have to ditch them. You need fabulous new gear for your new bedroom suite. I'll take you shopping,' Sophie offered. 'La Perla do amazing pieces.'

'That stuff costs a fortune,' Julie said.

'Julie, you're loaded. You can buy anything you want,' Sophie reminded her.

Julie blushed and changed the subject. 'Is anyone hungry? Harry insisted on ordering a ridiculous amount of food from some posh caterer so we have tons.'

While the others made their way to the table, Louise pulled Julie aside. 'Look, I know having money is new to you, but you need to enjoy it. Stop being so defensive – we're all thrilled for you.'

Julie's eyes filled. 'I just feel . . . embarrassed about all this. It seems so over the top.'

'Julie, you of all people deserve it. Besides,' Louise said, watching as the triplets started a water fight, 'the boys will trash it and make it feel like home in no time.'

Julie squeezed her sister's arm. 'You're right. Is Clara OK?'

Louise turned to look at her little daughter, who was curled up on the couch with her fingers in her ears, reading a book. 'She's not used to so much noise.'

There was an almighty crash as one of the triplets rugby-tackled his brother and knocked over a platter of food.

Julie ushered them out into the garden.

Anne shook her head. 'They are pure wild. They need a firm hand.'

'They're just high-spirited,' Harry said. 'Besides, they'll be calmer once school starts tomorrow. You know, Castle Academy's considered the best in the country – the sports facilities are second to none.'

'I think that's the tenth time he's mentioned it,' George whispered.

'Are the triplets excited?' Sophie asked Harry, trying to cover her father's mumblings.

'Not as excited as their father,' Julie muttered.

'Incredibly excited. They can't wait,' Harry enthused. 'The best thing about coming into money is being able to give the boys the best education.'

'I want to go to Castle Academy with the boys,' Tom said, pulling at his mother's leg.

Julie picked up her youngest son and kissed him. 'I know, pet, but you can't go until you're seven.' Sophie's phone beeped. She read the message and her face fell.

'What's wrong?' Julie asked.

'Jess wants to stay with Jack and Pippa tonight. She's supposed to come home at six. I always do a movie night on Sunday and get her to bed early for school. But now she's begging to stay. If I say no, I'll be the worst mother in the world. I'm sick of it – she never wants to be with me any more. It's all about Jack and Pippa.'

'Oh, Sophie, that's rotten.'

She sighed. 'Yes, it bloody is. I need to meet someone so I can move on with my life.'

Julie patted her shoulder. 'You will, you're gorgeous.'

Harry clinked his glass. 'I just want to make a toast. Welcome, all of you, to our new home. Julie and I are starting a very exciting chapter in our lives and I know it's going to be a lot better than before.'

Julie looked down into her glass of expensive champagne. She'd liked her old life. She'd been very happy. All this change frightened her. What was this next chapter going to bring?

Exclusive
Bonus Content

RICHARD AND JUDY
Thorntons
SUMMER
BOOK CLUB
2014
EXCLUSIVE TO
WHSmith

**Read on for author interview,
book club questions and much more...**

Richard and Judy ask
Sinéad Moriarty

Emma finds it hard adapting to London life. Did you, when you moved there for a while from Ireland? Can you distil for us the essential differences in the social mood of Dublin and London?

Like Emma, I found it difficult moving to London. I didn't have any children at the time, but I struggled to find a job and to make friends. After many failed interviews I got a job on a magazine that wrote about printing presses – beggars can't be choosers. The editor said he hired me because I was the only candidate who took their coat off! With this new job, I began to find my feet and make friends through work. Six months later I had settled into London life and spent six wonderful years living there. But when I was writing about Emma, those initial feelings of loneliness came back to me. One of the things that surprised me most was that no one in my apartment block ever spoke to me in the lift. I'd always get in and say a big friendly 'hi' and smile widely at people, but they behaved as if they couldn't see me. In those early days I did it on the tube too. Now I know that smiling at people on the tube is just not done unless you want people to think you're a bit strange. Looking back, my desperation to make friends must have been so obvious. No wonder everyone stared blankly over my head or buried their heads in their books!

This book opens with the Oxford Dictionary's definition of trust. You really put poor Emma through the wringer on this whole issue, didn't you! Jealousy and doubt are hugely powerful human themes — were they the mainstays of your plot even before you worked out the finer details?

All of my books start with an issue or subject matter that I'm interested in. I think the issue of trust is something that everyone can relate to, whether it's trust within a marriage or friendship or siblings . . . Having seen a lot of relationships around me change and face new challenges, I wanted to look at the feelings of doubt that can seep into a marriage when it is put under pressure. It's amazing how just one seed of doubt being planted in your head when you're feeling vulnerable can blow up into a huge issue. What happens when you start doubting your partner? Can you ever go back to trusting them implicitly when your faith in them has been broken?

All your books rely on 'family' as the canvases on which to paint your stories. You seem very fluent with the whole area of family tensions, rivalries, loves and loyalties. How so?

Move into my house and you'll soon see!

I'm only joking, but I think all families contain deep wells of stories and emotions. Every family has secrets, tensions, loyalties, loves and wounds. Then, when you get married, you become part of a new family full of their own issues. (Although my husband claims his family is a lot more 'normal' than mine . . . needless to say I disagree!)

The beauty of family life is that it is never dull. I think the relationships within families are fascinating. You think you know someone really well and then if you see them interacting with their families, they can be so different. I also think it's true that where you come in the family plays a huge part in the person you grow up to be – youngest, middle, eldest, etc. Your placement within a family can be key to the person you become as an adult. It forms the way you look at the world and the way you feel about yourself. (In case you're wondering, I'm the youngest!)

No matter how serious the underlying topics of your novels, you always inject humour in the unlikeliest places. Is that knowingly based on the traditional connection between tragedy and comedy in literature and the arts?

I'm afraid to say it's done unwittingly. It just feels natural. Life is tragedy and comedy mixed together. I firmly believe that being able to laugh when times are hard can save your sanity. I remember when my friend's mum died and the gravediggers went on strike. She and her sisters had to start shovelling the mud in their high heels and best coats. They all ended up roaring with laughter through their tears and to this day the memory makes them smile. The best humour so often stems from the darkest places. I know my sense of humour has kept me sane during times of stress and I am grateful for it. I also really want to entertain my readers. My ultimate goal is to pull at readers' heartstrings but also to make them laugh. If I can do that, then I know I've written a good story.

Download our podcast at http://lstn.at/rjmadaboutyou

Do you have any questions that you would like to ask Sinéad Moriarty? Visit our website – whsmith.co.uk/richardandjudy – to post your questions.

Richard and Judy Book Club – Questions for Discussion

The Richard and Judy Book Club, exclusively with WHSmith, is all about getting you involved and sharing our passion for reading. Here are some questions to help you or your book group get started. Go to our website to discuss these questions, post your own and share your views with the rest of the book club.

- What would you say was the state of James and Emma's marriage at the start of the novel?
- Discuss all aspects of trust – or lack of trust – in the novel.
- Do you think that James and Emma will be able to go back to 'normal' after what has happened? Will it make their relationship weaker or stronger?
- How do you think Moriarty balances humour and tension in the novel?

For information about setting up, registering or joining a local book club, go to www.richardandjudy.co.uk.

Can Love Survive When Trust is Gone?

I've known the characters in *Mad about You*, Emma and James Hamilton, for over ten years. In fact, my very first novel, *The Baby Trail*, was about Emma's struggle with infertility and how her desperation to get pregnant led her to do some crazy things – handstands after sex being the least of them! I was trying – and failing – to get pregnant at the time too and I wanted to write a story that captured how infertility consumes your life. Writing it was immensely cathartic and I truly believe it helped me get rid of a lot of my own angst and sadness. I was pregnant at the launch of *The Baby Trail* and I am very happy to say that I now have three lovely children. As you can imagine, Emma and James have a very special place in my heart.

I wrote two further novels about the Hamiltons and then moved on to other themes and novels. But they always stayed with me – like very good friends – and from time to time I wondered how they might be getting on. After a few years of being a mother myself, and sharing stories with friends, I realized there was a lot about being a parent that I could never have imagined back in the days when I was dying for a baby. Like my husband and I, Emma and James had desperately wanted children and then it had happened. Did having children make their life perfect and was everything suddenly idyllic?

I think every parent will know the answer.

Not quite!

We hear it all the time: marriages need to be looked after and worked on. We also know that that's easier said than done. Children take up a lot of time and energy and couples often stop making an effort with one another. Weeks can go by when all you talk about is who is going to get up with the baby, who forgot to buy nappies and whose turn it is to put the bins out. Romance and sex are replaced with grunts and arguments and endless discussions about how little sleep you're getting.

In *Mad about You* we meet Emma and James after ten years of marriage and watch what happens when their relationship comes under pressure: the recession means a change of job for James and a big move for the family. They both struggle to understand one another's challenges with their new life. And then, just when Emma is at her lowest ebb, something happens that makes her start to doubt James and doubt their marriage. The heart of the novel is about trust and what happens in a relationship when that is undermined.

The theme of the novel came to me over coffee in a friend's kitchen (that's what happens with writers – you never know when inspiration will strike!). I had called around to see my friend and her neighbour happened to be there. She began to tell me the story of what happened in her life when her husband was stalked by a 'stranger'. She explained how her trust in him began to fade and no matter how much he reassured her she began to doubt him.

It made me wonder. How would I feel in those circumstances? How much do we really trust our partners? Even the best relationships get stale, so what would happen if your husband began to receive saucy texts? Would you really believe he had no idea who was sending them? Or would a seed of doubt be planted in your mind?

Another area of trust I wanted to explore in *Mad about You* was the trust between parents and childminders. A friend of mine, a mother of four, jokes that she chose her first childminder after a rigorous and lengthy interview process. But by the time Baby No. 4 came along she would have handed him to a stranger at a bus stop for a few hours of peace.

When you think about it, the fact that we leave the most precious and vulnerable people in our lives – our children – with babysitters and childminders, who we sometimes barely know, is really very odd. How can we ever fully trust the people that are minding our children? How can we be sure that they are the best person for the job?

Writing *Mad about You* was a lovely experience. I got to know Emma and James again and the themes of the novel reminded me just how precious my family is to me and to never take them for granted.

Ways to get involved

The two of us are absolutely passionate about reading and there's something immensely satisfying about discussing books amongst friends and family.

We'd love you to be part of these conversations so do please visit our website to discuss this book, and any of our other Book Club choices. There is so much to discover and so many ways to get involved – here are just some of them:

- Subscribe to our author podcast series
- Read extracts of all the Book Club books
- Read our personal reviews and post your own on our website or post your short review on Twitter #RJBookClub
- Share your thoughts and discuss the books with us, the authors and other readers
- Set up, register or join a local book club

For more information go to our website now and be a part of Britain's biggest and best book club – whsmith.co.uk/richardandjudy. See you there!

 Richard and Judy Book Club

 @RJBookClubNews

Our latest Book Club titles

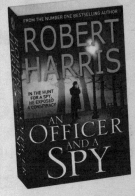

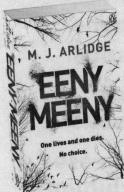

RICHARD AND JUDY
Thorntons
SUMMER
BOOK CLUB
2014
EXCLUSIVE TO
WHSmith

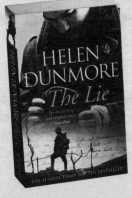